Capitol Angst

D.C. White

ISBN: 0983735514
ISBN-13: 9780983735519

DEDICATION

To my awesome husband. Thanks for writing this with me, I couldn't have done it without you. Thank you for all the evenings we spent dreaming and adding to the mystery, they have been awesome. I so look forward to spending more time with you, dreaming up characters and giving them life.

TABLE OF CONTENTS

D.C. White

ACKNOWLEDGMENTS

First and foremost, I thank my husband and each of my four children. Thank you for your support of whatever I try. To my girls, even though this type of book isn't your type, thank you for supporting me in this. I promise to let my oldest son know when it comes out in film so he too can see what was written. And thanks to my youngest son, my marketing guru.

I want to thank my sister and her friend Jon for their support and enthusiasm and reading what wasn't ready to be read. Thanks, for that was a huge challenge.

To the multitude of friends that gave their time to read, my deepest thanks, you kept me moving in the right direction, your time was well spent.

Prologue

"Why are you doing this. Do you know who I am?" he yells at his abductor. "You don't need to do this, I promise I won't say anything to anyone" he screams as he feels the first of many slices to his body. Waking up lying on a metal table, naked on a cold January morning, in a room devoid of anything but knives and torture instruments, Bill prepares to meet his maker. The bastard, I don't even know him. Who would have thought that I'd go this way, he thinks as his captor continues slicing his skin. First his legs, now his arms, he thinks while opening his mouth to scream, a burning sensation consuming him. His vision gets cloudy, the pain bringing him to the edge of consciousness.

"Wake up" he hears, and then he feels something like acid touch his arms. As Bill slowly reaches consciousness, pain greets him like an old enemy. He opens his mouth to scream only to find it filled with a foul tasting substance. A rag, he stuffed my mouth with a rag, he realizes. This is really happening, it's not a nightmare.

"There you are" an old hippie throwback says when he notices bright blue eyes staring at him in fear and loathing. With a smile showing rotted teeth, broken to the gum line in places and a stench that smells like rotted food, his captor slowly moves his knife into view, knife point moving closer and closer to his right eye. With a quick stabbing motion, he jabs the eye socket and in agonizing pain Bill escapes into the dark, never to surface again. "That gets them every time" his captor murmurs with a smirk and continues with the job of separating man from skin. Those sure were pretty blue eyes, he thinks as he examines the right one, now residing on a tray with his knives.

ONE

Friday morning, four fifty-seven a.m. Meow, Meeoow, Meeeooooow, Meeeeoooooow . . . All right, Prissy," replies an exasperated Norma as she struggles with her walker, to get to the front door. "Stop your scratching and digging at the door, I'll let you out as soon as I get there."

Frustrated with the heavy door and all the safety locks that her son had installed just last year, ever since her previously safe neighborhood had become a lot more dangerous to live in, Norma finally gets the door open.

"Oh Prissy, what's that mess on the floor? That looks like blood. Did you kill another squirrel? You know how I hate it when you go out and kill those poor little defenseless animals. Don't you get enough food around here?" she asks, not finding it unusual at all to talk to Prissy. As she opens the door wider to investigate, she lets out a blood curdling scream and turns to get to the phone, to dial nine-one-one.

What's wrong with me? My chest feels funny. I'm dizzy. Everything seems slow. "Oooh" she moans as she collapses to the floor just as she reaches the phone, pulling it onto the floor with her but just out of reach. Luckily, she's wearing the 'I've-fallen-and-can't-get-up chain' that her son Bill insisted she have, just for this reason. So tall and handsome, I can see him so clearly now. He's not going to be happy about this. I didn't shut the door she thinks while she grabs the chain and pushes the button. That's the last thought she'll ever have and the last thing she'll ever see. She's saved some pain, never knowing that it's her son that's hanging on the door, skinned like a rab-

3

bit.

A call comes in to squad twenty two of the Metro DCFD "This is Anna from Life Watch. We've received an alert from a ninety three-year-old woman that lives alone. We've tried to reach her unsuccessfully. She's on heart medication, so we're requesting an ambulance to be dispatched. The address is one-one-three-four Decatan Street." As the ambulance arrives at the home, the driver and paramedic, Skeet, notices an unmarked police car already on scene and an officer that appears to be throwing up beside it. After Skeet gets out with his partner, EMT Patricia Keller, they approach the officer first and see its Bob Gaitlin, a thirty-year veteran of the force, and a friend of Skeet's brother.

"Bob, what's going on?" Skeet asks. Bob looks up, pale and gray and looking much older than his fifty eight years.

"Skeet, in all my time on the force, I've never seen anything like this. I haven't been sick like this at a crime scene since I was a rookie. I was just driving through the neighborhood when I heard the call come in on the radio, and I thought may-be I could help.

"Come on, Bob" Skeet says "it's just a little old lady. We'll take care of it. Cops are such wimps," he says quietly to his partner, Pat. Before Bob gets the chance to say anything else, Skeet and Pat approach the Brownstone, seeing what caused Bob to lose his breakfast. There, hanging on the front door, is what appears to be the skin of a human body.

As Bob comes up behind them he says, "I've called the detectives and the CSU; they're on the way. In the meantime, we need to get in there and check on the woman that lives here. She must be a mess. We'll have to move carefully though, no disrupting the crime scene. The detectives will have my hide if you do, since I'm letting you so close."

"Too late," Pat answers after peeking into the foyer of the house, and seeing the old woman lying there. "It looks like we have another one for the coroner."

Lieutenant Kathleen Thomas, department head of the homicide division, D.C. Metro One, and her partner, Detective Desdemona Rowald (Des), show up to start the crime scene.

"Set up a perimeter, establish the crime scene and start the sign-in procedures before we get overwhelmed" Lieutenant Thomas orders.

"Alright Des, let's start the scene. We need to take a closer look at the body. I believe we have a male" she says "age undetermined at this time. The skin, not being on the body, is so wrinkled it's hard to tell. The hair on the head is pretty gray though and military short. Oh, man, check this out" she says, and "somebody grab that cat, he needs to go in with the medical examiners team. Hopefully he didn't eat much.

"Hmm, they left the eyes. Now that took some time, but why attach them to the groin area? The eyes aren't attached to the skin normally, and never in the groin. Although you know what they say" she says with a smirk."Nice blue color though. Too bad the guy that owned them lost them, and what happened to the body that goes in the skin?" Kat asks Detective Des.

"Notify the Medical Examiner's office, the scene is on the one thousand block of Decatan Street. It looks like a street that houses upper-pay-scale people.

"This is not your normal murder neighborhood, I wonder how the body on the door and the old woman are connected?" she murmurs looking at Detective Des.

"How is it possible to totally skin a person, and take everything except the skin? It's got to be some kind of message. Just what is it and who is it directed at?" Kat says as she walks backwards from the door, trying not to contaminate the crime scene. Several police cars with lights flashing, and sirens screaming, fly around the corner. After screeching to a halt, the officers jump out of their vehicles in excitement, everyone wanting to see what the big deal is.

"Alright" Kat begins "can I get your attention, everyone? I need the following Officers: Scott, Johnson, Biggs, and Stuart to start interviewing witnesses. I want to know everything, absolutely everything. Did anyone see or hear anything last night? If so, what was it? What about animals, does anyone have any pets that started acting up at anytime in the night?

"It looks like the murder took place awhile ago" she informs them. "I'm going to need your reports at D.C. Metro One, as soon as possible. I'd like them within the next four or five hours. We need to get started on this before the killer has enough time to get too far. Unfortunately he's already got a lead. Lord knows how far away he is by now" she adds in disgust. As the Officers leave to start questioning witnesses, the medical examiner's office shows up.

"Good morning, Doctor Zorgath, you look good as usual. How is it that you can always be dressed and ready no matter what the time?" she teases. He's wearing a beautiful navy blue suit, probably silk, a gray shirt the color of smoke and one of his famous ties. This one has a navy background with small gray squares in varying sizes all over the front, probably silk, since that seems to be his favorite material. His trademark black hair with every hair in place, the spiked top messy, but sexy.

She did her usual jump out of bed, rush through the shower and threw on some wrinkled cloths. Then she pulled her slightly damp hair back into a pony. With a naked face and a glance in the mirror she's ready to go. There's no one she wants to impress this early in the morning, anyway. She doesn't realize that she looks about fifteen and like she's ready for some kind of high school sport.

"People never surprise me anymore with the ingenuity they use for the most evil of crimes. Let's get this skin down, be careful with the eyes, Samantha" orders Dr. Zorgath."That's a unique signature, wouldn't you say, Lieutenant?" he questions as he starts investigating the crime scene, making note of the same things that Kat had noted. He order's his techs to bag the hands and bring the push pins in that were used to attach them to the door. "Be careful with the feet, bag them also, and make sure you get pictures of everything and every angle, especially the eye placement."

As the team gathers samples from the door, porch, sidewalk, anything that looks out of place, Dr. Zorgath walks over to Kat and starts talking."This one was nasty; the killers seem to get weirder all the time. Let's hope this is the only one like it. I'd hate to see anyone else go through this, Lieutenant. Unfortunately, I can't tell you much from this scene, but I can say definitively that this is not the real crime scene. There's not enough blood or noticeable struggle for this type of crime. I'll get a lot more information at the morgue when he's on my table. It won't take as long as other autopsies since we haven't got a body (so to speak) to look at" he says as they load the skin up from the door and put the eyes in special containers with lids, to protect them.

"I've gone over the scene, initially" Kat says. "It's going to be difficult to gain much insight into this. When I'm done here, I'm heading back into the office. I need to contact the Police Department in Staleyville, PA. They've had a similar murder up there. It might give us a few ideas as to what went on here."

Kat heads back to D.C Metro One to start looking for answers. Once in the car, she starts thinking out loud.

"What's the name of the owner of the house? Has anything suspicious happened in that neighborhood? Contact Staleyville Police Department and find out how similar the murder in Staleyville was compared to this one," she orders.

"On it, Lieutenant," Des promises.

"There's never any parking in this damn area" she complains in frustration. After circling the block three times, she finally finds a space out front, squeezes into it, gets out and auto locks the car all while muttering in disgust "you can't be too careful around here."

"It's always so noisy in here" she complains as she makes her way to the fourth floor squad room, "perps yelling and fighting with the officers that arrested them. Someone smells ripe, like they haven't showered in a year" she adds, disgusted. "This place is the closest thing to home that I have. Where else would you see transvestites in unbelievably tall heels and micro skirts? Drunks puking or sleeping as the need arises, and gang bangers lining the walls? Yeah, there's no place like home," she admits with a grin.

At least being a Lieutenant has its privileges. It gives me an office to work out of instead of being stuck in the bullpen with everyone else. It's damn near impossible to think in the bullpen. Not that my office is a prize. It's stark, dingy old white walls, a small desk next to the window which looks at the back of the Smithsonian, a broken down office desk chair that's seen better days, and a computer that works sometimes, it's a jackpot. At least I'm not looking at the dump. There's no place like home, Dorothy, no place like . . . It could definitely be worse.

Kat heads over by the bull pen for a cup of that rot gut coffee that flows so freely in police departments. I sure miss the days when I had time to go to Mike's Coffee house. I wonder how he's been. I haven't talked to him in at least a month. I really need to put that on my mental list of things to do, she decides guiltily, as she heads back to her office.

"I have Detective Bob Monroe of the Staleyville Police Department on line two," says Detective Des.

"Okay, I'll get it in my office, thanks" Kat replies.

"This is Lieutenant Thomas of D.C Metro One, is this Detective Monroe?"

"Yes it is, Lieutenant. How can I help you?" he asks in a southern twang.

"Detective, are you there?" she asks.

"Oh, yeah, sorry, my mind flashed back to the scene. I'm having a hard time not seeing that skin" he admits.

"That's all right; can we focus on the crime now? I have a few questions. We may have had a similar occurrence in D.C, but I'm not sure what the connection is. Can you give me a little information about the case?"

"Sure, I'd be happy to" he offers. "Staleyville is one of the smallest towns in Pennsylvania. We're located at the bottom of the Alleghany Mountains in southern PA, surrounded by some of the most beautiful country God created. The only strangers we normally see are those passing through on vacation.

"We don't normally experience one unusual death and definitely not one as dramatic as this one. It really shook us all up. We're just small town folk here, Lieutenant" he explains.

"Yeah" she agrees "but we're not small town folk here, and we don't normally see something this nasty either. I guess we're on the same page with this one. What can you tell me, Detective?"

"The victim was a thirty-eight year old man, by the name of

Tom Mason. He lived just outside of town in a small ramshackle house. He kept to his own, wasn't the real friendly type, although he did do a lot of handyman repairs and such for the folks around here. He was pretty well known in his own right. He wasn't rich, not even close, which was pretty apparent by where he lived. Although I guess some rich folks get kind of recluse and hide the fact of their wealth, but that wasn't Tom's case. Anyway, he didn't have a lot of friends in the area, either."

"A guy that lived just down the road from him, Mike Walker, found him as he was driving by. He routinely drove past Tom's after his weekly visit to the store here in town. It scared the b'jesus out of him when he saw him. Whoever did this, they skinned him like a rabbit" Detective Monroe repeats in a shaken voice. "I've never seen anything like that, not in my whole life. We haven't found the body yet. Actually, we don't have a clue where it could be, we're just hoping some kid doesn't come across it somewhere" finishes Detective Monroe.

"Do you have a coroner in town?" Kat inquires.

"Hell no, Lieutenant, excuse my language. This town's too small for that. We sent the victim to the coroner is Althena. That town's a lot bigger than we are. That's where all homicides go from this area."

"Have you received the report back from the Althena coroner, yet?" she questions.

"Yeah, we just got it back yesterday," he admits.

"Is there any way that you can fax or e-mail me a copy, Detective?"

"Sure, I can fax it over to you right away."

"Great, I appreciate it. Thanks for your time, Detective and if there's anything that you hear or that comes up regarding this case, could you let me know?"

"Sure thing, Lieutenant" he promises.

"Des, can you come in here? I didn't get much information from the Staleyville P.D. They didn't have much. It sounded like this threw them for a loop down there. It's a small town, maybe three police officers in the whole town, and I would imagine Detective Monroe's the only detective in town. Anyway, he's going to fax us a copy of their coroner's report so we can compare it to ours" she says. "We need to head over to the coroner's office and see what they've got so far."

"The traffic across D.C. at eight a.m. sucks," she complains to Des while trying to maneuver around all the people that seem to be sightseeing this morning. Everyone's trying to get somewhere, but not very fast. "It's a good thing I'm not a road cop" she mutters in frustration as she tries to move through the somewhat narrow streets. "Damn it, did you see that guy, he just freakin cut me off, then turned around and flipped me off like it was my fault. Where do people get the balls? If I wasn't a cop, I'd chase him down and teach him some manners" Kat says.

"Alright, there's a spot. Let me get into it before another asshole beats me to it. Let's head in" she demands as she tries to get out of the car before a passing car takes off her door.

"Think Dr. Zorgath is done with the body yet?" Des asks.

"I don't know, probably pretty close. Let's hope he's got some information for us."

Entering the medical examiners offices, Des mutters in disgust "You can actually taste death in the air."

"Yeah, that's why I'm always ready with gum. I'd rather taste that then death," Kat admits.

"This is my least favorite thing to do. You think all the dead bodies in here have spirits floating around, following us? It really feels creepy" Des admits nervously.

"No, and I think you said that last time we were here" Kat replies with a grin.

Entering the hallowed halls of autopsy, Kat finds Dr. Zorgath working on the 'body' from her case this morning. "So what have you got, Doctor, anything useful?" she asks.

"Well, let's see, the body isn't a body" he says in a teasing tone.

"No kidding." Kat snorts out a laugh.

"Yes, well anyway, I've been able to get a few prints off the skin. There were also a couple of hairs that didn't belong. They were too long and the wrong color, so I've sent them for processing. We may be able to get a DNA sample from at least one of them. Also, I'm running the fingerprints through CODIS right now; hopefully it won't take long to finish. This was definitely a male, and with the fingerprints on the skin's hands, I was able to identify the body."

"Meet Mr. William Blaketon, the former House Majority Leader. Bet you weren't expecting that, were you, Kat?" Dr. Zorgath inquires teasingly. Kat is one of his favorite murder cops.

"Actually I was, since the old lady that owned the home and probably died because of seeing him hanging on the door was Norma Blaketon, William Blaketon's mom" she responds sadly.

"So, how did you get the prints off the hands of the skin, or don't I want to know?" inquires Des.

"Probably not, but it's a relatively simple procedure. We just cut off the tips of the index fingers, and thumbs of both hands. Then I placed them over my gloved ones and viola. Fingerprints plump enough to run through CODIS," he says with teasing look.

"Awww, man, gross" Des cries "I think I'm gonna be sick" she mutters as she runs from the autopsy suite, a hand over her mouth.

"I also finished the autopsy on the old woman" he continues as he turns to Kat. "She died from a cardiac infarct also known as a heart attack, probably caused by the trauma of seeing the skin on the door. And yes, it was Bill Blaketon's mom," he repeats what Kat had told him. "The poor thing, the only good thing was she probably didn't know that it was her son since her death came pretty quickly."

"Good, thanks Doctor, and would you please stop making my partner sick? While we're waiting for the last results, I have a couple of questions" Kat says.

"Alright, bring em on" he offers in eager anticipation.

"First, can a body live without its skin, and second, how long can a body live without its skin?"

"Well, those are good questions even though they sound rather weird. The body can only sustain life for a short time without the skin, and that would be a small part of the skin, not all of it. The skin is essentially the largest organ of the body. There are so many blood vessels affected, the person will bleed out in short order, but in actuality, you can live for a short time, say maybe ten minutes, depending, of course, on how much of the skin has been removed. It's an extremely nasty, very unpleasant way to die. Not that any murders are pleasant, but with all those blood vessels and the thousands of nerve endings affected, ouch. Those would all have to be unattached, usually by way of a knife. It's comparable to the skinning of a fish, but a lot more difficult and it would also be a pretty painful way to die."

A creepy sound starts making a racket in the background. "Hold on, let me get the phone, Kat."

Jeeze, she thinks with a shiver "you'd think he'd change that ring tone, make it a little less loud and spooky sounding, wouldn't you?" Kat mutters to Des.

"I know it scares the crap out of me every time I hear it" Des admits, having returned from hugging the toilet bowl.

"Yes, you're sure? Okay, let me pass that info on. Thanks. That was Selma in the lab. She got a hit on CODIS for the fingerprints we found on the body. They belong to a man named Elroy Wade. He's from a small town in Ohio. All the pertinent information is being sent to your email by my directive Kat, so you should have everything you need. At least now, hopefully, you can find justice for this dead man and his poor dead mother" he remarks as he shakes his head, astounded by the murder and who found it.

"Thanks Doctor, I appreciate the time. We need to go. Call me if you get something else," Kat requests.

"Do you think we could stop for some food?" Des asks hopefully. "This body, beautiful as it is, needs sustenance" she says with a grin. "Plus, I just lost breakfast and I need to refill."

"Fine, what do you want?" Kat asks as she takes off from her parking spot in front of the M.E.'s office at a speed which is just slightly illegal.

"Come on, Kat, slow down or I'll have to give you a ticket," Des warns teasingly as she bites her lip to keep from smiling.

"Bite me" Kat says. "You want to eat? Then shut up. You

only get one pass for food. After that, we wait till tonight."

"Alright, whatever, how about that Chinese place on Reynolds Road? It's on the way, and they do take out. I'll call and order, it's always ready in 'ten minute' Des adds with a laugh.

After picking up lunch, Kat heads back to her office, turns on her computer, clicks through all the safety programs to get to her email, all while trying not to contaminate everything with duck sauce.

Come on, come on, I need that info. Okay, here it is. Hmm, Elroy Wade, that name sounds a little familiar. Who knows, with all the names we go through here it could be anyone. Let's see, who you are Elroy Wade? A fifty-eight year old male, ex biker, loner, lives in a small Ohio town called Mt. Buckhorn. So where's Mt. Buckhorn? Get me the map, Des," Kat yells.

After flipping through all the pages and passing the map of Ohio three times, Des takes the map back, turns it to the right page, and gives it back to Kat with a smirk on her face.

"Thanks, smart ass. I would have found it. I was trying to finish my egg roll. Okay, it's just south of Toledo. Not a big name town, kind of unknown, just your mediocre Midwest town" she says to Des.

"What brings you to D.C, Mr. Wade?" Kat murmurs. "Let's contact the Althena coroner, and see if they found any evidence from their crime scene. Set up an evidence board while you're at it. I believe we're going to need it. I have a feeling this one's going to be big."

"Yes sir, I'm on it.

"Kat, I just got off the phone with the medical examiner in Althena, a Dr. Coleman. He claims they found some DNA on the body, but they haven't received the reports back yet."

"Of course not" Kat gripes."Small town, elected official, money problems."

"Yep" Des says, "they had to send it to Philly for testing, and a city that size, things tend to get put on the back burner. The victim in P.A. wasn't anyone important, just a small town hick, so that gets put on hold, same old, same old."

"Why don't you call Philly, and see if you can light a fire

under them.Tell them this is a top priority case, and that we're suspicious of a possible copy cat, maybe even a serial killer. We need to know now, one way or the other, yada, yada, yada. After you're done, meet me in the bull pen, we'll see if any of the officers got anything during the witness interviews."

"Okay" agrees Des "give me five, and I'll meet you there."

Kat walks down the narrow hall, thinking about skinning a human and how long it could take, how long before death would occur. I'll have to thank Dr. Zorgath for answering my questions about the skinning. Eyes narrow, she walks into the bullpen. "Okay, Officer Biggs, did you get anything from the witnesses?"

"Yes, Lieutenant," Biggs says as Des walks in and takes a seat in the back of the room."I spoke with the woman that lives four houses down, same side of the street. She said she heard some kind of commotion, but it was in the middle of the night, and she was in bed. She said there's always something going on in that neighborhood anymore, so she never bothers to go check it out."

"Did she say what exactly she heard?" Kat questions in a dry tone of voice.

"Oh, yeah, she said it was some kind of noise, maybe a scream, but it didn't last very long, so she thought it was just some kids messing around. She never even got out of bed, Lieutenant. People just don't want to get involved anymore. They're too afraid, especially the elderly."

"Okay, thanks. Officer Johnson, got anything?"

"No Lieutenant. I knocked on all the doors of the houses on the opposite side of the crime scene; no one answered. They were either not home, or like Jimmy said, they don't want anything to do with it. Too many fear retribution."

"Alright then, Officer Stuart, please tell me you got something.

"Um, well, I actually did get something, Lieutenant."

"Okay, WHAT IS IT?" Kat yells in frustration, feeling her blood start to boil while watching the day go to hell.

"Well, the woman that lives next door, she actually saw something. First she heard something, and then she actually went to the window to look, but not before she turned off all her lights, so no one could see her looking, if you know what I mean."

"Officer Stuart, the point?"

"Oh, sorry Lieutenant; she said she saw a man, average size, but heavy through the middle. He was wearing a black coat, and had a knit hat pulled down over his head. He had longer hair in the back that stuck out of the bottom of the hat, and it looked pretty scraggly, light colored, maybe gray. She said she could see it because of the moonlight; it made it bright enough that she could see, but she couldn't see his face, although he didn't seem to be fighting with anyone, just clumsy maybe."

"She said it looked like the other person just kind of fell to the ground. But the black-coated guy, he helped him get up and they limped together towards the neighbor's house. She just thought they had a little spat and got over it. Then she went back to bed. She said it didn't seem bad enough to be a murder or anything. Maybe a lover's spat, but nothing really bad."

"Okay, thanks Officer Stuart."

"Officer Scott? What have you got"?

He stands up, pulls out his pocket notebook, flips to the right page, and proceeds to read. "Well, I interviewed a man by the name of John Campbell. He said he sleeps on the other side of the house, so didn't see anything, but he said he heard plenty. Someone screamed once, pretty loud, and then there was a lot of yelling, and some music. He said it seemed like an hour, but he didn't have his watch on, said he doesn't wear it to bed. Goes to bed at ten o'clock every night, and bragged that was the reason for his old age and good health. He said he was sleeping when the noise woke him. He's ninety years old and swears he doesn't get up in the middle of the night for anything, even pounding at his door, which he wanted to file a formal complaint about. He said it's "happening all the time anymore and that the neighborhood's gone to hell," his words Lieutenant, not mine."That's all he had to say on this subject, but he sure could go on about other stuff. He seemed like a lonely old guy" Officer Scott says, his voice dwindling after seeing the expression on the Lieutenant's face.

"Alright, thanks everyone, if you hear anymore, keep me informed. Let's go, Des, we have things to do."

While walking back to her office, Kat orders Des "Call Althena back, and call Philly again. I'll be glad to talk to them. I'm done waiting. In the meantime, I want a little more information on Elroy Wade."

Why does that name sound familiar, Kat wonders? After typing it into her computer's data base, the name Bad Ass comes up, a nickname for the perp. Bad Ass; I remember. It was about twelve years ago when I went up against one of the bikers from that group that was in Mike's Coffee Shop, Snakes group, and when I left he followed me and had the gall to try to attack me.

Yeah, Snake thought he came to my rescue, idiot, she thinks with a grin. A nice guy, I'm glad he's been in my life off and on for the past eleven years. He has some awesome eyes, I could drown in them she admits wistfully to herself, wishing he'd see her in a different light. Oh well, that Bad Ass dude must have got caught after succeeding with someone else after his failure with me. And now she thinks sadly of the woman he was probably successful with.

After more typing, "Bingo, her name was Beth Simmons, age nineteen, University of Nevada, 1999, raped, brutalized, rapist Elroy Wade, convicted and sent to Ely State Prison, Ely, Nevada. He was paroled a year ago" Kat reads.

"Well, well, Elroy, been a busy man, haven't you. Let's see, where did you go after prison? Home address listed as 17249 Blossom Road, Mt. Buckhorn, Ohio. Yep, same info I heard from Dr. Zorgath earlier. I wonder why he moved to Ohio, that's a boon dock destination; he must have some kind of connection there."

"Lieutenant, I got it. The information from Philly's in, they got a match. The suspect's name is Elroy Wade, from Mt. Buckhorn, Ohio. Same suspect as the one here."

"Okay, my suspicions confirmed," Kat replies. "We need to talk to the Captain. It looks like we could have a potential serial killer on the loose."

Kat picks up the phone and dials her captain's office, requesting a meeting. "Give me five minutes Kat, and then come on up" he commands. "Des, we need to go; you're with me."

They head toward the elevators up to the second floor. The captain's office is in the newly remodeled section of Metro One. After the elevator opens, Kat gives out a little appreciatory whistle. Clean, new, bright. "Nice place" she says. "I wonder who their decorator was, not that it matters; no one's going to re-decorate the working rooms of the precinct where all the criminals hang out. Who's going to spend a fortune only to have drunks puking and pissing everywhere" she says in grim amusement. Des just smirks.

The captain's secretary sees them coming and gives them a little wave. Kat's known her for years; she went to college with her for a year, was in some of the same classes. "Hey, Leslie, how's it going?"Kat asks.

"All good with me, the Captain say's you're to go on in when you get here."

"Thanks, Leslie, I'll talk to you later."

"Sure, Kat, see ya."

Kat had just lifted her hand to knock when the door opened from the inside and there stood Captain David Hall. Tall, blonde, built. Unfortunately, he's been happily married to Denise for the past ten years, a beautiful wife and two awesome kids. All the good ones are taken she thinks as she enters his office with Des trailing behind.

Des has always gotten tongue tied around the Captain. I do believe she still has a crush, Kat thinks with a smile.

"Please sit," orders the Captain. After everyone sits, the Captain says "Okay, give me the good news about the murder this morning. Tell me you know who did it, and where we can apprehend him, Kat."

"Yes sir, the murdered victim was Congressman William Blaketon, age sixty-one, House Majority Leader of the U.S. Congress, and the elderly woman that found him was his ninety-three year old mother, Norma Blaketon."

"Ouch, that sucks" exclaims Captain Hall. "What else do we know?" he asks.

"We've contacted Staleyville PD and found out that their

murder victim from one week ago was Tom Mason, a thirty-eight year old handyman with no known connections to William Blaketon. We do know that the fingerprints from a man by the name of Elroy Wade of Mt. Buckhorn, Ohio, were found on both the body of Blaketon and of Mason. We called Mt. Buckhorn Police Department and requested they go to his address and informed them that he is a person of interest in two murders. We've also put out an APB with the Ohio State Police, the Pennsylvania State Police, and the Staleyville Police Department, the Capitol Police Department, Washington D. C. State Police and the local Leo's. Hopefully he'll fall into one of those nets."

"In the meantime, the next step is to contact the Capitol Police Department, Special Investigations Unit and the FBI BAU, Metro Headquarters. It looks like this could be a serial killer in progress. Two kills, one week apart. Hopefully he's done, but we can't be sure, so we need to find him as fast as possible. I've had officer's combing the neighborhood looking for witnesses, unfortunately, the neighborhood consists of the elderly and no-one saw anything useful" Kat finishes formally, the tone she uses in front of superiors.

"Thank you, Lieutenant, keep me apprised of any changes, and call the Capitol Police to set up a time to meet. Maybe you should aim for tomorrow morning. Now, it looks like you need to take off before you fall on your face. You've been at this since early this morning. It's now getting after seven, so go home and come back refreshed, ready to meet the agents."

TWO

Tall, dark and handsome walks into Metro One Homicide Division, Saturday morning at seven a.m.

"I'm looking for Lieutenant Kathleen Thomas" he says to the first officer he see's, rookie Officer Scott. "She's back there in her office" Officer Scott responds with a wave in the general direction of the back wall of the bullpen. Capitol Police Deputy Chief Devon Callander just shrugs and walks toward the back of the room.

"I'd be happy to show you" offers Officer Kim Patterson as she jumps up from her desk in the center of the bullpen, almost falling in her haste to help him. After gaining control of her feet, and turning a bright shade of red, she shows him to the Lieutenant's office. Who is that guy she wonders as she stares at the door that was just closed between her and him.I wouldn't mind his shoes under my bed in the morning. I wonder if he's married.

"Looks like you got it bad, Patterson. You know, you could always hook up with me" offers Officer Johnson suggestively.

"Drop dead," says Patterson "cause that's what it would take to interest me. You, dead."

"F*** you, Patterson" Johnson replies and looks back down at his desk, dwelling on the day he'll get even.

Kat feels at a big disadvantage, since she's sitting at her desk when Callander walks in, introduces himself, and then shuts the door. Nice, Kat thinks, tall, dark and handsome. This could get fun she decides, rising and reaching out to shake his hand while introducing herself."I'm Lieutenant Thomas; please have a seat."

He accepts, with thanks. "Lt Thomas, please call me Devon, that's what my friends call me, and since we may be working together closely, formality can get in the way."

"Sure, thanks" she replies "You can call me Kat" she offers.

She takes a seat and thinks, WOW, that's Capitol Police Deputy Chief? No way. This is gonna be interesting, she mentally rubs her hands together.

"Do I know you?" she asks. "You look familiar, but I'm not sure from where or when" she admits.

"I don't remember meeting you" Devon replies cautiously. "I'm a quadruplet, so you may have met my brother Eli. He works out of the Los Angeles FBI office, he's an SSA with the FBI" he says with eyebrows raised in query.

"No, I don't think so, unless he was in D.C. she replies, "I've never been to California."

He moves forward, he's heard the "have we met" at least a million times before. His looks are the type that makes people think they've met him before, and it gets a little old after awhile.

"So, Lieutenant, what have you got? I heard about a skinned body found on Decatan yesterday morning. Have you received anything back about that yet?"he asks, steering the conversation back to work.

"Yeah, we have some information. The victim was Congressman William Blaketon, the House Majority Leader, and the woman that found him and most likely died because of what she saw was his ninety-three-year-old mother, Norma."

"Awe, that's awful," he replies in sympathy.

"Yeah, it was a sad thing."

"So when were you planning on notifying the Capitol Police of this crime? This is my jurisdiction."

"I know, and I was just now preparing to notify you, but you beat me to it. Anyway, the reason we stalled notifying you was because of a murder that occurred a week ago in Staleyville, PA, that has a similar MO to the William Blaketon murder.

The person found dead was from Staleyville, PA. The victim was skinned the same way; it looks like the same calling card. The traveling distance is only about an hour forty-five, give or take" she estimates."I assume that the Capitol Police had already heard about the Staleyville murder?" she inquires politely.

"Well, actually no, we weren't contacted" he admits. "That's quite a connection, any idea who the murderer is?"

"Yep, we got that information yesterday and put out an APB in the two states and D.C.: in the home state of the killer, the first victim's murder state, and, of course, in D.C. The suspect was identified with DNA, and prints were found on both bodies. Our suspect's name is Elroy Wade. He's a fifty-eight-year-old ex-con from Elwood Prison in Texas; an ex-biker nicknamed 'Bad Ass.' We're not sure where the biker group hales from, but we do know that Elroy's home-town is Mt. Buckhorn, Ohio. At least it has been since he got out of prison last year. We haven't been able to locate him yet, but we're hoping to in the very near future."

"This is a priority case, Deputy Chief, don't you think?" she inquires in a calm but firm voice.

"Yeah, I'd have to say from what you've just told me it could be a serial killer, or possibly a copycat killer but we can't rule out terrorism either, because of the victim's political position" he explains. "Have you done a search to see if there were any other murders with the same MO that occurred since the suspects release from Elwood Prison? What were the prison charges against Wade, anyway?" he asks.

"It was for the rape of a nineteen-year-old woman in Texas, and, of course, we've run the search, Deputy Chief. We may not be Fed's, but we're no small town boon-dock here" she replies with a smirk. "You know, when I heard the name, I remembered something. It's been about twelve years now, since I was attacked here in D.C. while walking to class at Capitol Hill Community College. I'd forgotten about it, since it was such a long time ago, and I didn't get hurt, so I just kind of let it drop from my mind, until now.

"The reason I'm remembering it now is, I believe his nickname was Bad Ass. At least that's what the bikers called him, so I guess it could be the same guy."I thought his name was familiar when I first heard it. Elroy Wade, AKA Bad Ass. If it's the same guy, I got pretty lucky back then, I guess," she admits. "I was only fifteen at the time but I could take care of myself and fortunately for me, he didn't know that. If it is the same guy, he grabbed me off the sidewalk and pulled me into an alley.

I'm pretty sure his plans were rape, but he never got the chance. I actually had the upper hand before another biker named Snake, stepped in, beat the crap out of an already injured Bad Ass and warned me about walking around D.C. on my own and not paying attention. Jeeze, I haven't thought about that in years" she admits.

"Hold on a minute" Devon says."You were fifteen you said and on your way to class at Capitol Hill Community College. What were you, a child prodigy?

"Well, actually, I was a little advanced for my age" she admits. "But the point is, I believe I met Elroy Wade twelve years ago.

I need to get something to eat, man. I haven't eaten in two days. I can't just walk into a store though, Elroy thinks. Someone might see me and get suspicious. Maybe some little old lady left her door open. I could find some food easy that way, and get some company, too. I hate staying in the shadows; I had to do that too long in prison. You really don't want anyone to notice you in prison; he thinks as he breaks into a cold sweat. Those damn times still make me sick to my stomach, even though it was over a year ago. I'm never going back to prison, he promises himself. I'd rather die. I'm glad those days are over, he thinks in relief. D.C. sure brings back the memories and not all good.

We used to come out here, back then, for some mighty fine drugs, he remembers. I miss those biker days, the "Waco's Revenge" group. That group should have been mine, he thinks in anger, and it would have been except for that bastard Snake.

Just because he was younger; and started the group, big

deal. He actually ordered everyone around and expected to be followed. We used to be like bros back then; they was family, he remembers wistfully.

At least they've been throwing me some work once in a while, they owe me that much. So what if I change things up a little, have a little fun? I'm doing fine, I did my time. Geez, I shoulda been a poet he thinks as he smirks in the dark. I should never have got caught; I ever find out who snitched, they're dead meat. I still think they should have let me back in, those bastards. I was a good biker; I pretty much ran that group. Snake or no Snake, they needed me, he decides.

Now, all I have to do is wait for the dark, and find me some dinner, and then some fun in that order. This is gonna be a great night, I can feel it. He rubs his hands together and settles in to wait.

Thirty five minutes later, Elroy doesn't know what hit him, one minute he's hunkered down, the next he's laid out by a shadow while a blade is being stuck in and out of his stomach, the fire the knife is leaving causing his breath to catch. He knows he's bleeding out, but he still watches as the killer tries to move his ass to the car.

I'm glad I got bigger in prison, he thinks as his vision slowly fades, I ain't makin it any easier on that asshole he decides, his last thought "guess I don't get dinner."

"So, when did you graduate from high school, Lieutenant?" he inquires.

"I was fourteen," she admits with a shrug."What's the big deal Deputy Chief?"

"That's genius level," he murmurs.

"Yeah, so . . ."?

"Nothing" Devon replies."I was just thinking out loud. Pardon my rudeness, Lieutenant. So, there's no word on the suspect yet? No leads, no one has called anything in, saw him or anything?" he asks.

"Nope, no report of any sightings, as of now," she answers shortly.

"I'm sure we'll hear something soon" he says."Can we go

visit the crime scene, Lieutenant?" he inquires.

"Sure, give me just a minute to let my partner know where I'll be," she says in agreement. She picks up her phone, tells Des what's going on. "No, you aren't going," she remarks as she gets up, grabs her coat, says "let's go" and they both leave. All the way through the bull pen there's an unusual stillness in the air and a lot of furtive glances at the Deputy Chief that's walking behind Kat. Yeah, Kat thinks, I'd be staring too. This is going to be fun, she decides as she grins on the inside.

Once outside, she grabs the car keys out of her coat pocket and says "I'm driving, my cars right over here."

Devon offers, "We can take my car."

"Mine's closer, besides I hate riding shotgun," she responds. Once they pile in, she takes off like it's the Indy. Devon grabs the stability handle above the door, and groans.

"Earth to Devon, are you with me here? You've been kind of quiet since we left the station," Kat remarks.

"Oh, sorry, Lieutenant, I was thinking," he admits, glad that she can't read minds.

"Okay, here we are," she says as she pulls up to a nice two story Brownstone where crime scene tape is flapping in the wind, creating a grotesque picture in this elderly neighborhood.

"You wouldn't think this was a neighborhood where these things happened," he says thoughtfully.

"Yeah, on the surface it looks like an upper crust neighborhood. Unfortunately, its past its better days and the riff raff have moved in. Looks can be deceiving," she admits quietly.

As they both get out of the warm car, they stand facing in the freezing cold weather, the wind whipping their hair, a little sleet mixed in with the snow that's falling in a steady, accumulative fashion. "Looks like we're in for some more nasty weather," she remarks. "We don't usually get too much of this here, so it's going to cause problems later for traffic. Fortunately for us, it's Saturday, a less busy day in D.C. Hopefully by Tuesday, the worst day of the week for traffic, this will have blown through, otherwise, it could be a nightmare," she says while Devon shakes his head in agreement. "Let's get this done so we can get back in the car. I hate this weather," she complains.

"Okay" he agrees as he wanders around the perimeter, stares at the door where the skin was hung, and thinks about the poor guy that was killed in such a brutal way. We need to get this bastard, before he decides this was fun and does it again. "Okay, I'm through here, Lieutenant; let's get out of here," he decides.

As they head back to Metro One, he starts thinking about what needs to be done next. "I'm going to call the FBI. I'll get them working on the serial angle while I work on the terrorist angle. We're going to have to question the House of Rep's and see if they have any ideas about what might have gone on. Unfortunately, it's the weekend, and they won't be back in session until Monday and on Monday, it'll probably be a skeleton crew."

"Didn't you notice the lack of media attention? They usually know about this stuff before the police, but we've been able to keep it under wraps for twenty four hours plus," she brags with a grin, pretty proud of that accomplishment, knowing that it's not something that's easily done.

Devon laughs, impressed with that feat, "not too many can pull the cover over the media's eyes anymore, with everything that's digital" he admits.

"Oh" she says, "that quiet neighborhood that you remarked on, it was full of old people. Old people usually mean no cell phones, no computers, no eye witnesses either which sucks, but it does keep things on the downside. There's a little good about it, a little bad. Luckily, there were fingerprints. The public won't know about this happening until the news breaks sometime later today," she says as she pulls up in front of Metro One.

"Shit, I guess they know now" she mutters as she maneuvers around four different media vans all with tall antennas on top, their star reporters standing around shuddering with cold while waiting for someone to come out to interview. Rule is they're not allowed in the station for interviews, they learned that lesson a few years ago. "Here they come" she says as she gets out of her car to head in to the station.

"Lieutenant, Lieutenant Thomas, LIEUTENANT Thomas,

I have some questions," Sydney Norwood yells over the commotion, the most well known newscaster in D.C., from WKTL Channel 7 News, Metro Area as she pushes her way to the front with five cameramen trying to keep up. "Lieutenant, is it true that Congressman William Blaketon was killed yesterday, found by his mother and that there was a similar murder in Pennsylvania just one week before this one? Do you think we're looking at the same killer, Lieutenant? Have you found out anymore about this murder? How long till someone is apprehended? Do you think the public should be worried about this happening in their neighborhoods? Do we have a serial killer, Lieutenant?"

Well, we may have put a lid on it and had a temporary reprieve, but the cats out of the bag now, Kat thinks in disgust. I really hate the media, she admits to herself. Now that they know, it's going to be crazy trying to keep them from following every little thing I do and now that they're going to know the Capitol Police and the FBI's involved. It's going to be a media circus, she thinks on a groan.

Okay, here goes she decides as she and Deputy Chief Callander move into the spotlight together. "Can I have your attention please?" she yells at the anchors and cameramen. "I will give a brief statement, so pay attention, because as you know, I don't repeat myself. You get it the first time; that's your only chance. This is Deputy Chief Devon Callander of the Capitol Police. A murder occurred on Friday, time of death approximately two thirty a.m., on the one thousand block of Decatan Street. The victim, Congressman William Blaketon, was discovered by his mother at approximately four-forty-five a.m. while letting out her cat. The sight so upset her, we believe she suffered a massive heart attack and died at the scene." Questions come flying in; gasps are heard throughout the media.

"Lieutenant, is it true the victim was skinned, that you found only his skin and that his actual body is still missing? Do you think this could be organized crime?" yells Sidney. "We've never had this type of murder in D.C. before. Should the public, the House of Representatives, the Senate, even the President be concerned for their lives?" she asks insistently.

"I'll let you address Deputy Chief Devon Callander with those questions; he may be able to offer more insight into that area than I can."

"The investigation is ongoing at this time; we are actively pursuing any information pertaining to this crime. Since this is an active case, I am not at liberty to discuss this subject in any detail, but I do want to thank you in advance for your understanding. I want to say, the Capitol Police are at present looking into a possible copycat killer. We will be calling in a few different specialty departments today. That's all for now, thank you," he says and amidst screams, yells, light bulbs flashing and a general feeling of chaos, Kat and Devon escape into Metro One.

THREE

"Thanks for throwing me to the wolves, Lieutenant, I appreciate it" Devon remarks dryly. "Next time you decide to pull something like that, a heads up would be nice."

Kat just looks at him amusingly and says, "Sure, sure, *what . . . ever*! But I thought the Capitol Police were trained to handle such things" she adds with a smirk. "As long as I don't have to handle it, I'm good."

"Alright, let me make a few calls" he says and turns away to talk while Kat picks up the reports that were laid on her desk in her absence.

"Alright, cool" she says. What she sees may help a little. When Devon gets off the phone, he notices her looking at something,

"What have you got there?" he asks.

"It's a report, and it gives some history on Elroy Wade. It says he spent about seven years with a biker group, there's not much information during that time. It does make mention that he's an experienced taxidermist, not professionally, mostly just for friends or friends of friends. It doesn't look like there's any real money in it, just chump change thrown in his direction. Enough I suppose, to keep him from starving or dying of thirst" she adds with a smirk. "That information seems to have come from this past year, something he's been doing in Ohio.

"Of course, during those biker days, they probably would have taken care of each other, at least I would assume. He didn't have to do anything really. He just followed the group and went along with whatever undertaking they came across and decided to do. It sounds like he's always been a follower, she says. He definitely isn't leader material" Kat continues while thinking out loud.

"During his biker years, I would guess drugs would have been their method for obtaining enough of a cash flow to keep the gang going, since there's a lot of money in that. Enough to support everyone in the gang and keep everyone fed while still maintaining some cash. It's not cheap to buy those types of bikes, the loaded Harley's that they seem to prefer, so whatever they were doing I'm sure it wasn't legal. There's no money in legal things, especially not enough to keep a whole group going" she admits.

"I don't suppose you have an address for the biker group? I phoned my office and asked for the serial killer unit to meet tomorrow morning, here at Metro, if that's okay with you? Then I'm planning on getting the organized criminal investigative group in this with us. I want to make sure that we've got all the bases covered.

"I would also like to suggest that we take a ride to Staleyville, PA, tomorrow afternoon after we meet with the other agents. I'd like to talk to the officer in charge of that case and also the coroner that handled the body. Can you reach them and set it up?" Devon asks.

"Absolutely, Deputy Chief, that's not a problem" Kat promises "but since tomorrow is Sunday we'll have to set up a special meeting time with the Detective in charge and the Coroner. I'm sure they want this guy as bad as we do, so that shouldn't be a problem.

"There are a few things about the D.C. case that the media doesn't know, which will help us determine if the crime scenes are from the same killer. Hopefully we won't experience a leak," he says."We can leave here about noon tomorrow, if that's alright with you?" Devon asks quietly.

"It sounds good to me. Now I think I'll head out, no lunch, breakfast either for that matter. This has been one of those days" she remarks with fatigue."I'll see you here tomorrow Devon. Just pull the office door shut when you leave; it's already locked" she adds as she leaves.

"I'm Lieutenant Kat Thomas, this is my partner Detective

Rowald of D.C. Metro One Police, and this is Deputy Chief Devon Callander of the Capitol Police Department" Kat says as she reaches out to shake hands.

"Welcome to Staleyville, Pennsylvania. I'm Detective Bob Monroe," he adds as he shakes hands all around, "and this is Dr. Jimmy Cornwall, of the Althena Medical Examiner's office."

"Glad to meet you. That was a long drive you just made and not in the best of weather, either. I wasn't sure if you'd actually make it here today. I know a lot of people that wouldn't travel any distance with the weather the way it was. Near blizzard conditions for awhile for us, although I'm not sure what it's like in D.C. I don't think you normally get the same amounts of snow that we do" says Dr. Cornwall.

"Actually, no, we normally get just an inch maybe two; although I'm sure we had more than that when we left today. I think there's more now, but we can't let that stop us," Kat assures them. "We have a murder to solve."

"Would you like some coffee or anything before we get started here?" offers Bob.

"No thanks, we'll just get this done so we don't take up your whole day off. What can you tell us, Bob, about the murder? Have you received any details that weren't in the report?" Devon asks.

"There were a few small details that weren't included. We like to keep some of the things away from the public if we can, but for such a small town like we are, this became the quickest spreading gossip in all my years on the force. I think some people knew about this faster than I could drive out to the site.

"Anyway, poor guy, no one should have to die like that. What we didn't tell anyone, so only me, my boss the Sheriff (he apologizes, by the way, for not being able to be here today to meet you, he had a previous engagement), and the Althena coroner here, Jimmy Cornwall, know is this: he was actually attached to the front door by push pins. If that isn't sick, I don't know what is" he says in disgust. "First to be skinned and then push pinned," Bob just shakes his head in disbelief.

"I can take you to the crime scene if you're interested" offers Bob.

"That would be great" Devon accepts, enthusiastically. "Before we head out, are you staying in town tonight, Bob asks. We have a real nice Bed and Breakfast just outside of town; it's clean, with good food. I happen to know the owner personally, and if you want, I can call him up and let him know to expect you," he offers.

"No, but thanks Detective, we have to get back to D.C. tonight," Kat replies.

"The victim in DC was a politician, Congressman Bill Blaketon. Everyone heard about this on the news last night, so there're going to be a lot of upset people on Capitol Hill tomorrow. We'll probably have our hands full. We need to interview all of them about this, maybe hold some hands as well," she says with a sigh.

"Yeah" echoes Detective Rowald.

"Well if you want, we can go out to the crime scene and talk on the way. It's only about a four mile drive. It is backwoods, which means the roads aren't great under normal circumstances and after a snow like we just had, it's dicey. We can all go in my vehicle; it's got four wheel drive," offers Deputy Monroe.

"Thanks," Devon says in relief "we appreciate it."

"I guess I was expecting something a little different" Kat admits after viewing the crime scene in disbelief. "It looks like one of those hunting shacks I've seen on TV" she adds.

"The victim actually lived here all the time?" Devon inquires.

"These are really primitive surroundings; I'm surprised anyone found him out here, especially as fast as they did" Kat says thoughtfully.

"Yeah, it might not look like much, but it was all he seemed to need. That door right there, you can see the blood stains on it, that's where he was left. We haven't found the body yet. I'm not even sure where it could have been put, but if it was anywhere in the surrounding woods it's probably become someone's dinner. We have bears and mountain lions in this area, and they don't miss that kind of stuff lying around. The smell will call to them making for a nice easy meal and they don't leave anything behind, they eat everything. So I guess what I'm saying is, the hope of actually finding the body is pretty slim" he admits.

"It doesn't look like all the blood was right here. Did you notice if there was a more primary crime scene Bob?" Kat asks. "It would have had a lot more blood, soaking into the ground, maybe with leaves and grass trampled down?"

"Did you find any other evidence that wasn't in the report, Dr. Cornwall?" Devon inquires.

"Well, not including the fingerprints we found on the body, and the push pins that were used, we did find some hair that didn't belong and we recovered some DNA from under his fingernails. It looked like he fought his attacker pretty good. From the looks of the skin, a stab wound to the chest was the cause of death. He didn't suffer too much, it was a relatively quick death, he probably bled out within about minute" Dr. Cornwall assures everyone. "He wouldn't have known what was being done to his body, that's for sure."

"This is the only crime scene we found, but we've had close to a foot of snow a week for the past month," Bob admits uncomfortably "and that makes crimes scenes around here hard to find, because as you can see it's pretty much a wilderness out here."

"Yeah," Kat agrees with disappointment.

"Well," Kat says after getting back to D.C. "what are we going to release to the press, Deputy Chief? We need to keep to the facts and be able to calm the fears of the public and at the same time inform them that we believe there are a few commonalities with these murders. All our evidence is pointing to the two murders having one killer. We've searched all the databases around and haven't found any matching murders with the same MO. I'd like to get him before he can commit another murder. At least we know who he is, now we just need to find him" Kat says to Devon as she walks to the Captains office.

"Captain, I have a report for you on the capitol murder. All the evidence that we've obtained meshes with the medical examiners for both Pennsylvania and Metro. Elroy Wade's prints were the only ones that were obtained from both crime scenes. We also found hairs on the skin of both victims, those also belonging to Elroy Wade. His DNA was found in the system, since he was convicted of rape more than ten years ago in Texas. He was released last year, after serving his ten-year sentence. All we need to do now is find him before he commits another crime. An APB was issued for Elroy Wade to the Metro Police Department" reports Kat "and a teletype has gone out for all police in the U.S."

"Good work, Lieutenant Thomas, Deputy Chief Callander" remarks Captain Hall. "We have an interview with the press in fifteen minutes. They've been pounding on the doors for the better part of the day for some news" he warns them. "I expect the both of you, and your partner present, for this release."

"Yes, sir," Kat responds.

"Another thing, Lieutenant; I expect your presence on Capitol Hill tomorrow. The House will be in session, and I'm sure all hell's going to break loose. This hits them pretty closely since it's one of their own. We also need to interview all the members of the House. Someone may have seen this guy hanging around. What we don't know is why. Why William Blaketon, and why Tom Mason? What did they have in common? What made the suspect choose them?" Captain Hall asks. "Unfortunately, those are questions we don't have answers for yet."

"It's crazy in this room" Kat yells to Des, Deputy Chief Devon Callander, and FBI SSA Mallory Callander. Who could have known that Deputy Chief Callander would have siblings in the FBI? Not only quadruplet siblings, but all are federal agents. One's in charge of the serial killer unit, and from what Devon said yesterday, he's got a brother in California that's in charge of the West Coast counter terrorism unit.

I wonder where the last brother is. He hasn't mentioned anything about his other brother. He must not have followed his other siblings into police work, she thinks. I wonder why he wasn't mentioned. Maybe he's the black sheep of the Callander siblings, every family has one. I'll just bet that's an interesting story.

"I'll start with the Speaker of the House; you can start anywhere you want. We need to talk to all of these people as soon as possible" Kat reminds everyone quickly.

"Oh, shhhh, the Speaker of the House is getting ready to say something" Des whispers.

"Thank you for being here this morning," Virginia Moore, Speaker of the House announces."You have probably heard about the murder of our fellow congressman, William Blaketon, and the death of his poor mother, Norma. It was a terrible shock to all of us. From what I've heard, this was a random murder. The police have already identified the person responsible and are working frantically to locate this person. I'm sure no one here needs worry, they did reassure me that it was random," she says.

"There are police and FBI throughout the room at this moment. They would like to ask each and every person here not to leave until you have spoken with a Metro One Police Officer, a Capitol Hill Police Officer, or an FBI agent. I would also like to let everyone know that there will be a memorial service for Bill on Wednesday morning at ten a.m. at the Chapel on the Hill, with internment at Capitol Hill Cemetery. Both Bill and his mother are being cremated, so the memorial service will be for both since there is no family left for either Bill or his mother, after his father passed on over ten years ago.

"So, as Speaker of the House, and with the president's wishes, we would like you to keep the flowers down to a minimum. We're recommending donations be made to a favorite charity in their names. Thank you for your time, and please remember, don't leave until you've talked with an officer," she concludes.

"Alright everybody, let's tone this down. It's been a long day, and we need to head back to Metro One to complete the reports on everyone's response to the murder. I'm hoping we got some information on the sighting of our perp. The sooner we get this guy, the happier I'm going to be" Kat admits. It sure would be nice to close this up before the funeral, but I have a feeling that's not going to happen, she thinks.

FOUR

"I haven't seen this many people, wearing black, all in the same place, ever. It looks like a room full of penguins" Des murmurs.

"Let's hope the suspect decides he needs to see this, to bask in the knowledge that he created this moment. We need everyone to fan out and intermingle; we want to catch this guy if he shows up" Devon reminds everyone. "Kat, you take the front, right side, I'll take the left front and Mallory, you mingle in the middle. Both of you let your own teams know what the plan is. Everyone else, pick an area. Des, you monitor the back doors. If the suspect decides to show up, he has to come in somewhere.

"All entrances and exits need to be covered. It looks like it's going to start any time now. The President and Vice-President should be here any minute. Yep, there they are, coming in the front side doors. Of course the Secret Service is going to be heavy today."

"Who's that woman with them? It's not either of their wives" Des whispers to Kat.

"Wait a minute, isn't that Jane Martin?" Kat says."The woman who escaped while being held hostage in Iran, you know, that investigative journalist? Didn't they appoint her to the Department of Homeland Security after her ordeal in Iran; something about Terrorism Support?"

I'd already been here for five years, Kat remembers while taking her seat near the President for the funeral. Remembered hearing how the President pushed to get Jane Martin into that position; how he had to coax Bob Verahne to actually create the position for her.

"Honestly Bob, I think you should give Jane a thought. This position sounds like its right in her field of expertise, the president says."

"How so, Mr. President, since my take is she's just an ex-investigational reporter that was held as a hostage. She was lucky enough to escape with her life, and once home, she has done nothing but television interviews. She's not back to investigating anything, so she really gave that up, which tells me that she's not as unaffected as you say. How could that be a rehabilitated hostage? To me, that's someone with their head in the sand, who's cashing in on the fact that she's still alive. The media has grabbed her, and made her a prima donna. I don't see her doing this position any good" he responds in disagreement.

"I'm sorry you feel that way Bob. But I know if given the chance, she'd be perfect. Who wouldn't trust her? Who won't relate to her? She was there, she survived it, and she moved forward. She looks just like any other American, average, not movie star pretty, unassuming, single.A vocal Christian, held in high regard by the Minister of the largest non-denominational church in the world. I say she's perfect!" the President stresses.

"Okay, Mr. President, I'll interview her. But I can't guarantee anything, yet."

"Fine, that's all I'm asking Bob, just give her a chance."

"I'm Jane Martin, sir. You wanted to see me" Jane asks of Bob Verahne.

"Yes, I did" Bob admits."The President told me a little bit about your past, and I thought you might be just the person that we've been looking for, for a position that's open on my staff."

"What position, sir" Jane asks respectfully.

"Well, with everything that's happened in the past, since the 9/11 attack; we've been building a group of people to try to handle the repercussions of problems for those that were close to the terrorist attacks. They've been actual hostage releases, or were affected, but not physically harmed, by them. The damage is more in the psychological damage, collateral damage control area.

"Anyway, the position is for a subject matter expert (SME) on hostage rehabilitation.We want to be able to help people affected by hostage issues, and enable them to re-enter the world as normal, contributing members of society. We, this Cabinet, were formed at the President's request. Our goal is to create a team that will act as agents to the public, and help in a way that will give them back hope and direction."

"After your own attack on foreign soil, and the fact that you were held for six months by those Muslim extremists, and then your ability to escape, to have done as well as you have is a remarkable feat. You are to be commended, Ms. Martin, for the strength of character that you've demonstrated to the United States, and the world. People won't soon forget what you went through, and how well you came through it.

"You'll always be remembered as a heroine, you could even be a poster child for the people of the world. You offer them hope. You've been called a guiding light by the media."

"Thank you sir, that's the nicest thing anyone's ever said to me" she replies with a shy glance down. "I don't know what to say" she murmurs.

"I understand that your specialty area is investigative journalism, and that you did extremely well in that area prior to your confinement. You could make a difference in a lot of people's lives and not even leave the safety of your own country.

"I think this position would allow you the freedom of movement, that you seem to prefer, while giving you an anchor in this somewhat crazy world" he offers.

"It sounds like the perfect job Sir, but, can I think about it for a little bit. It's not something I've ever thought about before, and it's really come out of left field" she admits.

"I understand Jane, so yes, please, take a few days and then let me know" he offers with a smile. I think the President may have been right, Bob acknowledges to himself, there's just something about her.

"I never would have thought that she'd be here today" Kat says to Des. "She shows up at the oddest times, and she definitely keeps powerful company. She's been near the president for a few years now. He's kind of taken her under his wing. It's pretty hard to even get near her since she's being protected by the Secret Service, too. Not that it matters, she's just a little thing. She's certainly not considered a threat to anything that's happened."

"She probably hasn't heard, or seen anything, she's watched so closely" Devon replies.

"Okay people, let's do this" Kat orders quietly.

Phew, they are certainly a long winded group, Kat thinks as she listens to the closing sentences. You'd think all these people were best friends, with all the tears flowing so easily. They wouldn't want to miss a media moment, and I know that's where they're all headed, she thinks cynically. It was nice they blocked the media for a while, unfortunately, our times up and here comes the circus.

"Poor Jane, she looks like she took that pretty hard, wouldn't you say Mrs. Delrose?" Kat asks the House Minority Leader, as she reaches her. "How well did you know Bill Blaketon, Mrs. Delrose?" inquires Kat.

"Please, call me Karen, Lieutenant".

"Thank you, Karen; so were you close to him, to Bill Blaketon?" she asks.

"Well, I feel like we were close, since we held similar positions. I've known Bill a long time. It's a terrible thing that happened to him, and it just makes me sick" Karen adds with a sniffle."We're all going to miss him, even though he was a little pompous, on occasion. I need to get out of here Lieutenant, please excuse me" she mumbles.

"Sure Karen, I have all I need right now. If you think of anything more, here's my card. Please, give me a call" Kat requests.

"I'll be sure to, Lieutenant, I promise."

"Okay, I've been at worse services, any sign of anyone that looked out of place?" Kat inquires with hope. "My area was good, how about your people Devon, Mallory?"

"Nope, at least nobody glaringly different at first glance" Mallory says. "There was definitely no Elroy Wade. There's no way he could have hid, not even in one of those penguin suits. He would have stood out like a beacon in the night. Ex-biker dudes don't clean up that well" she adds.

"Alright, we need to get on the road. Let's start looking again, hit some of the bars around town, and see if anyone's seen him, or someone that looks like him. It's going on a week now. We need to get this guy, before he hits again" Kat reminds them all. With flashes of light everywhere, blinding everyone coming out of The Chapel on the Hill, they meet a mob on the outside steps.

"Shit" Kat says. "I was hoping the media interviews would be over before we got out here."

"Lieutenant, is it true you still haven't caught Elroy Wade? Do you think he's still in D.C.? What are your feelings that he'll strike again? We know this was murder number two; do the House of Representatives, the Senate, need to be afraid for their lives?"

"What about the President, does he need to worry? What's the connection between these murders? Is this a Capitol Hill killer?" came the questions fast and furious, from Sidney of WKTL TV, News Channel 7 while she's surrounded by a mob of press, all jostling for the front while yelling questions, trying to get answers before anyone else. This is big news, it's not every day a U.S. Congressman is killed, and never in the manner that he was.

The media has to be in a panic, to be first with the news, ratings and all that. Not that Sidney ever needs to worry about that, Kat thinks. She's a shark when it comes to the news; she always seems to get the information first. She must have a heck of a network, or some mighty fine moles, either way, she's good. Maybe I should use some of that ability, Kat thinks, it couldn't hurt, she decides as she moves forward to start leaking some info to the press. Besides, they get around faster than most of the agencies in town.

"Hi Sidney, looks like you met Deputy Chief Callander already. I was just coming over to introduce you" Kat admits with a knowing smile.

"Yep" Sidney replies with a grin "we introduced ourselves, and we're just talking about the murder, and some small tidbits of info."

"Well, Deputy Chief Callander, I hope you're not giving away any of our secrets about this murder" Kat responds teasingly.

"We were just discussing how similar the two murders are, and how much the media could help us in locating our suspect."

"A couple special news bulletins would probably work" Devon says, seemingly ignorant of the undercurrents in the discussion."Maybe one at the lunch hour and then again at dinner, what do you think Sidney?" he inquires.

"Sounds good to me" Kat adds with a smirk, feeling a winning situation after looking at Sidney's hard smile."I need to get going, I have things to do" she informs Sidney, and with Devon agreeing to that announcement, they both take their leave."Talk to you later, Sidney" Kat and Devon promise as they escape the press.

"So, how about a late lunch" Devon asks as they walk toward Metro One.

"Sure" she agrees "how about the Mohave Restaurant. They do a pretty good salad bar, if you're interested, plus they're quick. I eat there a lot since I'm usually running around town on one investigation or another."

"It sounds good to me," Devon says.

After Kat is greeted like a long lost friend by the maître'd at the Mohave, they take their seats in a corner table of the restaurant. "I guess you do eat here a lot" he says "since everyone seems to know you."

"Yeah, they're like an extended family. Everyone's always trying to take care of me," she admits."I suppose because I've been eating here since I was fifteen."

"So, where are you from Kat, D.C?" he asks.

"No, I'm from a small rural town, on the other side of Richmond. But I haven't been back there in twelve years, so I guess D.C. is my home now."

"But what about your parents, don't you keep in touch with them?" he asks in confusion.

"They both died together in a car accident when I was fifteen, so I've been on my own since. I'm quite capable of taking care of myself, Devon, in spite of the fact that everyone's always trying take care of me. I put myself through college, and paid for that with a small life insurance policy that my parents left. I worked some odd jobs, when I needed to. I did fine" she says with determination.

"What about you, Devon, you said you were a quadruplet?"

"Yeah, I have two brothers and a sister" he replies. "We aren't identical, but we look a lot alike. All of us have the same dark hair, the same blue eyes. But my brothers and I look so much alike, we could actually be identical. At a quick glance, we probably are for a lot of people, but thankfully there's something slightly different about each one of us, so those close to us can tell."

"You mentioned you have two brothers and that one is with the FBI in California, but what about the other one?" she inquires. "You've never said anything about him."

"Well, my brother Jacob, I haven't seen since I was seventeen. He took off after high school, and hasn't kept in touch with my parents, or his brothers or sister. He always was a hot head, hung around the wrong groups. I think he started to get into the drug scene. H wasn't interested in sports, or any of the things that Eli and I were, so we kind of drifted apart, sometime around our tenth grade year. He did graduate, but the same day that he got his diploma, he grabbed his stuff, and poof. He hasn't been heard from since" he admits brusquely.

"That's sad" she responds to the story. "I'll bet your parents miss him" she murmurs.

"Oh yeah, Dad calls me the same day and time every week, just to check. I hate to upset them, but there's been nothing. I don't even know if he's still alive. After fifteen years of nothing, I'm not going to hold out any hope" he responds.

"Yeah" she admits "that's a long time."

"So, enough about me, anyone special in your life right now?" he asks as he looks into her eyes with male appreciation.

41

"No, I haven't had the time lately, to even think about any-one. Work's been keeping me pretty busy" she admits.

"Well, we'll have to change that" he remarks.

"We just got a tip in" Kat informs Devon from Metro One after returning from a nice lunch. "Back to reality, work calls. We need to take off now, but I'll fill you in as we walk to the car. Des you're with me" she says. "The owner of the In Peace livestock hauler trucking company out of D.C. called. He was making his delivery to the pet cemetery "Best Friends Crema-tory and Cemetery" in Canterville, Pennsylvania, which is a town about twenty five miles south of Staleyville, where the first murder took place."

"Anyway, when he arrived, after picking up a couple of dead horses, he pulls back to the crematory building like he's supposed to. He normally tips his truck, to slide the animals out of the truck bed. It's a high walled truck bed, you can't see over it, he says, and it has an automatic tarp that closes at the push of a button, in the cab. He never see's the animals, until he starts to unload them, and he did say he can't keep them in the bed too long, because of the smell.

"He was emptying his bed, when one of the workers started yelling for him to stop. He pushed the stop button, but the mo-mentum had carried the rest of the dead animals out of the bed, and onto the ground. The workers started screaming, because they saw a human body included in the bunch, a human body san's skin" Kat finishes with excitement.

"It sounds like it could be our first big break" he replies en-thusiastically. "How long does it take to get there?" he asks.

"Maybe a little over an hour, probably less, if I'm driving" she replies with a grin and a light in her eyes.

Best Friends Crematory and Cemetery is located in an out of the way place, in a beautiful wooded area, with huge cupids guarding the gate to the Cemetery, and tiny head stones, mark-ing each of the precious animal's burial plots.

"It looks like a very upscale cemetery" Kat observes.

"This place is nicer than some of the people cemeteries I've seen" Des says in surprise.

"Yeah, no expense is spared when it's a favorite pet, but when it comes to grandma, well, any old place will do" Kat adds with disgust.

"That sign there says the Crematory is straight back" Devon informs them. "I see the big hauler truck, let's see what we've got" he says. With a whistle, he acknowledges the fact that there is indeed a human body mixed among the animals. The smell of death is in the air.

"Gross" Des admits, gagging.

"Want some gum, anyone?" Kat offers all around. "It's the only way I can function with that smell" she admits as Des takes a bunch and starts chewing quickly. "It helps me to focus on anything, besides the smell" Kat admits, her face bleached of color.

"That looks like it could be our victim, but which one is it" she wonders. "We had two with no skin, which one is this one? We need to notify the local police, and get this show on the road" she informs them. "Des, you contact the police, I'm going over there to talk to the owner of the trucking company" Kat says as Devon follows along.

"Who's the owner of that truck over there?" Kat asks of the men standing around. They all look pretty shaken up, and a few probably lost their lunch.

"I am, Ms" replies a middle aged looking man with brown hair and glasses.

"I'm Lieutenant Thomas of D.C Metro One Police, and this is Deputy Chief Devon Callander of the Capitol Police. What's your name sir?" inquires Kat.

"Oh, sorry, I'm Mike Andrews, I own the company 'In Peace.' I haul dead livestock to this cemetery, two sometimes three times a week. I've been doing this for almost twenty-seven years, and never had a dead human body show up. Maybe it's time to retire" he adds in a shaken voice.

"Mike, tell me, do you know anyone that could put something like that in your truck?" Kat asks.

"No, Lieutenant. I can't even begin to think of anyone that could have done something like this. It's disgusting" Mike states.

43

"Yeah, gross" echoes everyone standing around.

"This looks like it could be a murder victim that was killed in Washington recently. He was killed by removing the skin, and eyes. But the killer took the body and left the skin. It looks like he may have given it to you, sir. Have you ever heard of Elroy Wade?" she asks.

"Who, no, never" Mike exclaims.

"How about William Blaketon?" she continues.

"No" he assures her.

"You've never heard of William Blaketon, Mike, you're sure? His names been on all the local news channels, and the national news channels for close to a week now?" she exclaims.

"I had heard about the murders, Lieutenant. The news was pretty graphic as to what it would probably look like. That's why I called, to let you know what was happening here. I've never really paid attention to the names of the actual victims" he admits.

"What's your connection to either the victim or the killer, then?" she demands, getting a little more irritated."You think you were randomly chosen, sir, to have your truck used in a murder? After all, the body was found in your truck. I thought you emptied it more frequently than this, didn't you say three times a week, Mike?" she demands brusquely.

"Yes Lieutenant, I did, but we had all that snow last week and I couldn't make it. We had a lot in D.C., but Canterville had a lot more. The roads were too bad for me to come all the way here" he admits.

"Okay, I understand that, Mike.

So, when was the last time you came here with a load, and emptied your truck?" Devon asks as he takes over the questioning.

"Well, I did get here one time last week, but it was on Monday, the day before the snow started. I haven't been here since, right guys?" he demands in a panic.

"Yeah, he's usually here two or three times a week, but not last week" replies the group in a hushed tone.

"Alright, thanks" Kat says as a police vehicle comes driving down the road towards them, with lights on, but no sirens. Kat moves to intercept the officer while Devon stays for more questioning.

"Officer, I'm Lieutenant Thomas of D.C. Metro One Police Department. We believe that we've found the body of a missing murder victim from Washington D.C. Can you notify the medical examiner for me? We need to get this body moved before any more evidence is destroyed?"

"Right away, Lieutenant" replies Canterville Police Officer Garrett.

"The medical examiner is Dr. Louise Shirdon, I'll call her right away" he stammers after a quick glance at the dead body. He's no more than a rooky, but he'll do okay, if he doesn't lose his lunch, she thinks watching his color change from red to gray. At least he's got good manners, knows rank, and shows some respect for the Officer in charge.

"You didn't go back to the garage, where you park your work vehicle, Mike? Not all week long?" Devon asks.

"No sir, there wasn't any need. There were no pick up calls, so there was no need to go in, my truck was empty."

"Do you own the building that houses your truck?" he asks.

"No Sir, I rent a space big enough to house the truck. I don't need a lot of room, since I do all my office work out of my house. It's just a small part of a big building, but it's big enough for what I need, and the price is right. I always empty my truck before I park it and I wash it out. I don't want to smell up my parking area. The owner wouldn't like that, I doubt. I perform a service Sir, I would never hurt anyone" he insists.

"Right" Devon replies to the hint of panic in Mike's voice. "Don't go anywhere, I may need to talk to you more" he informs him.

"No Sir, I'll be right here" he promises.

"Lieutenant, Detective, anything new?" Devon asks.

"We just had the officer call in the medical examiner, she's on her way" Kat informs him."It's not an extremely small town, but it is relatively quiet, so I have high hopes she'll be able to get to this right away" Kat replies as Des shakes her head in agreement.

"I think she just pulled in at the front gates, Lieutenant" Des informs her.

"Yep, there she is. Thanks officer, for your help."

"No problem, Lieutenant" he replies "glad to be of service."

"Dr. Shirdon, I'm Lieutenant Kat Thomas, from D.C. Metro One Police Department, this is Deputy Chief Devon Callander of the FBI, and over here is my partner Detective Rowald, from D.C. Metro One.

"We're all here in response to a call we received, from the livestock hauler standing right over there with the other workers. I'm not sure if you've heard about the D.C. murder, but I do know that it was broadcast on the national news, and it was a pretty gruesome murder. I believe that the human body mixed in with the horses, could be the body from D.C." she finishes.

"Yes, it looks like a body that's been skinned, but I can't tell you anything until I perform the autopsy. I should be able to start that today Lieutenant, although it may take a few days to get all the tests back. I'll at least be able to give you cause of death, and probably even time. Will that help?"

"Absolutely, Dr. Shirdon, everything helps, and is appreciated" Kat replies earnestly.

Dr. Shirdon orders her team to "bag the remains, be careful not to contaminate them any further. It's going to be hard enough as it is."

"Alright, let's head out" Kat informs her group. "Before we go, Mike, I need a contact number for you. I'm going to need to look at your garage, when we get back to D.C. Who's the owner of the building, Mike?" she asks quickly.

"His name is Addy Thayer. He's a middle aged man, nice guy. He's never given me any trouble, even when I thought I was going to be late a couple times with the rent, he just smiled and shrugged it off. He knows I'm good for it" Mike smiles.

"How long has he been the owner?" Kat asks.

"Well, he's had it for maybe the last ten years. Before that, it was his uncle's, but he got sick and sold it to Addy. It worked out for everyone. Like I said, Addie's a heck of a guy" Mike says.

"Thanks Mike, we'll be in touch" she reassures him. "Let's head out to the Coroner's office" she suggests to Devon and Des. "It doesn't matter what town you're in, the Coroner's office is always the same. Small, dark, and smells like death" Kat says.

"I don't know how these people do this, day in and day out" Des says in disgust."It creep's me out to come in here" she admits.

"I told you to wait in the car Des, you didn't have to come in here" Kat reminds her as she lowers her voice to make her partner nervous.

"Kat, don't do that" pleads Des in a scared voice.

"Alright" she laughs while Devon grins."Don't want you passing out on the Coroner, she might mistake you for a victim" she teases her with a laugh.

FIVE

"Dr. Shirdon, may we come in?" Kat inquires as she peek's her head around the entrance door of the autopsy suite.

"Absolutely, Officers" replies Dr. Shirdon, who's standing by the table on which the body is laid out. She looks a lot different in all her medical clothes, with a mask on. You can only see her eyes, and she's got a face shield over them.

"I've started on the autopsy, as you can see. The body has started to break down, but I'm going to say time of death was around six days ago, cause of death appears to be a hole, right here in the sternum area. A stab to the heart is the most likely cause of death. The weapon used was a blade, approximately six inches long, possibly a stiletto of some sort, maybe a switch blade pocket knife. However, it was not the same weapon that was used to remove the skin. That knife was much sharper than the stiletto that was used, with a smooth blade. So I'm ruling the stab to the heart as cause, time six days ago.

"It's going to take longer to identify the body, since it will have to be through DNA testing, there are no fingerprints left. The job of removing the skin looks almost professional, though. Someone has either done this before, or something similar. Someone in the medical profession could do this, although I would expect a better job of one in my profession" she says arrogantly. "The eyes also have been removed, enucleated is the term for that. That took some work. It also looks like whoever did this, took the optic nerves as well. Unfortunately, bad news is that this can be done alive, and even though I hope it wasn't, I'll be able to tell you more when I get to that part of the autopsy" the Dr. admits.

"Shit, I never thought of that" Kat says. "So, what you're

saying is, the stab occurred before the victim was skinned, is that right Doctor?" she asks.

"Yes, I believe so. I see nothing to indicate that it was the other way around" she replies.

"Okay, after the stab, they removed his eyes, is that what you're saying Dr.? Kat asks.

"That, I can't be sure of Lieutenant. It's very possible that the eyes were taken first. The killer would have liked the thrill of causing pain, while the victim could see his murderer and be tormented.

"I believe a lot of killers enjoy that. I'll have to examine the wounds, to know which were caused first. Leave me your contact information, and when I finish with the autopsy, I'll call you to let you know. I should have more information for you probably by tomorrow, Lieutenant."

"That's excellent Dr. and thank you for your cooperation," Kat says.

"It's been very nice working with you" Devon says as they turn to leave.

"Let's head back to Metro One. It's only about four in the afternoon and with an hour and a half drive, we still have time to update the Captain with this new information."

"Alright" Devon agrees.

"Can we eat? It's been like ten hours since my last meal?" Des complains.

"Fine" Kat says, irritated. "It seems like we spend a lot of time eating, or planning on eating" she complains. "We'll get some fast food, and eat as we drive."

"Captain, I have an updated report for you" Kat informs him after she knocks on his door, upon arrival at Metro One.

"Please Lieutenant, let's hear it" he replies.

"Yes sir. We recovered the body from the Pet Crematorium in Canterville PA, this morning. We contacted the Coroner in Canterville, and she is, at this time, completing the autopsy on the John Doe. She did report cause of death as being a stab wound to the heart, probably by a blade six inches long, possibly of the switch blade variety. She's investigating the eyes, sir, believing that they may have been removed before the victim was dead."

"Jeeze, Lieutenant" the Captain says "this sounds more and more like a sociopath all the time. That's not going to comfort the public. Let's leave that detail out. We'll keep that one close, and release anything else that isn't so graphic. There are kids out there. They listen to the news too. There's no since in upsetting them, giving them nightmares, or giving anyone else any ideas. I'd hate to be responsible for another murder with the same MO, all because we leaked too much information" the Captain muses.

"I agree Captain, and I'm sure Deputy Chief Callander will also."

"See that you notify him tonight, before he has the chance to share the info, Lieutenant" orders the Captain.

"Yes, sir" she replies.

"You're dismissed, Lieutenant."

"Thank you, sir."

Kat had just gotten home, taken off her boots from work, and started changing into her favorite outfit. Old worn flannel pants from her police academy days, and a tank top that somehow ended up tied dyed in different shades of green. She hears pounding on her door, just as she finishes dressing. "Hold on, I'm coming" she yells as she grabs her weapon, and heads down the hall from the bedroom. After looking through her peep hole to see who it is, she throws open her door. "How did you get my address, Devon?" she demands while holding her weapon in one hand, and the door knob in the other.

"I'm Capitol Police, Kat, I can find anyone. It's what we do, remember?" he answers with a grin.

"Oh, yeah, right" she mumbles, feeling stupid. "So what do you want, I'm done for the day" she says. "I just want to sit down, and not think for a while, maybe eat something that's not on the run" she admits.

"I was hoping you weren't busy" he explains "how about we order pizza? I haven't eaten yet either."

"All right, come on in, if you must" she invites begrudgingly. "You'll have to excuse the mess. I haven't been home long enough to clean ever since this case started, a week ago."

"I hear you" he agrees."I'm not even sure what my place looks like anymore, but it sure isn't as clean as your place" he admires."Nice colors."

"Thanks" Kat says."I don't usually have people over. Actually, you're the first person to come over here in probably a year. I think the last company I had was Des. I don't share my home with many people" she admits shyly.

"Devon, can you get the door please?" she yells, busy in the kitchen opening a bottle of wine.

"One large supreme pizza, sir" announces a red headed curly haired teenager, lime green ear buds hanging around his neck, wearing baggy jeans and a brilliant orange hoody sweatshirt, with the pizza parlor logo on the front, and those tennis shoes with the wheels in the back. Devon hands him a twenty, says keep the change, and shuts the door.

"You can put that on the coffee table, if you want. We'll eat comfortable. I don't want to sit at the table tonight" she explains.

"Sounds good to me" he admits.

"That was perfect" she groans as she licks the rest of the sauce off the thumb of her right hand.

"Small, delicate fingers" Devon says as he strokes her left hand."No rings, Kat?" he asks.

"No, they get in the way, they're a hazard. They get caught on things, like hair, coat pockets, you know, they get in the way."

"Yeah" he says agreeably as he turns to face her while moving a little closer.

"Wow, I ate too much" she says nervously when she see's Devon lean in a little closer.

"What's the matter Kat, am I making you nervous?" he teases. "There's nothing to be nervous about, you know" he insists.

"I know that, Devon" she replies. "I'm just not used to being this close to anyone" she admits, as she moves back into her own space.

"You can't tell me you've never had a boyfriend?" he remarks in surprise."There's no way that's possible. You're too pretty to have not attracted the opposite sex" he exclaims.

"Oh, I've had boyfriends, when I was at the academy. But the relationships didn't last. I guess I've just put everything into my job, for the past few years" she admits sheepishly.

"Well, how about we change that a little" he murmurs. "I'm attracted to you" he says as he moves in to lightly kiss her lips, and then turn a small kiss into a long kiss, with tongues stroking. "I'd like to get to know you better" he groans as she responds to his kiss with a tongue thrust of her own. He turns, and presses her back into the bright red couch as the kiss deepens.

Suddenly, her cell phone rings."Shit, not now" she groans "come on, leave me alone."

"You better get that, it could be important" he reminds her.

"Yeah, I know" she mutters in disgust and moves to find her phone."Where the hell did I put that phone? Oh, I see it, it's on the table" she says as she hurriedly gets up, trips over her shoes and after almost falling, she reaches it. "Hello?" she grumbles.

"Kat, I hate to bother you in your off time, but we have a problem."

"What is it Captain" she inquires smoothing her hair, as if the Captain can see through the phone.

"We have another dead Congressman, Kat. Her daughter found her lying on the floor of her study. She dialed 911, and dispatch sent a squad and an officer from Metro One. Once the medics discovered her dead, the medical examiner was dispatched, but since it's the second congressman to die in a week, I think you need to be there. It's doesn't look as if it's murder, at least not at first sight. The medical examiner will determine cause at autopsy, but I'd still be more comfortable if you were there. Treat it as a crime scene until we hear otherwise" he orders.

"Which Congressman, Sir?" she inquires.

"It's Congresswoman Karen Delrose; she lives at two seven seven eight Potomac Avenue."

"Right, I'm on my way Sir."

"Thanks Kat. Keep me informed" he orders her.

"Yes Sir" she replies. "Devon, you heard? I need to call Des."

Kat drops the phone on the coffee table, almost hitting the last piece of pizza, and informs Devon of the dead Congresswoman.

"Right, I think we're set, let's go," she says. "We better take both our cars. I don't want anyone to know we spent the evening together" she says anxiously.

"What, why?" he asks in confusion. "It's not against the law, for two people to see each other in their off time."

"I know" she admits "but I don't date co-workers, that's one of my long standing rules."

"I'm not a co-worker" he exclaims.

"Well, I disagree" she argues. "We're working on the same case right now, so that makes us co-workers."

"Alright, technically, maybe we are. But in reality, we're not" he insists.

"Well 'technically' is all I need" she says. "We are co-workers, and that's my final comment on that" she insists.

"Well, excuse me, but you can't make that kind of decision, Kat" he insists. "It affects both of us; therefore, we both have to agree, and I don't agree" he states in a firm tone.

"I can't talk about this now, I have a crime scene to get to" she replies uneasily.

"Fine" he says as he rolls his eyes.

As Kat pulls up to two seven seven eight Potomac Avenue and parks next to the medical examiners body wagon, Devon pulls in also.

"That was a quick ride" he admits.

"Shhh" she says, glancing quickly around looking for witnesses, "we're just now meeting here, remember."

"Stop it Kat, there's no one around to hear us anyway" he responds in disgust. "You're making more out of this than you need to" he insists.

"Fine, let's go and see what's inside" she says with dignity and not a little hurt.

SIX

"Hi Dr. Zorgath, what have you got?" Kat asks after she enters the study and starts to wander around.

"Well" he says "it looks like she just collapsed, right here, and never got back up. She's so young to have died of natural causes" he says to Kat "It's been known to happen, though. I'll be able to understand more, after I get her back to autopsy. This is such a shame, wasn't she the Minority Leader for the House?" he asks in confusion."I don't keep up too closely with politics, and before you say anything," he says defensively."I find politics rather boring, too many hypocrites" he explains with a sheepish smile.

"Yea, I know what you mean. I've never been too interested in politics myself" she admits.

Devon just shakes his head at both of them."We live and work in the political capital of the free world, and neither one of you know much about politics. That's sad" he admonishes.

"Yeah, she was the Minority Leader for the House, and William Blaketon was the Majority Leader for the House" Kat says.

"And now, it looks like there's a connection" Devon adds.

"We had better treat this as a crime scene, Dr. I'll call the Captain and inform him" Kat says.

"Must have leaked the news somewhere" she remarks to Devon, as they walk through the bull pen."Otherwise, we'd never be this crazy, at this time in the morning."

Officer Patterson overhears Kat as she walks by, and tells her "It's all over the news already, the phones are going nuts. I think every congressman has called, and the White House wants to be informed as soon as we know anything, Lieutenant."

"Yeah, I kind of figured" she replies."I'll head down to give the Captain my report. You're welcome to come, if you're so inclined" she offers Devon, but he declines the offer with the question,

"If I could use your office, I need to make a couple of calls, too."

"Sure, it's open, help yourself" Kat replies tiredly.

Kat finishes her report to the Captain, having little information at this time. When she gets back to her office, the serial killer unit from the FBI along with the anti-terrorist group is all talking at the same time.

"Devon" she says loudly to be heard over all the noise in the background."We have a conference room available. Let's move everyone there. It's bigger and there's seating for everyone."

"Thanks Kat" he replies gratefully."Listen up everyone, we're going to take this to the conference room, we need to talk." Once the roar subsides and everyone's got some coffee to get things going, Kat's able to give her update.

"Look, I know this is confusing, but we have, as you've probably already heard, a dead Congresswoman Karen Delrose. She was the House Minority Leader. The medical examiner will be performing an autopsy this morning, to determine cause of death.

At first sight, this did not look like a murder. She was lying on the floor of her study, peacefully asleep. It really did look like natural causes. However, a woman of forty eight doesn't normally die of natural causes, so we need to wait for the official ruling. Hopefully, before noon but I'm not going to hold my breath" she admits with a sigh."This was nothing like the first murder, that murder was obvious, with just the skin showing up. We did find a body close to a week later, at least it was like the body that could have been left from that murder, but we're still waiting for that identification. It should be coming in sometime today" she informs them all.

"There was a media leak somehow last night, so the majority of D.C. Metro One was called in to do damage control. The phones, as you may have noticed when you came in, have not stopped ringing since last night. The people of D.C. are getting scared. This is the second politician to die, one week after the first. Since I don't believe in coincidences, we're treating it as a murder; we just need to figure out why? Why two congressmen, what do they have in common besides politics, why those particular congressmen?

"First, the House Majority Leader is murdered, and now the House Minority Leader is found dead. That's just too much of a coincidence, at least for me" she admits.

"Who called in the Congresswoman's collapse?" inquires Agent Mallory Callander.

"The daughter of the deceased, phoned in the emergency. When she couldn't reach her mother, she got concerned, so she dialed 911.The DCFD showed up along with a Metro One Officer, which is a routine dispatch. They found the Congresswoman, and after finding a lack of vital signs, they then called in the medical examiner. I was then called in, suspicious death ruling. The rest, you know" she replies.

"There's not much we can do, aside from canvassing the neighborhood of Congresswoman Delrose. Talk to anyone who may have heard, or seen anything strange last night, and once we get a ruling, we can start a formal investigation.

"In the meantime, we've got an ongoing open murder investigation to try to close. We still have not located Elroy Wade, the suspected murderer of William Blaketon. And now it looks like Capitol Hill is going to have another funeral. We'll need all the manpower we can get for this next funeral. There are a lot of people in the House of Representatives, not to mention all of the Senate and Congress. We have a lot of people to talk to regarding the Congresswoman, so let's get moving" she orders "we have work to do."

Devon's cell rings as he's leaving to meet the congressional leaders."Hey, this is shadow, Dev".

"Hold on" he says as he recognizes his snitch, and moves into an empty office to talk.

"Okay" Devon says "talk. What have you got?"

"Well, you know the killer of that congressman, that guy that was skinned?" Shadow asks in a low voice.

"Yes I know, go on" Devon says.

"Well, the guy that did that, he's an old biker dude."

"Yeah" Devon says "I already have that information, I need something I don't already know."

"Hold on, wait a minute, I'm getting to it" Shadow replies anxiously."I found out where he's been laying low" he exclaims."He's staying in a downtown tenement area. For his address, I get fifty" Shadow demands.

"Only if it turns out to be true" Devon agrees.

"It's true, you know me" whines Shadow.

"Yeah, I know you; that would be why I said if it's true."

"Fine, meet me outside the tenement, One-four-seven-two-eight Borlin Road, and we'll talk" he replies after thinking it over for a minute.

"I'll be there in fifteen minutes, so you better be there when I get there, or no fifty and you better have good information, or no fifty. You know how it works" Devon adds.

"Yeah, I'll be there, you just have the money" Shadow demands before he hangs up.

Devon pulls up to the tenement, in a part of Washington that never see's tourists. It's dark, old, quiet he notices, and deserted.

"Ah, there you are Shadow" a slight person in dark ill fitting clothes wanders over."I wondered if you were going to be a no show, but I figured you'd want the fifty. So, where's our hidden murderer" Devon demands.

"No way" says Shadow "the fifty first."

"The murderer" Devon says as he holds the fifty just of Shadow's reach."Shadow, you need to get a little taller" he teases with a grin."I don't think you can jump high enough to reach this fifty" he says as Shadow reaches in his coat, grabs his metal arm extender, reaches up quickly and grabs the fifty, just as Devon reaches into his jacket for his weapon, in response to Shadows move.

"I don't need to grow any, Devon" he laughs.

"Okay, you win" Devon admits "but don't ever pull that

again, I could have shot you for that. So, where is this guy?"

"See that drab old red door, the fourth one down on the other side, the one that's so faded it's hardly red anymore?" Shadow points out.

"Yeah, I see it".

"He's in there, hiding from everyone. He's been there for the better part of the week now, or so my sources tell me. He has to be sick of hiding out in there, there's nothing left of these places. No way for the heat to work, no electricity either. People break in so they can either hide, or get out of the weather," Shadow says."Thanks for the fifty," he laughs as he walks quickly away in the opposite direction."See you around Deputy Chief" he yells and salutes jauntily.

Devon takes out his cell, and makes the call to Kat."Hey, I've got a lead on where our murderer may be hiding" he says, when she answers her phone."I'm at the old east side tenements of D.C. He's supposedly hiding, in the fourth one down. I wanted to let you know. I thought you'd be interested in meeting me here" he offers."I'll wait for you to get here, before going in. It's only fair, since we've been working this crime together, pretty much from the start" he says quickly.

"I'm on my way" Kat replies "give me five minutes. I'm not far from there right now."

"Fine, I'll just look around a little, and check out the area. I'll wait for you before I go in."

Devon walks down to the red door house, walks up the steps and stops, looking. It sure doesn't look like anyone's been around here for awhile, but he notices the front door is open a little bit, just before he realizes there's a smell like rotten eggs, gas. He takes his weapon out of its harness, steps up to the door, and feels a click under his right foot.

"Shit, son of a bitch" he yells as the house explodes in front of his eyes.

The front door hit's Devon and sends them both flying into the air and onto the ground in front of the house. Luckily, D.C. just got about seven inches of snow, and it was still soft, so it helped to cushion his landing, just as Kat pulls up.

She screams and runs for Devon, moves the door that's

burning and smoking, and finds him unconscious but breathing. As she pulls her radio off her collar to notify dispatch, he groans."Hold on Devon" she hurriedly says as she finishes letting dispatch know that an ambulance is needed; there's an officer down, there's been a house explosion, with a fire spreading quickly throughout the residence. She kneels down to take care of Devon, and watch for rescue to get there.

The sirens are getting louder finally, letting her know that they're getting close to the scene. She breathes a sigh of relief as she see's rescue and fire come around the corner.

Skeet jumps out, grabs his bag and tells his partner to grab the gurney."It looks like we're going to need it" he says."We need to get this guy away from the house, before there's another explosion. Thanks Officer, I've got him now."

"His name is Deputy Chief Devon Callander of the Capitol Police" she replies."You take good care of him, okay" she insists nervously.

"Yeah, I've got him Lieutenant, he'll be okay. I promise we'll take good care of him" he reassures her as she stands back to give him room to work.

Captain Hall shows up, and walks over to Kat to see how Devon is "it looks like all of Washington's firefighters showed for this."

"It's a big thing. The house, the fourth down, blew up. It happened as I was pulling up to the sidewalk. Devon had just called me, and told me he had a tip come in from one of his informants. Our murderer was supposed to be hiding out in the house with the red door. It looks like Devon had gone over to that house to look in, as least from what I can tell sir, because the house blew up. If our suspect was in there when it exploded, he probably isn't identifiable" she admits in disappointment."I'm not sure how bad Devon; I mean Deputy Chief Callander is, so I'll follow them to the hospital. The arson investigator's going to be busy for awhile here, there's not much I can do" she admits.

Captain Hall agrees and remarks "I'll head back to the station, give a briefing to the staff and try to hold off the media for as long as possible" he offers.

"Thanks Captain, I appreciate it. I'll let you know what's going on as soon as I know anything" she replies.

"I'm fine," Devon insists for the tenth time in ten minutes. "Just let me out of here. I have to get back to work."

"I'm sorry Deputy Chief" replies his nurse, Sally, "but you can't go anywhere yet, you just woke up from being knocked out, in that explosion. The Doctor's ordered some tests, just to make sure there's no damage."

"I said I'm fine" he replies forcefully.

"Well, yes you did, but that doesn't change the fact that we're going to be running some tests. Head injuries are a dangerous thing." she warns "You can't be too careful with them, plus you have bruised ribs, a sprained shoulder and a couple of small cuts and bruises on your face, so you'll just have to dig deep for some patience, and wait till the Doctor says you can go" she announces with a smile.

"Damn it" he grouses. I had to get a stubborn nurse, not an easy one. I really hate hospitals, there's got to be some way to escape from this place. They don't even have food that's edible here, besides, I was getting close, that's got to be why I ended up here. I hope they can still find Elroy, if he was in that house. Shadow is usually good for his word, so if he was, is there anything left?

"You can go back now, Lieutenant" Sally, the triage nurse says, as she checks into the visitors waiting area and see's Lieutenant Thomas, along with a real pretty, black haired woman. "Good luck with him" she warns. "He's not the easiest patient we've ever had. You can find him in cubical three."

"Thanks Sally, I appreciate it" Kat says as she and Mallory take off for cubical three.

"Devon, are you decent" Kat inquires as she walks into cubical three.

"Yeah, as decent as I can be in this stupid gown, it covers nothing. Can't you spring me Kat, I don't need to be here" he swears."Ahh, Mal" he groans, "I'm sorry you had to hear about this through the grapevine. I would rather have told you myself" he apologizes to his sister.

"As long as you're okay, Devon, I don't care how I heard

the news. You scared fifty new gray hairs onto my head with this latest injury, though" she sniffles.

"I know Mal and I'm sorry."

"Just get back to normal, that's all I want, and don't be surprised when Eli calls because I had to tell him, you know? He would have killed me, if he would have found out through other channels."

"Yeah, Mal, I know" Devon admits, chagrined.

"Are you being released soon?" Mal asks hopefully.

"Nope, sorry, they said he needed some brain tests, not that they'll find anything, can't find something when there's nothing there" Kat replies with a snicker.

"Yeah, right" he says."They'll find a brain the size of Einstein's" he grimaces after chuckling at Kat, irritating his bruised ribs.

"So, did you plan this Devon? Is that why you called me? You said you'd wait for me to go into the house, and then when I pull up, you get blown up" she accuses."Was that the plan?" Kat demands angrily."You know better than going up to a possible hide out, without back up. Yet you did it anyway. It just makes me wonder why" she continues with her tirade. "You knew I was going to be there any minute, yet you couldn't wait, tough guy? You need to stop trying to be the hero, Devon. You're going to get yourself killed."

"Stop, please Kat, I don't need the lecture. I was just standing on the step waiting for you. I'm glad you weren't there though, because then only one of us was hurt, instead of both! Besides" he tries to reassure her "I'll be out of here in no time. It didn't hurt me too much, just a couple of bruised ribs and my right shoulder's a little painful, but overall, I'm not too bad.

"Yeah" she snorts "you still need to have some testing done. It'll be a couple of days, before you're released" she guesses.

"No way" he predicts "they wouldn't."

"We'll see" she replies with a smug smile.

"So, did you see anything by the front door?" she asks.

"No, but when I stepped up to the door, I noticed it was slightly open, and then I felt a click under my right foot. I knew then that I was screwed. I think it was a switch that was wired to whatever caused the explosion. Which means I was set up, damn it" he admits.

"You would have realized that sooner, if your brains hadn't been scrambled for awhile. You are not going to do that again" Kat says."I can't take another day like today. Look, I need to go. I have people to talk to" she adds in a rush.

"Wait" he yells at her quickly retreating back "you can't just leave me like this".

"Oh, yeah, I can" she yells back."I'll see you later" she promises. She just grins at the nurse and waves, leaving the problem of Devon to the pros.

Kat goes back to the burning house "Chief Walker, what can you tell me about the explosion?" Kat asks.

"Devon informed me that he felt a click under his foot when he went to stand in front of the door. He believes it was from a switch that was wired to some type of explosive device. Have you found anything like that?" she asks him.

"Not yet, but we just got the fire out about a half hour ago, so the investigations just starting. We had to stop the fire in the houses on either side of the main house; they started to go up like dried timber, which is what they technically are" the Chief admits.

"Do you mind if I go in with you?" she asks.

"Sure, but let me check out the inside before you come in. I won't be responsible for another injury here" he warns her.

"There was supposed to be a suspect that was hiding in the house, that's why Deputy Chief Callander was here to begin with. He got a tip from one of his snitches, and he says that he may have been set up. Any sign of a person in there?" she asks anxiously.

"So far, no, but there is a small section that's not burned as badly, we'll go in the back, there's less damage. Here, cover your nose and mouth with this face mask. It's going to be hard enough to breathe in there, and without it, Lieutenant, no guarantees. I don't want to lose any one else at this scene" he insists.

After breathing through the material for a few minutes, the smell of burning starts to permeate everything. Smoke is still wafting through the air, when they finally see something that could be of interest.

"There's a lump over there, behind that separator wall, Lieutenant" yells the Chief.

"I see it, I'm headed over there" she yells back, the only way you can hear through the mask. "Shit, gross, oh man, it's what's left of a body, and it's still smoking?" she says as she shines her flashlight onto the lump. "Talk about stench" she mutters, while trying to hold her breath.

"Can we get this dead body out of here, Chief?" she begs. "I can't breathe in here" she admits.

"Yeah, let me get the medic's in here, they can deal with it" he responds.

"Thanks, that's greatly appreciated" she says, gagging.

"It's an interesting burn pattern in here" the Chief says. "Looks like someone opened a natural gas main, wired it and when Deputy Chief Callander stepped on the switch, it caused a spark which blew the gas main. Obviously not enough gas pooled to level the place. He's lucky to be alive though, most people don't survive this kind of explosion," the chief admits. "I think the front door, blowing him off the porch, probably saved his life. He's a lucky guy, Lieutenant, a very lucky guy" the Captain admits.

"Yeah, I think so too, unfortunately, HE doesn't think so, he just wants out of the hospital" she complains. "Thanks Chief, I'm going to head out now. I need to call the medical examiner's office. He needs to take this dead body in and see who it belongs to" she announces.

"Sure Lieutenant, and if you need anything else, just call me" the Chief offers.

"Shit, looks like the media couldn't wait at Metro One for the release" she mutters, as four different news vehicles pull up at the curb. Everyone's pushing everyone else, she observes.

"Stop" she yells. "This is a crime scene. You may not cross the yellow crime scene tape" she says as she pulls her radio off and calls dispatch. "We need some officers here at the tenement, for crowd control. The media's shown up, en-mass. We need them now" she informs them. "I need to speak to Captain

Hall, dispatch; can you have him call my cell phone, please?"

"Of course Lieutenant," dispatch promises, "out."

"This is Captain Hall, Lieutenant, what's up?"

"We just removed a body from the burning house, Captain. It could be our suspect. We're still waiting for the medical examiners van to show up. Once he retrieves the body, I can head in. It will be a waiting game then, until he can ID the body. It was purportedly our suspect, in the skinning murder" she admits. "The medical examiner's here, I'll see you in about a half hour" Kat promises and hangs up.

"Hey Dr. Zorgath, long time no see" Kat says with a grin.

"Yeah Lieutenant, I think we've seen each other too much lately, don't you?"

"Absolutely" she agrees."No offense or anything, but I hope not to see you again for a long time" she admits.

"You're reading my mind again, Lieutenant. So, what do we have here?"

"This was supposedly our suspect, from the skinning murder."

SEVEN

"This day flew," Kat thinks as she makes her way to her favorite coffee shop. "Let's see, first the Congresswoman's death, then the house explosion, the hospital wait, the burned body found, the public notified. I think I'll head over and see Mike. I could use a break."

"Hi Mike" Kat yells as she walks in the front door.

"Kat, long time, for crying out loud" he exclaims as he sees her standing at the counter for a latte. "Where have you been hiding yourself?" he demands gruffly.

"Yeah, I know, I know and I'm sorry" she answers sheepishly. "I've been hung up lately with that murder that occurred. We still can't answer the questions the public have. But we're getting closer" she reassures him.

"Is everything okay, Kat?" he asks with concern. "You look a little shook up, maybe a little sad."

"Yeah, I am, to both I guess. Have you been following the news at all?" she asks.

"I saw some footage today, an explosion that occurred in one of those old tenement buildings. Is that what you're talking about?" he asks.

"Yeah, the officer that got hurt, he's the Capitol Police's Deputy Chief that I've been working with for the past week" she says. "He's going to be okay, but it really shook me up, Mike. I had just pulled up when the house exploded. It looks like it was set-up for someone to get killed. It was such a close call for Devon" she replies still shaken. "He's really lucky he wasn't killed" she exclaims, voice shaky.

"You sound pretty upset, let me get you your favorite drink. Go on over there and sit and we can talk" he orders.

"Thanks Mike, that's just what I need" she admits.

"Here you go Kat, enjoy. So what's going on, besides work?" he questions after he takes a seat across from her.

"Well, I think I made a mistake by getting too involved with Devon" she admits sheepishly.

"That's the Capitol Police Deputy Chief that got hurt today?" he inquires.

"Yeah"

"You're allowed to have a personal life Kat, all work and no play!"

"Yeah, yeah, I know Mike."

"Well it's about time you had a relationship outside of work" Mike adds.

"I know, I know, but we're working together on this case, so that makes him a co-worker. You know how I feel about dating co-workers Mike" she reminds him.

"Yeah, I do, but you're really not co-workers. He's with the Capitol Police, not Metro."

"You sound just like him" she complains in a whine.

"It's just common sense Kat, no big deal. If you like each other, then you should see each other" he says.

The door chimes as someone else walks in. "I see business is going good, Mike" she says with a little enthusiasm.

"Yeah, hold that thought, I'll be right back. I should have called in my part-timer early today, since business has been steady all day. I think it has something to do with the cold, and the snow that's coming again. Whatever the reason, I like it" Mike says with a laugh.

Kat looks over at the line for coffee, and see's someone who looks familiar. Wow, this feels like déjà vu, she thinks. I first met him twelve years ago, by running face first into his chest.

"Kitten, glad my timing's so good. I was hoping you'd be around. How the heck are you, you look great?" Snake says as he looks her up and down. She's gets more beautiful all the time, he observes.

"So what have you been doing for the past few years?" he inquires with a grin.

"Well, let's see. I'm a cop with D.C. Metro One Police" Kat explains in pride.

"No way" he exclaims. "How did a smart girl like you end up working for pennies? I figured you'd be a huge business owner, or a lawyer, maybe even work on Wall Street. But a cop, that's hard to believe" he responds in surprise.

"Not really" she replies in defense "I always wanted to be a cop, you know. I just had to wait till I was twenty one before they'd even let me attend the police academy, but now I'm in the job that I always wanted to be in she replies happily. How about you Snake? I never knew where you were from, or what you even did for a living."

"Well, you know, back in the day I was a biker with that little group you saw me with. But then I got tired of it, settled down, opened my own shop.

"I'm the proud owner of Custom Bikes, Little Waco, Texas, and I do pretty well" he brags. "Sometimes I miss the freedom of just riding, I admit. But most times, I like the grounded feeling of having my own business. I do well enough, I don't have to worry about money any more, not since my bike shop is so popular" he adds with false modesty and a devil may care grin.

"You seemed a little serious when I came in Kitten. A problem, is someone giving you a hard time again?" He asks with a growl. "Just tell me who and I'll take care of them for you" he offers.

"Actually no, my temporary partner, well sort of partner, was hurt this morning in an explosion, in an old tenement building on the east end of D.C. He came really close to getting killed" she finishes quietly.

"Sounds to me like you might like this guy" he asks quietly.

"Yeah, I guess I do. He's U.S. Capitol Police Deputy Chief Devon Callander." When Snake hears that name, he leans forward with a strange expression on his face "anyway, we've been working pretty close, for a week now" she continues, not noticing the sudden interest that Snake's demonstrating.

"Devon Callander, that's the name you just said, right?" he

asks in surprise.

"Yeah, that's his name, why? You seem a little excited, do you know Deputy Chief Callander?" she asks suspiciously.

"Well, I guess you could say I know him. He's my brother, one of the four of us. My mother had quadruplets, three boys, and a girl. I haven't seen him since I was seventeen, and a rebel. I was so bad, I left home the day I got my diploma, and I haven't contacted them since. You said he was injured, how bad?" Snake demands.

"He's going to be okay" she responds to the anxiety she hears in his voice, "he's in the hospital for now. Do you want to see him?" she asks quietly.

"Yeah, I think I do" he answers her in surprise."It's going to be a big surprise, but yeah, I'd like to see him."

"Okay then, follow me. I was heading there anyway, so I'll show you where he is" she offers.

Bye, Mike, I gotta go!" Kat yells as they walk out of the shop.

"Here we are" Kat informs him as she gets out of her vehicle and he gets out of his. "No more bikes?" she teases.

"Oh yeah, I'll always have a bike, it's just too cold in D.C right now for me to ride" he admits with a grin.

"Yeah, that's true, it's freakin cold, and the worst snow year we've had that I can remember. Devon was in the ER most of the day, but after all his testing was complete, they were going to move him to a private room. There were just too many agents and cops, you know, trying to visit him. It was causing too much of a disruption for the other patients. Now he's on floor two, room two eleven. I'll go with you, since I haven't seen him since they moved him, but I'll warn you now, he's not a very good patient" she says as they get off the elevator on floor two.

"Devon, can I come in?" Kat asks as she opens the door a couple of inches and knocks at the same time.

"Of course Kat, please save me" he replies in frustration. "You can come in and get me out of here."

"Oh, did they release you, because that's the only way you're getting out of here" she promises teasingly. "Besides, I brought someone to see you" she warns as she walks in followed by Snake.

"*Jacob*" Devon exclaims, after doing a double take. "Is that really you?" he questions, with a shake of his head.

"Yeah, it's me. I heard you were hurt, and I was in town so I thought I'd look you up. So, you're the Capitol Police Deputy Chief, huh?" he inquires.

"Yeah, Capitol Police, how about you Jacob, what do you do?"

"Actually, I own a Custom Bike shop out in Texas, doing pretty good with it too, plus it keeps me busy, and around the things I like the best, bikes" he replies to Devon's questioning look.

"Wow, you look so different" Devon remarks "taller than you were when you left, bigger, meaner."

"I think he looks like you Devon, with long hair. I thought you looked familiar when I first met you, remember. I just didn't realize it was because of Snake. Snake, your real name is Jacob?" she asks inquiringly.

"Wow" Devon says, quietly."This is a bit much to take in, all at once. I haven't seen you since the day we graduated from high school. I think we all actually thought you were dead. It's been such a long time. They call you Snake now?" he repeats in disbelief.

"How about Mom and Dad, how are they?" Jacob asks quietly.

"Why do you want to know?" Devon demands. "You left all of us, not the other way around, and you didn't care enough all these years, to check in with any of us. So I'm not sure it's any of your business" he finishes bitterly.

"Oh, come on Devon" Kat exclaims shocked "he's here now, don't you think you should give him a chance?"

"No, I don't" he replies. "He created this problem himself. I'm not sure he should be allowed to cause anymore heartache" he adds angrily.

After lying there in silence for awhile, thinking, Devon decides "Okay fine, but I'm not telling you where you can find them. They're good. Dad still calls me about once a week to see if I've heard from you. All those years and he's never given up hope. He's retired now, they both are, but in good health. Retirement didn't slow Mom down though, it actually made her busier" Devon admits with a slight smile. "She can't say no to all those volunteer jobs. And now that they're retired, it actually freed up time for her to volunteer more" he admits in exasperation.

"That's nice" Snake says thoughtfully. "I might like to see them, while I'm in D.C." he admits quietly.

"I'm not sure" Devon replies."You can't just stop in. It would be too much of a shock for them both. I don't think you want either of them to drop from a heart attack, just because you want to see them. How about I let you know, after I talk to Mal and Eli? Just leave me a way to reach you" he says dismissively.

"Sure" Snake agrees. "I'm going to go anyway, so the two of you can talk" he decides. "Bye kitten, I'll be in touch. We have some catching up to do" he promises as he strolls out the door.

"Well Devon, that was weird. I never would have connected the two of you, especially as siblings. You've never mentioned Jacob, but I knew there were four of you, you just never talked about him" she exclaims.

"That's because he left when he was seventeen, Kat. I had nothing to say about him. It was like he dropped off the face of the earth. I know my parents never got over him leaving, and like I said, my Dad still calls me once a week to see if I've heard from him. The answers always been no, until now. I'm not sure how I'm going to tell them that he's in town, alive and well, and not dead" he admits. "Kat, how do you know him? It sounded like you knew each other pretty well" he says suspiciously.

"You remember when I was attacked, about twelve years ago? I told you about it when I heard Elroy Wades name. You remember, because I thought the name sounded familiar. Well it was, since Elroy Wade was also called Bad Ass, by the biker group that he rode with. They all came into my friend Mikes Coffee Shop one day. I was in there getting my morning Latte before class at Capitol Hill College, and I literally ran into

Snake when I was leaving.

"One minute there was no-one behind me in line, then when I turned around, he was right there and I ran into him. I actually almost scalded him with my coffee. He grabbed me, so I didn't fall, then he teased me because I was so short, and he called me kitten. Well, I was rude. I used to get riled pretty easy when I was young, so I told him my name was NOT kitten, that my friends called me Kat. They're my initials.

"Anyway, he started calling me kitty Kat, but I was in a hurry, so I let it go, figuring I'd never see him again anyway. After I left, and was half way to school, Bad Ass jumped out of an alley, grabbed me by my ponytail, and started to drag me back into the alley. I started screaming, because it hurt and scared me, but I got it under control. I was beating him up pretty good when Snake came running into the alley.

"He said he had heard the scream, because he was outside looking for Bad Ass. He came running, finished beating up Bad Ass, until he was sure that he couldn't hurt me again. I think he felt kind of protective of me. I only saw him a couple more times and then nothing till today" she admits. "Look, I need to get to the office, but I'll come back later to check in on you, I promise."

"Fine, I'm sure I'll still be here, especially if the same nurse is on" he says tiredly.

"Detective, report" orders Kat after she walks into Metro One's bull pen.

"Yes, Lieutenant, I received the Medical Examiners report, about the body we found in PA, the one without the skin".

"And . . . Kat says, "you want a drum roll, or something?"

"Uh, no Sir, well, you aren't going to like this, but the coroner says the body does NOT match our murder victim. It doesn't match the murdered victim in Pennsylvania either."

"What?" she exclaims. "It's not a match to either? Damn it, we have another body, so where's the skin?" she asks of anyone in the general vicinity. "I can't believe we don't have a freakin match. Son of a bitch! Alright, what else" she asks suspiciously.

"Well, they haven't found anything on the Congresswoman that was found dead this morning, either."

"Well shit, you have anything positive to report, Detective?"

"Yeah, the Coroner did say the final report for the congresswoman won't be completed until tomorrow, because he's running toxicology tests on the blood, looking for anything that could have caused this."

"Okay" she admits "that's something anyway. Anything else?" she asks.

"No, Lieutenant, I think that covers everything I have, at the moment."

"We need to begin the questioning on Capitol Hill" Kat decides. "Let's get a team set up, so we can get this going. It looks like it's going to be a long day, since it's going to take time and we have so many people we have to talk to."

"Yes sir. When is Deputy Chief Callander being released?"

"Today sometime" Kat replies."His family will take care of him I'm sure, his sister and brothers. Oh, I didn't tell you. Devon's brother came in from Texas yesterday."

"Yes sir, I expected that. He works out of the Los Angeles field office, and is the head of the anti-terrorist Unit out of Los Angeles?"

"No, I said Texas, not Los Angeles. I'm sure his one brother is from LA, but the brother I'm talking about is the one Devon never talked about, the one that left when he was seventeen. He showed up yesterday at Mike's, and we talked a little."

"Wait, you talked? Why, how did you know him, were you just talking to anyone?"

"No, you remember I told you about when I was attacked, when I was fifteen? Well, he's the biker that came to my rescue. So we were catching up on old times and new times, and he found out his brother was the Deputy Chief injured in the explosion."

"Wow, that was good timing" Des exclaims.

"Yeah, it makes me suspicious. I don't believe in coincidences, you know, and this was pretty coincidental" she admits.

"The House of Representatives is in session, Lieutenant. You can't go in there right now" she's informed by the Capitol Police Officer standing guard in the hall. "We're investigating the untimely death of the House Minority leader. That trumps this session, so if you'll move out of the way, I need to get to work."

"Could I have everyone's attention please" Kat demands once she gains entrance to the House. "In case you haven't heard, there's been another death. Ms. Karen Delrose was found collapsed at her home, late last night. She was DOA when the medics got there. The Medic and a Metro One officer found her unresponsive, in her office on the first floor of her home. The coroner is conducting an autopsy at this time, with the cause of death being unknown as of yet. We're going to need to talk to everyone that knew Ms. Delrose, so please do not leave until you've spoken with one of the officers" she informs the House.

"Shhhh, quiet down everyone, I know these are scary times, but I don't believe anyone has anything to worry about. These deaths are nothing alike. So please, let's keep the roar down, it would be best for everyone concerned. Thank you" Kat says. "The officers will be wandering around talking to individuals, so please be patient and we will get to you, I promise. Anything that you can tell us about Ms. Delrose, will not be a waste of your time. Thank you again" Kat says and moves to start the questioning.

"Ms. Martin, can you explain to me how you knew Ms. Delrose?" Kat asks politely when she reaches her side.

"Yes Sir. I've met all of the people in the House of Representatives, the Senate and the Congress. I had a difficult experience overseas a few years ago, and because of that experience, the Department of Homeland Security hired me as a terrorism support professional and now everyone seems to know me.

"I was just a small town girl, but these people, they're the nicest people I've ever met, including the President, and Vice President, Lieutenant. They actually feel like family to me now, even though I've only known them for a short time" she admits with a slight blush.

She seems like a small town girl, a little overwhelmed by all the attention she's been receiving, Kat thinks. Strange, but even I feel like taking her under my wing. She seems to have quite a thing about her, shy, reserved, angelic, she thinks. "So, how did you say you know Ms. Delrose, Jane?"

"We talked for hours; I've had dinner at her beautiful home, and she treated me like a sister. It's going to be terribly hard without her" Jane admits, with tears running down her cheeks."It's okay Jane, I'm sorry you had to go through this" Kat replies sadly.

Looks like the Speaker of the House is headed this way, and not real happy either."Madame Speaker, what can I do for you?" Kat asks.

"I, no, I mean everyone in this building, watched you talk to Jane, what did you say to her?" Virginia asks suspiciously. "She's crying, surely you don't believe Jane capable of doing harm, to anyone, do you Lieutenant? I can assure you, it's not possible. We all watch out for her, she's been through enough in her past, and she doesn't need to face anything more, including the questioning of all of us, regarding Karen Delrose the speaker says abruptly.

"The President called, Jane, and he wants you to meet him in the rose room, at the White House. He says it's important, and asked that you leave right away."

"Of course Madame Speaker, I'll go as soon as the Lieutenant is finished questioning me. She didn't do anything to me, Mrs. Moore" Jane reassures the speaker quickly.

"Call me Virginia, dear" requests Virginia Moore.

"Thank you, Virginia" Jane acknowledges with a blush.

"She was just asking me how I knew Karen and well, I remembered the last time we spoke. I was at a dinner at her house; one she had so kindly asked me to attend. That thought made me start crying, Virginia. I cherish all my friends, and when something happens to any one of them, it's a terrible thing" she sniffs.

"Yes, you're so right Jane" Virginia says as she gives Jane a hug and moves her towards the door. "We'll talk later" Virginia promises "when you feel more up to it. Take care dear. Bye-bye now" Virginia says.

"Excuse me Madame Speaker, but I wasn't finished questioning Jane. She seems like a very nice person, not someone I would put down as a suspect, but this is my investigation, so next time, stay out of it" Kat demands.

"Of course Lieutenant, you have my word" reassures Virginia.

"Thank you" she replies before turning to start more questioning.

"Detective, we're done here I think, finally. What was your take on the House?" Kat asks.

"They all seemed pretty nervous, Sir, and I don't understand why, you'd think they knew what killed Karen Delrose. But I don't see how that's possible, since we don't even know how she died" Des admits in confusion.

"Hopefully tomorrow, we'll have some answers" Des says quietly "but my take would be someone knows something, Sir. They're scared someone will find out what it is they know."

"Yeah, that's my take too, Detective. I wonder just what it is that they know" Kat murmurs while scanning the room. "If someone knows something, we'll find it Detective, you can take that to the bank" she promises.

"Alright, let's head back to Metro One. I'm done here for the day" she decides. "I do believe it's time for a little R & R. I think I'll go check up on Devon, after I give the media another statement. Let's go" she says with a big sigh. Tired to the bone she decides, this has been a freaky two weeks. Hmmm, why did they both die on the same day, she wonders, another connection? Well, well, what do you know, we have another common denominator. But why, she wonders. We need to find Elroy, hopefully before he does this again. We have three deaths now, and we need to stop this, before they take out the whole congress.

"I'd like to speak to Devon Callander, please. He's in room two-eleven."

"I'm sorry Ms., he was released today."

"What, when?" Kat asks in surprise.

"It was right after lunch, his brother and sister came for him Ms. He seemed pretty glad to be going home, from what I saw of his face."

"Well, okay, thanks for the information" she replies while thinking.

"Did he go home, and where is home" she wonders, annoyed. I'll have to look that up tomorrow. For now, I'm going home. I'm sick of the snow, the cold, and the cold meals. It's time for a change, she decides. How come he didn't call me to let me know he was discharged? Hopefully I'll see him tomorrow she decides as she pulls up to her apartment.

"Devon, what are you doing" Kat asks as she hurries to the door of her apartment. "You shouldn't be out here, it's too cold, you just got out of the hospital, you know."

"I'm fine" he insists. "I wanted to see you but when I called the office they said that you had left for the day. I wasn't sure where you were headed, but I was hoping it was here. I've only been out here for about two minutes, total. I'm fine right now, but I wouldn't mind an invite in" Devon wheedles.

"Of course, come on in. I'm going to do the dinner thing" she offers with a grin. "I hope you're hungry, because I'm starving" she warns.

"I could eat" he agrees.

"All right, here we go, oh, I forgot about the mess. Oh well, please excuse. I haven't had time lately, for anything but work" she admits sheepishly.

"Yeah, I know, plus you were short handed while I was in the hospital. I'll work extra hard to make up for it" he promises as he pulls her closer. "Mmm, Eskimo kiss, your nose is freezing, Kat! Come here, let me warm you" he offers, with hidden promise.

Kat feels a lump in her throat, clears it, and hugs him back. "Devon, I was so scared when I saw that house explode, with you right there at the front door. I keep seeing it over and over" she admits with a sniffle.

"Shhh, it's okay Kat, I'm fine, see, and everything seems to be working the way it should."

"Yeah, I can feel that everything's working" she whispers huskily.

"Well" whispers Devon "then let me show you just how well I am" and he grabs her by the hand, and pulls her towards the back of the apartment where he knows the bedroom is. She steers him into the right room, where he backs her against the bed, pushes her over onto her back, and joins her slowly. "Kat" he says "I've been thinking about this since I was here last time" he admits with a groan.

Kat's heart rate slams into high gear, sounding like a jackhammer, after the first kiss. She feels like she's suffocating, all the air in the room has been sucked out. Ooooh yeah, she thinks, this is good, real good as Devon slips her out of her cloths so fast she doesn't even notice, till she feels the breeze.

Well, we can't have this all one sided and starts to unbutton his jeans, pulls his shirt off and slides his jeans to the floor. Wow, she thinks, admiring that broad chest, with a few small bruises, narrow stomach, tight butt, and rock hard thighs. As she reaches for his jockey's to release him, he groans in excitement.

The things he's doing to her should be illegal, she decides. She sighs in pleasure as he slides off her, so he can reach better, and starts slowly touching her neck with his lips, her lips, her collar bone, the valley between her breasts, her nipples.

"Ooohhh" Kat groans in pleasure, as he continues to move down her body. Lips follow hands, his mouth and hands are everywhere at once, it seems. He licks and nips, then licks again, healing any small twinges that he may have created.

I can't catch my breath, Kat's last thought as he slides even lower. As he feels her tightening, he spreads her legs wider and thrusts into her.

"Ooohhh" she moans as he starts the rhythm that's as old as time.

He holds her tightly as she runs her hands down that strong back, that muscular buttock, while he thrusts in and out until she can't breathe again, and her mind starts to spin out of control. Then with a deep groan, he gives one last mind blowing thrust, and joins her in the largest, longest climax she's ever had.

As they both lay there breathing like they ran a marathon, she sighs deeply in contentment. He slides off her so he doesn't crush her, and pulls her to his chest, not ready to give her up yet.

"Mmmm, that was amazing. I've never felt anything like that before" she murmurs huskily.

"My pleasure" he answers sleepily "we can practice more in just a little bit" he promises, causing Kat to smile and begin to drift off, knowing a sense of peace she hasn't felt in a long time.

EIGHT

The alarm clock is what finally wakes them, after a warm and peaceful night. Kat groans as she tries to beat the alarm clock to death, but keeps missing it. Oh yeah, it's on the other dresser, she remembers. "Wake up Kat, its five thirty already" her alarm clock says. "Wow, hold on" she says as she half falls out of bed, and hops on one leg to reach the alarm. "I forgot I moved it, because I was hitting the snooze too many times, and had to run out of here for work every morning" she says on a groan as she stands in front of the dresser after turning off the alarm, and gazes in the mirror at Devon, in her bed.

I could get used to this she thinks. "Guess we better get ready for the day" she announces. "We've got a murder to solve."

"Yeah" Devon agrees as he yawns "time to go to work. Where did you find that talking alarm clock?"

Kat looks at him and then moves to the door saying "it was a gift. I'm showering first" she says as she runs out of the bedroom.

"Hey" Devon yells "no fair."

"Too bad, I got here first" she says as she rushes into the bathroom.

She's almost done showering when the curtain's drawn back, and Devon steps in. "You were taking too long" he says with a wicked grin "here, let me help you!" He grabs the soap and proceeds to show her just how easy it is for him to reach all those places that she can't. It's a while later when they both leave the shower, clean and relaxed. It's going to be a good day she thinks with a soft smile.

"We better wear suits today" she reminds Devon, "it's the funeral, for the House Minority Leader. We have to be there at nine."

"I'll have to meet you there, since I didn't come prepared for a funeral. All of my suits are at home."

"Alright" she agrees. "See you in a few."

"It looks almost exactly the same as one week ago, she says after meeting at the front of the Chapel on the Hill. It's really strange, having two funerals, a week apart. I hope this is the end of this for awhile. I really don't want anyone else to die."

"I think I'll go up to the front" she informs Des."I want to stand by the Speaker of the House this time. Everyone else, let's do the same as last week. Watch for anything unusual, anyone acting strangely, and remember, we need to talk to everyone again when this is over" she reminds them as she turns and heads to the front.

"Good Morning, Mrs. Moore" Kat says in greeting.

"Lieutenant" she acknowledges."It's not such a good morning, as far as I'm concerned. This is the second death Lieutenant and a young woman this time. Forty-eight years old is not old enough to drop dead, not as far as I'm concerned" states the Speaker of the House "so you can talk till you're blue in the face, and I will never believe that this was a death from "natural causes.""

"We're still investigating this death, Mrs. Moore, and if it wasn't from natural causes, we'll find out, trust me" Kat insists."The medical examiner is very thorough. I don't want anything like this to happen again, either" Kat reassures her.

"Thank you Lieutenant, for going the extra mile for us, it's appreciated. Now, if you'll excuse me, I need to say a few things to open the service."

"Absolutely" Kat murmurs.

Kat scans the room, looking for who's standing with whom and who's absent, who looks happy or sad. That murderer is in this room, she thinks I'm just not sure who, where, or why. There's Jane again. This time she's standing next to that tall handsome blonde. I don't remember who he is. I don't think I'm the one that talked with him last time we interviewed them.

Hmm, they look pretty close, she's smiling and blushing at him, and he's leaning down to talk to her. They look almost like a couple she thinks. I think there's something there, and if they're not in a relationship now, then they will be soon she thinks. I need to know who that is.

"Excuse me everyone, we need to quiet down a little, and show some respect for the deceased. I have been re-assured by D.C. Metro One Homicide and our Capitol Police, that they are thoroughly investigating this death. As I told them, Karen was too young to just collapse, which is pretty much what they say happened. I was reassured that they are treating this as a homicide, until they have further information. I'm sure we'll all miss Karen Delrose, she was a feisty woman who spoke her mind. She did like to rock the boat. But it kept us thinking, which I believe was her ultimate goal" Virginia says with a shake of her head, in unbelief. "This is her official memorial service. There will be a closed funeral for Karen Delrose, at her family's request. Now the Reverend Matthews will continue on."

The service was short, tasteful, and to the point, as was appropriate, and it honored Ms. Delrose and her position as Minority Leader for the House of Representatives. I did notice fewer tears for this funeral, than for the last funeral, William Blaketon's funeral. Granted, there were totally different circumstances surrounding that death. His was definitely murder, and the circumstances were horrific. Bad enough to upset the sturdiest of souls Kat thinks while waiting to leave.

"We're done here" Kat decides as all the members of the different Police, FBI and DHS units gather together at the back of the church after the questioning is completed. "I'll hold a briefing in conference room C at Metro One in one hour. We can share notes, thoughts and opinions with each other, then head out for the day. I know the list I have to get done just keeps getting longer with every one of these services" she says quietly and receiving many heartfelt nods.

"Detective, we have an hour to get something done. Let's

head to the coroner's office. He may have gotten something in by now, although he did promise to call me when he had anything new. Just in case there is something, we'll have that much more to share at the briefing. I saw that Devon left with his sister and some of her unit, so I'll drive" Kat says to Des.

"You always drive" Des accuses.

"Of course I do, I have rank, remember" Kat reminds her, with a grin.

Traffic in D.C was relatively light for the morning, so the trip took less time than usual, Kat thinks happily. Let's hope the return trip to Metro will be as smooth."Dr. Zorgath, you in there?" Kat yells over the sound of water running, and a loud saw.

"Yes Kat, come on in" she hears faintly.

"Phew, it's loud in here" she complains."Can we go somewhere to talk" she yells just as someone switches of the saw and her voice comes out in a yell."Oops, sorry" she says sheepishly, a blush blooming on her face.

"Not a problem Lieutenant, we've all done the same thing at one time or another" he reassures her."What can I do for you?" he asks kindly.

"I was hoping you'd gotten something back from toxicology on the Delrose death"

"I haven't received anything yet, but let me call Selma in the lab and double check. Hold on just a second."

Kat wanders around the autopsy suite while Dr. Zorgath finishes his talk. When he hangs up, he goes over to where Kat's standing, staring at a body. "Poor kid, what happened to him?" she asks with sympathy.

"Cancer" he says."I hate it when kids turn up in here. This isn't a place for kids. Kids should be out in the sun shine, playing in their back yards, not lying on a table in my morgue" he says sadly.

"Anyway, I talked to Selma and there hasn't been anything reported on toxicology, at least so far. A couple of the more advanced tests haven't been completed yet. Those should be done within the next 24 hours, at the latest. I'm sorry, Lieutenant, I know how much you want those results, but we can only work as fast as the testing allows us. I promise to call as soon as I have anything."

"Thanks Doctor. Let's go Des."

"Can I have your attention in here?" Kat asks loudly."I just returned from the medical examiner's office, hoping for some information on toxicology for Karen Delrose. The more complex of the testing isn't completed yet, but he's estimating within the next 24 hours. I have nothing new to report there. How did the questioning of the house members go" she asks. "I know I didn't get much, except maybe the unpopularity of Karen Delrose with her co-constituents. She definitely wasn't a very popular house minority leader, which makes me wonder how she ended up with that position. Anyway, Agent Mallory Callander, do you have anything?"

"I noticed the same thing, Lieutenant. She definitely wasn't a contender for the Miss Congeniality award. None of the people I spoke with liked her. They all complained that she was a loose cannon. I agree I'm not sure either how she landed that position."

"Deputy Chief Callander, your input?" Kat asks.

"I spoke with the House Majority Whip. He didn't have anything negative to say about Karen. Actually, he seemed rather fond of her. Could have been sexual, I guess, but I'm not sure of that, that's just supposition."

"Anyone else? No one? Alright, if no one has anything else, you're dismissed. Let's get out there and get some answers."

"Devon, can I see you?" Kat asks as the room clears out.

"Sure Kat. I'll talk to you later, Mallory" he promises.

"We need to go to the storage building of that livestock hauler, the one the skinned body was found in the other day. I thought you'd want to be involved in the questioning" she offers.

"Absolutely, thanks" replies Devon.

"It shouldn't take long to get there since it's only on the east side of D.C. Of course, with the stupid weather we seem to be having, it might take an extra few minutes to maneuver around in the thick slush that's on the roads. I'll drive" she says quickly.

"Not this time Lieutenant, we'll take my SUV; it's got four wheel drive" he says.

"Oh, alright, if we must" she agrees begrudgingly."There it is, I think" she says after the long slushy drive, spotting a nicely preserved brick building with three garage doors on the front. "The owner's name is Abdul Adl Thayer. Let's go see who this owner is" she says as they get out of the car.

"There's a doorbell, let's see if he's here. It has an all closed up look to it" observes Devon.

"Yeah hopefully the trip wasn't for nothing" Kat says.

"Hello" says the speaker next to the door bell."Who's there?" inquires the voice.

"Police" Kat says into the speaker.

"We need to talk to you sir. Could you open the door, please?" she asks.

"Sure Officer, one moment" replies the voice at the other end of the speaker. As they wait, the garage door starts opening soundlessly."Wow" Kat says "that's amazing, it's so quiet."

"Hi, I'm Abdul Thayer, but everyone calls me Addy."

"We'd like to ask you some questions, sir" Kat says.

"No problem Officer. What can I do for you" he asks.

"That's Lieutenant" Kat corrects him.

"Oh, sorry, my mistake, Lieutenant. Would you like to come in out of the snow?" he offers.

"Thanks" they respond together "it's pretty crappy out here" Kat says.

"Mr. Thayer, I have some questions about Mike Andrews, owner of the livestock hauler, the one that parks in this building" she begins after scanning the garage.

"Yes, I know him, he's a good guy" Addy says.

"How long has he parked his vehicle in your garage?" Kat asks.

"Well, I've owned this business for the last fifteen years, ever since my Uncle got sick, and decided to retire and move out of state. He now lives in sunny Florida. Anyway, Mike's been renting that space since before I became owner. I've never had a problem with him, he always pay's his rent on time, and he only parks clean trucks. I would have had a problem otherwise. I don't want to smell rotting animal carcasses" he says.

"So he's the epitome of a great renter, but don't you ever talk to him on personal matters?" she questions.

"We talk when I'm here and he's here; but we don't socialize, if that's what you mean Lieutenant"

"Yeah, I guess that's what I mean" she says.

"Have you had any break-ins, Mr. Thayer?" Devon inquires.

"No Sir, there have been no problems with this place. Not since I took over. Not even before then I don't believe, but I can ask my Uncle next time I talk to him, if you wish" he offers.

"No, I don't think that will be necessary, Mr. Thayer. You said that you took over this business fifteen years ago, I think that's far enough back."

"Could you give us a quick tour of the garage that Mike parks his truck in? Kat asks.

"Sure, just follow me. The doors are at the back of each room. There's just a small door that leads to a hallway, and then to all three garage spaces. I always have renters for my garages" he admits proudly. "I'm one of the few storage-parking facilities in D.C that keeps the bays heated. Not real warm, mind you" Addy explains, "but way above freezing. If I lose one renter, another is always on the waiting list. Here's the bay were Mike keeps his animal hauler."

"He's not here right now" Des observes.

"No" Addy says in agreement. "He had a pick-up and delivery to make today. Said it couldn't wait, but he'll probably be back by night fall" he offers. "He usually is, but with the way it's snowing right now, I'll bet he's a lot later than normal."

"Thanks for answering all the questions, Mr. Thayer, we appreciate your time."

"It was my pleasure Lieutenant. Anytime you need something, you just call me, here's my business card" he offers.

"Thank you Mr. Thayer."

"We got nothing with that visit" she grouches as they pile into the car "it's like we're constantly starting over."

"Yeah" everyone agrees, discouraged.

"He seemed helpful enough, but there's just something about Addy; I'm not sure what, call it my gut, but there's something there. I'm going to keep my ear to the ground. You never know when you might hear something worth listening to" Kat says.

"Yeah, I'll look a little deeper, too" Devon replies. "I felt something back there, too. Usually if my gut says watch, there's a reason" he says.

"We're almost back to Metro One. I hope there's some information waiting for us" Kat says. "Des, check incoming and let me know, I'll be in my office" she orders.

"I'm heading over to the Capitol Police Complex, but I'll talk to you later" Devon says as they pile out of his SUV.

"Okay, see you" she replies then quickly walks into the building.

"Lieutenant, there's something here from the Coroner."

"What is it?" she asks.

"Looks like some toxicology tests were finished" she says after looking over the papers.

"Alright" Kat exclaims with excitement "let's have a look. Hmmm, yeah, hmm, okay" Kat mumbles as she finishes reading the report. "We have a trace of a poison, called chironex fleckeri, from a box jelly fish. It usually works so fast that it doesn't leave a trace in the body, and it's deadly" she states after reading the report. "This is a break. We have a murder weapon here for Karen Delrose" she says excitedly.

"Now why would anyone want to kill Karen Delrose" Kat wonders out loud. She was relatively young, with a daughter and a son. I didn't see the son so I am assuming he's at college somewhere. I'll have to ask the daughter, she decides. "This could be a break, at least in the Delrose death. Now all we have to do is figure out who and why. Let's take a ride to the coroner's office again" she tells Des. "I'm going to need to talk to the FBI; it looks like we may just have some type of serial killer working in the D.C. area."

"Dr. Zorgath, good afternoon, can we talk for a couple of minutes again?" Kat asks quietly.

"Sure, I'm not busy at the moment. A little earlier and it would have been impossible, since there was a fatal multiple car pile-up on interstate ninety five this morning, and we were swamped. But right now, I'm not busy" he says with a smile for his favorite Lieutenant.

"Great" Kat replies with a smile. "Not about the pile up, but that you're not busy right now. I received the info you faxed over, on the toxicology reports for Karen Delrose. Can you explain to me what exactly the poison chironex fleckeri does?" she asks.

"Sure" Doctor Zorgath says. "It actually stops the heart suddenly, long enough to kill the victim, but it also dissipates so rapidly, that it's almost impossible to detect in the blood or even in any body parts. "Unfortunately for them, during the autopsy I tested a part of the brain that things move through slowly. There was a small trace left. Because she was found quickly after death, it didn't have time to clear out of everywhere. However, that's the only part of her body that showed any sign of the drug" explains the Dr.

"Awesome, Dr. Zorgath, you were thinking quickly on your feet, as usual," Kat compliments.

"Yes, indeed" he drawls in that southern voice of his,

The one that always gives me the chills, Kat thinks with a grin.

"It was the speed of the autopsy that allowed me the time for the sample that we needed, to find this actual drug. Another ten minutes or so, and it would have been gone. I didn't think a woman of her age, and general health, would just drop dead so I wanted answers. She was a young, and vivacious human being, one that someone wanted rid of. I found the cause Lieutenant, now you get to find the killer. We work well together, don't you think?" he inquires with a smile. "It takes some well organized and smarter than average people to catch a smarter than average killer" he says to Kat. "Why else would he know about that poison?" he asks "He did his homework with this one, or you've got a person with a strong medical background, doing the crime. That would be a disgrace to the medical profession, since we take an oath to protect and serve, not destroy."

"Thank you Dr. Zorgath. I need to get this information back to the office and share it with the other Agents. We have a killer to catch" Kat says determinedly.

"Des, get Deputy Chief Callander and the Agent Mallory Callander on the line. We need to set up a time for an information exchange, and also for a media release. I don't want to share everything with the media yet, but we need to notify them of the basics" she says.

"Alright everyone, I called this meeting because we have some information from the coroner's office that you just might be interested in" Kat reports in the conference room at Metro One. "We were informed earlier of the results of the autopsy on Karen Delrose. Her death has been declared by the coroner's office as a murder. He found that she was given a poison called chironex fleckeri. This poison stops the heart cold. Symptoms are normally nonexistent and untraceable, by even the most modern technology. It's a drug that dissipates quickly with time. Fortunately for us, the coroner was able to get to work quickly with this case, and obtain enough of a sample that testing was successful. He actually found the poison. We now have the proof we needed to confirm murder, not natural causes, and we now have someone to look for beside's Elroy Wade" she finishes.

"Let's get the noise level down, we have work to do" Devon announces loudly."From what the medical examiner said, someone with medical knowledge, or a friend of someone with medical knowledge, could have had something to do with this. With internet availability, practically anyone could have done this" he says. "Sure, they would have needed to know a little about the internet. But even my friends five year old know how to type a question in, and find answers. Granted, a five year old wouldn't know about anatomy, chemistry, physiology, or any of the more refined ways to search. But an adult definitely would. Now we have questions we need answers for. Hopefully it will give us some leads."

"Mallory, you're head of the serial killer unit, what are your thoughts on this?" Kat asks.

"Seldom do serial killers stray this far from their initial murder style" she admits. With three murders with similar M.O.'s; two sets of skin without the bodies and one body without skin. So yeah, we could definitely be looking at a serial killer. Unfortunately, unless this latest murder was made to look different on purpose to throw everyone off the murderer, then we're leaning towards something not serial, maybe terrorism. I'm not sure, that would be Deputy Chief Callander's area of expertise" she adds.

"It could be terrorism, I've known them to do some extremely strange things. Skinning first, and then some kind of drug that's untraceable, those are opposite ends of the spectrum even for a terrorist" Devon admits.

"What about organized crime?" Kat asks."They've been known to go to those great lengths. They actually get a kick out of confusing the police. They'd probably take pride in just the thought of creating chaos with the public, while sending a message to whatever group they've targeted. So, the million dollar question right now is, what's the message, and who is it directed at?"

"I think we need to talk to the House of Representatives again, since they seem to be the main focus" Devon suggests.

"I agree Devon and thank you." Kat says. "What we need to keep in mind though, is whoever is doing this, is gaining something from it. No one does anything without getting something in return. But what's their agenda?

"We need to start a comparison on the two congressmen that are dead, and look into anything that connects them, money, family, history or whatever. I don't care if it's a Saturday night poker game. If anything connects them, we need to know. So let's get that board in here" Kat orders "we need to catch this bastard as soon as possible."

"I need to write this report up and get it to the Captain" Kat explains to Des "so he can handle the media."

"Um, Lieutenant, there's a police officer from Mt. Buckhorn, Ohio on the line. He says it's important" Des says to Kat.

"Okay thanks. I'll take that in my office."

"This is Lieutenant Thomas, how can I help you?" she inquires after grabbing the phone.

"Lieutenant, we're at Elroy Wade's house, looking around. In his garage we found a set up for taxidermy. It looks like it's quite an advanced set up" she's informed. "Anyway, we located some human skin. It's been nailed into an upright position and it looks like it's being cured like they do with cow or dear skin, for leather. We're not sure why, but it's pretty disgusting. I'll send some pictures to you as soon as we get them" she's assured. "We have the coroner en-route right now, so it shouldn't be long before I can get those pictures to you" the officer promises.

"Thank you. Officer?" Kat says in an inquiring tone.

"Oh, sorry. Officer Grant" he replies.

"Thank you, Officer Grant. I'll be waiting for those pictures" she promises.

"Heads up, everyone" Kat says, as she walks back into the conference room. It's still a little noisy, but everyone's busy, she notices. "I just got off the phone with the police in Mt. Buckhorn, the home town of Elroy Wade. They were at his house doing a search, and they found a set up for taxidermy. They found skin that looks like it came from a human body and it was being preserved," she informs them.

"Oh, gross" says someone in the back of the room.

"Yeah, I'd have to agree with that assessment. Anyway, they're going to get pictures as soon as the coroner gets there and email them to me. We just might be able to do a comparison with the skin that we found here, in D.C., and the one from Staleyville, Pennsylvania."

"Hopefully, we'll be able to get some closure, although it may be the skin from the dead body that was found at the pet crematory in Pennsylvania last week. Anyway, things look like they're getting tied up. I'm going to get some information from our medical examiner on the body that was recovered from the explosion in the east end tenements. As soon as I know anything, I'll let you know" she promises.

"Doctor, I have one more question, which I should have

asked you while I was still there" Kat mentions to Dr. Zorgath who's on the other end of the line."That dead body from the explosion the other day, have you got anything on that yet?" she asks.

"Yes, I did, thanks for reminding me. It's been swamped in here" he says in a flustered voice.

"That victim's name was Elroy Wade. He was killed before the explosion" he says as he looks over the report.

"What" Kat repeats "he wasn't killed in the explosion?"

"Nope" Dr. Zorgath replies."He was killed by multiple stab wounds, six to be precise, to the torso. There was no sign of smoke inhalation, so the burns over his body were post-mortem. He never felt the fire" he finishes."Are you still with me, Kat?" Dr. Zorgath asks when he hears nothing on the other end.

"Yeah, I was thinking, sorry. That means we now have a murderer for our murderer. Shit! That casts doubt over a lot of the theory we built: about the murderer of William Blaketon, Tom Mason, and the unknown dead body that we found in the pet cemetery in Pennsylvania. I better get back to our conference room, we may need to start over" she says discouraged."Thanks for your time Doctor, see you around. Not too soon though, I hope" she says teasingly.

"Ditto" Dr. Zorgath says.

Let's get this show on the road Kat decides as she heads up to the Captains floor, spotting Sidney in the waiting area.

"Hey Sidney, what are you doing here?" Kat asks.

"I heard there was a break in the case and I wanted to see you personally about it" Sidney admits.

"Yeah, there was one" Kat agrees "but I need to report to the Captain first, then we can talk" she promises."If you'll give me about ten minutes, I'll be back."

"Sounds good" Sidney replies in the affirmative."I'll be watching for you. In the mean time, I'll work on something for a release" she says as Kat walks towards the Captains door.

"Go right on in, Lieutenant, the Captains been waiting for you" Leslie informs Kat when she gets close enough.

"Thanks Leslie, Captain?" Kat inquires as she knocks

lightly while pushing the door open to the Captains office.

"Come in Lieutenant, have a seat."

"Thanks Captain. I've just received some information regarding Karen Delrose. It's been determined that she didn't die of natural causes, like we believed previously. Dr. Zorgath actually found a poison that induced cardiac arrest, but is usually untraceable. He told me he got lucky, that the autopsy he did was done quicker than most, and because of that he was able to obtain a sample of tissue from the brain that still had a residue of the poison in it. He also said that the poison travel's quickly throughout the body, but slows down in the brain. It lasts only about ten minutes longer there, than in the rest of the body. He was in that ten minute window period and the results proved without a doubt that she died by poison."

"Excellent work" Captain Hall responds. "Tell Dr. Zorgath for me excellent work."

"I will" she promises. "Also, the burned body from the east end tenement was identified. The remains belonged to Elroy Wade."

"Shit" the Captain exclaims "that was good work, but not what I wanted to hear, so what's the verdict?"

"He was murdered Sir, and according to Dr. Zorgath, he didn't die from the fire, he was stabbed in the abdomen six times. The cause of death was the stabbing" she admits.

"Hmm, odd" he responds.

"Yes Sir" she replies. "I believe he was killed and dumped at the tenements. Then a call came in to Deputy Chief Devon Callander via cell phone from one of his snitches, informing him that Elroy Wade was in that house. It looks like it was set-up, either to harm or kill Deputy Chief Callander. The arson investigator confirmed that Devon stepped on a wired switch that caused the explosion. He also informed me that the main gas line for that building was turned on and a small leak was left. The switch activated a spark on the wall near the gas line, and as soon as someone stepped on the switch, it blew up. Deputy Chief Callander was very lucky not to be killed."

"Indeed Lieutenant. Has Deputy Chief Callander gotten a hold of his snitch yet?" the Captain inquires.

"No, not yet sir. He sent a message out to him, but he hasn't received any response yet. That's his first priority, I believe. Unfortunately, with the information breaking all at once, we're all a little busy" she admits to the Captain. "Captain, the media's waiting for a briefing, are you scheduled for one soon?"

"Yeah, I planned on a media release in thirty minutes. We want to leak some information, but not enough to panic the public" he admits. "At least we can let them know that the serial killer is dead, but unfortunately, there are some complications in this case. I'll also inform them that Metro One's finest, along with multiple federal agencies, are working around the clock to take care of the problem. As far as we can see, there's nothing for the citizens to worry about."

"Yes Sir, thank you. If that's all then, I need to get back to work."

"That's all, Lieutenant; please keep me apprised of any updates" the Captain says in dismissal.

"Sidney, the Captain's preparing a media briefing. He'll be out in a couple of minutes. Unfortunately, I've got to go. I'll talk to you soon, I promise" Kat says as she hurries b away.

"Devon, did I miss anything?" Kat asks as she walks back into the conference room.

"Nope, so far we're talking with all the members of the House of Representatives, unfortunately there's been nothing new with that yet" he admits.

"Lieutenant, I have a call for you" Detective Des says.

"Alright, I'll take that in my office" she informs her. "I'll be right back, Devon."

"This is Lieutenant Thomas, can I help you?"

"Yes Lieutenant, this is Virginia Moore, the Speaker of the House" she's informed.

"I remember, Mrs. Moore. How can I help you?" she asks.

"I just received a call from Ellen Stewart."

"I'm sorry Mrs. Moore, who is Ellen Stewart" Kat inquires politely.

"She's the wife of Jeff Stewart, the House Majority Whip" Virginia informs her.

"Okay, is this supposed to mean something to me, Mrs.

93

Moore?" she asks politely.

"It will when you listen, Lieutenant" Virginia Moore says in exasperation.

"Sorry, I'm listening Mrs. Moore" Kat assures her.

"Ellen just called from Maui, where she and her husband are vacationing for two weeks."

"Alright, and" Kat prompts impatiently.

"She was hysterical, Lieutenant. She claimed her husband drowned in the ocean while swimming."

"Excuse me, could you repeat that, Mrs. Moore?" Kat says in disbelief.

"She claimed that Jeff was dead and that he died while swimming in the ocean" Virginia repeats.

"When did this happen, Mrs. Moore? Kat asks, stunned, as she slowly sinks into her chair.

"Well, she said it happened about two hours ago. She hadn't called earlier because she went to the hospital with the rescue squad, while they were trying to resuscitate him. But they were unsuccessful, Lieutenant" Virginia finishes tearfully.

"Oh" Kat says in shock. "Mrs. Moore, can I get a number on Maui to reach Mrs. Stewart?" she asks, thinking another murder. "I'm afraid I'm going to need to speak with her personally. Also, please expect an officer to show up at your office today, we're going to need a statement from you too, on the exact message that you received from Mrs. Stewart" she warns.

"Fine Lieutenant, I'll be expecting someone" Virginia assures her.

"Thank you, Mrs. Moore, for the information. I'll be in touch" Kat says slowly as she hangs up.

"Listen up everyone" Kat announces as she walks back into the conference room. "I just received a very strange phone call from the Speaker of the House, Mrs. Virginia Moore. She called to inform me that she received a phone call from Mrs. Jeff Stewart, informing her that Jeff died in a swimming accident off the coast of Maui."

"Jeff Stewart was the House Majority Whip. They've have been vacationing there for the past few days. She informed Mrs. Moore that rescue tried and failed to resuscitate him en-route to the hospital, and that he was confirmed dead approximately two hours ago. How many of you believe in coincidences?" Kat asks. No hands were raised "that's what I figured; I don't believe in coincidences either" she remarks. "It looks like we have another suspicious death in the House of Representatives. Now I'm getting a real bad feeling about this" she admits.

"We need to start thinking in the terms of politics, not just murders. It has to be connected, there's no way this is random" Kat insists. "I guess our next questions should be: what had they done recently, what were they responsible for, who didn't like them, what kind of opposition did they encounter, who gave them a hard time. I'm sure there will be a lot more questions that need answers" she observes. "But at least that's a good starting point. Devon, Mallory can I see you both in my office?" she requests when she's finished with the update.

"We'll be right there" Devon promises.

"Okay, this is what I believe needs to be done first" Kat says when she shuts her office door."I'm heading for Maui; I need to see the scene, talk with anyone that may have seen anything, talk with the medical examiner, the paramedics first on scene and so forth. You two want to accompany me?" she asks."We have a lot of work to do. This makes three murders in the House of Representatives, in three weeks. We have no idea who's responsible for this, but I have a bad feeling that this isn't going to stop. Something's really wrong up on the hill" she says."We need to find out who's doing this, and why. I need to clear my trip through the Captain, and you two need to get clearance from your boss, so I'll let you know what time we leave" she offers.

"Wait" Devon says."We have a jet for work purposes, let me arrange the flight and let you know the time" he offers.

"That would be great" Kat says in relief. "I'm sure the Captain would rather do that then have to pay, since budgets are so tight with all the cuts. A free ride would be perfect. After I talk to the Captain, then I'm heading out to pack a few things, the sooner we can leave the faster we might get some answers. I'll let everyone know in the conference room while you arrange the trip" she offers.

"Deputy Chief Devon Callander, Agent Mallory Callander and I are getting ready to fly out within the next few hours" Kat informs the officers in the conference room."We'll be gone about three days. We need to see the scene, talk with witnesses and discuss this with the local coroner. As soon as we have that information, we'll call you and you can get started at this end" she announces.

"In the mean time, keep up with the questioning of the House of Representatives. We need to figure out what's happening. I'm going to leave Detective Rowald in charge here in my absence, so if you need anything, please let her know."

NINE

"That was a long flight" Kat mumbles around yawn."I'm glad it's over but at least I did get some rest, finally. I hope you both got some too?"

"Yeah, we're ready to go. Let's start at the hotel where the Stewarts were staying and then we can go from there. We have a lot to get accomplished in a short amount of time, so it looks like the rest we had on the plane will be the last we see for a couple of days" Devon warns them.

"Wow, will you look at that view" Kat says in awe."I've never seen anything so gorgeous."

"Haven't you ever been here, Kat?" Devon asks in surprise.

"Nope, I've never had time to vacation" she admits sheepishly "nor are my funds the type to swing one of these vacations. You don't make a lot of money working for the police, Devon" she reminds him.

"Yeah, that's true, but it's too bad, you'd have had a blast here" he predicts.

"Look at this hotel, it this looks like the Taj Mahal" she exclaims.

"Well, not quite, but close" he admits with a grin, enjoying her excitement."I'll start with the desk, you start at the bar Kat and you Mallory, question the housekeeping staff. We need to see his rooms also" he reminds her.

Kat enters a dark bar where the view is breathtaking and the ambiance is sexy."Are you the bartender?" she asks as she walks up to the bar.

"Yes Ms. I am. What can I get you?" he asks.

"Nothing to drink, thanks, but I do have a few questions. I'm Lieutenant Thomas with Metro One Police in Washington D.C. I have a few questions about Mr. Jeff Stewart" she explains.

"I'm afraid I don't know a Jeff Stewart, Lieutenant. You sure are a long way from home" he says.

"Yes, I am" she admits with a grin."Jeff Stewart is the gentleman that died swimming yesterday. Do you know anything about that? I didn't get your name, sir" she admits.

"It's Casey, and yeah, I heard about that" he answers, but now seems a little nervous.

"Was he in here a lot?" Kat asks.

"Quite a bit, Lieutenant; as a matter of fact, he was in here yesterday. It did look like he was going swimming, because he asked for his drink to be put in a plastic glass. He must have been going to the beach. Real glass isn't allowed on the beach, safety reasons, you understand."

"Yeah" she replies in agreement.

"Did you notice anything strange yesterday, when he was in here?"

"Not really, he seemed fine, he wasn't acting strange or anything and he was friendly. There really wasn't anything different that I noticed" he admits.

"He never said anything out of the normal?"

"No, nothing" he admits, now moving his hands constantly.

"You seem a little nervous, did I say something to upset you?" she asks.

"No, I'm just not used to talking with the police."

"Yeah, I can understand that" she acknowledges with a smile."Has there been anyone in here lately that you didn't recognize, that kind of stood out?"

"I don't think so." he says."Wait! There was a group of businessmen in here about four days ago. I was surprised that they were here, because I asked them if they were staying in the hotel. I was going to start a tab up for them, but they said they were staying a mile down the road at the Vista Hotel. I was actually surprised by that, because they have a nice bar of their own there but they'd come all the way over here to sit in this bar. It didn't make sense to me, if you know what I mean?" Casey admits.

"Yeah, I do. Did you notice if they spoke to Mr. Stewart at all?"

"I really didn't pay any attention, but they could have. I mean, they were all in here at the same time, and one of the waitresses spent a lot of time on the suits" he adds thoughtfully. "I thought it was for the big tips. Some of the suits leave real big tips if you cater to them, and she was definitely catering to them, almost exclusively. She didn't take care of any other customers when they were here" he adds after thinking about it.

"What's her name and is she working now?"

"No, she'll be here tonight though. She's on night's this week. Her name's Linda Mattlow, she's tall, long blonde hair, built (if you know what I mean) and real pretty. She's got a thousand watt smile that can light up this room. She's the most popular waitress we have" he says.

"What time does she come on tonight?"

"She should be here about eight."

"Thanks, I'll come back later, and Casey, you should give it a shot if you like her that much" Kat remarks as she walks away.

Devon's pretty successful at the front desk with the check in clerk. A cute twenty something with a knockout smile and a body that rocks, Kat thinks jealously. Of course, Devon's talking and smiling. Men, she thinks, that's why I'm single. None of them can behave."They always have to flirt," she mutters as she walks up to the desk. I'm hardly at my best after a twelve hour flight, she thinks huffily. Besides, we have no strings, right? We just sleep together.

"Kat, this is Torri Emerald, she works the desk here, days, and Ron Small takes over nights. She remembers Jeff and Ellen and says they seemed like nice people, they never gave her or any of the other staff any trouble. Actually, they weren't very demanding at all, she says."

"That's good" Kat replies shortly.

"Did you see a group of businessmen come in here a couple of days ago" Kat asks "and then go into the bar?"

"Yes, I did. I thought it was strange that they came to our bar, but we do have a nice one so I just thought that was why. Did they do something wrong?" Torri asks in alarm.

"No, no, just inquiring. The bartender said the same thing and that he thought it was odd too, especially since they told him they were staying at the Vista. He couldn't understand why they came here, when they have such a nice bar over there. He also noticed that one of his waitresses was glued to their table, so I wondered if she knew them, before they came here."

"Did you ask her" was Devon's response.

"No, she works tonight; so I'll come back then and talk to her."

"Let's head out to the Fire Department then. I want to talk to the paramedics that answered that call" Devon says.

"I think if you walk around back, you'll find them" Kat says. "It looks deserted but I can hear something outback. Hey, there you are" she says as she wanders around to the back of the building.

"Did you need something" asks one of the firefighters as he dribbles the basketball to the hoop.

"Looks like a good game going on" she says.

"Actually, we have some questions we need answered" Devon says shortly. He'd seen the look on Kat's face.

"What are they, sir?" asks one of the firefighters.

"You took a call, day before yesterday, for a drowning victim over by the Grand View Hotel?"

"Yeah, we took the call" admits the firefighter.

"When you got to the beach, how did you find him?"

"Well" answers the oldest of the paramedics "it was a little strange. He was lying on the sand and there were people standing all around. His wife, I think it was his wife, she was trying to give him CPR, but she wasn't doing it right. There didn't seem to be anyone else that had offered to help. That was unusual. Seldom do you come across a scene like that with no one helping. Usually too many people are trying to help."

"But not that day" another firefighter says in confusion."I

100

just put it down to inexperience. They are a lot of people out there that don't know how to give CPR, which I think is criminal, but to be doing it wrong, now that was sad, real sad" he finishes.

"Yeah, who knows, if someone capable was doing the CPR he might have made it" responds another firefighter."Poor guy, he didn't stand a chance."

"Did you notice anything else that was strange at that scene Mr.?" Devon asks.

"Oh, sorry sir; I'm Matt, Matt Caden."

"Thanks Matt, anything else strange at the scene?"

"Well not really, the wife, she tried CPR like I said, but when we got there he wasn't breathing. His lips were already blue by that time. I thought it was more than a drowning, like a sting from a jelly fish. Sometimes that happens, and if you're allergic you can die. But I didn't notice any spots on his body, any marks from a sting. We started CPR, loaded him on the back board, and ran to the squad with him. We continued with the CPR until we handed him over to the ER Doctor. They took over, but we stayed for a little bit. Unfortunately, they couldn't get him back. We hate it when one of our rescues doesn't make it. It's pretty depressing for us when we can't help."

"I can understand that" Devon says."Was there anything else that seemed off to you about the victim, Matt?"

"No, just the blue lips. I thought that was strange, but everything else, including the people watching, seemed normal."

"Thanks Matt. Here's my card, call me if you think of anything else" Devon asks.

"Will do, sir," Matt responds with a small salute.

"If you're here very long Ms., you might want to get some sun block. You have a really fair complexion. We wouldn't want you to get burnt, that can be pretty painful. You know, there was something else that I noticed" Matt says into the silence.

"What's that?" Devon asks.

"He wasn't burned sir, sun burned, and I didn't see any sunscreen around. If you're here a couple of days without sunscreen, you definitely get burned" the paramedic says thoughtfully.

"Hmm" Devon replies "thanks Matt."

"Let's see if the coroner's available, or would you rather stay at the fire department with the medics?" Devon asks snidely.

Kat laughs, then acts innocent when she turns to Devon with the remark "of course I want to go to the coroner's office, I have questions for him. I'm here to work and I need some answers. D.C is waiting to hear something and we don't have a lot of time, the deaths are appearing seven days apart" she reminds him.

"The medical examiner's name is Kenike Laimana, and his office is attached to the hospital" Devon informs her en-route. "I asked Torri about it before we left earlier. She said to just go in the back, it's a closer walk to his office."

"Alright" Kat says agreeably "here we are. Dr. Laimana, are you in there?" Kat yells after
stepping up to the open window.

"Yes, come in" replies a voice from inside.

"Dr. Laimana, I'm Lieutenant Thomas and this is Capitol Police Deputy Chief Callander."We're here from Washington D.C."

"To what do I owe this honor?" inquires Dr. Laimana suspiciously.

"We need some information on the death of Jeff Stewart. He was brought in yesterday, death by drowning" Kat says as a reminder.

"Yes, yes, I remember the name" remarks Dr. Laimana.

He must only stand about five-five Kat thinks. He's about my height, not a very big guy, but he's definitely Hawaiian, that dark hair, dark skin, and a name born of this state. Yep, he's definitely a native.

"Did you happen to finish the autopsy on Mr. Stewart, yet?"

"Yes, I did Lieutenant. The official cause of death for Mr. Stewart is drowning. An unfortunate accident" he says sadly.

"Are you positive there was nothing unusual about this drowning, Doctor?" Kat asks.

"Not that I'm aware of" he replies "should there have been,

Lieutenant?"

"I wouldn't know that, it's not my area of expertise. We do seem to have a rash of death's occurring in the House of Representatives, though. When we heard about Mr. Stewart's death, we flew out here immediately.

"Let me pull his report, hold on. Alice, can you pull the report for me on Jeff Stewart? He's the most recent drowning victim" he reminds her.

"Sure, here it is Doctor."

"Thank you, Alice. Now, let's see" Doctor Laimana says. "Everything looked normal; he had no cancer, no heart disease, the brain looked normal. He was actually one of the healthier drowning victims I've seen" he adds with a sad shake of his head. "A shame, he probably could have lived a long life" the Doctor says with a sigh.

"Dr. Laimana, did you run any toxicology tests on Mr. Stewart?" Kat asks quietly.

"Of course, that's standard operating procedure, Lieutenant. Let's see, we have most of the reports back already, but not all of them. The ones we have back all have negative in the findings box" he says as he shows them the paper.

"Did any of them check for a short term chemical that can poison or cause death?"

"No, those are expensive tests and we only request them when there are suspicious circumstances surrounding the death. This one wasn't suspicious, it was a drowning" the Doctor says emphatically.

"Doctor, is there any way that you can run those tests now?" Devon asks, before Kat let's her temper get the better of her.

"I'm not sure. It would depend on if the body is still here. Let me make a call" he offers. "Alice, call the holding room please and see if Jeff Stewart's body is still there" Dr. Laimana requests.

"Certainly Doctor; I'll get right back to you" she assures him.

"Thank you, Alice. She's going to call me back with that information."

"If the body hasn't been requested yet, for either shipment

or by a funeral home, then we can probably get those tests done" he offers."If not, then you'll need to contact whoever has the body and then have it brought back here or to the coroner in the city they took him to. The tests can be run as long as the funeral home has not embalmed the body for burial."

"Dr. Laimana?" the intercom statics to life.

"Yes Alice."

"The body has already been released. It's being flown back to the Washington D.C. area as we speak."

"Thank you, Alice" the Doctor says."There you have it. You'll have to contact the next of kin and find out if you can get the tests done before he reaches the funeral home. The funeral home is usually informed prior to landing and is waiting on the tarmac to receive the body. That way, everything is done quickly. Since there's such a short amount of time to prepare the body before decomposition begins, the embalming slows the process long enough to allow for a funeral service" he explains.

"Thank you Doctor. I guess we better hurry. We might be able to catch the plane before it takes off" Kat says.

"Good" the Doctor says. "It was nice meeting you."

"And you" reply Devon and Kat.

"Well, that was good and bad information. Do you think they left yet?" she asks.

"Let's hope not."

"I'll drive, that way you can call Mallory and see what she's found out, and let her know that we're heading for the airport. Tell her to meet us at the front gates of the hotel, maybe we can stop Jeff Stewart's body from leaving the airport terminal, if we can get there in time" Kat says.

"We may need to jump on the plane and head back to Washington" he says. After picking up Mallory at the hotel "I better call the pilot too, so he's ready when we get there. Hopefully we'll catch that plane, before anyone has time to do anything to that body."

"No, I think, aw . . . shit, that planes taking off. We missed it" Kat yells as she pounds on the dashboard with her fist."We need to go inside the airport and see if the pilot of that plane can be reached, see where it's landing" she says quickly."We can contact the airport and put a stop to anyone taking the body. Also, ask them to check for funeral homes waiting for a plane."

"I can do that" Mallory offers. "I'll send someone out to the airport personally, it's always better than a call, I hate getting put on hold" she admits."I didn't get a lot of information from the Hotel staff. Housekeeping has pretty tight lips, so they must get good tips. No one admitted to seeing anything and I probably talked to a hundred employees" she admits in disgust."How about you two? Did you get anything?" she asks.

"Well, the bartender implied something suspicious was going on with the men from the other hotel. There were a group of businessmen, from the hotel down the street that came into the bar for drinks one day last week. One of the waitresses seemed unusually familiar with them, to the exclusion of any other customers, or so the bartender said but he could have been jealous."

"Hmm" Mallory says "intriguing."

"Also" Kat says "the fire department thought the drowning was more than a drowning because of not only the lack of help at the crime scene but the blue lips that the drowning victim had. They said that was odd. It looked to them more like a poisoning, like maybe a jellyfish sting or something, or even an allergic reaction to some type of sting."

"The medical examiner didn't run the specific toxicology tests for poison, because the drowning was not suspicious appearing, and those tests are extremely expensive. He holds an elected position, and they won't re-elect if he spends frivolously ('he didn't say that, that was my take'). That's where we are now. We have to catch the body that just left this airstrip before the funeral home gets it, so we can have those tests run."

"I'll make the calls" Mallory offers as they head into to the terminal.

"All right Devon, what's next?" Kat asks.

"We need to find out what funeral home is waiting. I'll contact the wife; hopefully she'll talk to us. If not, we wait for Mallory to come through" he admits.

"I just got off the phone with Dulles's and we may have a problem" Mallory says after finding them in the terminal.

"What, what problem?" they ask in tandem.

"Well, the Department of Homeland Security was informed of this newest death. They want to up the security level because they believe these are acts of terrorism. They've assumed control over the investigation and are awaiting the plane with the Congressman's body."

"Shit" they both exclaim.

"That is NOT good news" Kat complains. "I can just hear the Captain now. Stop the investigation, this is now the responsibility of the Department of Homeland Security. I'll now be the last to hear anything. This just isn't right" she complains."I don't care, this is my case, and I will find the murderer's" she mutters.

"Now Kat, you know you'll follow orders, you have to" Devon says to remind her."Besides, if the Department Homeland Security's in charge, that puts me in charge. This is a Federal problem now. It was only a matter of time until we took the case. I've been monitoring and working this case almost as long as you" he reminds her."It has to be this way Kat, but don't worry. I won't kick you out in the cold. I figured we'd work it together. Highly unusual for us, I know, but it can be done and I'm willing" he offers."You have some good ideas and a lot of knowledge. I'm not afraid to use you" he admits with a small smile.

"No, you're not" she adds with a knowing grin.

Mallory just stares at them, well, well, what's going on there. How come I'm just now noticing this, she wonders.

"I hate to interrupt, but I think we should head back to the hotel and see if that waitress is working tonight" Mallory suggests. "We can at least continue this investigation before we're technically informed of the takeover by the Department of Homeland Security" she reminds them with a small smile.

"Yeah, I'm all for that" Kat exclaims."Let's hit the road. Maybe we can close the case before the Department of Homeland Security has the chance to take it over officially" she says with a grin.

"Kat, this is the last time you're driving. Hey, slow down. From now on, this is my case and I'll drive" he says frustrated. "At least I can pretty much guarantee that we'll get from point A to point B alive. If not, it won't be my fault" he growls.

"If we don't" Kat argues, "it won't be my fault either. I'm a very good driver" she insists.

"Doing ninety-five in a fifty-five doesn't seem safe to me. Not to mention, you could be stopped. Then waste time trying to get out of a ticket, while our waitress leaves to a town unknown, never to be heard from again" he goes on with a pained look on his face.

"Fine, I'll slow down. Now can we talk about something else?" Kat asks.

"My, you two get along famously" Mallory says with a knowing smile. Kat groans and gives Devon a look. 'Don't go there' she says with her eyes. With a sigh of relief, she pulls up to the hotel.

"We're here, let's see if she is" Kat says as she jumps out of the car. "First, let me change my hair to a wig and put on some glasses. I questioned the bartender, so he'll know who I am."

"We'll all go into the bar like we're tourists and order some drinks, then maybe dinner. You never know what we'll pick up undercover" Devon decides.

"Alright" Kat agrees "let's do it."

TEN

All three walk in together, talking as if they're tourists and saw the sights, and take a seat at a table in the corner.

The lighting is dim and the tall blonde waitress see's them seat themselves in her area and looks over with a smile. "I'll be right there folks" she calls. "What can I get for you all?" the pretty blonde waitress asks while wearing a short tight mini and a blinding smile."I'm your waitress tonight, my names Linda" she offers.

"We've been out sightseeing all day" Kat says with a deep sigh "my feet are killing me, I'm starving, and I could definitely use a drink" she confesses. "So let's start with a drink and then maybe some dinner?" she asks hopefully.

"Sure, you poor thing" the waitress exclaims."I can get you started right way, what would you like?" she asks.

"I'd like a pina colada" Kat admits.

"Yeah" Mallory says in agreement "me too" while Devon just orders a whiskey, neat.

"I'll be right back" the waitress promises.

"Thanks" they all say.

"It looks like she might have taken the bait" Devon murmurs.

"Yeah, why wouldn't she?" Kat asks "it's what we are, at least I am" she admits with a grin.

When the waitress comes back, Mallory starts telling her how upset they all were that the "poor man from room one sixty eight drowned this week. What a terrible thing to happen" she finishes in a shocked voice. "Did you hear anything about that, did you know the man?" she asks.

"Well, yeah, he was in here just before he drowned, had a drink, um, let me think. It was a martini, dry with a twist of lime" Linda states.

"Wow, you actually remember what he drank" Devon says in awe.

"I don't normally, but he was here for about a week and he always ordered the same drink" she admits."Kevin, he's the other bartender, he would see him walk in, and mix his drink right away, then I would grab it, and usually had it to the table just as he was sitting down" she grins."It was like a game between us" she admits as she blushes "he remembers the drinks and I remember what the customer likes, it's team work."

"Do a lot of people drown out here?" Mallory asks nervously.

"Oh, no, we don't have many people drowning. I'd hate for you to get the wrong idea about this beautiful island. Occasionally, someone goes out a little too far and usually by the time anyone can get to them, it's too late" she explains with sadness. "Will there be anything else?" she asks.

"No, we're good for now" they all chime together "thanks."

"That went well" Devon admits quietly.

"Team work, huh? Maybe in more ways than one" Kat says suspiciously.

"Hey" Kat says urgently "that group of businessmen just walked in the side door. They're taking the table next to the door, and Linda's already headed right for them, almost like she was waiting for them" she says."This could be the break we've been looking for" she whispers with excitement.

"Yeah, let's hope it's what we've been waiting for" Devon replies in agreement.

"I wonder if she'll ever get back to us" Kat questions."I really could use some food" she admits sheepishly.

"Let's watch and see" Devon murmurs. "I want to see the interaction between Linda, the businessmen and the bartender" he says.

"Yep, he had their drinks all ready for them; she's already taking them over" Kat whispers.

"That guy on the other side facing us, he looks familiar" Mallory whispers. "I wonder where I've seen him."

"Hey, what are you doing Kat?" Mallory asks quietly but urgently.

"I'm just going to take his picture. You can send it to your office and run a facial recognition program on it, right?" she asks.

"Yeah, but you really don't want them to see you doing it, that may scare them away" she insists.

"I know" Kat says "I didn't start this job yesterday, you know."

"That was a good one, what's your email?" Kat asks urgently "I'll send it over."

"Do it quick, because one of them noticed you taking the picture and he's talking quickly to the others. Oh-oh, he's getting up, wait, they're all getting up and leaving out the side door" Mallory groans. "Damn it Kat, you scared them away!"

"At least I got the picture. I hope you get a hit, Mal. I also sent you a picture of Linda; you can run that one, too. Now, I think you should take a picture of Devon and me, over by the bar, and try to get the bartender in it at the same time" she suggests, "you know, vacationers in Maui, need lots of pictures."

"I hope that works!" Devon snaps in anger.

"Amen to that" Mallory says.

"You know, it's not that late, how about we tail the businessmen, see where they're going?" Kat asks hopefully. "We might get lucky; learn something about them that can help us with the congressman's death. Besides, we're leaving as soon as the pilot gets everything ready, so we only have a little time."

"Fine, let's go" they agree.

"Hey, wait a minute, I thought you wanted food?" Linda reminds them when they all get up to leave. "We did, but we have to go now. Sorry, we'll probably be back later" Devon promises with a wink.

"Do you see, wait, there they are" Kat says urgently. "Devon, why don't you follow them in and see where they go; Mallory and I will follow you in and see what we can find out at the check in desk" Kat offers.

"All right, I'll call your cell phone Mallory and let you know the room number" he says.

"Good, I'll be waiting" Mal promises.

"Check out the cute guy clerk" Kat whispers."He looks pretty young; we should be able to find out what we need."

"Yeah, he looks like an easy mark" Mal admits."There's Devon, hold on" she says before answering the call.

"Room two thirty six" Devon says.

"Thanks, let's see who's registered for that room" Mallory says.

"I'll take the clerk, you wait for an opening" Kat says. "Sir, can you help me" Kat asks with a little embarrassed grin."I dropped my earring outside and I can't find it. Could you help me please?"

"Sure miss, let me get a flashlight" the clerk says.

"Oh, thank you so much. These are my grandmother's earrings and I'll be so upset if I've lost one" she admits.

"No problem, we'll find it" the clerk reassures her as he grabs a flashlight and with Kat following, goes outside the front entrance to help.

Mallory slides around to the back of the desk to check the computer for reservation information. Devon wanders back into the lobby as Mallory finishes and comes back out from behind the counter.

"What's Kat doing?" he asks.

"She pretended to lose her grandmothers earring and the kid's helping her find it."

"Good, what did you get?"

"The reservation is for Tom Walters from Waco, Texas" she replies.

"Good, that gives us a starting point at least" Devon says.

"Yeah, let's go help find the earring" Mallory suggests "and then we can get going."

"Hey, is this what you're looking for?" Devon asks, holding up a small shiny earring.

"Oh, where did you get it?" Kat cries in relief."Thanks for trying to find it, I appreciate it" she says to the young clerk and kisses his cheek.

"You're welcome" he stammers as he blushes and hurries back into the hotel.

"I called the pilot; he's ready anytime we are" Devon says. "Let's go."

"Well, this was quite a day" Mallory admits after boarding the plane. "Let's see if there's anything to eat, and then some sleep" she says "I'm beat."

"Me too" yawns Kat. "I think sleep first, then food" she decides as she puts her seat back to get comfortable. "A short nap, then I'll be fine" she mumbles.

"Morning sleepy head" Devon says "I wondered if you were ever going to wake up" he adds teasingly.

"Sorry, I needed some sleep" Kat admits."Now, I just need the restroom. I'll throw a little water on my face, and I'll be fine" she promises. "Some coffee would be good" she hints as she struggles with her seat, and moves her numb legs.

"I stayed in the same spot too long" she complains. "How long till D.C.?"

"About an hour, maybe a little less" Devon replies to her inquiry.

"Good, we need to find out what's going on, we've been gone too long."

"Let's hope no one else died while we were gone" Mallory says.

"Yeah" Kat agrees "Let's hope."

"The businessmen from the other hotel, the one that was registered, his home address was Waco, Texas" Devon announces.

"What?" Kat exclaims. "Waco, you're sure?"

"Yep, that's what it said in the computer" Mallory confirms. "Why? You seem surprised by that, should that mean something to us?" she asks.

"Well, I'd never heard of Waco, not until a few days ago" Kat admits.

"Were did you hear it?" Devon asks.

"Snake" she says flatly. "Snake told me that's where his bike shop is, Waco, Texas."

"Hold on a minute, who's Snake?" Mallory asks.

Kat just looks at Devon with a questioning look.

"Umm, Mallory, it's a long story, but, Snake is Jacob" Devon says, shifting in his seat a little.

"Who?" Mallory asks in confusion.

"Jacob, your, I mean our, brother" he says.

"What" Mallory cries, "you've seen Jacob?" she questions Devon in shock."When, when did you see him?" she demands.

"When I was in the hospital last week" he admits. "Actually, Kat brought him to see me."

"Kat, how do you know Jacob?" she asks in confusion.

"I met him about twelve years ago" she replies."He kinda helped me out, stopped me from being attacked" she admits with a shrug."I've seen him a few times in the past; whenever he comes back to D.C he looks me up. We usually sit down and chat. Well, he came back to D.C. this year, and looked me up at my friend Mike's coffee shop. That's where we met originally. I was on my way to class, and I literally ran into him on my way out. We talked a little and then I left, and was jumped by a guy from his biker group. He heard me scream, came running and then proceeded to beat the crap out of the guy that jumped me. None other than Elroy Wade, in person" she admits with a shrug.

"Okay, hold on, I'm a little confused" Mallory admits. "You're talking about my brother Jacob, whom I haven't seen in fifteen years and you're saying you saw him in D.C.?" she inquires.

"Yes" Kat affirms."Last week, he showed up in Mike's coffee shop. Mike's like an older brother to me" Kat explains "has been since I was fifteen. So I try to go there at least once a week. He worries if I don't keep in touch. Unfortunately, I've been so busy with the murder, and now the deaths of the congressmen, that I missed a few weeks. But I did get in there last week. Mike and I were talking when the door dinged and in walked Snake, um, I mean Jacob" she explains.

"How does he look, Devon?" Mallory asks with excitement.

"He looked okay" Devon admits grudgingly."Scruffy, with long hair, but he looked okay. Life seems to be going good for him. He said he owns a custom bike shop in Texas, been settled there for about seven years or so."

"He said he got tired of riding and wanted to establish a home base. He's not married, had a girl back home, but not anymore, he said. He wants me to tell Mom and Dad, he thought he actually might be able to see them, but I told him I had to talk to you and Eli first. I did remind him though, that he was the one to leave, not us. He said he'd be in town a little while and to let him know. I'm not sure, though" Devon admits, "I don't want Mom or Dad hurt again" he murmurs.

"Devon, that's not up to you, nor is it up to us, it's their right to see their son" Mallory cries. "If he wants to see them, he should. You know they've been looking for him for fifteen years. Dad's never given up looking. Didn't you say Dad called you every week to see if you've heard from him?" she reminds him.

"Yeah, he does" Devon mutters.

"Well, how could you think to stop him from seeing them?" she demands."Have you let Eli know yet? Were you going to tell me?" she asks harshly.

"I was, I just haven't had the chance, we've been working a case, you know" Devon says in defense. "I'm not the bad guy here" he reminds Mallory "so stop treating me likes it's my fault. He's the one that left" he mutters in anger.

"I know, I'm not treating you like it's your fault he left. But for not saying anything to me about seeing him, that's your fault" she declares."You need to call Eli and let him know. He needs to hear that you've seen and talked to Jacob" Mallory insists.

"Fine, I'll call him, just as soon as we land" he promises.

"Okay, now can we talk about the case?" Kat demands.

"Yeah, sure, talk" Devon replies sullenly.

"I've never been a coincidence believer" Kat admits "but having heard the town of Waco, Texas two times in a little over a week, that's just too much to expect me to swallow, there's got to be a connection" she states emphatically."What is it?" she wonders out loud.

"Yeah, that's too much coincidence, I'm with you on that,

how are they connected" Mallory asks in puzzlement.

"I think I need to talk to Snake again, see how this could be connected and see if he knows that businessman" Kat decides. "This is starting to give me a bad feeling" Kat murmurs "a real bad feeling."

"Is it ever going to stop snowing this year" Kat complains with a shiver as they get off the plane in D.C."I wish I'd have had a heavier coat" she mutters shivering."This is nuts. I don't think we've ever gotten this much snow, not since I've lived here" she admits."It's not going to make our investigation any easier, that's for sure."

"No, it sucks" agrees Devon."Let's get the car; hopefully it'll warm up fast" he replies.

"Yeah, I hope!" Kat says.

"Mallory, I'll drop you, where do you want to go?" Devon asks.

"Just drop me at home; I want to clean up before I head into the office."

"Alright, Kat, where to?" he asks.

"Just drop me at the station. I'll clean up later" she decides. "I need to speak with my captain as soon as possible."

"Fine, let's go. It looks like it may take a little longer than normal though, look at the traffic." "I don't believe anyone in D.C. knows how to drive in this stuff. What a mess" he exclaims as traffic is stopped, three across and the snow is coming down so hard that visibility is about fifteen feet."This is a freakin blizzard" he exclaims.

"Yeah, it's bad out" Kat says "I sure wish we were still on Maui" she says wistfully.

"Great, this is not good for us right now" Mallory states "we still have to catch a killer."

"Yeah, and I need to speak with anyone still at the House of Representatives" Kat decides."I want to see what's going on there."

"Wait" Devon says "you're not on the case anymore, remember?" he reminds her.

"I know, but I'm still going to get the killer" she promises. "Whether they want me to or not, it's my case until I close it" she insists.

"Here you go Kat, I'll call you later. I need to check in at work after I drop Mall off" Devon says.

"Yeah, see ya" Kat says as she braces for the wind and slips and slides her way to the front door of Metro One.

"Hey" Des exclaims "you made it! I was worried you wouldn't be able to land in this."

"It lightened up a little, it's a lot worse here than it was at Dulles" Kat admits. "It's a blizzard out there!"

"Yeah" Des agrees "it's been doing this on and off for the last three days" she complains."It's hard to get anything done in this weather."

"Is the captain in his office, do you know?" Kat inquires.

"He's waiting to see you, his orders are for you to report to him as soon as you get here" she says.

"I figured, I'm on my way" she says as she heads for the elevator. "Is the captain in?" Kat asks Leslie when she reaches his office.

"Yes, Lieutenant, he's waiting for you, go right on in."

"Thanks" Kat says quietly.

"Captain" Kat says as she slowly pushes the door open. He's sitting at his desk with the blizzard blowing behind him in his big window. "I just got in" she says.

"Good" he replies "have a seat Lieutenant."

"Yes sir."

"We have a change in the case you've been working on" he begins.

"Yes Sir. What is it?"

"The Department of Homeland Security has taken over the case, Lieutenant. I've discussed this thoroughly with the Director of The Department of Homeland Security and we have decided to allow you to continue investigating as long as you work with the Capitol Police and the FBI. I believe that would be to our advantage. You've been on this case since day one. I believed it would benefit the investigation for you to stay on it. That's our decision. You'll be working with the Feds from here on out, until this case is solved. Any questions?"

"No, Sir."

"You're dismissed, Lieutenant, good job" he adds as she rises to leave the office.

"Detective, meet me in my office" Kat orders as she walks past Detective Des' cubicle.

"Yes Sir."

"Has anything been going on here while I was gone?"

"Not really, we've run all the leads we had, Lieutenant. Nothing new came in. We've spoken to eighty five percent of the House of Representatives, and no one seems to know anything. They all seemed terribly shocked about the death in Maui; if there was someone that knew something, they didn't show it" she replies.

"Thank you, Des" Kat says. "I have a couple of names I need run from Waco, Texas. You can get started on that today. I'll be in and out, since I've been ordered to work with the feds now that the department of homeland security has taken over the authority of the case. However, there's no reason why you and I can't work on this also. I'll just give whatever we find to the Feds. I don't care who solves it as long as it's solved" she declares. "The names are Jacob Callander and Tom Walters; run them and see what you can find" she orders.

"Yes Sir."

"Call me with anything you get" Kat says.

"Yes Sir" Des replies.

"Oh, and thanks Des, for keeping things in check here, I appreciate it."

"You're welcome Lieutenant."

"I'll be back later" she says as she hurries out of the office.

ELEVEN

Kat walks out into winds of thirty five miles per hour, blowing snow and only ten degree's but it feels like minus fifty. Wish I could have enjoyed Maui more; it sure was a lot nicer there than it is here. You should have a least spent a little time on the beach, you idiot. Oh well, back to reality. Once home, she runs the water for a hot shower. I need to warm up. Damn it's cold out there.

"Kat, it's Devon, did you get any more info about the murders?" he asks after she answers her phone.

"We're waiting on the toxicology reports from Dr. Zorgath, remember?"

"Did he say how long?"

"Nope, probably a couple of days, though."

"Fine, I guess we'll have to wait."

"I'm going to head over to the House and talk to whoever's there" she informs him during the lull on the line.

"I want to, too, so how about if I pick you up? Say about fifteen minutes, if you can be ready?"

"Yeah, I can be ready"

"All right, I'll see you in a few, then."

After rushing through the dressing ritual, throwing her coat and boots on, she rushes out the door just as Devon pulls up.

"I've got Detective Rowald running the two names from Maui" Kat informs him after she jumps in to the warm car.

"I have them being run, too" he admits.

"Oh, well, I guess since I was in charge of this for so long, I'm still thinking of this as my case, sorry" she admits, chagrined "I'll change that, I promise. I should have called you to check first."

"Damn, it's miserable out, I hope we aren't making this trip for nothing" he mutters. "There had better be someone at the House tonight. I know they work strange hours, so hopefully there's someone there. Sorry but it's going to take a little longer than normal to get there, between the weather and the bad roads."

"I figured, since it's a freakin blizzard out here" she gripes. Just as they gain a foot, they lose one."I'm surprised they didn't put out a road advisory and an emergency level to help people decide when to get off the roads, before they get killed."

"We made it and there's a parking spot, right in front. My lucky day" he admits with a grin.

"Let's go" she yells to be heard above the wind after getting out of the car.

"It looks like a couple of people are still here. There's Jane. I'm surprised to see her here, since she's usually surrounded by the Secret Service" Kat says.

"Jane" Kat says as she walks over to her."I'm surprised to see you here."

"Yes, Lieutenant, I'm still here. I spend a lot of time in this building, I like to think that these people are my closest friends" she admits with a sincere smile.

"I know what you mean. What did you think of the accident in Maui, with Jeff Stewart?"

"Oh, that was just horrible" Jane responds, voice quivering. "It's so sad, I feel so bad for his lovely wife. What a terrible thing to happen, and on vacation no less" she admits.

"Yeah, it was terrible." What is it about her that I don't like? Kat wonders. She seems nice enough, always smiling, and very quiet. She doesn't seem to like to stand out, even though she does, and she's always smiling. It's that smile that's always in place, seldom does it seem to reach her eyes, but most people don't seem to notice that, maybe it's just me and my suspicious brain. I just don't like her. Still, when my gut says something, I try to listen; it doesn't usually let me down. "Any comment Jane, on what seems to be happening in the House of Representatives? There have been three deaths in three weeks, I'm not very comfortable with those odds" Kat admits.

"You don't think someone is deliberately hurting the congressmen, do you?" Jane asks nervously.

"Well, I have to take all things into consideration when investigating a crime. Mr. Blakely died from murder, obviously. Next it was Karen Delrose, suspicious causes and now Jeff Stewart. That's three deaths in three weeks. I've never believed in coincidences, Jane" Kat assures her.

"My, when you put them together like that it sounds ominous, it scares me a little" she admits with a nervous smile.

"You probably shouldn't worry, since you don't hold a seat in the House" she assures her.

"Yes, that's true, I don't hold a seat" she agrees, voice dwindling. The same smile's still there, but it sure doesn't reach her eyes, Kat notices. I'll have to watch her, she just doesn't fit. Something's definitely not right there.

"Overall, everyone I spoke with had good things to say about Jeff Stewart" Kat tells Devon after they meet near the doors to leave.

"How about some dinner, Kat" Devon asks. "We can talk work while we eat, I haven't had a decent meal in days" Devon complains.

"Fine with me, your choice this time" she says.

"I know this little pub that has the greatest bar burgers in the Metro area" he says hopefully.

"Okay" she agrees "I'm in."

"Nice place, Devon" she admits after the five minute travel. "I wonder why I never noticed this place before. A dark, cozy atmosphere, candles lit on every table, table cloths of red and white, homey, with a real wood fireplace, and most of the place to ourselves. I like it" she says.

"It's only slow because of the weather, this place is usually hopping. Let's take advantage of it, and sit by the fire, take the chill off. You can never get this seat on a normal night" he admits.

"Well then, I'm glad we came." Kat says as the waiter walks up to the table.

"Can I take your order?" the waiter asks.

"Yes please. I'll have a Killians" she requests.

"Make that two" Devon adds.

"Do you know what you want to eat yet, Miss?"

"Yeah. I've been told that you have the best bar burgers in the Metro area" she admits with a smile. "I want to check that out, so I'll take one, well done with fries on the side."

"Yes Ms, and you Sir?"

"I'll have the same."

"Very good, it will only be a few minutes" he promises.

"Thanks."

"Okay, now we can talk."

"I spoke with a few of the House members. They all had good things to say about Jeff Stewart. The consensus is he was a nice guy, known for rocking the boat a little. He just helped pass a ruling on placing a fine on the oil Barrens in the Middle East. He didn't want the United States to pay a higher amount for its oil. The barrens in the Middle East got angry; with their profits being cut into, they wanted to increase the tax base again. Jeff went against that, brought all his House friends into the mix, and they got it passed. So, now we have a motive, but who's behind this? I hope we'll know a lot more when we find out who that businessman in Maui was, the one that lives in Texas. I'm hoping we'll know more about him soon. With both offices looking into this, we should have answers fast" she says in satisfaction.

"Here are your burgers" announces the waiter as he walks up to the table, tray in hand. "Ketchup, mustard, anything else that I can get for you?" he asks.

"Yes, I'd like some ketchup please. Thanks" she says when he sets the bottle on the table. "Hmmm Hmmm Hmm, this is delicious" she mumbles around a mouth full. "Devon, thanks for bringing me here" she says after swallowing.

"My pleasure" he says with a grin.

"Where was I" she asks, after putting her burger down to breathe.

"You were talking about Jeff Stewart and the Arab oil."

"That's right. Anyway, he did get that bill passed, which I'm sure pissed off a lot of people including the ones overseas.

But other than that, it sounds like he was well liked by everyone."

"I noticed you talking to Jane tonight" Devon says thoughtfully.

"Yeah, we chatted a bit" she says. "She seems to be a very nice person, but for some reason, I keep getting the feeling that I don't like her. It's almost as if she's a good fake, not sincere, even though no one else seems to have my problem. I'm going to keep my likes and dislikes about her to myself for a while. What's your take Devon?"

"I agree; there seems to be something there, but I haven't been able to put my finger on what it is either. I'm just going to watch her, and have a background check done. Although, with the secret service, and the president involved, I'm sure they've already run a check and found nothing. She seems privy to everything at the White House."

"I'm done in for the day, we flew all night, and I feel like I haven't slept in days. I'm not going to be much good for anyone until I get some more sleep" Kat announces around a yawn.

"I'm pretty tired myself" he agrees. "Let's go, I'll take you home" he offers as he throws some money on the table for the check.

"Thanks" murmurs Kat. Is he going to stay? I'm tired, but not too tired, she thinks to herself as she grins behind his back. God, he's good looking. "It's pretty bad out Devon, why don't you stay at my place, its closer?"

"You know if I stay, you aren't going to get as much sleep as you want" he warns her with a leer.

"Yeah, I was counting on it" she laughs.

The ringing of a cell phone wakes them up from a short sleep. "I'm not ready to get up yet" Kat grouches.

"I know, me either" Devon adds with a yawn.

"Just ignore it" she says as she snuggles back into the covers and lays her head on his shoulder. "This is way comfy. I'm not getting up yet."

"Kat, you need to move, I have to get that" he insists.

"Why, just let them leave a voice mail." she says.

"I would, but we're working a case, remember" he says as he slides out from under Kat's head "it could be important."

"I guess" she mumbles as she digs further down in the blankets.

"Yes, sir, I'll be right there." Devon says before hanging up.

"You need to get up Kat. It was my boss, and something's come back about the case."

"Fine" she says as she gets out of bed and flounces to the bathroom. "I need a shower and coffee, then maybe I'll be able to talk" she says as she gets in the shower and adjusts it to a hotter temperature. "I want to be warm for at least a few minutes today" she says to Devon.

"All right, it's all yours" she says as she walks back into the bedroom.

"Thanks Kat. I made coffee, it's in the kitchen" he tells her.

"Thank you, you are awesome" she sings. A good start to the day, she decides.

"So, what did your boss say?" she asks over the sound of the shower.

"They got some results back from the medical examiner, on Jeff Stewart" he yells.

"Is it anything good?" Kat yells back.

"Don't know, I told my boss I'd be in within the next half hour."

"Okay, I'm almost ready" she says as Devon walks up behind her, hot from the shower and wraps his arms around her waist. "Devon, stop, you're getting me wet" she complains.

"Just a little snuggle" he chuckles "water never hurt anyone, Kat; you'll be fine" he grins, unrepentant.

"Don't forget, we have a funeral this morning" she reminds him.

"Yeah, yeah, I haven't forgotten."

"Stop, just put your clothes on, we need to go."

"Yeah, I know, I just wanted to make this last longer" he admits.

"Don't worry, we'll try this again real soon" she promises dreamily. "I'm not done with you yet, either" she admits with a smirk.

"Okay, I'm ready, let's start the day" he says after he's finished dressing and puts on his weapon.

"Jeeze, Devon, you take longer to dress than some prima donna teenager" she teases when he's finally ready.

"Sorry, this is not my normal speed. I'm just a little tired this morning, that's all" he admits."Someone wouldn't let me sleep much last night" he complains, a sparkle in his eye.

"Yeah, right" she says with a blush."You wouldn't let me sleep last night" she clarifies.

"No" Devon says "it was you, not me."

"Whatever" she says "let's go, we have work to do."

Ten minutes later they walk into the home base of the Capitol Police and into Devon's office.

"Wow, this is my first time seeing your office. You have more room here than we do up town in the conference room."

"Yeah" he admits "Fed's, you know."

"Yeah, I know" she says with disgust.

"Okay, let's see what they have. This report says that Jeff Stewart died from a very rare form of poison, found only on the coast of Australia, in the chironex fleckeri, or in plain English, the Box Jelly Fish. The article claims that it has the most deadly venom in the world."

"What? How can poison from Australia's coast, be found in the body of a man in Maui? They don't swim that far, I'm sure" she says in disbelief.

"No, I bet it came from a human source, through a different method than a sting. Let's see what this is. I'll do a search. Wait, here it is. It says that the sting from one of these has enough venom in it to kill up to sixty humans in three minutes. Wow" Devon exclaims.

You think someone released this in the water off Maui?" Kat asks, confused.

"No, I think someone poisoned him some other way, maybe in his food or a drink, with the venom from one of these. It says within three minutes, so he could have taken a drink, then gone out to the water to swim, and in three minutes been far enough out for it to look like a drowning accident, no sting marks or injection sites, everything is clean."

"The toxin is so fast, it's got to be hard to trace and I'm sure you need the right equipment for that" Devon says while deep in thought "so it's a good thing that his body was checked by the D.C. Medical Examiner, there's no way that Maui has the equipment sophisticated enough to run this test" Devon claims. "So yeah, looks like we moved up in the game of death. Now, all we have to do is figure out who, and how."

"This helps a lot" Kat says.

"Let's start digging on the guy from Waco. By the way, did you happen to get Snakes number? I think we need to talk." Devon says, determined.

"I'll call him and tell him to meet us at the coffee shop, he'll probably be a lot more comfortable there. There are no threats, and not too many cops, that always keeps bikers happy, I mean ex-bikers" she grins.

"Hi kitten" Snake exclaims as she and Devon walk into Mike's coffee shop together, about twenty minutes later.

"Snake, looking good" she says "nice black leather, but aren't they cold this time of year?"

"No, they're lined with flannel, nice and toasty" he admits with a smile as he closes the distance between them and picks Kat up to give her a big hug.

`   "How's your visit to D.C going?" she asks.

"Good, but I'm ready for some sunshine" he admits as he set's her down gently and turns to greet his brother with a hand clasp. "This crap outside reminds me why I live in Texas. Sure, we get a little snow, but over-all it's very mild and sunny. I miss the sun. I'm sick of freezing, I'd sure rather be biking in Texas" he admits.

"Yeah, I'll bet you would" Devon says sarcastically.

"Stop it Devon. We need Snake to talk to us; you're just pissing him off with those kinds of comments."

"Don't worry Kitten, that's why I don't see these people much. They're so full of themselves; they couldn't care less about me. I take care of myself, I don't need family to butt in" Snake says, disgusted.

It's all a front. Families, it's hard to comprehend, mines

been gone since I was fifteen. "Hi Mike, how's business going" she asks with a smile at seeing her good friend again.

"It was going good, but the weather has slowed it down a lot. I'm hoping this starts to clear up soon. I can't afford it for much longer. So where have you been Kat? We're used to you visiting, coming over for dinner once in a while, you know?" Mike reminds her gently.

"Yeah, I know Mike; send my apologies to Kathy please. I've been busy for the last few weeks. Crime doesn't stop just because we have bad weather" she admits.

"That's true, but I was hoping it had slowed down for you."

"No such luck Mike, if anything, it's been busier" she answers.

"Can I have my usual, you want anything Devon?" Kat asks.

"Yes, I'll take a plain coffee, black" he says.

"Snake, how about you, you want a latte?" Kat asks with a grin.

"No thanks, I'm good, I got mine just before you walked in, brat" he informs her with a smirk.

"Okay, let's have a seat then. Mike if you'll excuse us for a little bit, we need to talk to Snake about work" Kat asks quietly.

"Sure, I'll be in the back if anyone needs anything" he offers as he shuts the door between the front and the back.

"Looks like we'll have the place to ourselves for a little while" comments Kat.

"Snake, have you ever heard of Tom Walters? He's from Waco, Texas" Kat asks.

"Yeah, I know him. Why?" he asks.

"Well, he was on the island of Maui while we were there, with a bunch of suits. He wasn't staying at the same hotel, but I did get a picture of him and it came back with a hit. I wondered if you knew him since he's from the same town as you."

"I do know him, but not because he's from the same town. I've done business with him" he admits.

"Really, what kind of business" Devon asks suspiciously.

"Bike business, that's the only kind of business I do" drawls

126

Snake.

"Yeah, right" Devon scoffs in disbelief.

"Devon, stop, I told you, you can't talk to people that way and I don't care if he is your brother. He's helping out the Metro One Police department with an investigation."

"Actually, the Capitol Police is in charge, remember Kat" Devon says snidely.

"How could I forget when you keep reminding me, at least twenty times a day" she snaps.

"Kid's, kids, let's bring this back down to a civil level." Snake suggests.

"Fine, you said you know Walters?" Devon asks.

"Yeah, I've done business with him. He's a very good customer." Snake says quietly.

"How so" Devon asks.

"Well, he's this mega rich guy, oil I think. Anyway, he orders custom bikes from me, usually about four times a year. They're always for different people and different events."

"Wow, that's a lot of business from one customer" Devon exclaims.

"Yeah, it is, I told you he was a good customer."

"How much does a custom bike run?" Devon inquires.

"Normally, the ones he orders are loaded, so they cost a lot more" Snake admits. "They usually run around a hundred-twenty-five-thousand" Snake says. "American dollars" he adds with a smile.

"What" cries Devon "that's a shit load of money for a bike?"

"Yeah, it is, but it's a completely custom bike so it's worth every penny. All the bikes I sell only gain in worth as they age, not the other way around. I've never had a bike go for less than ninety thousand and that was close to basic for a custom bike. So yeah, he's a good customer. What about him? Snake asks. "How does he tie in with the murders, just because he was on Maui? He vacations there at least once a year" he says. "I know, because he always brings me pictures of his vacations. He also spreads the word about my bikes and I get orders from all over the world because of him. I won't do anything to make him angry, I don't want to lose his business" he states firmly.

"Do you think he could be walking on the other side of the law?" Kat asks carefully. "It seemed way to coincidental for him to be on that island when the Congressman drowned" she admits."So what do you think Snake, could he be doing illegal things?" she asks.

"Have you ever thought he might be doing illegal business?" Devon asks.

"Well, I guess anything's possible" he says thoughtfully."I'm not sure what kind of illegal business it would be" he ponders as he rubs his lower lip with his thumb."I could check on that for you, I guess" he offers.

"Thanks Snake, if you could do that, I'd appreciate it. He might talk to you easier than us" Kat says.

"That's for sure" he agrees."I don't know many people who willingly talk to the Fed's or the local LEO's. Most people would rather be bitten by a viper than talk to the cops."

"Yeah, I just don't get that" she complains."We're just trying to keep people safe."

"Uh huh, right. It's guilty till proven innocent now, that's not the way it's supposed to be" he states.

"That's not true, but we don't have time to debate this right now, we can save it and revisit it at a future date, if you wish" she offers.

"There're those claws again" Snake smiles."You do have quite a scratch, Kitten" he admits.

"Yes I do" she admits."I'm a cop" she reminds him.

"When do you think you'll talk with Westfield?" she asks.

"Well, I guess I could fly out and see him, or give him a call."

"The call would probably be better since there's no flying out of here for a while, at least until the weather clears" Devon reminds them.

"You're just going to cold call him? Won't that raise alarms" she wonders out loud.

"No, I have a bike he wants, that's almost done. I call him all the time to keep him updated on how the bike's coming. So, that's not a problem."

"Great, we'll be at the House of Representatives for the funeral this morning and probably most of today since we need to finish interviewing them about this latest death. But give our cell phones a call when you get something and leave a voice mail. We'll call you back as soon as we can."

"We have to go Devon; it's almost nine thirty and the funeral starts at ten. We don't want to be late."

"Fine, let's go."

"I'll talk to you later, Snake" she promises."Maybe we can do dinner, I'll let you know."

"Good lord, this wind takes your breath away as soon as you open the door. It feels like it's twenty below zero out here" she cries.

Once in the car, she has to blow into her hands to get her fingers to start feeling again. With eyes watering, she groans as the pins and needles start."At least I can feel them now" she admits.

"Yeah, mine too" he agrees."That is so damn painful" he gripes as he rubs his hands."Let's see if we can get to the House before the funerals over."

"It's pretty bad out here, I can't see anything ahead of us now, can you?" she asks.

"Not much. There's a slight glow for tail lights, which will have to work" he mutters."Let's hope no one hits us. Hopefully, everyone can see our taillights. We only have about two miles to go, we should get there before it's over. I hope everyone showed up. If they were smart though, they'd have canceled it till better weather" Devon says.

"Yeah, but you know they didn't, his wife needs closure" she reminds him.

"We made it, and of course there's no parking, so hold on. I'll go down that street over there. There might be something down there."

"Just go into the parking garage, I'll pay. At least it's out of the worst of the snow."

"Fine" he agrees."Here we go, second story, out of the direct wind. Good thinking Kat" he says.

"Thanks, now let's get in there, it's five after ten. It already started, so we'll have to sneak in the back." Just as they enter the back the Speaker of the House finishes her little speech and the Minister rises to begin the services.

"We normally have this type of gathering at the Chapel on the Hill, but because of the declining weather and the amount of people involved, we thought this would be easier. Thank you all for coming. Jeff Stewart was a good man, a wonderful husband and dedicated father and Congressman. He will be missed."

Kat's mind wanders as she starts thinking about comparisons, why three deaths in the House of Representative, how could they be connected. Who's in charge of this? Is it at this level or is it higher, she wonders. It's got to be higher, I spoke with everyone here at least two times, not including today, and I didn't sense any hostility or notice anyone with anger big enough to kill. Whoever it is could be sociopathic, but I don't think so. You'd think that type of person would have a sign on their foreheads or have four eyes or something to distinguish them from normal. Nothing seemed abnormal here. Who didn't show up for this thing, she wonders as she looks around. It's going to be impossible to tell, with so many people here.

I wonder where Jane is, she thinks. I haven't seen her in here yet. She didn't miss the other two, but she is pretty small, she usually sit's with the President and he's not here for this one. Some kind of pre-scheduled meeting at the White House for him and the Vice President, so they couldn't be here, but Jane should have been.

Oh, wait, there she is, she's sitting next to the Speaker of the House. That figures, the third most powerful person in the States.

Hmmm, she thinks as she flashes back to the last funeral. She was sitting by Jeff Stewart at the last funeral, isn't that weird, she thinks.

"Devon" Kat whispers "Jane's sitting next to the Speaker of the House today."

"Yeah" he whispers back "so what?"

"Well, at the last funeral, she was sitting by Jeff Stewart. Don't you find that's a little coincidental? I mean, let me think, who was she sitting by at the first funeral?" The President, re-members Kat; that was the first time she ever saw or met Jane. She sat with the President and the Vice President and was sur-rounded by the Secret Service. Hmm, thinks Kat. No connec-tion there, I guess.

"Is this service ever going to end?" she asks.

"Shhh, it's almost over" he replies in a whisper,"This is the closing prayer."

Finally, Kat thinks."Alright, let's get to the doors so no one can leave until we've talked to them. I see Mallory and her group over on the left, and some of my guys are here, there's Detective Des" Kat says."Let's do this."

TWELVE

"Jane, can I speak with you?" Kat asks.

"Certainly Lieutenant, what can I help you with?"

"I just have a couple of questions for you today. How well did you know Jeff Stewart?" she inquires.

"Well, I knew him pretty well, he was a super person. He was always so friendly and caring, he's definitely going to be missed" she replies with tears in her eyes, her small mouth quivering in sadness."We're all going to miss him so much, Lieutenant. Believe it or not, the House of Representatives is like a family. Most of these people work together for at least half their life, so they become like family and just like family, they always stick together."

"Of course, there were small disagreements on occasion, but nothing that would cause one member to want to harm another." she states passionately.

"Thank you, Jane, for talking with me."

"I want to help, Lieutenant, as much as I can. I don't want to see anyone else die. This is just terrible, but if there's nothing else Lieutenant, I have an appointment at the White House."

"Thanks Jane, I'm through here" Kat says.I'm so sick of talking to these people, Kat thinks as the last of them leave the building.

"It's still snowing, but I can see the people out there walking down the sidewalks so it's letting up a little" Devin admits."Its light out at least, it looks like the sun's going to come out pretty soon."

"Wow, I've never seen so much snow" Kat says in awe."It covers everything and makes it look soft and round. Shit, did you see that little kid, hey, pick up that kid mister! He's not as tall as the snow banks; he's going to suffocate in there" she yells. The man just laughs and picks up the kid who squirms until he puts him down again.

"He likes it" the man says with a shrug and a grin. "I won't let him disappear, I promise" he laughs.

"It's going to take a few days to dig out of this, but hopefully it's over for the month now." Devon says. "Let's head back to the station" Devon suggests. "We need to check in, see if there's anything new and check for anything from Jacob. Granted, we're exclusive on this case, but that doesn't mean we need to be out of the loop. I prefer to work with everyone and help where needed. It keeps the lines of communications open."

"I agree" Kat says. "I'll be over to your headquarters later" she promises "since I need to go into Metro for awhile."

"I'll drop you, then" he offers.

"Thanks for the ride Devon. I'll call you later" Kat says as she gets out of the car.

"Morning, Des. How'd we do at the House today?" Kat asks.

"It seems like everyone really liked Jeff Stewart. I didn't speak with anyone that had even a small amount of dissatisfaction with him, it was really strange. Nobody's that popular, to my way of thinking, it's almost as if the House of Representatives have closed themselves off to the public. They're definitely treating this as a terrible accident and not looking at it as a murder because they kept saying things like, a terrible accident, bad timing and all that. It was strange. What about you, Lieutenant?" Des asks.

"I spoke with quite a few of them and had the same feeling, they've closed ranks. I wonder who was responsible for that. It could have been Virginia Moore, the Speaker of the House, I guess. Maybe a directive came down from the White House.

They're probably thinking that we don't want the public in a panic just because there's some nut job out there killing off the House of Representatives. I can actually envision that being discussed in the oval office" Des says.

"Yes, it looks that way, at least to me. Someone with authority gave a directive, no public panic" Kat says.

"We still have a murderer to catch, and it's not Elroy Wade either. He's dead, but he did kill the House Majority Leader, William Blaketon. So let's see, Des. The first was the House Majority Leader, then the House Minority Leader, and this latest one, the House Majority Whip. If there is another one, who could it be?" she says. "I wonder if we should give a heads up to the House Minority Whip" she thinks out loud. "Those are parallel connections, but I still think I'll talk to Devon about it. If there is another one, it's going to happen tomorrow, all the murders have been exactly one week apart, that's the weird part. It's as if the murderer has a preset agenda, and is keeping to it with the every week thing. So how can we warn anyone, when we haven't got a clue as to who's going to be next? It kind of makes sense, but then again, it doesn't. Let's hope we get a break in the case before anyone else has to die. Who's benefitting from these murders? Who's replacing the dead Congressmen? The answer has to be there, I just can't see it clearly, yet."

"Des, I'm heading out to capitol headquarters. You can reach me by phone if you need me." Finally arriving at capitol headquarters, the roads a slush pile, cars stuck everywhere, Kat parks in the garage. Making her way to Devon's office through the busy lobby and into the guarded inner sanctum, she spots Devon and wanders over to catch up with the news.

"Devon, I was thinking, who replaced the dead Congressmen? What do all the replacements have in common and what did all the dead ones have in common, besides being the nicest, most popular, etc? There hasn't been anything negative that's been said about any of the deceased. It's almost as if they got a directive from the oval office, stating; keep all opinions to yourselves, to close ranks, in other words."

"That's what it felt like today, there has to be a connection" he says thoughtfully.

"Anything new on your end?" she asks.

"Well, I've talked to all the Representatives that I could and you're right, they all seem to be tight lipped and non-opinionated about everything that's going on in the House. I think you're right about the directive. Public panic is a problem and this is an election year, so they certainly don't want the public to see them in a negative light."

"Actually, that's how I'm starting to think, too. So what's next, then?"

"We've talked to all the people at the House but what about the ones that didn't make it to the House for the last funeral? I guess it's time to start going door to door" he decides.

"Okay" she says "it's going to take a long time, since some of them were out of state, and due to snow problems they haven't made it back to D.C. yet."

"True, but it's clearing up now, so they should get Dulles open and running close to schedule sometime this afternoon. That means the Senators and Congressmen will start trickling back in, hopefully by tonight, tomorrow at the latest" he estimates.

"I think we should go over all the evidence from all three deaths, and start comparing them" she suggests."We need to see if there is some microscopic thing that can connect them. Let's try that, and we'll get fresh eyes on this. It could be we're missing something right under our noses, but because we've looked at it so long, we just can't see it anymore. I'll ask Mallory to work with us on this."

"Wait; hold on" Devon says "that looks like my brother coming up the stairs. Eli" he yell's "what the hell are you doing here" he asks as he grab's his brother in a hug."I didn't know you were coming into town" Devon declares.

"Yeah, I've been trying to get here for two days, but the flight was cancelled three times. You have a shit load of snow out there" he observes in distaste."This is why I like California" he mutters, "I've never liked snow very much."

"Yeah, I know" Devon grins "you've always been too wimpy for the snow."

"And who's this?" Eli asks as he zooms in on Kat.

"Oh, sorry" Devon says."This is Lieutenant Kathleen Thomas from D.C. Metro One."

"It's nice to meet you Lieutenant, I'm Eli Callander, Devon's and"

"Mallory's brother" Mal finishes for Eli as she walks up to him to grab him in a hug."I didn't know you were coming in" she admits.

"Well, after you called me and told me about Jacob being in town, I decided to come out and check up on him, I haven't seen him in fifteen years, either" he admits sheepishly.

"I haven't seen him yet either" she informs him.

"We've been a little busy with the murders on Capitol Hill, so I haven't had time to set up a meet with him, but now that you're here, maybe we can all get together" Devon decides."Kat, maybe you could reach him, you set it up last time" Devon says hopefully.

"I'll give it a try" she responds.

"Kat?" Eli asks in confusion."I thought your name was Kathleen?"

"It is, but I go by Kat. I use the initials of my given name, Kathleen Ann Thomas. I've been called Kat since my early teen years, my dad started it" she adds with a smile, her green eyes sparkling.

"I'll give Snake a call" she promises as she walks away.

"Snake?" Eli says "who's Snake?"

"That would be your brother, Jacob" Mallory responds, as she watches Devon watch Kat walk away.

"Jacob is going by Snake?" Eli says in confusion."Why doesn't he just go by Jacob?"

"Maybe because he's an ex-biker; he also looks like a biker" Mallory says dryly.

"Wow" Eli responds "I've really been out of the loop. Anything else I should know?"

"Well, he knew Kat from twelve years ago, when she was a fifteen year old college student at Capitol Hill Community College. He actually helped her when she was attacked by a future rapist-murderer" Mallory says as she gets into her storytelling mode. "They've seen each other a couple of times in the past twelve years, he'd stop in to see her at her friend Mike's coffee house when he was in the D.C area, just to say hi, or so Kat says. They have a friendship there, but nothing more, by choice

I believe. He sees her as a little sister type friend, and she sees him as the big brother type."

"It's getting late, how about all of us go out somewhere and wind down, get a little dinner?" Devon asks.

"I'm in," says Mallory, "me too," Eli says with Kat, at the same time.

"Alright then, let's head out, we have a lot of catching up to do."

"Did you reach Jacob?" Devon asks Kat. "Yeah, he's free tonight too, so when we decide where we're going, I'll let him know to meet us there."

"Excellent" says Eli, and Mallory's agreeable with that.

"Let's go someplace comfortable, where we can eat and talk" Devon suggests.

"What about that little Italian place, on New Hampshire Avenue?" Kat asks. "They have good food, and they're not usually swamped, so we can talk, and eat in comfort. Besides, Italian is everybody's favorite. At least it's my favorite" she admits with a sheepish look.

"Okay, give him a call Kat and we'll head over there" Devon says.

"Let's sit in the back" Kat recommends after they get there "that way we won't be disturbed by everyone coming in and out of this place. Hey, Snakes here already" she says as she walks towards the back. Seated at a long table, Snake stands out in the atmosphere, with his long black hair, five o'clock shadow and his leather jacket, he looks exactly likes he sounds, one hundred percent pure biker with a lot of danger mixed in.

"Hi kitten, how are you?" he grins as he stands for his big hug from Kat.

"I'm good, how about you?"

"Great" he replies as he prepares to greet his brothers and his sister.

"Lord, look at you" he says, when he catches sight of Mallory. "You got beautiful, Mallory" he says softly.

"Thanks Jacob" she replies with a hug for the brother she hasn't seen in fifteen years. "It's been a long time, bro. It's really good to see you. We all feared for your life for a long time.

You need to keep in touch more often" Mallory admonishes.

"Yeah, I guess it's time" he agrees."I will" he promises reassuringly to Mallory.

"Eli, you look good" he admits, offering his hand to his brother.

"Jacob, long time, I can't believe I'm actually seeing you, finally. After all these years. Biker dude, huh" Eli queries, "that's so hard to believe" he admits.

"Yeah, I've been one since I left fifteen years ago. It was a good life, but I got tired of it, and stopped the group after about seven years of riding together. I got sick of having no home base, so when I finally settled, I settled in Waco, Texas. It's been good" he admits.

"Let's sit down everyone and order, then we can talk" Devon suggests.

"What would everyone like?" asks the waitress after everyone is seated. "Let's start with drinks and then I'll come back for your food order" she suggests.

"Okay, let's have some wine, everyone okay with that? We'll take three bottles of cabernet sauvignon" Devon says.

"Great, I'll be right back with that."

All is quiet while looking over the menu until the waitress gets back with the glasses and wine. "Would you like to order now?" she asks after distributing the glasses and opening the wine.

"What's your special today?" Kat asks.

"We have the spaghetti and meatballs today. Everyone seems to like that dish" the waitress replies.

"Okay, I'm in" Kat says enthusiastically, and after everyone agrees to the order she leaves.

"So Jacob, life has been good for you?" Eli asks.

"Oh yeah, it's been real good."

"We missed you a lot" he admits. Devon remains very quiet during their welcome home speeches.

"So, when can I see Mom and Dad?" Jacob asks.

"You haven't seen them yet" Mallory asks "why not?"

"Well, Devon's not sure I should see them, he thinks that I'll hurt them by leaving again."

"Devon" Mallory says "you can't stop him from seeing his own parents. If he wants to see them he should. You know they've missed him all this time. How could you think to stop him" she cries in disbelief.

"I was just thinking about Mom and Dad and how hard they took it when he first left" Devon admits sheepishly."I don't want to see them hurt again."

"If he doesn't see them and they find out he was in D.C. they'll never forgive you" Eli states.

"I won't tell, and neither should you" Devon replies in anger.

"I'm not going to hope to not tell them, I may forget someday when I'm talking to them and let the cat out of the bag" Mallory says."You want to take a chance and not tell them, you go ahead, but I'm telling Jacob where they live. They need to see him, Devon. They love him too and they have more right to seeing him than any of us!" Mallory says stubbornly."We can go with him for the first visit, so they have us for support, it might make it easier" she offers.

"Fine" he says quietly after being rebuffed by Mallory and Eli.

"Dinners here" Kat says in relief after seeing the waitress head their way."Let's eat, I'm starving. Food's been slim lately, what with the murders and the blizzard. It's time to enjoy. We can talk more after" she promises. There's sudden silence around the table, which shows that everyone has been working too much lately and not eating or relaxing as much as they should. Working around murder is tough, she thinks. All work and no play.

"This was a great idea Kat" Eli says, "Thanks"

"I've never been to this place before" Mallory admits "but they're good, real good" she says and groans around a mouthful of food.

"Good choice" Devon says while Jacob agrees.

"So what's next?" Eli asks. "It's too late to go to Mom and Dad's. They're probably relaxing for the evening."

"Can we set up a time for Sunday?" Jacob inquires.

"What about for lunch on Sunday?" Mallory suggests.

"They're only about ten minutes outside of D.C. proper, so we should be able to get there and back quickly, how about you Jacob?"

"Yeah, lunch works for me, I really can't wait to see them" he admits.

"You waited fifteen years" Devon says angrily.

"Yeah, I know Devon, but I want to see them now" Jacob answers in the same tone."I've changed, whether you want to believe it or not."

"Fine, so what will you call yourself to them" he inquires snidely.

"They'll call me Jacob, just like everyone here did, except for Kat. I go by both names, so either name is fine" he admits.

"Alright everyone, it's getting late, and we have work tomorrow, so I'm going to head out" Devon decides tiredly.

"Yeah, me too" agrees Kat. "See you tomorrow."

THIRTEEN

"Kat, can I come up tonight?" Devon asks pleadingly.

"I expected you to want to, I was actually hoping you would" she admits with a smile of satisfaction. As she opens the door of her apartment, Devon puts his hands on her shoulders and starts to rub out some of the knots that formed during the stressful day and evening they just had.

Oooh, she moans. "That feels so good, but be careful, you'll put me to sleep" she warns.

"That's not quite what I had in mind" he answers with a squeeze.

"Let's take a shower" she suggests.

"Later" he replies as he picks her up to take her to the bedroom. Once in the bedroom he slowly lowers her to her feet as he starts a leisurely move down her body, undressing her as he goes, sucking and kissing exposed skin as he undresses her.

"I want to see all of you" he murmurs between long kisses and little nips, as he soothes with his tongue anywhere he nips. As her heart starts to pound harder and harder, a dizzying feeling in her head, she lets go of any further thoughts. With her heart beating rapidly, her breath non-existent, she wants more. Slowly he lowers her to the bed, covering her with his body, now there's skin touching skin everywhere as he sips from her lips.

"I could get used to this" Devon murmurs quietly.

"Mmmm, me too" she says with a sigh.

"I can't move. I'll get up in a minute" he promises.

"What is that damn noise" she wonders as music fills the

room, the rolling stones screaming out the speakers of the clock radio.

Shit, it can't be that time already. I just shut my eyes a minute ago. As she moves her legs to slide out of bed, she finds someone's arm trapping her. "Huh" she groans and spies Devon, sleeping next to her. "Shit" she says frustrated "we did it again" she complains to the sleeping Devon. "I'm in the shower first and this time, stay out till I'm done. We don't have time for anything else today, we're going to be late," she adds.

"My, didn't you get up on the wrong side of the bed today" Devon teases.

"It's not you" she admits, "it's the freakin time, and aren't you little Mr. Sunshine?" she remarks.

"Yeah, I had a great night" he admits. "I thought you did too."

"Yeah, yeah, I did, I just hate mornings" she announces as she marches into the bathroom and shuts the door with a little bang.

"Wow" he says with a roll of the eyes.

"Detective, join me in my office" Kat orders as she walks past Des' desk.

"Right away, sir" Des replies.

"Any news?" she asks after Des walks into her office.

"Not yet, no one's been able to breach the wall that the House has erected around them."

"Damn" Kat swears. "Don't those people understand that they're all in danger, until we find this maniac" she demands.

"Is everything alright Lieutenant" Des asks worriedly. "You seem to be in a rather foul mood this morning, not a normal thing for you."

"I think I'm just tired, too many hours on this murder with no answers, it starts to get to you after a while."

"I know, but you can't take it personally Sir."

"I know" Kat grumbles "but until we get this asshole, I'm going to be taking all of this personal, I can't help it. He struck on my watch, and I can't tolerate that."

"I know" Des says "I'm sorry."

"Oh, stop" Kat says with a growl "leave, I have work I need to do."

"Yes Sir" Des says quietly and walks out.

Aw shit, now I've hurt her feelings. Damn it, I didn't mean to do that. I'll fix it later; she decides and looks over her desk full of clutter. After typing up her report for the Captain, she heads out.

"I'm going to the Captain's office with my report and then I'm headed back to Devon's office, want to come along Des?" Kat inquires as a peace offering.

"Yes Sir."

"Then let's roll."

After exiting the elevator on the Captains floor, Kat walks over to Leslie's desk and waits quietly for her to get off the phone.

"Go on in Kat, he's been waiting" Leslie informs her.

"Thanks Leslie."

"Captain, I have my report and any news that could be gleaned from the Department of Homeland Security's head-quarters" she states after he answers his door.

"I'm listening, Lieutenant."

"As of this morning, we are no closer to the murderer than we were a week ago. We have three dead congressmen, all dead from different means. We've run watch lists, looked into organized crime, terrorism and a sociopath but have received nothing from those lists. We did get a name of a businessman that was in Maui at the time of the last death, have run him down to Texas and we also have a businessman that has done business with this person. He's going to try to find something out about this guy, if there's a connection. We did inform the House and the President that if the killer keeps to his schedule there'll be another murder today.

"No one knows who, what, where, when, why or how yet. We were hoping to have more definitive information by now. Unfortunately, the next murder may have already taken place, and we just haven't heard about it yet."

"Damn" groans the Captain "not good news, Lieutenant."

"No Sir. I'll report back to you as soon as I have anything more."

"Thank you Lieutenant."

"Let's head over to Capitol Police headquarters" Kat says to Des after leaving the captains office.

"It's almost lunch time, you want to grab something?" Des asks hopefully.

"Yeah, let's make it to go; I don't have time to sit."

"Okay, how about the Mickey D's across the street here?"

"Fine" Kat says, feeling anxious. "I feel like something's happening" she admits to Des "let's hurry."

Walking quickly into Capitol headquarters while swallowing the last of her Big Mac, and not breaking into a run, was difficult for Kat; the sense of urgency that something was wrong propelling her forward.

"Devon" she calls as she gets off the elevator. "What's going on?"

"Nothing yet" he admits quietly, "but my gut says something's happened already. It's just a matter of finding out what."

"I agree, oops, hold on, there's breaking news on the news channel. Let's go over and see what it is."

"There's been a plane crash in Virginia, a small plane, with four people on board. No possible survivors" it says. "No identification of who was flying, but we'll will keep you up to date as soon as the information is available."

"Okay, so there was a plane crash, hopefully it's not one of the Congressmen."

"Yeah, let's hope."

"Hold on, they're back already."

"The plane was a private plane, a Cessna, and the pilot was, shit, son of a bitch" Devon yells, "Virginia Moore, the Speaker of the House. Damn it, it's happened again, who the hell is killing all the Congressmen?" he exclaims. "Well, now we know" he admits to Kat "who the next victim is, the Speaker of the freakin House. What the Hell is the connection" he demands. "Are we going to bury one a week all year" he worries, "that will certainly cause a bit of a commotion in the House? I think we better get over there, because as soon as they hear this, all hell's going to break loose."

"It probably already has" Kat agrees.

"Mallory, grab your group, I've already informed mine to head over to the Capitol. Kat, call yours in, we need everyone extra sent to the Capitol."

After three hours at the Capitol, Kat meets Devon at the front door.

"That was as chaotic as I thought it would be" Kat says after leaving the Capitol.

"It was, and more, there seemed to be a lot of shocked people standing around. I can't understand how they could be so shocked, it's not like this was the first one. Didn't we warn them to be on the lookout, that we expected another murder, from whoever this was?" Devon demands.

"Yeah, we did, but the truth of the matter is, I don't think they believed us. I really believe they thought all of these things were coincidences and that they were safe from any more attempts. Idiots" she declares angrily.

"Let's head to Virginia" Devon suggests. "We need to see what happened and the National Transportation Safety Board (NTSB) should be on site going over what's left of the plane and gathering evidence and body parts or what's left of them."

"It won't be pretty" she admits.

"Wow, leave it to the media" she says as they pull up two hours later, to the field in Virginia where the plane came down. "I didn't know Virginia Moore had a pilot's license" she admits. "Moneyed, privileged people, they do whatever they want. I'm thinking politics pays too well" she says. "It seems to pay too much if these people can afford to do pretty much anything they want to."

"Let's get out there, close enough to the crime scene to be safe from the media. They're out in full force today. It's going to be hard to keep them out of here, but we need to at least try. Let the NTSB take care of any releases today, it's their crime scene" Devon reminds her.

"Captain Brooks" Devon yells across the crime scene tape.

"Yes, Sir, what can I do for you?"

"I'm Deputy Chief Devon Callander of the Capitol Police, and this is Lieutenant Kat Thomas of D.C Metro One Police along with her partner, Detective Des Rowald. We just came out to see the crash site. As you know, we've been working on a spree of murders in D.C. and believe that this crash is somehow connected. We aren't sure how they're tied together, but we believe they are, so what can you tell us Captain?"

"Come on over Deputy Chief, Lieutenant. I do have an announcement but this isn't for media release yet. The plane crash wasn't a crash."

"What do you mean, Sir?" Kat asks in surprise.

"The plane didn't crash, it exploded in the air."

"Excuse me" Kat says, confused.

"Some type of explosive material may have been used, or the fuel could have leaked with pretty much the same results, but since the damage and distance of debris is so large it couldn't have been from a crash, an explosion is most likely the answer. We won't have hard evidence for awhile, but I believe it will be ruled an explosion."

"Shit" Devon exclaims."It's going to be hard to find evidence from an explosion."

"Yep, I'm sorry Deputy Chief; we may never know the cause of this. We can definitively say if it was gas or something else, but probably not exactly why. If it was staged as a fuel leak, they could have set that up and made it look like the fuel exploded.

"With such a strong explosion we may never recover the evidence, which probably disintegrated in the explosion, anyway. Unfortunately, there's been debris found in almost a two mile radius."

"What about the bodies" Kat asks with a sense of dread.

"The same Lieutenant, I'm sorry. We've found some small pieces and parts. Enough to run DNA but nothing large enough to identify, although we do know that Virginia Moore was scheduled to fly her private Cessna, and that she filed her flight plan yesterday with air traffic control. Everything was approved and the small airport that she used has assured us that she requested clearance today. At zero eight a.m. she took off, and everything appeared normal, no problems. However, we checked and her plane never arrived at its destination. Her husband and two children were scheduled to fly with her. All boarded this morning, so when the explosion occurred, all four people on board were killed" he informs them, sadly.

"This is bad" Kay says. "This takes the D.C. murder tally from three to seven for a total, inclusive of the Speaker of the House's family. This is big Devon, bigger than I thought, at least."

"It sure looks like it. Let's head back, we need to contact the Department of Homeland Security, exchange some information. They may have the toxicology reports back from the Stewart case, so let's hope they have something. I'm starting to get a little nervous, we need to step up this whole case. I don't want to lose anyone else and the clock is ticking. One week, we only have one week to find this person, or group of people, whatever. Someone's killing off the Congressmen."

The drive back to D.C. was quiet, both Devon and Kat contemplating inwardly on the murders. What they could have done differently to stop this whole mess, or at least lesson the number of deaths.

"There's one" Kat says as she scans the street for parking.

"No" Devon decides "I'm parking in the garage, just in case it snows again. I want to be able to get out if I need to, and the snow plows will bury me in the street."

"I'm a little sick of this weather" Kat complains.

"Yeah, me too it sure isn't helping the investigation."

Mallory greets Devon when he walks into the bull pen at the Capitol Police headquarters. "It looks like all hells broken lose here" he says.

"It has, every Federal Agency is now involved in the investigation. The Department of Homeland Security has taken complete control of the case, since the plane crash this morning. Everyone's demanding answers, starting at the top with the President. He's scheduled to have a press conference this morning at eleven am, live. Every channel will be covering it. It's grown huge, since this latest incident" Mallory informs them.

"Let's talk, in my office."

"Sure" she says in surprise and confusion. After Kat, Mal-

147

lory and Devon enter his office he shuts the door and gives Mallory a report on the situation they found at the crash site. "The NTSB notified us this morning that the plane didn't crash, it exploded in the air. The debris radius was too large for this to be just a crash."

"Crap" she exclaims. "I wasn't expecting that information" she says as she sits down.

"We have a big problem, Devon" Mallory says.

"Yeah, I know. We have a killer out there, whether it's one person or a group, that's been taking out a Congressman or Congresswoman once a week for four weeks now. We only have seven days before the next congressman could be killed, and we have no pattern other than once a week.

"So far, all the deaths have been different. I believe that knocks sociopath down on the list. It looks like a terrorism group or organized crime, although it's a strange thought. Usually terrorists like to take credit for the destruction they create, yet we haven't heard anything from anyone during this whole process.

"It's strange, but I don't think we can rule out anything yet, we can't take a sociopath totally out of the picture, he could be running the group. I know they usually don't work with others, but there are occasions when they do. There could be a group, at least something with some structure, otherwise, how are they finding all these ways and where are they getting their knowledge on who's going to be where? We also need to know, who did the Speaker of the House talk with prior to her flight? Who knew where she was going to be and when?

"It's not a coincidence that it happens wherever these people are at the time, first Blaketon in D.C., then Delrose at home in D.C., next Stewart in Maui and now Moore in Virginia. Someone's on the inside Devon, they have to be, to have gained all this personal knowledge on each of the congressmen" Mal says.

"It certainly looks like an inside job. So we go back out, and question each person that's been in the House of Representatives or even on Capitol Hill. Find a common denominator between these cases, it needs to be done fast. The clock is ticking" Devon says.

"Let's gather the teams and head out, no one leaves until everyone's been questioned" Kat says with finality.

"I've spoken with over two hundred people" she admits at nine o'clock that night. "I don't think there's anyone left that hasn't been questioned. Let's head back to the office and gather all the information that was obtained in the questioning, compare notes. It's going to be a team effort that brings this killer down. We'll get him, whoever he is" she says tiredly.

"Let's turn the conference room into a war room, for the duration of this murder situation. It'll be easier to keep up with everyone and compare everything. The last thing we need is to let something slide, especially if it brings the murderer down."

"Good idea, Kat" agrees Mallory, Eli, and Devon.

"Eli, thanks for joining us. We need all the help we can get" Devon says. "The Department of Homeland Security raised their level today to red. No one is going to come into this country, or get out, without their knowledge. It may give us a little breathing room, but we'll also have to tread through more paper trails; and detour around more people to get where we need to be. We still need the extra help. I'm hoping someone comes across something that looks too normal or is obvious, but I won't hold my breath. I don't know about everyone else, but I can't think straight anymore and I don't remember eating anything today, so I need food, energy and maybe a few hours of sleep. I won't be good for anyone if I collapse." Devon says.

"I'm feeling the same way" Mallory says along with Kat and Eli.

"Okay, let's hope we find something still open, then its sleep for a little while" he decides.

"Thanks everyone, I'll see you around six a.m." Devon promises after dinner. "We'll meet back up in my office, but for now, I'm hitting the bed" Devon announces.

"Us too, see you Devon" they reply as they get in their cars and leave.

"Kat, let's go get some sleep. Mind if I stay at your place?"

"Sure, but I'm so tired it will be sleep only tonight, nothing extra."

"I know, but at least I can hold you" he murmurs in fatigue.

"Yeah, that sounds good." They get through the living room and into the bedroom with the unmade bed, and with a yawn Kat drops to the bed rolls over onto her stomach, and is instantly asleep. Devon climbs in with her and before he can pull up the covers he's out too.

"That alarm clock is the most annoying thing I've ever heard" he groans as he tries to find it in the dark.

"Just a few more minutes" pleads Kat "I'm still tired" she whines.

"Yeah, me too" he complains, "but we have to get up. Everyone will be waiting for us by the time we get there."

"Fine" she snaps "I'll put on coffee, I need coffee."

"Thanks, I'll run through the shower."

"Good" she says "we'll switch when you're done."

"I have some bread, do you want some toast?" she yells over the shower.

"Thanks, that would be great" he yells back. An hour later, they walk into Devon's office, looking a little less fatigued.

"I think we need to find out some stuff, let's ask everyone to gather in the war room" Devon commands.

"Will do" Kat says.

"Alright everyone, let's compare some notes from yesterday" Devon starts."Is there a connection between the four dead congressmen, anyone? There has to be some connection, we need to look a little deeper if no one has a theory" he insists.

"Sir, I've looked into the backgrounds of all four, they are not all from the same party and they were mostly well liked, except for the Speaker of the House, sir. She was tolerated, according to everyone I spoke with yesterday. They were all strong willed but fair, they also worked closely with their constituents; tried to keep in touch with what the people wanted. That's kind of unusual in these times, sir, if I may say so."

"Please, facts only, no opinions please, opinions can drag you off track" Devon says "anyone else?"

"We need more information people, there has to be something that makes them connected!" "Find out if anyone talked with anyone, passed anything like bills, in particular" he directs.

"Sir, I remember reading something a couple of weeks ago about Mr. Stewart; he wrote a bill that would affect an Oil Cartel in Iran, by placing an embargo on their oil. It would have been a costly bill for them, since they would have had to pay special taxes for price gouging the American's. He said he had proof that they were gouging by raising the price per barrel unfairly. There were quite a few people not happy with this bill, sir. I don't think the bill went any further, but he did try to institute it."

"Good, that's something, actually that's a lot. It gives motive to terrorists to at least remove him, but how come no one mentioned this earlier?" he asks. "We should have heard of this a week ago. All right, let's see what connects the four congressmen, go back, and break up into groups and everyone start investigating the backgrounds of all of the dead congressmen" he commands.

Just as Devon turns to go to his office, Jacob walks in. "I think we need to talk Devon" Jacob insists.

"Is this business Jacob, because I'm busy right now. I can't deal with anything personal at the moment."

"Yeah, its business" he replies seriously."You could deal with personal if you weren't so busy trying to escape from the past all the time" he informs Devon in a derogatory manner.

"Not now" growls Devon.

"Okay" as he shuts the office door he asks "what do you want, Jacob?"

"I made a few calls for you, to Tom Walters in Texas" he informs him.

"That's right, he's the businessman millionaire that buys overpriced bikes from you about four times a year" Devon says in a spiteful manner.

"My bikes are NOT overpriced," Jacob replies in anger."I was doing you a favor by contacting him and you're going to tell me my bikes are overpriced? I don't think so" Jacob says as he turns around to leave.

"Wait" Devon says apologetically "I'm sorry, that was uncalled for."

"Damn straight it was, but I'll give you a break. I know you're working pretty much around the clock with these murders."

"Yeah, I am, thanks Jacob. So you spoke with Tom Walters, the businessman and?"

"It looks like he's the majority holder of a very large oil cartel working out of Texas. It's possible he has overseas contacts, and anything overseas usually points to Arab. He could be connected to a terrorist group."

"That's two clues now that point in the same direction. Thanks Jacob, for coming in to let me know."

"Tell Kat I said hey" Jacob says as he leaves.

"I will" Devon promises "as soon as she gets back here; she's over at Metro One. Everyone's trying to juggle everything else with these murders, so we're all a little swamped right now. But this is the priority, we'll get whoever is at the bottom of this, or should I say top. I'll have her call you Jacob, you still at the same place?"

"Yeah, I'll be there but tell her to phone this number" he says as he hands Devon a card with a number written on it. "It's my new cell phone; I just got it yesterday, since I'm out of the hotel room most of the day. I thought I better get this so I can be reached, pretty much all the time."

"Good thinking, thanks" Devon says "I'll be in touch."

FOURTEEN

"Devon, what's new?" Kat asks as she walks into his office.

"Well, a couple of things. One, they believe that Jeff Stewart tried to pass some kind of bill against an oil cartel in Iran. Two, Jacob was in about an hour ago with an update on that business man from Texas, Tom Walters. He's the majority holder of an oil cartel in Texas with connections to the Arab Cartel in Iran."

"Yes" Kat says with excitement and an arm pump. "They're connected somewhere, so now we have a direction. You know, I think we should go back and talk to Addy, he's Arab I believe. Maybe we didn't ask him the right questions" she says thoughtfully.

"It looks like we might have a connection in more than one place" he agrees. "Alright, let's let the team's know what we're doing and tell them to look in that area. Maybe we can find a few more ties to the same thing."

"Have you let Mallory know about the potential connection?" she asks Devon as they head out to the garage.

"Yeah, I called her, she's been slammed with all of this too, but she was really excited by this connection."

"Me too" she agrees, "it's finally a break, I don't want to get my hopes up too much, and I need to keep an open mind because I don't want to miss anything; I want everyone involved with this. No one's getting away with murder, not while I'm around."

"Let's go, I parked in the garage. The cities having a hard time keeping all the parking areas cleaned up. I didn't want my car hit by a plow driver" Devon admits.

"Yeah, it's been one of those months" she agrees.

"It looks like the building's empty. I sure hope he's around here somewhere" Devon says after pulling up at Addy's garages. "Let's try the office first, then we can start searching for him."

"Hmm, it looks like he left in a hurry. The computers are still on, the lights are on at the desk" she says suspiciously.

"There are some phone messages, the lights still blinking. Let's check those out" he suggests. "Unfortunately, if we find anything on them, we won't be able to use them, since we'll have needed a search warrant first."

"If we find anything, we won't tell anyone, we'll just go with it ourselves" she says. "We don't have time to wait for a warrant."

"True" he agrees "let's try it. Message one was deleted, two, Abdul, you must call me at the first opportunity. This is important, you know who this is, and you know my number, call me right away.'

"Hmm" Kat says "that sounded slightly threatening, didn't it?"

"Yeah, it did. What's the number, does it show?" he asks curiously.

"Let me write it down, it's an overseas number, I think."

"Call Mallory, and see if she can run that number. Let's see who this person is."

"She'll get back to us when she gets an answer" Devon says to Kat's look of inquiry.

"Good, now let's see if we can find Mr. Thayer" she says a she rubs her hands together.

"The first two garages are empty; even Mike's truck is gone. It looks like it's been gone all day, so he might have had a delivery," she says.

"It's weird" Devon says "everything's so still. Where do you think he is?" Devon asks.

"I don't know, but I don't like it. I'll bet this isn't good.

That message was from over an hour ago and it had been listened to, so Addy got the message. It looks like he left fast, too. Let's finish the rest of the garages" she says. "The door opens in the back, to a hallway, remember? Let's look back there, you take low" she says quietly.

"Fine" he replies as they both get out their service weapons.

"Clear" Kat calls.

"There's the staircase for the upstairs" Devon says quietly "let's check it out, he might be up there."

"Looks like we found something" she says as they see blood drops on the stairs, about half way up. "I don't think this is going to turn out good."

"Shh" Devon whispers. "I thought I heard something." He motions for Kat to wait and lets her know that he's going first and he's going low. Kat moves into position behind him and they sweep the area with their eyes and their guns.

"Shit" she says quietly "there he is."

"He almost made it to the back room" Devon says.

"Whoever did this was a pro. One bullet to the brain, looks like a professional hit" Kat says quietly.

"Damn it, no answered questions. It's all clear" he says.

"The only one here is Addy, and he won't be answering any questions now" Kat says in disappointment. "I'll call it in."

"Thanks, in the meantime, let's see what we can find. Maybe the killer left us a memento" he says with hope. After searching through his personal effects and finding nothing, they decide to wait for the crime scene unit to get there and finish.

"The medical examiner's here" Kat says. "I'll go show him where we are."

"Thanks" Devon replies as his cell phone rings.

"Dr. Zorgath, the body's upstairs" Kat informs him.

"Thanks Kat" says Steven Zorgath, a southern gentleman all the way. "After you" he says.

"Thanks" she replies as she climbs the stairs and shows him the small living room that Addy was found in.

"He was headed for the backroom, probably for safety" Kat speculates "but he never made it."

"Yes, it looks like a clean shot to the head will be cause of death, poor guy. I'll bet he was pretty scared.

"This is a nice little room; it's well taken care of, really nice natural lighting. All those windows, and the sheer curtains to allow the sun to come in" says Dr. Zorgath with his southern drawl."He also used color very nicely, bright, modern yet comfortable. It was definitely a welcoming room. It looks like he had collections too" he says after staring at a beautiful hand carved hummingbird."This was his home." After tagging and bagging they start to search for any type of evidence.

"Don't forget to take the phone system downstairs and his computer, we might be able to get something from that."

"We have a threatening message from an unknown caller, from about two hours ago. I called ahead to Mallory with the number and she's running a trace as we speak, to see where the call originated from" Kat says. "Right now, that's our biggest lead" she says to Dr. Zorgath.

"Okay, we'll get this poor man back to autopsy and see what he can tell us. Hopefully I'll know something by later this afternoon."

"Thanks Doc. We'll be in touch."

"I think we need a brainstorming session" Kat says to Devon on their way back to headquarters. "We need to contact Mallory and Eli, and maybe Snake to round out the group. Let's see if we can get more information if we're all together."

"All right, I'll schedule it, how about seven this evening?"

"That's fine with me" she replies."We can meet at that Italian place we had dinner at last week."

"Was it last week already" he groans."Time flies when you're chasing killers" she says.

"And we have been supper busy. This has got to crack open soon. Who's going to figure it out first? I hope we get a break tonight, we only have five more days before D Day. If the killer stays on schedule, it will happen in five more days, so who's going to be next? There seems to be no rhyme or reason to anything anymore." she says to Devon, thoughtfully.

"Hi everyone" Kat says as she walks into *Angelo's*."I just got off the phone with the Department of Homeland Security. They received the toxicology report back on Jeff Stewart. He died from the poison of a large jelly fish, but he wasn't stung" she says in suspense.

"Well, how did he get the poison in him then?" Devon asks in confusion.

"Well, first, the Jelly fish's natural habitat is not around Maui, but around Australia."

"What?"cries Mallory "Someone transported that thing all the way to Maui and he gets accidently stung" she says in confusion.

"No, now don't jump to conclusions with this one" Kat says with a grin. "He was poisoned by drinking it" she announces.

"But I thought that poison such as this couldn't kill you if ingested?" Mallory says in confusion.

"That's true, but it can kill you if it gets into your blood stream."

"Yeah, but the last anatomy class I attended didn't show a blood connection through the stomach. Has something changed in anatomy since seventh grade?" Devon asks sarcastically.

"No" she admits with a laugh."But there are other ways for it to be absorbed into
the blood stream when drinking it. Remember the waitress from the hotel, how she said he went in there every day for the same drink?"

"Yeah" replies Mallory."Wait" she says."He always ordered the same drink, right? It was a martini, dry with a twist of lime" she quotes as if she memorized the discussion with the waitress.

"The alcohol weakened the poison but the lime didn't, and Jeff always sucked on his lime before drinking the drink. The lime was loaded with the poison from the jelly fish. The poison is so deadly from that particular fish that one sting, or the amount of poison from one sting, can kill up to sixty people, Kat says.

"He had the full amount, but it has to go into the bloodstream. What they don't tell you is, if you have a bad tooth, a cavity, then the poison can enter the blood stream that way. Enough of the poison to kill a man, not as fast as the actual sting but someone that sucks on it, gets it into a cavity and goes swimming and bam, dead" announces Kat.

"Wow" Devon mumbles as he shakes his head. "So we have a congressman that was killed by a poison that is normally found in the Australian waters, but he died off the coast of Maui, so this was no accidental drowning" he says.

"That's right, he was murdered. Now we have congressman number three, murdered, that's three of four. We just might get this person or group of persons soon" Kat adds with hope.

"Now we wait for the NTSB to rule on Congresswoman Moore's plane explosion. We have a tentative ruling, but it's not official yet" Kat reminds them all. "They did tell us at the sight that the plane exploded in the air. We know that planes don't normally explode in the air, even with a fuel leak, so they already believe that this wasn't accidental. It's not official and god forbid the media gets a hold of this, so keep it down in here" Kat warns. "The media's been following me around all day. I don't know about you" she says "but I think quiet is good. With all the noise in the room, they shouldn't be able to overhear what we're talking about if we keep it quiet. Did you guys order without me?" she asks.

"Yep, it's on its way" Devon says.

"So what am I eating" she asks suspiciously.

"Oh, we thought you'd like the Eggplant Parmesan" Devon says with a small grin.

"WHAT, you ordered me vegetables?" she demands in dismay.

"No" Devon snorts, "we got you the fatted calf."

"Come on, I'm starving, what am I having?"

"The same as last time" Mallory answers before Devon gets another chance.

"Stop it Devon, she wasn't raised with brothers, so she doesn't know how to handle the kidding."

"Yeah, I'm sorry Kat. I was just kidding."

"It's okay; I can take a joke with the best of them" she admits with a grin. "Anyone have any more information on the second death, Congresswoman Karen Delrose? She was murdered, but with a different type of poison. One that's almost impossible to trace, but thanks to Dr. Zorgath and his brilliance, he found it. Another loose end tied up" Kat remarks. "So, what do all these Senators and Congressmen have in common" she asks "any theories?"

"Actually, we were talking just before you got here and there seems to be a tie to all of them with the Arabs" Devon says.

"How so" Kat inquires. "I know about Jeff Stewart's tie, because of his decision to try for a bill that would hurt the Arab Oil Cartel, but what does everyone else have that connects them? I can even see a tie between Abdul Adl Thayer (Addy), since he was Arab, but I'm still working on his tie to the congressman's death. As far as I know, he had nothing to do with the congressman. That needs to be more thoroughly looked into."

"I'm working on that" Mallory promises.

"As am I" seconds Eli. "Since he was from my part of the country, there must be something that will tie them. I put some people in Los Angeles on it. I might as well keep them working, even if I'm in D.C."

"Here you go everyone" the waitress says as she delivers the long anticipated food. "Sorry it took so long. I can't believe how busy it is in here tonight. Word must have gotten out," she says happily, thinking of the tips she'll be getting.

"What about the first dead Congressman" Devon demands after the waitress leaves. "How is he connected to all of this? His murder was straight out of a horror novel, so why would they go so far off course with this one?"

"Well, that's probably why" Jacob answers.

"Okay, Jacob, why" Devon says "enlighten me."

"You were looking for a serial killer, weren't you? If you'd have been able to tie this to the Arabs that fast, do you think they would have been able to get the other three?"

"I'm not sure" Mallory says "since we haven't a clue right now who's going to be next. There are still some gray areas in the theory of the Arabs. We need a lot more information before we can determine if it really is the Arabs, plus this is a political bomb."

"You can't even theorize that it's the Arabs without throwing down the virtual gauntlet" Jacob warns.

"It would be political suicide for this country, if this weren't factual" Mallory explains to Kat.

"Yeah, we know how delicate the balance is between the Middle East and the United States; it wouldn't take much at all to rock that boat. Hey" Kat whispers,"I just saw Sidney Norwood come in here. She's a shark when it comes to news. We don't want her to even think we're talking business, so let's stop business and start with the personal stuff.

"So Snake, have you seen your parents yet?" Kat asks.

"Not yet, but I'm hoping we can set up a time tonight, while everyone's here."

"Yeah, that would be a good idea, since you're all together. What do you think, Devon?"

"Fine, I'll call them tomorrow and set up a time."

"No. Why don't you call them now" Kat suggests. "Everyone's here, you'll all know when you're available."

"Fine" he says aggravated, as he takes out his cell phone.

"Hi Mom, how are you" Devon inquires after she answers.

"Good, Devon, how are you? You haven't called in a long time, is everything alright?"

"Yeah mom, it's good. I've just been busy lately. Are you and Dad going to be home on Sunday?" he inquires tentatively.

"Yes, we will" she says "after church of course."

"Of course. Eli's in town working a case, and Mallory and I thought we could all get together and visit" he admits with a smile in his voice.

"That would be wonderful" she responds in excitement "It'll be like a party, I'll even feed everyone!"

"I was hoping you'd say that. How about one o'clock then?"

"Perfect. I'll let your dad know that you'll all be here on Sunday, I can't wait" she cries excitedly.

"Good, then we'll see you Sunday" he says as he hangs up.

"You heard it's all set up. We'll meet at the corner of Ashwood Road and Trumbell Drive, and then we'll go. I don't want you going there alone Jacob. I want the three of us to buffer everything, so it's not such a shock. Kat, I think you should join us" he says.

"I don't know Devon, this is a family matter, and I don't want to be a fifth wheel."

"You won't be one, but since you've known Jacob so long it might be beneficial to my parents for you to talk with them also."

"If you think it's a good idea" she agrees reluctantly "I'll be glad to go."

"Fine, I'll pick you up and we'll meet the others at Ashwood and Trumbell, one p.m." he reminds everyone. "Oh, and don't be late, mom wouldn't like that. I want to start this all of on the right foot. Now, it's time to call it a night. Sleep is a commodity that has been short lately and I'm starting to feel it" Devon admits. Everyone agrees as they divvy up the check, throw money on the table for the waitress and start the mass exodus to the front door. "See you all tomorrow" Kat says. "Well, that went well" she says as she turns to go.

"Hold on a minute. Since I seem to be sleeping mostly at your place anyway, I thought I'd follow you" Devon says.

"Fine with me" she grins and her eyes sparkle as she thinks, I'm tired, but not that tired.

"Lieutenant Thomas, Lieutenant" shit thinks Kat. I wanted a quick escape. I didn't want Sydney to see me, much less with Devon, in a restaurant at this time of night. That's just what I need, the media putting the two of us together in a personal way. I don't want anyone to know, especially my co-workers, she thinks with dread. I've been so careful, damn it!

Of course she had to come in here for dinner or was she tipped off, Kat wonders. I hate coincidences. No, she found out we were going to be here, she decides as she goes over to her and takes on an aggressive demeanor. "Sydney, are you following me?" she questions in a low voice, anger simmering just below the surface.

"No, Lieutenant I would never do that" Sidney denies with a cat like smile.

"Yeah, I think you were. This restaurant is off the beaten path, so why would you be here?"

"Why Lieutenant, it's got wonderful Italian food. It's one of my favorites, so why wouldn't I know about it?"

"That's true" Kat admits "but why tonight, while I'm here? When I find out your source, they'll get fired" she informs her. "No one at Metro One is allowed to disclose this type of information. If they'll tell you where I am, they'll tell you other things. We can't have employees that don't know how to follow the rules, Sidney. So you just got someone fired; and one of your snitches, no less. I'll find out who it was, Sidney. You better be a good friend and let them know that Kat is hunting them down. Night now" she says as she turns and leaves.

"Wow" he says "that was pretty harsh, Kat."

"Yeah well, she can take it. I was serious Devon. No one discloses anything in my office. There's no room for someone like that in law enforcement. You have to be able to follow orders and not open your mouth. Those have always been the rules, and I won't tolerate anyone breaking them."

"So I see" he murmurs, trying to pacify her. "Okay, calm down now, we just had a nice meal and now we're going to cuddle, so let's be happy again" he cajoles.

"Oh, I will" she snips angrily "just give me a few minutes. That really made my blood boil" she admits in anger.

FIFTEEN

"We need to go out to the debris site" she informs him the next morning as she's waiting for the coffee pot to stop gurgling. "There's something we're missing and it has to be at the site. We've looked everywhere else."

"Okay then, let's go. It's about a two hour drive, so we should be able to get there way before lunch" he estimates.

"Good, let me get Des, she needs to be involved in this" Kat explains."Detective" Kat says after Des answers the phone "we're heading out to the site of the plane incident. You need to be in on this. We'll pick you up in ten minutes."

"Yes Sir".

"Okay, all set" she says once Des gets in the car.

"Deputy Chief, good morning" Des says after getting in the car.

"Detective, morning" replies Devon.

"Now that the niceties are finished, can we talk about this investigation?" Kat inquires.

"Kat, you're still in a bad mood from last night?" Devon asks.

"Yeah, I guess so; I'll deal with that later, after we get back from the site"

"Is something wrong Lieutenant?" inquires Des hesitatingly.

"No, I mean, kind of. Someone in the Department gave some information out to a reporter on my whereabouts last evening."

"Oh oh, who would do something like that, Sir?"

"That's what I'm going to find out Detective."

"Any idea who's responsible?" Des asks carefully.

"Yeah, I have an idea. Someone's going to get fired for this one. It's too dangerous to slip information to a news anchor about an ongoing case."

"Yes Sir" replies Des.

"I'll find out for sure who it was, there's no getting out of it this time" she says.

"Does that mean it's happened before?" Devon asks in surprise.

"Yeah" she admits. "But it was more minor than this, so I let it go. Not this time, this time his ass is mine" Kat claims in a furious tone.

"Let's talk about something else" he suggests.

"Fine then; about the crash, site debris site, whatever it's being called. We need to talk with NTSB and see if they've come up with anything more. We also need something that will tie this in with the rest of the murders" she says, counting off the things that need completed. "There has to be something."

After a long two hours of near solitude "good, the NTSB is still on site along with some local Leo's. I'll start with the NTSB and work my way to the Local's" Kat decides.

"Yes sir" Des answers. "Where do you want me?" she asks.

"You start with the locals and we'll meet in the middle" Kat decides. "Devon, are you going to wander around and talk to everyone? Your Capitol Police badge will probably get you more information than I can get with my Metro One badge."

"Sure, I wanted to talk to everyone here, anyway" he says agreeably.

"Thanks" Kat says. "I'll meet you back here in a couple of hours."

"Sir" Kat calls, "I'm Lieutenant Thomas out of Metro One D.C" Kat yells across the field towards the NTSB Agent.

"Yes Lieutenant, what can I do for you?" asks a man of about sixty who's going through some of the planes pieces and parts.

"I was wondering if you've found anything suspicious; anything that may point you in the direction of the cause of the crash, sir."

"This plane didn't crash Lieutenant, it exploded in the sky" he states firmly.

"Ouch" Kat says.

"Yeah, it was fast, it's doubtful anyone new anything. It happened and poof, they were gone, just that fast Lieutenant."

"Do you have any idea why it exploded?"

"Well, I've been looking at some of the debris and it's a little confusing. First I think I understand and then I look at something else and it changes my mind. So far, my decision is something blew it up. I haven't been able to find some of the things that would point to an on board detonation. My thoughts are, maybe a rocket launcher? It could have been a surface to air missile, but that's not official yet, Lieutenant" the NTSB Agent Randy says.

"Oh" she replies in disappointment.

"If you and your partners would, I need someone to do a perimeter search. Say out to two miles around the debris area? There just aren't enough people to send them out to do a search of that magnitude" he admits."There are other NTSB Agents coming in today, but not for a while. This is small town USA, literally" he says quietly."There's a lot of ground to cover, but it needs to be done" he sighs.

"No problem, we'll get started on that right away. I want to stop this murder spree before it gets to anyone else. We're on the clock here and time's running out."

"Thank you Lieutenant. I appreciate it."

"You're welcome. We'll be back when we're through" she promises as she turns and walks towards Devon. "Devon, Des, let's go" she says when she gets near enough they can hear.

"Where are we going?" Devon asks "I wasn't through interviewing everyone."

"The NTSB Agent asked if we would do a perimeter search, and I told him we can help out with that. We're going to go out and start looking at everything within a two mile radius. He has thoughts that it might have been a surface to air missile that took out the plane. But he needs evidence. For an explosion of this magnitude, debris is scattered probably within a two mile radius, he said."

"Kat, this is the last time I'm reminding you, this is now my case and you're just along for the ride. Feds trump locals, now."

"Yeah, yeah, how can I forget when you keep reminding me" she says in a huff.

"Well, I need to remind you, you keep trying to run the show. I can't let you do that anymore" he reminds her heatedly.

"Fine" she replies "enough, consider me reminded" she says sarcastically. "I really don't care who runs it, I just want the bastards that did this."

"Yeah, right" he mumbles. "You want the lead. Let's head south" he decides. "We'll start there and travel west, then north, then east, and back to the site."

"Fine" she says.

"There's a driveway up ahead" Des says "It looks like a farm of some type."

"Good, let's check it out" Devon says.

"It doesn't look like anyone lives here anymore" murmurs Des in disappointment after seeing the place up close.

"Things do look pretty ramshackle around here" Devon admits as he gets out of the car.

"I'll knock at the house door, you guys take the barn" he orders.

"Fine" Kat says as they pile out of the car.

"Are you gonna be silent all day Lieutenant?" Des asks quietly.

"Yep" she says.

Devon walks in and scans the building, "there's nothing here either" he remarks emotionlessly. "The house was empty. It doesn't look like anyone's been here in a long time."

"Yeah, it's the same out here" Kat admits.

"Let's head out to the next, then." After driving about a quarter mile, they find another driveway and start down it.

"Well at least this looks like someone's been here lately."

"Yeah" they both agree.

"The snow down the driveway is trampled down, like something was driven over it" he observes. As they round a small curve in the driveway, there's a two story house, well maintained. Snow shoveled off the walkway and off of the front porch. Smoke is curling gently out of the top of a chimney, and there's a newer Jeep sitting parked next to the detached garage. "This is nice" he says.

"Yeah" Kat says. Devon just grimaces and walks to the house door.

"Let's see if anyone's home." After waiting a minute or more, someone finally opens the front door. A wizened old man stares out of his shiny wrinkled face with a questioning look in his pale blue eyes.

"Can I help you folks?" he asks in a mild voice.

"Yes sir. I'm Deputy Chief Callander from the Capitol Police, in D.C." The old man's eyes get wide when he realizes he's talking to a federal agent on his own front porch.

"Oh dear" says the little old man "please come in, come in, it's cold out there."

"Thanks" they all repeat as they walk into the front of the house. Looks like a sitting room, Kat thinks. An old fashioned couch and chair with small end tables and white lace doilies, milk glass lamps, some pictures of a beautiful woman with a couple of kids on the wall, all set around a cast iron stove that at the moment looks cold.

I bet this is nice in the evenings, she thinks with a smile in her mind. I love old people, so many stories they have, they're awesome to listen to when they get in the story telling mode. I wish I had some grandparents to enjoy. I'd spend a lot of time just talking to them, she thinks.

"No sir, I didn't see anything" Kat's brought back to the present in a rush as she realizes the questions had started, and she'd been daydreaming, "but some stuff came floating down from the sky. I found a couple of things and just put them in a pile in the garage. I wasn't sure what they were, or if anyone might need them, but they're yours if you want them" he offers.

"Thank you, Sir."

"I'm just Charlie" he says.

"Okay then Charlie, did you see anything or hear anything yesterday?" Devon asks as Kat listens.

"Well, my hearings not as good as it used to be" Charlie admits "but I did hear a bang. It was around ten in the morning. I was just straightening up the house, a little dusting and such when actually I heard the bang. It was pretty loud. Loud enough to rattle the windows a little" he explains. "I didn't think much of it though, because we have that old mine just down the road a ways, and they sometimes dynamite in there, so that's what I thought it was."

"Wow, an old mine, what kind of mine is it" Des asks excitedly.

"It's an old iron-ore mine, not gold, if that's what you were thinking" Charlie laughs good-humoredly.

"Oh" Des says as she blushes "no sir, I mean Charlie, I was just curious."

"Thank you Charlie. Can we see the stuff you put in the garage now?" Devon requests politely.

"Sure, let me get my boots on and then I'll take you over there myself'"

"Thanks."

As they all troupe through the snow, Kat looks behind her wistfully, memorizing the little farm house and the warm and cozy sitting room of a little old man.

"Here it is" he announces after he gets the garage door open.

It's pretty full of stuff. That would be why he parks his Jeep outside in the snow. He looks like a collector. Funny how the house was nice but definitely not overly crowded like the garage is. How does he find anything in here? Kat wonders.

Garage must not be heated. It's too cold out here for Charlie to do anything with the stuff in here. Probably gets so busy in the spring, summer and fall with outside chores that he never gets a chance to do anything in here. He just adds to the mess by storing everything in the garage.

"Here it is" he says after searching through a small box that was set by the door when you first walked into the garage. He hands some pieces to Kat. Some type of plastic, metal, it's hard to tell, but they were definitely ragged with sharp edges.

"Thanks Charlie. Where exactly did you find these?" Devon asks.

"One of them was down near the mailbox, at the beginning of the drive" he says. "The other landed on the roof of my jeep. I'm not sure what they are, but I saved them anyway. I save most things, you just never know" he admits with a blush.

"That's true" Devon responds with male camaraderie."Can you tell me anything else about the noise you heard, and when you found these items?"

"No, I don't think so. I just heard the noise and then I found these a couple of hours later, that was all" he says quietly. "This doesn't have anything to do with that plane crash, does it?" Charlie asks."That was a terrible, sad thing" he says.

"We aren't sure" Devon answers "but that's what we're investigating right now, so thank you for saving these. Thanks for inviting us into your home Charlie, we all appreciate it. Have a good day now" Devon says as they get back into their car.

"Nice old guy" he says.

"Yeah" Kat responds.

"Let's see what we have here" he decides at the next driveway.

"Wow, who would have thought, this looks like a fancy ranch way out in the middle of nowhere" Des says.

"Yeah, it actually looks like a horse ranch. See the huge barn back and to the right?"

"Yep" Des says.

"There are heat stacks coming out of the roof with smoke curling out of them, which means it's heated. That must be where they keep their horses."

"This is a really nice house" Des murmurs.

"Yeah, a three story, probably ten bedrooms. There are multiple outbuildings, and everything is in immaculate condition. A huge circular driveway with a drive that branches off the main house driveway, headed toward the horse barn," Devon says.

"Let's head up to the main house" he suggests as everyone piles out of the car. As they wait for the door to be opened they glance towards the barn where there seems to be a delivery of some sort happening.

A small woman opens the door to the main house inquiring "Can I help you?"

"Yes, I'm Deputy Chief Callander of the Capitol Police in D.C and this is Lieutenant Thomas and Detective Rowald of D.C. Metro One Police. We'd like to ask you some questions about a plane crash that occurred yesterday, about a mile and a half from here."

"I'm Debra, the housekeeper, come on in. I'll let Mr. Jackman know that you're here."

"Thank you" he says as they all move into the warmth of the foyer of the house.

"If you'll follow me, I'll show you to the sitting room" she says as she walks toward the room to the right of the entry door. "Please have a seat." she instructs."Can I get you anything, coffee or tea maybe?"

"Coffee would be great" Devon accepts while Kat wanders the room not saying a word and Des stands staring out the large front window.

"Wow, it's hard to comprehend that people actually live this way" Des remarks "with a housekeeper and all" after the housekeeper left the room."Must be nice" she comments. "This place is gorgeous" she says as a gentleman of about forty five enters the room. Tall and blonde with brilliant blue eyes; muscular in worn jeans, and a button down jean shirt. A cowboy hat that's tipped back showing off a strong forehead, with arched brows and a grin on his lips.

"I'm Mark Jackman, glad you like the place'" he says. "What can I do for you?" he questions as he scans the room and his gaze stops on Kat with purely male interest.

"I'm Deputy Chief Devon Callander of the Capitol Police and this is Lieutenant Kat Thomas and Detective Des Rowald of the D.C. Metro One Police Department. We're investigating the plane crash that happened yesterday and have a few questions we'd like to ask, if you're not too busy" Devon informs him.

"Sure, I have time for the police. I'll be glad to do whatever it takes to figure out what happened. That was a terrible thing" he admits "the Congresswoman and her whole family, gone, just terrible" he repeats with a shake of his head.

"Please, have a seat" he orders as his housekeeper walks back in carrying a tray filled with coffee and cookies. After she places it on the coffee table, he continues, "thank you Debra, please help yourselves. Now, what can I help you with, Deputy Chief?"

"Did you see or hear anything, Mr. Jackman?"

"Please, call me Mark."

"Thanks Mark" Devon replies.

"I did as a matter of fact, I saw something" he replies."I was riding, out in the back forty, as we like to call them, alone. I noticed a small plane flying overhead. It seemed like it was fine, didn't sound different, it sounded just like a normal small engine plane, probably a Cessna. I have one that looks similar to it, so I would have noticed if there was anything unusual about its noise. Like I said, it sounded normal and it was flying at the normal height for a recent takeoff. It looked like whoever was flying it, knew what they were doing.

"Anyway, it was just a plane, when all of a sudden, I saw something streak towards it. It was so fast it was hard to comprehend what I was seeing. But whatever it was, hit it mid-section and then there was this huge explosion. I actually watched it blow up and spiral towards the ground in thousands of pieces. I wasn't sure where it hit, but it was apparent that someone shot it down. I've decided I won't be flying mine anytime soon. I don't want some freak shooting mine down, too" he remarks.

"Why didn't you call this in, Mark?" Devon asks.

"I did call it in" he says "as soon as I got back to the barn. I don't wear my cell phone when I'm riding. I like to ride to escape from all the city stuff and I can always talk to whoever needs me, after my ride."

"Yes Sir. Do you remember who you reported it too?" Devon asks.

"I called the local police department and reported it. I assumed you were notified by them" he replies, a question in his voice.

"Actually no, I haven't heard from the local police at all"

171

Devon admits in disgust.

"How far from the house were you when this occurred?" Kat asks.

"Let's see, maybe a mile from the house."

"You were riding, you said?" Kat continues.

"Yes, I generally ride every day, no matter the weather" he replies.

"You said about a mile, what direction were you in, sir?"

"I was south west of this house."

"Okay, one mile south west from where we are, right at this moment?" Kat clarifies.

"Yes Lieutenant."

"At what time would you say this occurred?" she asks.

"It was about, oh, ten in the morning, or so" Mark says.

"Did you notice if anything from the explosion landed on your property" Devon inquires.

"Yes, I'm sure it did. I had a couple of my horse handlers go out and look to see if they could find anything. They actually did, but it was pretty late last evening when they finally got back, so they were told to put everything they found in the old barn behind the new horse barn. I'll take you out there in a little bit" he offers "if you want."

"Did you notify anyone of this?" Devin asks.

"Not yet" he replies. "I haven't personally seen the stuff, so I haven't called anyone yet" he admits. "After I see it, I'll decide if it needs to be handed in. For all I know, it's just junk that people have thrown around for years, not something from the plane explosion."

"If you're ready, can we head out to the old barn" Devon asks.

"You might want to drive" Mark advises "since it's quite a ways behind the new barn."

"Alright, thanks" replies Devon as he heads out with everyone else.

"Nice guy" Des admits.

"Oh yeah" Kat agrees "and good looking, too. Rich and handsome, not too shabby" she adds as Devon glares at her. After driving close to half a mile behind the new barn, they come across the old barn.

"It's in pretty good shape" Des remarks. "I wonder why they built a new one."

"Who knows, the rich have money to burn, so why not" Devon replies, envy in every word.

"The door's over here" Mark says as they all pile out of the car again.

"What have we got?" Devon asks.

"They put the stuff they found over towards that large pull up door. Wow" Mark whistles" I guess they did find some stuff." Lying on the floor near the overhead door are large pieces of debris.

"It looks like it could be part of the fuselage" Devon remarks.

"This looks like it could have been a piece of a seat" Des says as she walks around the rather large pile of stuff.

"That could be pieces of an engine, too" observes Kat. "I think we'd better call Randy, the NTSB Agent at the site, and let him know what we have here. He's going to want to see this" Kat exclaims.

"I'll go outside and give him a call" Devon says.

"I didn't realize they found this kind of stuff, or I would have come out here last night. It was pretty late when they got back, so I didn't question them much about it" Mark admits."I figured it could wait. I feel terrible that I haven't been out here until now to see this stuff. I could have reported it a lot sooner."

"Don't worry about it. You're reporting it now" Kat responds soothingly.

"Thanks Lieutenant, but I still feel somewhat responsible for holding up the investigation. You can be sure from now on, if there's something to look at, I won't wait. I'll look right away, especially when there's something wrong."

"He's on his way" Devon says when he returns to the barn. "Mark, a quick question?" he asks.

"Yes, what is it?"

"That live stock hauler that you use, have you used him for a long time?" Devon asks.

"Oh, you mean the dead horse people?"

"Yeah, they're the ones" reiterates Devon.

"Oh, I've used them for probably twenty years or so, why?" he asks.

"Well, they were part of an investigation a few weeks ago and I just thought it was kind of coincidental, that's all" Devon replies as both Kat and Des look at him in shock.

"They're here" Kat says in disbelief "right now?"

"Yes, it looks like they're picking up at the barn behind this one."

"Yes, they are, Deputy Chief. Is there a problem with that?" Mark asks.

"No, no problem sir. How long have they been here?" he questions him.

"They were supposed to pick up yesterday. With the plane thing, they weren't able to make it, the roads were jammed up. They called and scheduled themselves for this morning. They've only been here about a half hour. It usually doesn't take them long, and they still have to get to Pennsylvania with the dead bodies, so they like to be out of here by noon at the latest, they always deliver to a pet cemetery in Canterville."

"How did the horses die, if you don't mind my asking?"

"No sir. I had two that were really old, they were put out to pasture but with all the bad weather we had, they just couldn't handle it. I put them out to pasture a week ago and they never returned. We went searching for them a couple of days ago and found them both, dead in a snow drift. I'll miss them. Horses live for about twenty years, so they become very much part of the family. It's always hard on us when they die."

"That I can believe" replies Devon.

"So does everyone with horses around here, use the same livestock hauler?" he asks.

"Yeah, there aren't a lot of them around, so you have to use what you can. Mike's a pretty good guy, though. He's never given me a bit of trouble. He's always reasonable and fast, and he usually gets out here within twenty-four hours of being notified. Like I said, he arrives in the morning and is gone pretty quick. No one has to see what he has. His truck sides are high and he has that electric tarp that keeps things covered. I've never noticed any bad odors from his truck, so yeah, he does a good job."

"I think I hear a car" Devon says "it might be the NTSB Agents showing up for the plane parts."

"It is" Mark admits as he looks around the door frame. "There they are. Come on in this way guys, we're all in here" he shouts.

After examining and exclaiming over the pieces and parts that were discovered, everyone loads up and leaves.

"Thanks Mark" Devon says."We'll get back to you with anything else, and if you find more, please give me a call" he requests as he hands him his business card.

"No problem" Mark says as he watches them leave.

"I don't like coincidences, either" Devon says to Kat, "and that livestock hauler was just too much of a coincidence for me."

"Yeah, I agree" she admits. "That was no coincidence, not to my way of thinking. Now what?" she inquires of Devon. "There's only us, and we can't be everywhere at once, so what do you want to do?"

"I called for back-up while I went out of the barn to get a hold of the NTSB Agents. They should be arriving with-in the next forty-five minutes or so. Unfortunately, they had to come from D.C. since there wasn't anyone closer, and that's a longer drive. We can hang around and follow Mike when he leaves, or we can let back-up find him and question him, maybe bring him in" replies Devon. "Kat, I think you should call Metro One and get a background done on Mark Jackman. Let's see if he is what he portrays he is" Devon says.

"Sure. Des, run it" Kat says.

"Yes Sir."

"That was quite a bit of plane wreckage, Devon" Kat says speculatively. "Hopefully they'll be able to determine what happened. From what Mark explained, it sounded like a surface to air missile that hit the plane. If it was, who initiated it? This just opens up more questions. We have so many directions now, we need to buckle down and get some answers. We're losing time every day we don't solve this problem.

"I think we need to contact DHS and update them on what's going on." Devon admits.

"I agree" Kat says. "Let's head back to D.C. and get some things on the ground running. Like I said, time is not our friend. We may have another person dead soon if we can't stop this group. I say group because there's too many differences in all these murders. Whoever's in charge must have done all this on purpose, just to confuse the hell out of the police."

"It's starting to feel that way" Devon admits. "It's the 'keep 'em chasing their tale motto.' It's almost like a chess game, and we're at the 'check' point. Its check mate next, but when" he mutters "and how?"

SIXTEEN

"I'll drop you both" Devon offers."I'll be at headquarters for the rest of the afternoon" he says.

"Alright" Kat agrees. "I have lots to get done here, so keep me updated, please."

"Of course. Don't forget you promised to go to my mother's this Sunday, with the rest of us. Is that still on?" he inquires.

"Of course, if I said I will, you can depend on it."

"Thanks Kat" he says, "I'll call" he promises.

"Des, I'm headed to my office; I need to write up a report for the Captain. I'm sure he's anxious to know what's going on."

"Yes Sir. You're going to his parents house on Sunday, Kat?" Des asks carefully.

"Yes" she says abruptly. "I said I would, so I will. Sunday is when Snake is going to see his parents for the first time in fifteen years. He asked if I would go and so did Devon, both for different reasons, but with the same outcome. So I'll go. I don't want to talk about this anymore and please, this is just between the two of us. It goes no further" she warns.

"Yes Sir" Des agrees obediently.

"Captain" Kat says "I have my report."

"Good Lieutenant, bring it in."

"Sir, I've just returned from Virginia and the plane crash site."

"What did you find?"

"We have a witness in Virginia that actually saw something hit the plane, and cause it to explode."

"Really, who?" the Captain asks.

"It was a horse rancher, by the name of Mark Jackman. He owns a sizeable piece of land about a mile and a half from the plane crash site" Kat informs him. "He admitted to being out riding at the time of the crash, and actually said he saw something that was flying fast, hit the plane. He thought it could have been a ground to air missile."

"You've reported this to the department of homeland security, correct Lieutenant?"

"Yes sir. As soon as he notified me, we put the call in to DHS. He had some of his ranch hands go out on his property, and search for any debris, to protect his animals. They recovered quite a few sizable pieces, at least one from the fuselage, and some from the cabin. We informed NTSB of the debris, and they came out while we were there to pick it up.

"We have his promise, that if he finds more on his property, he'll contact us. While we were there, Deputy Chief Callander noticed a livestock hauler trucking company. The same company we came in contact with after the first murder. He was presumably picking up two dead horses. The horses had died from old age, and exposure. We asked Mr. Jackman about the hauler company, and he told us he'd been using them for about twenty years."

"All of us considered this too much of a coincidence, and decided to pull in some Agent's from the counter-terrorist group to do some tailing. They were told to watch everywhere he went, so they should be arriving anytime. This just happens to be the same livestock hauler that ended up with the skinned body in his truck. That body didn't match either of the ones that we had discovered; not the one from D.C or the one from Staleyville, Pennsylvania.

We still have an un-identified body with no skin and two bodies, skin only. His was also the company that stored his truck at the rental garage that Abdul Adl Thayer owned. That person was of Arab descent, and was found dead in his apartment over his rental garage, of a single gunshot wound to the head. It looked like a typical hit crime. We're closer to the answers and yet we have more questions now than we did this morning. Somehow, these things all tie themselves to the House of Representatives. Unfortunately, we're no closer to that answer than we were after the first murder four weeks ago."

"From everything we have, we know that the murders are occurring every week, and that they have all been killed in a different way. We don't know who could be next Captain, and time is running out for whoever's next on the list. It all does seem to be Middle East related, so we're following those lines of investigation. We've informed DHS of our findings, and are awaiting instructions from them."

"Very good Lieutenant" the Captain responds as he rubs his face in confusion."This case is going to be the downfall of this whole department. I can't put any more people on it than we already have. There are always crimes occurring, and we're responsible for the safety of the citizens of Metro D.C."

"Yes, Sir" she agrees.

"We can't focus on the crimes on Capitol Hill exclusively; however, you and whatever staff you have chosen are still responsible for this case and for working in conjunction with the Feds, Lieutenant."

"Yes Sir."

"Work faster Lieutenant, that's all I have to offer. We only have four days left until the week is up. We can't afford to let the House of Representatives panic. The public would join in on that quickly, and then we'd face public panic. The killers would have everything they wanted plus some."

"Yes Sir. We're working diligently and as quickly as possible on these murders. The answers are there, we just can't see them clearly because of all the things that have been thrown into the mix. The murderers are smart. They've layered us with multiple types of murders, so that we can't connect them. It's my opinion that whoever is responsible is a master mind. He knows how to plot, and he's good at follow through. I also believe that money isn't an issue, since he seems to have plenty of criminals to hire, and he knows who he wants, and what types of criminal to use."

"Thank you Lieutenant. Keep me informed when you have more. For now, get some rest. It won't do anyone any good if you collapse from this mess."

"Yes Sir. I'll get some down time tonight, and be back at it tomorrow" she promises.

"Good enough Lieutenant" he replies.

Finally a nice day, with sunshine: a balmy twenty-five degrees, and no snow in the forecast. Spring is almost here, Kat sings as she whips through her apartment, vacuuming. It's been about a month since I've been able to get this stuff done. At least I did all the laundry this morning and still had time to finish the cleaning. Fresh sheets, clean windows, it will be awesome at bed time. Not bad for a morning's work, considering I have to be at headquarters by noon to catch a ride to Devon's parents house. Why I ever agreed to go with all of them for this visit by Snake, I don't know. Well, actually I do, idiocy, that's always the reason. It really is a family matter, if only I wouldn't have agreed. Oh, well. I still have time for a shower and when I do come home later, at least it will be to a clean place. I'm definitely not used to dirt, she thinks with a grin.

"I told you I'd be here" she replies to Devon's remark. "I don't break promises unless a new case comes in, and I have to work. But I always call if that happens. It would be rude to do anything else."

"Sorry" he replies "I should have known."

"No problem. Let's go, since we have to be at the corners of Ashwood and Trumbell by one o'clock and it's about a twenty-five minute drive from here."

"I'm sorry I didn't get a chance to talk to you yesterday" he says.

"You're under no obligation to talk to me every day."

"Did you have a good day off, anyway" he asks.

"Yeah, I cleaned my apartment, did some laundry. You know the necessary evil stuff. But it always makes me feel good when I'm done with it" she says.

"I haven't had a chance to get that done at home lately. I think the dust mites might be taking over the apartment" he grimaces. "They'll probably be thick enough by the time this case is over to physically move the couch, out the front door. I just hope I'm there when they try" he says.

"Here we are" twenty minutes later."I see Mal is already here and there comes Eli. We just need Snake to show up. Oh, never mind, he's riding with Mallory" he says as he gets out to talk to everyone one last time before they move on to Mom and Dad's house. "Now remember, Jacob. You come in after the rest of us. I want to be able to buffer your trip home with Mom and Dad, so they don't have a heart attack."

"Fine" he agrees quietly."Whatever you decide" he murmurs.

"Well, I guess this is it" Devon says as he parks in front of a two story colonial on a nice quiet street on the outskirts of Arlington.

"Dad" Jacob says quietly, moving closer after his dad see's his face for the first time in fifteen years. He grabs his hand in a manly shake.

"Jacob" his Dad replies in shock."You look great" he says as he starts to tear up. "I never gave up hope that you would come back" he says gruffly.

"I know dad" Snake says with a lump in his throat.

"I've missed you son, so very much" he says as he steps forward to grab his long lost son in a bear hug.

Snake gives his Dad a hug and notices that he feels frail, so he steps back to get a really good look. Yeah, fifteen years show in his gray hair, the wrinkles around the eyes, and the slightly stooped shoulders that used to be ramrod straight from his ex-military bearing. He looks good though, just older. His eyes are still the same brilliant blue they always were, though they now contain tears that sparkle like diamonds. He hears a gasp and turns to see where it came from.

"Mom" he cries as he steps closer to his tall and thin mother."Mom, I'm home" he says as he grabs her up off the floor for a huge hug, and she cries and pats his back while her feet dangle. "I can't believe it's you" she sobs. "I've wondered and hoped all these years, but I was so afraid" she admits "that you were gone forever."

"I've wanted to come home" he murmurs "but I was afraid. I didn't want you to tell me to get out" he admits as he puts his mom back on the floor. "You look wonderful, Mom" he says "not a grey hair on your head and as young and beautiful as I remember."

"Thank you Jacob. I just can't believe you're here like this. It's a dream come true" she admits as she turns to face her three other children. "How long have you known" she asks with tears streaming down her face "I'm so happy" she announces.

"We've only known for about two weeks" Devon replies. "We've been working a case together, and Kat, I'm sorry Mom and Dad, I didn't get a chance to introduce you. This is Kathleen Thomas, she likes to be called Kat, She's a Lieutenant with the D.C Metro One Police Department.

"We've all been working a case together; Kat had met Jacob twelve years ago. He came into D.C a few weeks ago, and came across Kat in a coffee shop that she frequents. They were talking about the explosion. When he heard my name, and that I was the Capitol Police Deputy Chief that was hurt in that explosion he was shocked, and demanded to see me in the hospital. Since then, we've met twice. Once to reacquaint with each other, and the second to plan how to get together with you both so you could see him again, and here we are" he finishes.

"Oh, it's wonderful" she cries as she tries to stop the tears with the tissues she grabs from the box on the end table. "Joe, can you believe this?" she asks.

"No Hon, I can't, but I sure am happy" he says through his own tears as he grabs her hand and pulls her close. "Our whole family, together again, wow" he whispers "It's a dream come true."

"It's our prayers answered" she admits out loud. "I knew someday we'd be together again" she says to them all. "I just knew it" she repeats as Mallory and Eli move forward to share in the comfort and love with their parents.

Devon had already moved in to be closer to his dad and when his mom's finally free, he turns and hugs her."Thank you" she whispers to her first born son, Devon.

"It wasn't me, Mom" he denies.

"Yes it was" she corrects him "it's always you, dear. You've always taken care of Dad and I" she says, tears running freely down her face.

"Uh…hem" his Dad says as he clears his throat of tears. "Let's have some coffee, we can all go into the dining room" he suggests as he urges everyone forward.

"We'll have dinner real soon" Sandra Callander assures Kat.

"Oh, please, don't mind me Mrs. Callander" Kat insists "I'm fine."

"I know you are dear, and please call me Sandra."

"Thank you Sandra. Is there anything I can do to help?" she inquires hopefully.

"No, it's all complete; I just need to bring it all in."

"Let me help you with that then, please" Kat offers quickly.

"Oh, thank you Kat. The kitchen is right through here" she says as she goes to the door on the left of the large formal dining room, done in soothing greens and grays. A huge and shiny dark cherry table and chairs face a big picture window, which has a fabulous view of the back yard, and a beautiful view of a small lake.

"This is really a beautiful place" Kat says to Sandra.

"Thank you dear, we like it."

In the lull following a good meal, Kat remarks "Dinner was fantastic, Sandra. I don't think I'll be able to eat for a week" she moans and laughs."I love home cooking. I don't get to have it too often since work takes up such a large portion of my time. I find myself ordering out most of the time or grabbing fast food on my way here or there."

"Oh, that's dreadful" Sandra exclaims."There's nothing like a home cooked meal and they're so much better for you."

"That's so true" Kat agrees.

"Devon, isn't there a special announcement on the TV this afternoon, regarding the House of Representatives?" Mallory inquires.

"Yeah, it's on at three p.m. If we all go into the living room, we should be able to catch it" Devon says.

"All right, let's go then and see how they're going to change our investigation, again" Mallory says,

"It shouldn't change it at all" he insists.

"Yes, it will, you know it will" Kat exclaims. "We'll need to question the new replacements of the positions that were opened from the murders. We could possibly break open the case with the right leads from these three people."

"Three?" questions Mallory "there were four deaths."

"Yeah, but I haven't gotten a heads up on the Speaker of the House position, yet. It's possible that they'll do that today too, I'm not sure. I know for sure they're filling the three seats vacated by the murders, this afternoon" Kat says.

"Here it comes, it's on "World Vision Now" Devon says.

"We've never had to replace these three positions at the same time. This is a first for the United States" Kat says.

"Shhh, he's starting now" Devon says.

"Welcome to "World Vision Now" out of Washington, D.C. I'm Gerry Partell. We're live here on Capitol Hill at the House of Representatives. It's been a few difficult weeks since they had their first murder, and now the count is up to four. This has been a fearful time. No one is sure who's going to be next, and even if there is a next. I have with me here, Mr. George Malik, the Director of the Department of Homeland Security, who has assured us that they have everything under control, and are not expecting any more murders.

"Mr. Malik, what can you tell us about the person or persons responsible for the murders, in the House of Representatives?"

"Since this is an ongoing investigation, all that I can say at the moment is, we do have everything under control. There is no reason for anyone, be it from the President down to the newest member of the House of Representatives, be afraid for their life.

"We have increased security tenfold, and have not had a visual on any type of unusual movement. We are watching and listening everywhere. There hasn't even been any chatter. Normally, there's always chatter online. This is an unprecedented decision of the President. To handle the mass confusion the deaths created with the new appointments for those positions.

"One of our own employee's is helping the President make the decisions, since she holds a respectable position within the Department of Homeland Security. She's made a difference in the world for those that are overcoming terrorism.

"These murders, as far as I'm concerned, are nothing more than small town terrorism. The public needs to keep that in mind. We will go about the long tedious work of finding this mad man that has caused such disruption. Unfortunately, the public has been greatly affected by all that has happened. Jane, fortunately for us, helps those same people to overcome their fear, allowing them to move on and lead very productive lives. Her program is the benchmark for many other programs planned for in the future. We have listened, and studied those people moving into the newly opened positions in the House today. You can be assured that there is nothing in their background that could possibly cause this country any further trouble.

"We hope the general populace of this great country finds the courage to overcome, and admit they are in safe hands. We, at the Department of Homeland Security, do not take our positions lightly."

"Thank you Mr. Malik, for your time. It looks like it's time to go over to the House. Sydney, it's over to you."

"Thank you Gerry. Good Afternoon, ladies and gentlemen. I'm Sydney Norwood for WKTL Channel 7 News, the Metro Area. Live, we are covering the appointment of the house majority leader, the house minority leader and the house majority whip.

"Three positions that became open due to the unfortunate deaths of the three members of the House. They will be missed for their loyalty, hard work, dedication, and their untimely demise. The president of the United States will be coming out to do these appointments, personally. He feels the burden of his fellow politicians in the House of Representatives, and has asked to do the honors of announcing the new members. Those moving into these open positions. He should be stepping out in a matter of moments. It looks like he's getting to the podium now. Yes, he's starting."

"Good afternoon. This is a happy, yet sad time for me" the president of the United States, says. The announcement of the appointment of three great people who will work hard fulfilling the promise they made to you, the American people.

"The majority party leader, elected by their conference to represent this position as the new house majority leader, is Quinton Uqbahtor. He's a republican from Texas and a man of American Indian lineage.

"Next, the house minority leader, elected to this position by the minority party caucus, is Timothy Greenspan. He's a Republican from Maine, with fifteen years experience in the House. And finally, the new majority party whip elected by the congress is Christine Neuburg, a Democrat from Iowa whom was chosen for this position because of her twenty-five years of experience.

I know that these people will represent our American public to the best of their abilities.

SEVENTEEN

"Now, I have another announcement that I would like to make" the President announces with a secretive smile.

"I would like to introduce to you, the American public, the new Speaker of the House, Jane Ellen Martin. I have all the faith in the world that she will fill this position with complete dedication. She understands the magnitude and honor of this position, and will never do anything to cause embarrassment to our great country."

The camera swings back to Sydney, and catches the shock on her face before she realizes that she's live again.

"Sydney, where you expecting this" Gerry Partell from World Vision Now asks.

"Gerry, hi" Sydney says."No, I have to admit I was in no way expecting this announcement. It's truly unbelievable; I'm not even sure what the American public is going to think. This is about the new speaker of the house. She's the one known as "darling Jane,' she's strangely the most known and popular person in the United States. I take that back, in the World. Maybe now, the United States can begin its long overdue re-covery.

"The public has enough faith in her abilities, and they know she can change the world. I believe the people have embraced her because of what she endured, and how she maintained her innocence, and joy of life. It's astonishing. She's actually more popular than the Kennedy's were. In fact, I would compare her popularity with the obsessive love and joy the people had for the late Princess Di.

"For the past few years, she hasn't been able to go anywhere or do anything without the world knowing everything that's going on. She went from a small town girl to being world known. That's been an amazing feat while still maintaining the normalcy and sweetness that's been her personality the whole time, in spite of her unbelievable experiences in the past."

"Amazing" Gerry Partell says, news anchor for "World Vision Now" out of New York. "This has been an unbelievable day for Jane. We are so happy for her and we can't wait to see what her first act will be, as Speaker of the House. Back to you Sidney" Gerry says.

"Thank you Gerry. This is an unprecedented decision. She's never held a position in government, yet here she stands next to the two most powerful people of the free world. She's never even had any experience with this type of power. However, according to the constitution of the United States, the office of the Speaker of the House was created by the U S Constitution, and there is NO Constitutional requirement. That just means that she doesn't have to have political experience at all, to hold this position. The Speaker is the second in the line of succession (after the Vice-President) to follow the President should he become incapable to hold office, as dictated in the Presidential Succession Act of nineteen forty-seven. If anything were to happen to those two people, the President or the Vice President, she would hold the highest powered position in the country. A few years ago, no one knew
this small town Jane. The world has nicknamed her darling Jane."

"Over to you, Gerry" Sydney says.

"It's unbelievable" Gerry stammers. "I've never heard of anything like this ever happening before. To appoint someone to the Speaker of the House position as fast as she was appointed, it hasn't even been a full seven days yet since the speaker of the house died in that terrible fiery crash. If this is what the President wants, fine, but why such speed? Is there a reason why this wasn't debated over or pre-announced to the American public? Granted, she's probably the most popular person in the United States, maybe even the world" Gerry says into the cameras.

"I can't believe this" Devon yells. His family is in an uproar over this announcement.

"I can't believe it" Joe cries.

"Dad, have you ever heard of Jane Martin?" Devon asks.

"Not in the political arena, at least" Joe says."I have heard of her of course, when she was kidnapped four or five years ago, by one of those Muslim extremists groups. She was on every news channel for months after she was kidnapped, and then more months after she escaped. I think she's from Texas, but I'm not sure. I do know she has no political experience at all. Why would they appoint her? Surely there are many others more qualified" he demands in confusion.

"Yes, I'd say there are" agrees Sandra as she shakes her head."Strange things are happening" she murmurs as she watches Jacob stare at the television."He looks shell shocked" Sandra says quietly to Devon.

"What's up Jacob, what's wrong?" Devon asks.

"Shit" he replies as he scrubs both hands over his face, hard. "I know that dude, man."

"What?" demands Devon "What dude?"

"The one that just got appointed, the Majority Leader, you know, that Indian guy. He's not American Indian. He rides one of my bikes, and I know he's not Indian."

"Okay" Devon says "does it matter what he is?"

"Probably, since he lied" Jacob says.

"Well you know you can't believe the media."

"It wasn't the media that lied" Jacob says hotly "it was the President."

"Well, maybe someone gave wrong information" Devon offers in excuse.

"Maybe, but that businessman that I know in Texas, you know the one in the oil business" Jacob reminds him.

"What about him?" Devon asks. The whole family's now staring at them while they rehash this.

"He's the one that buy's four or so bikes a year?"

"Yeah, he orders them for other people and buys them from you, custom made. Go on, I remember" Devon says.

"Well, I remember that guy coming in to pick up his custom made bike from my shop. There's only one of that bike. I never copy one of my custom made bikes, and I know he's the one that has it. He's now the new majority leader."

"Okay" Devon says "why is all of this a problem?"

"Because he's not Indian" Jacob says in frustration.

"I know, you've said that twice now, so what's the big deal?"

"I happen to think it's a big deal when someone tries to pass themselves off as an American Indian when in actuality, he's Arab."

"WHAT?" Devon yells. "That can't be right."

"Yeah, bro, it's right. I don't know who told the President that he's Indian, but he's not. We talked a lot when he picked up his bike, he's Arab."

"Holy Shit" Devon says as he sinks into the nearest chair. "Kat, Mallory, Eli, we have a problem. We have to get to the bottom of this."

"Yeah" they all agree as they too, take a seat,

"We missed something, or we didn't take it seriously enough" Kat murmurs.

"This is bigger than four congressmen. We need to do backgrounds on every house member, and the senate, oh, shit, it looks like everyone. How the hell do we do this? This is way bigger than our departments. This is a Homeland Security issue" Kat says."If we can't figure this out, we're in big trouble as a country."

"Where do we start? We aren't going to be able to tell many people, we don't know who to trust." They all agree to that.

"What can we do without help" Mallory questions.

"We'll have to start our own task force, the four of us" Kat suggests.

Jacob just looks at her like she's gown two heads."Look, I've never worked in the law enforcement area, but I have worked against law enforcement."

"Jacob, you can't tell me you don't want to help us. This is the country you live in? Do you want it to stay the same or to be taken over by a different country? One that's oppressed, with no freedom, with fear of walking the streets" Mallory cries.

"Now Sis, don't jump to conclusions. All we know is that one of the new party members are not who they say they are. But we know nothing about the rest. It may be all above board. Our active imaginations are just working overtime, that's all" Devon says.

"Let's just start investigating on the Q" Eli suggests."That way we can follow all the leads, since these are active murder cases we've been working on and need to solve."

"We need to re-group. Let's sit at the table. Mom, Dad, you're welcome to join us, but it may cause you trouble. Just by listening to what we're about to say. I don't want to be responsible if something happens to you. Maybe we should take this somewhere else, and not involve Mom and Dad" Devon suggests.

"Now wait just a second Devon. You have never been responsible for either your mother or me. We'll decide if we want to help or not." Joe exclaims. "After all, this is our country too" he says heatedly.

"I know Dad, I know."

"Do you want in or out?" Eli asks.

"Of course we want to help" affirms Sandra."I see a lot of people during my volunteering time. I might be able to find out a little" she offers."Okay, Dad?"

"I've been thinking about getting out more, and this will be the perfect opportunity" he says firmly.

"Then let's make a list of what needs to be done" Kat says quietly.

"First things first" Devon says. "Can you get in touch with the new house majority leader, Jacob?"

"Probably, since I'm in D.C., and so is he. I doubt if he would think much of me contacting him. I guess I can do it on the pretext of how he likes the bike."

"That's good."

"Mallory, can you start running some backgrounds on the congressmen?"

"Absolutely" she agrees."I'll do it slow, just one or two at a time so I don't get any raised eyebrows."

"Good" Devon says "Eli, how about you?"

"I'm going to work on the plane explosion. Something's bothering me there" Eli admits."I don't believe in coincidences either and this is just way over the top" he says thoughtfully.

"Good" Devon says. "That will help. Kat, how about you" he asks.

"I'm going back to the beginning. Looking again at all the leads we had that fizzled out. Something may add up now, now that we have a specific direction to look in."

"Excellent" he says. "I'm going to start looking back into the terrorist angle; we must have missed something there, something big. Alright Mom and Dad, go out and start asking your questions, just make sure they aren't obvious."

"We will" Joe says as he grabs Sandra's hand in his while she nods her head in agreement.

"Let's head out, keep in touch and we'll schedule another meet where we can go over what we've learned. Maybe tomorrow night" Devon suggests "but we'll see. I'll call" he promises. "Kat I'll drop you at your car."

"Wow Lieutenant, you're working some strange hours" remarks Detective Des.

"Yeah, but I don't seem to be the only one" Kat remarks, tongue in cheek "since you're here as well."

"Yeah, I needed to tie up a few loose ends."

"Me too, and I thought I'd come in when it's quiet. Being Sunday, there's only a skeleton crew here. I'm going to enjoy the quiet. I'll be in my office" Kat says as she continues on.

Now, first murder, William Blaketon, skinned out body; murderer, Elroy Wade, deceased. Body found in burning house, identification is made by the Medical Examiner, Dr. Zorgath. Let's see that report. Yep, he identified the remains by DNA since the body was so badly burned. Cause of death, stab wounds to the abdomen. Time of death was approximately fourteen hours prior to being burned. No fingerprints from the killer, but I don't know about trace. Need to contact the medical examiner, for trace reports and toxicology.

Murder number two: Karen Delrose, minority leader. Her time of death was approximately two hours prior to the medical examiners arrival. Cause of death was poison. A slight trace found in the brain tissue. It was a rapid acting and disintegrating poison, difficult to find on normal autopsies. Specialty toxicology testing found it. Murder number three: Jeff Stewart, house majority whip. Cause of death, a fast acting poison from jellyfish, absorbed through the lime on his drink.

Check out bartender, waitress and group of businessmen. Back ground check on Addy needed even though he's deceased. He was a Muslim/Arab individual. Update the murder board with the new information. Call Mallory and request background on Addy Thayer. Background needed on bartender, waitress and every business man in group on Maui. Ask Snake for more information on the group of businessmen. Murder number four: the speaker of the house, Virginia Moore. Her cause of death was a small plane explosion, possible land to air missile. Re-interview Mark Jackman from the horse farm in Virginia.

I need to start at the beginning, she decides. Elroy Wade, who were you? You seem to be the one that started this all. I better contact Snake, she thinks as she pulls out her cell to call.

"Snake, it's Kat, I need to talk to you about Elroy Wade. Can we meet? How about at Mikes coffee shop? I can be there in fifteen minutes. Good, I'll see you there" she confirms. "Des I'm going to be out of here for awhile, I have some leads I want to follow up on. I'll see you later."

"Snake, thanks for meeting me" Kat says as she gives him a hug. "I have some questions about Elroy Wade for you."

"Shoot" he says as they take a seat in the corner.

"Hey Mike" Kat says as he waves at her from behind the counter.

"When did you first meet Elroy?"

"Oh, about fifteen years ago, I guess. He was riding with another guy from the group we formed and just got carried along. He wasn't Mr. Popularity, but he minded his own business most of the time, so we let him stay. Then he tried to rape you and we had to rethink his position with our group.

It wasn't long after we left the D.C. area, had actually just gotten back to Texas, when he did rape a college girl. He got caught, was arrested and sentenced to prison. He did ten years, and then got paroled. We wouldn't let him ride with us anymore. As far as we were concerned, he was done when he crossed the line. It was no great loss; none of us liked him much."

"Did the guy he rode with before you, have anything bad going on; what was his name and have you got any idea about his background" Kat asks.

"No" he says. "He's dead. He died in a bike crash about four years ago. We missed him, he was a good guy. The group that I hung with wasn't a bad group, we just looked it. I really don't know why Elroy rode with him; they were like night and day. Can't ask him now, either, since he's dead."

"Did you have any idea about Wades murdering capabilities?"

"No, he would never have been allowed to ride with us, if we'd had any inkling that he was a serial killer. He probably started doing that after he was released from prison. People change in prison. He would have never been able to hide that type of behavior from us" he insists.

"Hmm" Kat says, deep in thought. "So, did you notice any strange acquaintances while he was riding with you?"

"Yeah, all of his acquaintances were strange" he admits with a grin.

"No, I mean evil strange" she repeats, frustrated.

"Well, there was a guy, he'd show up at the weirdest times. Seemed like he always knew where we were and how to reach Elroy. It might have been Elroy keeping in touch with him and letting him know where we always were, I'm not sure" he says quietly as he thinks. "Yeah, it was probably Elroy contacting him, the bastard."

"About the guy that showed up at the weirdest times, what did he look like?"

"He was dark skinned, maybe a gypsy, or Muslim, I'm not sure of that. If he was, he had good English skills, although he looked the part of Muslim; a small beard, thin, short stature and dark eyes. I'm just not sure" he admits.

"What about a name, do you remember hearing his name?"

"Let me think" he groans. "You're not asking much, are you Kitten? Wait, it was Baroque or something like that. We called him rogue, that's it, rogue."

"No last name?" she asks in disappointment.

"No, we didn't use last names, just nick names. I'm Snake, Elroy was Bad Ass. Everyone had their own nickname."

"Shit" she mumbles. "Do you think you ever heard his last name?" she inquires.

"I may have at one time or another, but I can't think of it right now, to be honest."

"Okay, if you do remember it, can you call me?" Kat asks.

"Sure, I'll do that Kitten" he promises.

"Thanks Snake, I better go. I have a shit load to finish today."

"See ya Mike, I'll call" she promises as she rushes out the door.

Well, she thinks as she heads back to Metro One. Hopefully he'll come up with a last name for me so I can look that guy up. Just because Elroy Wade is dead doesn't mean the investigation stops. There's got to be something else we're missing. I'm sure there's something we're missing. Now, Karen Delrose's death was with some type of rare poison, I better stop and see the medical examiner; he might be able to enlighten me a little on the poison stuff.

The smell's a little strong today, she thinks as she walks through the autopsy area. "Dr. Zorgath, you in here anywhere?"

"Yeah, I'm in the back. Hey Kat, what can I do for you?" he asks as he works on a body.

"Oh, sorry, I didn't know you were busy."

"No problem" he says. "I multitask. I can do this and talk to you at the same time. So, what's up?"

"I wanted a little more information on the death of Karen Delrose. What can you tell me about the poison that was used on her?"

"Well, it was an extremely hard one to find, but thankfully I was suspicious and thought to run the extra toxicology tests. Otherwise we would never have found it. It comes from a fish found in Japan, actually, the blow fish. Tetrodotoxin is the official name of the poison."

"It can and is ingested in Japan when they eat the blow fish. The blow fish is considered a delicacy to the Japanese, but occasionally, someone will die from eating it. It has to be prepared meticulously and there's only a handful that can actually make the dish and not kill everyone that eats it. They even have to be licensed to cook it in Japan. I believe it's a secret that's handed down in families."

"Wow, okay" she says. "How would I find those capable of preparing this food?"

"That, my dear, is the million dollar question! I'm not sure, but you might visit a couple of the Japanese restaurants in the area and ask them. They may be able to guide you in the right direction."

"Good idea Doctor, thank you" she says as she turns and leaves.

Well, that was interesting she thinks as she leaves the last Japanese restaurant in D.C. They aren't allowed to sell blow fish or serve it outside of Japan. But thanks to the internet, you can obtain the poison. Isn't that just great she thinks in disgust. You can get pretty much anything you want off the internet.

So, I now know that it's available off the net, and of course, they guard illegal purchases like they guard the gold at Fort Knox. I need a search warrant to obtain what I know. How can I do that without informing DHS, since I'm not supposed to be working this case anymore? I'll get Devon on this; he might have a data geek that can get this information without a search warrant. That's strange, she thinks, two different deaths, both related to poison, both from a rare type of fish. The jelly fish near Australia, and the blow fish from Japan.

What do they both have in common, besides having been killed by rare poison? Both poisons were used to kill, both are from fish, both are internet available. Bingo, she thinks. I believe that's the common denominator.

I need to talk with Devon. If we can find where the poison was purchased from, we can get closer to our murderer. We also have the livestock hauler that was coincidently near two different crimes. With the unknown body that was in his truck, and then at the horse ranch in Virginia. What connects him besides dead horses, she wonders. That's weird, she thinks; there's a connection that I'm not seeing, but what is it? I need to re-visit the garage that he stores his truck in. There must be something we missed.

"Devon, are you busy" Kat asks as she walks into the Headquarters "I had a thought."

"Look out everyone, she had a thought, we're in trouble" he warns teasingly.

"Shut up" she says on a huff and with a grin. "I think we need to re-visit the garage where the livestock hauler parks his vehicle. I've been going over the murders from the beginning to the end. I talked with Snake about Elroy Wade, and his history. I also talked with the medical examiner for D.C. about the toxicology reports. There's a commonality for those two murders, the poison. Both poisons are available online, through the black market, but I can't access that. I was hoping that you had an internet geek that could get us some information. Like where can you get this and who purchased both? I know it's a long shot, but it's the only thing we have right now."

"Sure" he admits "we have a guy that can do that. I'll get him on it. It may take awhile, but at least it's a direction."

"Then I thought about the coincidence of the livestock hauler and his being at two separate places we happened to be at, during this investigation. I don't like that coincidence at all" Kat says "so I think we need to go back to the beginning with the livestock hauler. Are you in?" she asks.

"Of course, just let me make a call, and then we'll head out" he replies.

EIGHTEEN

"This place still looks deserted" Devon says as they pull up at the garage.

"Yeah, but you never know. Let's start with the garages and then we can move into the apartment area. At least the garages aren't empty today" she says. "Maybe we can get a break this time. We can go over the livestock haulers vehicle, since we've never been able to, at least not thoroughly. I'll take the passenger side" she offers.

"Deal" he says. "Look for anything, receipts or papers thrown about that might give us some information. He's got to be involved, at least with the skinned body deaths. It was just too coincidental to find a dead body in this truck."

"Yeah, I agree" she admits. "He's involved somehow."

"I think this might be something" she announces after looking through the entire glove compartment. "There's a receipt here for gas, on the same day as the murder was. Check out the time. We can compare times, but I know the date's the same; we'll back track from there. Did you hear that" Kat whispers as the hairs on her arms stand up.

"Yeah" he says quietly "it sounds like someone just got home."

"But there's no one that lives here" she says nervously. "Addy was the owner and he was killed. Let's check it out" she whispers.

"On one, you go high" he orders.

"Okay" she agrees.

"Halt" Devon yells "Federal Agent's. Stop and put your

hands in the air where I can see them" he continues as they both move forward to grab the man that's moving quickly towards the only way out. After catching him and wrestling him onto the floor, they're able to remove his mask and see just who it is.

"Addy?" questions a stunned Kat. "You're supposed to be dead!" she declares in shock.

"No officer, I am not dead" he says in his stilted English.

"So I see" she says in puzzlement. "But we both found your body here and the medical examiner came into this facility and declared you dead" she insists.

"No officer, that wasn't me" he insists.

"If it wasn't you, just who the hell was it?" Devon demands.

"It was my twin brother; he was shot in the head."

"Did you shoot him" she demands.

"No, I did not. I was hiding him from immigrations. They wanted to deport him and I promised when he came over here that I would help him to become a citizen, like I am."

"How could he have passed for you?" she asks in confusion.

"He was my identical twin. No one could tell us apart, not even my mother" he admits.

"Well" Kat says, thinking. "You're under arrest, Addie, for the murder of your twin brother." As she reads him his rights, Devon takes a quick look around to make sure there's no one else hiding out in the garages.

"Anyone else with you" Devon asks.

"No sir, I am here alone."

"Where have you been since you're brother was found here, shot to death, two weeks ago?" Kat demands.

"I have been afraid for my life, so I have been in hiding" he admits with chagrin.

"What were you afraid of?" she demands.

"I didn't know who shot him, and I was afraid they were after me, since I'm the citizen and no one knew about my brother, at least as far as I knew" he admits.

"We're going to have to take you downtown" Devon informs him, "we have a lot of questions that need answered."

"Yes Sir" Addy says meekly.

"I want to finish searching" Kat informs Devon. "I'll meet you back at headquarters" she promises.

"I called it in" Devon says. "I'll ride with him in the unit that shows up. Here are the keys to my SUV. You can bring it back when you're done.

"Fine" she says. "I should be back in about an hour. I just want to search a little more, see if I can find any more paper work in the truck. I want to find out where this guy is in this investigation. Something's not right here, but I just can't seem to put my finger on what it is. I'll see you later" she promises as she heads back into the hall. This place is a mess, she decides after finding the finger print powder all over everything, from the crime scene investigative unit.

"They sure don't clean up after themselves" she says, thinking out loud.

"No, they sure don't" a voice from behind her says. As she spins around to see who said that, something hard hits her in the head, knocking her out. When she starts to come to, she can feel a pounding in her head; her vision is kind of narrowed, like she's looking through a tunnel. After trying to move her hands to rub her head, she finds them tied behind her back.

What the hell, she thinks, what happened? Then remembers the voice she heard just before she got slammed in the head? That voice sounded familiar but I can't remember from where. She closes her eyes to keep the light out while trying to remember. It's too bright out there; it's giving me a headache. Just a few more minutes with my eyes closed she decides, then starts to go under again until she feels something hard hit her in the face.

"Ahhh" she screams "what the hell?"

"I can't let you go back to sleep, princess" says her abductor in a strangely familiar voice.

"I want to have a little fun with you, before you die" he admits. "But first" he hits her again in the face with his fist and as she sucks in her breath to scream, he stuffs a dirty old rag into her mouth so she can't make any noise. That bastard hit me on purpose to make me scream, she realizes as she opens her eyes to try to focus on the face behind the voice.

"You've been getting a little too close, Kat" her abductor announces in a too kind voice.

"How do you know my name?" she tries to say but can't because of the rag. Shit, I'm pretty much defenseless, she realizes in fear. This can't be good. I wonder how much time has passed. Maybe Devon will wonder where I am if I don't show up with his vehicle. That could work in my favor, she thinks with hope.

"I'm gonna enjoy this" he promises as he takes a knife off of the shelf next to where she's lying. As Kat looks around, she recognizes the room she's in. It's Addy's apartment, the one with the vibrant colors, the one with all the fingerprint powder all over everything. I was searching this room, she remembers, and complaining about the mess left, when I heard someone agree with me. Who the hell is this guy, she wonders in fear, while a knife is being used to remove her shirt. "Hold still now, you don't want me to cut you, do you?" he says breathlessly. "I just want a little peak, that's all" he promises in a thick voice.

Shit, she thinks, he's going to rape and then kill me. I don't want to go this way, she decides in a panic. What can I do, she wonders as she stares at him in fear? Move; I have to move, I can't let him do this to me. As she starts to kick out with her legs to hurt him, he stabs her in the thigh. When she screams and chokes on the gag, he laughs.

"I told you to hold still. It's your own fault that you're hurt" he tells her. "I won't hurt you again if you hold still" he promises with a smile, "but, go ahead and try. I don't mind hurting you and I'd like you to give me another reason to."

Her eyes are filled with tears from the pain in her thigh as she tries to focus on her attacker. He's that damn driver, that guy with the dead horses. I know him, she realizes.

"I see you've recognized me" he laughs as he sees the knowledge in her eyes. "Know what that means?" he taunts. "It means you have to go, you know who I am so you're going to have to die. But first, let's have some fun" he grins as he strips her of the rest of her clothes.

"So how's it feel to lay naked as a jay bird in front of me and not be able to do a damn thing about it" he asks as he cruelly pinches her nipples with his nails until they bleed. The pain is so intense she screams behind the gag, making very little noise. As she lays there, tears streaming down her face, into her hair, she watches his eyes focus in excitement, and then he starts touching her all over.

"I can't do this" she moans and gags. "I can't let him do this to me. This isn't the way to go; she decides as she lashes out surprisingly quickly and hits him in the groin, with her knee. He screams as he folds over in protection of his groin and she scoots backward to get away from him.

When he can breathe again, he threatens "get ready to die bitch. I'm going to enjoy this" he warns hatefully "Unfortunately, you won't like it one bit. I know how to hurt you in so many ways. Ways you could never dream possible" he says. She's moved far enough away that she can roll to her side, swing her legs up and get into a sitting position. As she scrambles to get to her feet, he starts moving too, and soon they're facing each other. He doesn't know that she's a third degree black belt, and under normal circumstances, can kill with a kick. But she's weak in the left leg from being stabbed, and from blood loss.

I can do this, she chants to herself as she glimpses movement in the hall outside of the room. Don't let him know, she warns herself, don't let him know. It looks like it might be Devon to the rescue. I hope it is she thinks in pain and fatigue. She still can't talk because of the gag, but she can move. If I move this way, it gives Devon a chance to surprise him and take him out. But I want him alive, Kat thinks. He might be responsible for a murder or two. I need to question him.

As he starts to move forward, Kat briefly looks behind him. He sees the move and turns abruptly around, spying Devon as he bursts into the room. The attacker's ready and he jumps at Devon knocking him into the wall, then he pushes past him and barrels out the door, into the hall and outside. "Damn it" Devon yells.

"You're hurt!" he cries when he sees the blood. Kat is shaking her head violently at Devon as he moves to where she's standing and removes the gag.

"Get him" she whispers harshly, her mouth as dry as the desert. With what little moisture she can summon, she begs him "Don't let him get away."

"I know who he is" Devon tells her as he tries to lead her to a chair while spying a knife, and using that to cut off her bonds.

"No, get him. We'll never find him if he gets too far away" she begs urgently.

"Are you okay?" he asks as he looks at her leg and all the blood she's lost.

"I'm okay, go get him, hurry" she says urgently.

"Alright, I'll be right back" he promises and runs out the door. As Kat goes to sit down, she grabs the table cloth and wraps it around her, her clothes lying in rags on the floor. This day has sucked, she thinks in fatigue, my leg is killing me.

With sirens blaring and feet pounding on the stairs, Kat is revived from her thinking when Devon rushes over and get's down on his knee to see if she's alright. "I'm fine" she says tiredly. "It's just a little knick" she says.

"Yeah, it looks like a flesh wound. The paramedics are on their way and we'll let them decide. Your face, Kat, it's a mess. Just how many times did he hit you?" he asks.

"I don't know; a couple of times I guess, why?"

"It looks like he used you as a punching bag" he says quietly. "I'm sure you'll be fine, but I think you're going to need to be taken in for x rays. Ah, here they are" he says in relief as the paramedics walk in and take over.

"We're going to have to transport you" they inform her. After having her vitals checked, putting a dressing on her leg and giving her a blanket, they load her on a gurney to carry her down stairs and put her in the squad while Devon's reassuring her he'll be right behind her.

"Captain Hall, this is Deputy Chief Callander. Kats been attacked and is injured. She'll be fine, but I wanted to notify you. She's being transported to the hospital as we speak. Yes, Sir, I'm headed there now. I'll meet you there."

"Mallory, its Devon. Kat's been attacked. She's on the way to the hospital. Could you let Eli and Snake know please, and also Mike? He's the guy that owns that coffee shop on Washington Avenue. Thanks, I'll see you there."

I'm going to kill that sonofabitch when I can get my hands on him. I should never have left her on her own, he chastises himself, and this is my fault.

"Is she okay?" he asks worriedly when he sees her with her eyes closed, being wheeled into the emergency room.

"Yeah" one of the paramedics says "she's sleeping, she's was pretty beat up" they remind him.

He's pacing the waiting room, while the Doctor is with her in the back, poking and prodding, hurting her more than she is already. When Malory and Eli walk in, and spot him they know that he's blaming himself for this.

"It's not your fault," Mallory tells Devon as she hurriedly grabs him in a hug. "She'll be okay" she says.

"Yeah, she will" he agrees "but the bastard that did this is not going to be so fortunate."

"Did you get him?" Eli asks.

"Oh yeah, I got him. I had to leave her to do it, but she was insistent that I get him. Truthfully, when I saw her, I didn't care if I got him, all I could see was her and what he'd done to her. It isn't pretty, but I think she'll be alright, at least I hope she will" he says in despair.

"What the hell happened" Snake demands when he walks into the waiting room.

"She was going over a crime scene; we both were, when a guy we thought was dead showed up. We find out his twin brother was the one killed, but no one knew about him because he's an illegal from Iran. The brother Addy is from here. No one knew anything about him, so when we saw Addie, we both thought we were seeing things."

"It was Kat and I that found the dead body of his twin. One shot to the forehead, hit man style. We had no idea that there were two of them, identical. I wonder how long they played that one." he mutters.

"What about Kat?" Snake demands roughly.

"I left with Addy but Kat wanted to spend a little more time looking through his apartment, and through the livestock haulers truck. She finished with the truck, and went upstairs to look in the apartment for anything we may have missed the first time through. While she was up there the livestock hauler snuck up behind her, and hit her on the head, knocking her out. Then he proceeded to tie her hands behind her back, and sat and waited for her to wake up. When she finally came to, he hit her in the face with his fists so that she would scream, and when she screamed, he stuffed a rag in her mouth. She must have tried to kick him or something, because he stabbed her in the thigh. It looked like a through and through. I think she'll be fine, but she did lose a lot of blood. She's a scrapper" he admits in admiration.

"She managed to kick him in the groin somehow and get far enough away from him to get herself on to her own two feet. She was facing him, naked and bloody when I got there. I'll never forget that sight" he admits miserably."It was heartbreaking. There she was, standing in front of him with a rag in her mouth, blood running down her leg, pooling at her foot. Her face a bloody mess, but she didn't back down" he says. "She's a tough one!"

"Did he rape her" Snake asks quietly.

"I don't think so" Devon replies "but we'll have to wait on the Doctor and ask him. I didn't want to ask her and upset her even more" he admits.

"Good thinking" Mallory says.

"Isn't that Mike" Eli asks Devon.

"Oh, yeah, I had Mallory call him. He's like family to Kat. I didn't want him to hear this on the news."

"Mike, she's going to be fine. I just wanted to make sure you heard about this through me and not through the media first" Devon says quickly.

"Has the doctor come out yet?" he asks in a shaken voice.

"Not yet, it should be any time" Devon assures him. "The media's piling up outside, waiting. I called her Captain, he should be here anytime. He can handle the interviews with the press. Devon says with another glance towards the back, where Kat is.

"There's Captain Hall now" Eli says.

"Captain" Devon says as he greets him by the door. "Thank

you for coming. We haven't talked with the doctor yet, so there's nothing official."

"How is she?" the Captain questions.

"As far as we know, she'll be fine. She's had a tough time of it, though" Devon admits. "There's the Doctor now" he says quickly, and they all walk forward to hear the news.

"She's going to be just fine" the Doctor reassures them, and everyone sighs with relief. "We're going to keep her overnight, since she did admit to being knocked out completely. She also admitted that she doesn't know how long she was out, but thinks it was maybe ten minutes or so. Whenever there's a loss of consciousness we like to monitor them" he says.

"What about her face, Doctor?" Devon asks worriedly.

"She has a lot of bruising and contusions, but they'll heal. It looks worse than it is" he reassures them.

"What about her leg?" Devon asks.

"She was stabbed, through and through. That's why it bled so much. I don't think there will be any permanent damage. It will take time to heal, but she should be back to normal in no time" he assures them "she's young and healthy. You'll be able to see her when they get her into a room upstairs. That will probably take about an hour or so, so if you want you can get some coffee in the hospital cafeteria. It's not bad in there and it's close" the doctor admits.

"Thank you, Doctor" Devon replies.

"You're welcome" he says as he leaves.

"The media's outside, waiting for an update" Eli reminds everyone.

"I'll take care of that" promises Captain Hall.

"Let's go get something to drink" Mallory suggests as she grabs Devon by one arm and Snake by the other. They all seem to be deep in thought.

After waiting nearly three hours, Devon gains access to Kat. "Kat" he says quietly "how are you feeling?"

"Like a bus ran over me" she answers as normally as possible.

"You look better" he admits.

"Better than what?" she asks "Better than dead?"

"No" he says exasperated "better that you did when I found you earlier. You weren't looking so hot earlier."

"Well, I don't look hot now, look at my face" she says in frustration. "Do you know how long it's going to be before I look normal again? These types of injuries take forever to heal."

"Not so long" he promises. "You'll be back to normal soon. How about the leg, how is it?"

"It's pretty painful" she says "more so than the rest of the injuries. Bastard stabbed me, and I wanted to kill him. He just pulled out his knife and stabbed me! Please tell me you got him" she demands.

"Oh yeah, I got him. I had to leave you to do it, but I got him, and he's going to pay for this" Devon promises in anger.

"Have you had a chance to talk more to Addy?" she asks.

"No, you've been on my mind too much. I couldn't really do anything until I saw you and talked to you" he says. "Now that I've seen you for myself, I feel better. Hopefully I'll get a chance to see him later today."

"You better" she says quickly. "The investigation must go on. I'll be back to it in a day or two" she promises.

"Yeah" he snorts. "I'll believe that when I see it" he says. "More like a month or so" he predicts. "I'm going to have to get going, there's a whole line of people waiting to see you."

"What" she says with eyes wide. "Who, why, I'm fine" she reassures him frantically.

"There're a lot of people that care about you, so of course they want to see you for themselves" he explains patiently. "They need to be reassured that you're okay, just like I did."

"But" she says.

"No buts" he replies with a warm squeeze to her hand. "You'll be fine. They told us only one or two people in here at a time, they don't want you worn out with visitors."

"So now I'm an invalid" she says disgruntled.

"Yep" he agrees cheerfully. "I finally have you where you can't escape; I could talk to you forever and you couldn't get away. Maybe I should" he adds with a grin as she gives him her most evil eye. "Alright, I'm going before you hit me, but

I'll see you later" he says with a gentle kiss to her swollen face.

"A little nap and I'll be fine" is her last thought before she slides into a healing sleep. When she opens her eyes, she expects to be home. It's a strange room she's facing, with Devon sound asleep in the chair next to the bed.

"What are you doing here" she whispers and he jerks awake.

"Sorry" he mumbles "I was waiting to see you" he says sleepily. "I must have fallen asleep."

"What time is it" she asks and he glances at his watch and says "shit."

"What's the matter?" she asks.

"Nothing, I must have been tired, it's four thirty in the morning already. I got here last night around ten thirty and you were sleeping, so I thought I'd just sit here and wait a few minutes to see if you woke. How are you feeling?" he inquires.

"Pretty crappy right at the moment, but I'll get better" she says tiredly.

"You will, but it's going to take time" he warns.

"I don't have time" she declares."I'm in the middle of a pretty large murder investigation" she reminds him.

"I know, I know" he says "so am I. But if you're not up to it, you're not up to it. You can't change the facts."

"I'll be up to it as soon as they release me" she warns him "and they better hurry up with that. I'm fine, there's nothing wrong with me that catching a murderer won't fix. I just need a shower and some clean clothes. Can you get me the clothes?" she asks.

"Sure, what do you want?"

"Just regular clothes" she says. "I want to feel normal and I need normal clothes to do that with"

"Alright, I'll pick some up, any toiletries you need?"

"Just my hair brush and a pony holder and oh yeah, my toothbrush would be nice" she admits.

"You got it. I'll go over to your apartment when I leave here and bring it all back when they release you, so you'll be all set" he smiles.

"Thanks" she says."Sorry I'm so bitchy this morning" she

admits.

"You're not bitchy, but you should be" he says "especially after everything that happened yesterday."

"Oops" says the nurse, as she wheels in the blood pressure stand."I didn't know you were here" she says.

"Yeah, I came in last night to check on her, and fell asleep. We both just surfaced a few minutes ago. Now she's chomping at the bit to get out of here" he explains.

"I'll bet" the nurse says "but you won't be released until later this morning" she advises."It's usually around nine or so, before the Doctor gets in, and signs the paperwork."

"Okay, then I have time to run out and get her stuff?"

"You sure do, plenty of time" she assures him.

"Well then, Kat, I'm going to take off and run those errands. I'll be back as soon as possible."

"Thanks Devon" she replies happily. "I appreciate it".

NINETEEN

"You look a lot better now, then you did a few hours ago" Devon admits as he brings in her clothes. "You look like you're almost ready to go" he adds as he hands her a bag with her clothes in it.

"I am" she declares."I'll just run into the bathroom, and change. The Doctor's already signed my release, so I'm all set. I want to get back to the office and get moving on this case, I don't have time to be lying around."

"I'll call the nurse and let her know you're ready" he offers. "I think they release you in a wheel chair, so we'll have to go out the back. The media's sitting out front waiting for you to make a statement" he warns.

"Oh no, not me and not today" she says adamantly.

"That's what I figured you'd say" he says with a grin.

"Wow" Des says to Kat as she walks through the bull pen area."You look terrible" she remarks worriedly.

"Yeah, I know" Kat admits "but at least I'm functioning now. It looks worse than it is" she reassures everyone in general, while Devon's walking behind her and shaking his head no.

"I should have been with you Lieutenant" Des replies guiltily.

"No, you shouldn't have been" Kat argues "I'm fine. I want the paperwork on my desk about Addy and about Mike" she informs her. "I need some answers, and I need them now. We're almost out of the seven day time frame before the next murder occurs. We only have today left, so we need to work fast here. I don't want to have to attend another funeral at the

Chapel on the Hill. Enough is enough" she declares.

"Yes Sir" Des responds.

"This is all I have. We're waiting on another report from the medical examiner. We requested him to do testing on Addy for comparison with his twin brother. We're going to prove who is who, sir."

"Excellent" Kat says. "Devon, stop hovering, I'm just going to work. You go ahead and go back to Capitol headquarters. I'll keep you informed of what's going on here" she promises as she rolls her eyes at Des.

"Someone's feeling a little protective" Des says quietly as Devon walks out the door.

"Tell me about it" Kat replies."He feels responsible" she says in disgust "no one's responsible for me except me. I've had enough though, I'm fine" she insists.

"The Captain wants to see you, as soon as you're settled in to your office again."

"I'll go right now, and you get me the medical examiner on the phone in about fifteen minutes. I should be back from the Captain's office by then" she says.

"Yes Sir" Des murmurs to Kat's back as she leaves the office, limping.

"Lieutenant" Des says as she knocks on the office door after Kat's returned from the Captains office. "The reports from the medical examiner's office are on your desk. Addy and his brother were so close in resemblance that it's understandable that the report stated that the murdered suspect was Addy. No one had any information on his twin, so there was nothing to compare it to. Now that they have both, they can differentiate."

"Thanks" Kat says."What about Mike Andrews, Des? What have you got on that bastard" she asks, fatigue in her every movement.

"He's in holding and will be until we figure out why he attacked you and what brought all this on. He didn't seem like the violent type" Des admits.

"We need to interview him, just not right now. I want to save that for later. Please just get me the reports on all four murders on the Hill. I want to go over them one more time, we're still missing something" Kat says.

"I know we are" Des agrees.

"Hey" Devon says as he walks into Kat's office.

"What are you doing here?" Kat asks in surprise. "I told you I'd call you."

"I'm done for the day; it's after eight, already" he remarks.

"What?" Kat says, appalled. "I didn't realize how much time had gone. I've been so busy."

"You probably didn't even eat yet, did you?" he asks.

"Actually I think, no, I guess not" she admits. "I've been busy" she says defensively.

"I know, but you need to eat or have you forgotten what happened to you yesterday."

"Not hardly" she replies sarcastically "since every time I look in the mirror, I'm reminded and if that isn't enough, every time I stand up to walk, my leg screams in anger. So, no, I haven't forgotten. That was a stupid question" she says. "Life goes on, and we have four murders to figure out. I've been cross checking all four murders and making a list of commonalities between them. You want to go over them" she asks.

"Not tonight" he says. "You need to eat and rest, since those were the Doctors orders when he released you today. I see you haven't bothered to follow them at all" he says dryly.

"Yes I have" she says defensively.

"How?" asks Devon with raised brows.

"I didn't go on any marathon runs or walks" she answers quickly.

"He didn't say not to do a marathon, what he did say was R E S T, but that word obviously isn't in your vocabulary."

"Sure it is" she replies. "I just haven't gotten to that page yet."

"Alright, miss smarty pants. Let's go and get some dinner and then its home and bed for you" he insists.

"Fine" she says. I am pretty tired she thinks, but no sense in letting him know he's right.

"We're going to the House of Representatives today" Devon says to the group.

Mallory agrees since today is the week anniversary, and the murder or murders seem to be on the one week cycle.

"Yeah, I agree" Kat says "but the murders never happen at the Capitol, they always seem to happen in off time for the Congressmen, so there really isn't any point in joining them at the Capitol."

"Sure there are" Devon disagrees."We can see who isn't there and maybe send some police to check on them."

"Do you realize how many House of Representatives there are?" she demands.

"No, how many?" he asks sarcastically.

"Well depending on the year and the election process, somewhere in the 430 area. Not that they all show up at the same time, but that's still a lot" she says.

"Yeah, I knew that, but we still need to do what we can. Sometimes a police presence can help or even stop a crime. I want to do something" he insists "anything, but at least something positive for a change."

"Alright" Eli and Mallory agree "Let's do this, then."

"We can re-interview while we're here, sometimes, in the heat of the moment people forget things. But if they wait a few days, it all becomes clearer as they dwell on it over and over. There may be new insight, something seen that they didn't realize was important. I think we could get whoever this is if we keep asking" Devon says.

"Hey, what about Jacob, anyone heard anything?" he asks.

"Not since yesterday" Mallory admits. "He was pretty upset about Kat, that's for sure, but I haven't heard anything from him since then."

"Let's hope he's staying out of trouble and letting the police handle things" Devon says in anger. "His lack of keeping in touch is nothing unusual but I would have thought he'd want to see Kat. See her for himself, and ask her how she's doing. I hope he's not getting into trouble. He's still such a hot head, some things just never change. Why don't you call him Kat? He seems to answer your calls fastest" he says.

"Yeah, he does" she agrees with a smile "he's my friend."

"I left a voicemail for Snake" she informs Devon."He'll call me back when he gets it. I'm going to talk with the new Speaker of the House" she says as she turns towards the podium. "I'll see you later" she promises.

"Jane, Madame Speaker of the House, congratulations on your appointment" Kat says.

"Thank you Kat" Jane replies. "What happened to you" she asks with sympathy "you look terrible."

"I was in a slight scuffle with a perpetrator yesterday. He thought he could hurt me, but I'm too tough for that" she grins, not realizing that the lighting in the building makes her look even worse, and she's still walking with a limp, favoring her left leg. With the overhead lighting, every mark and bruise on her face is standing out in stark relief.

"Have you had any strange conversations with anyone around here lately?" she questions.

"Not really" Jane admits "just the normal. I can tell you though, that everyone here, including me, has been a little nervous about today. We realize that the murders have been occurring every week for four weeks, and today's the day."

"Yeah" Kat admits "that's why we're all here."

"Who isn't here that should be?" Kat inquires."We were hoping that everyone would be here, but we also knew that probably wouldn't be the case. There's always someone either late or a no show."

"Well, there's a few people that are supposed to be here that I see aren't" Jane admits. "I hope that doesn't mean anything, though. I'd hate for anything bad to have happened to them" she admits in a quivering voice.

"Give me their names, and we'll try to locate them" Kat offers.

"Thanks" Jane says.

"Des, here are a few names that need to be called. They're supposed to be here and haven't arrived yet, so let's locate them" Kat orders.

"It's been nice talking with you Jane. Good luck with your new position. I'm glad we got someone with compassion in the seat. I need to start talking to the rest of the House, so I'll get back to you later" Kat promises her.

"Thank you Kat. I feel like we've become friends now and I also feel like I can call you if I ever need to talk. You can never have enough of those kinds of friends" Jane says warmly.

"Thank you Jane; that was one of the nicest compliments I've ever received."

Right, Kat thinks as she walks away as quickly as her bad leg allows. There's something wrong with that woman, she thinks. Her eyes tell a much different story than her mouth does. I'll have to keep my eyes on her. She gives me the chills when I listen to her. Something's just not right there.

"Well" Devon says during the debriefing, "so far there's been nothing that's happened today. Everyone that we've called, who was supposed to be there, answered their phones. Some were sick, but I believe the real reason they didn't show was fear. They actually expected something bad to happen to one of them. So they stayed home, and locked up like Fort Knox, but they all managed to stay alive. Maybe we did affect the murderer."

"And maybe he's locked up downstairs" Kat adds. "We haven't questioned Mike Andrews yet" she reminds them. "With him being locked up, we may have stopped another death. Let me give my Captain a report, and let him know that we're going to question Mike Andrews. He might like to watch that" she says. "Let's get him moved to interrogation and get started."

"Captain, I have my report for you" Kat says as she stands at his office door.

"Come in Lieutenant, have a seat" he commands.

"Thank you Sir" she says as she sits with relief, not wanting anyone to know just how bad she feels. "We stayed at the House of Representatives all afternoon Sir, and questioned everyone there, again" she admits. "We're no more enlightened then when we started, but I did get to know the new Speaker of the House. She seems different, but nice. However, I've got a bad vibe, so I'll be watching her closely" Kat says. "There's just something wrong there. I can't put my finger on it, but my gut says beware" she insists.

"How are you feeling?" inquires the Captain.

"I'm doing alright" she assures him. "A little discomfort, but nothing I can't handle" she claims.

"Good" he says.

"I wanted to thank you Captain, for coming to the hospital and handling all the media yesterday. I'm sure it was a zoo."

"You're welcome Kat. You are my Lieutenant, so of course I was there. Yesterday wasn't a good day for you. Since nothing has happened to any of the House members today, maybe we got ourselves the killer" he exclaims. "It's still day time and still the seven day mark, so I don't want to brag too early. There's still time for something to go wrong" he says.

"We're getting ready to question Mike Andrews, Sir. I wanted to let you know, in case you wanted to observe" she offers.

"Thank you Lieutenant, I would like to watch" he admits.

"We'll be starting as soon as I'm through here. He's being taken into interrogation as we speak."

"Who's doing the interrogation Lieutenant?"

"I am and Deputy Chief Devon Callander. We were both there and affected by him, so we felt it only right that we both do it."

"No" the Captain says."He attacked you personally, and injured you pretty severely, so you are not to interrogate him. Let Deputy Chief Callander handle this. You are officially taken out of the interrogation. I'm sorry Lieutenant" he says "but that's the way it has to be."

"Yes Sir" she replies, disappointed.

"You ready Devon?" Kat asks."The Captain has officially removed me from the interrogation. I'm apparently too close to this to be allowed to interrogate him. He's waiting in interrogation room three" she says.

"I'm sorry, but it's the right thing to do." he says, understanding. As they walk together to the elevator, he watches Kat out of the corner of his eye. She hates to admit when she's had enough, but you can see it in her body language. She's running on fumes now, but she'll make herself handle this even though he's going to be in her nightmares.

"Mr. Andrews, I'm Deputy Chief Devon Callander. I have

216

some questions I'd like to ask you."

"Yeah, what and where's that pretty Cop. I want her to interrogate me" he adds with a smirk "she's real pretty, especially without her clothes."

"You bastard" he yells "you keep your filthy mouth closed. You're going to jail for a long time for this one" he snaps. "Did you kill Addy Thayer's brother?" Devon starts the questioning.

"Who, wait, no way man, I had no idea he even had a brother" Mike denies. "Wasn't he shot or something?"

"I don't know. Why don't you tell me how you killed him Mike?" Devon demands.

"I didn't kill him." Mike says with finality.

"No way did I kill him. I don't like guns. They're too easy to trace. I prefer the knife, it's a little more personal and I like to get up close, in case you didn't notice that. Just ask that pretty cop, she'll tell you how much I like the knife."

Devon glares and grinds his teeth at the suspect. "So you like the knife, do you?" he inquires. "That's good to know, since we have three murders involving a knife and you just stated you prefer the knife."

"Wait a minute" Mike argues "I didn't kill those people. I had nothing to do with them."

"Well, you just admitted that you like to use a knife on people, and we have three people killed by a knife. It only follows that if we put two and two together we get you. Mike Andrews, you are under the arrest for the murder of. . . "

"Wait, wait" Mike yells. "I didn't do it" he exclaims. "You're not pinning those murders on me. No way, I didn't do it. I want a lawyer."

"Fine" Devon says "but you're still under arrest. Mike Andrews, you are under arrest for the murders of William Blaketon, Tom Mason and an unnamed subject, and also for attempted murder of a police officer." After he finishes the Miranda he escorts him to holding and informs the guard on duty to give him his phone call.

"Let's go" Devon says "I've had enough for today" he decides as he looks at Kat with concern. "You look exhausted. I knew working today wasn't a good idea, you should have been home, in bed and sleeping. You'll never recover if you don't take better care of yourself."

"Yeah" she admits with fatigue. "I think you just might be right this time" she says on a sigh.

"I'll make dinner tonight" he promises."Some chicken noodle soup and a grilled cheese sandwich coming right up" he declares with a smile. "It's not homemade soup" he admits as he hands her a tray "but it's hot and healing.

"Yeah, and it tastes perfect" she admits as she sighs with pleasure. "I was pretty hungry" she says as she starts spooning up the soup quickly.

"Hey, slow down" he exclaims "there's more if you want more."

"No, I just need to eat this as quickly as possible. I'm going to pass out in a couple of minutes and I need the food for healing."

"Yes you do, and you really need rest. I'm staying here tonight" he decides as he looks at her and sees the deep fatigue etched on her face."I don't want you to be alone yet" he says quietly.

"Thanks Devon. I don't want to be alone yet" she admits.

"You're exhausted; you've been through a lot in the past twenty-four hours."

"That's true" she admits as her eyes get heavier. "Thanks for taking care of me. I appreciate it. I wonder why Snake never called." Kat murmurs as sleep claims her.

TWENTY

"Wow, its morning already" she says as she wakes to find the sun coming up. Oh no, what time is it, she wonders. I'm going to be late she realizes when she sees it's after eight. "Shit" she says and winces when she moves her leg. "Ouch" she complains "that's really sore today." With a groan she realizes that her whole body hurts, and she still has to go to work. Damn it.

"Good morning sleepy head" Devon says when he sees her eyes are open.

"Devon, you're still here?" she says in surprise.

"Yeah, I am. I told you I wasn't leaving you last night" he reminds.

"Yeah you did, but it's not last night and I'm late this morning" she exclaims.

"No, you're fine. You aren't supposed to report for duty until at least noon. You went straight to work as soon as you were released from the hospital yesterday. Captain Hall called and told me to tell you he didn't want to see you until noon today. So, you're not late."

"I can't go to work at noon, that's just not right. I always start at seven not twelve. I'm not an invalid. Help me up" she demands with a groan.

"Listen to you" he says. "Help me up? You're not ready to be putting in fifteen hour days yet. You'll kill yourself and all for what Kat? You don't get special honors for always being at work at the right time. Besides, the right time is noon today. That's the Captains orders."

"Fine" she grumbles. "I need a shower, is that permitted, Mr. Jailer?"

"Of course, my lady, let me help you" he says with a mock English butler bow. "Remember not to get that wound in your leg wet, doctor's orders. There're stitches in it, so protect them."

"Fine, get me a piece of saran wrap." she says.

"Sure, hang on, I'll be right back. Good thinking. It looks like you've had to do this before" he says in suspicion after watching her put on the wrap and tape it securely in place.

"No, but I saw it on one of those Nat Geo shows, First Aid one-oh-one. You never know what you might need someday. I'm glad I watched it, it helped me today" she says with a smile.

"Need any help in the shower?" he asks a leer on his face.

"No" she laughs "I'm feeling better today but not good enough for that, unfortunately. Hopefully soon though" she adds with a wicked twinkle in her eyes. "I can't be laid up too long" she adds with a grin.

"What's on the agenda today" she yells over the sound of the running water.

"We have more investigating to do. We need to see if we can locate that brother of mine, Jacob" he replies.

"He never returned my call yesterday" she says. "I lost the last twelve hours or so" she admits. "Did he call while I was sleeping?"

"Nope, nothing" he assures her.

"Hmm, that's not like him, he always returns my calls. We better go out and look for him" she says worriedly; "I hope he's okay."

"Devon, stop, please, just give me that towel" she begs after trying to reach it and failing.

"Sure, here it is" he says as he starts to hand it over. "But first, a small kiss" he requests with a leering wiggle of his brows.

"Stop; just give me the towel, please. My good mood is rapidly deteriorating" she admits "because I'm worried about Snake."

"Fine" he says after handing her the towel, "we'll do it your way."

"Okay" he says. "If you're all set, I'll drive. I need to stop at home for a few minutes to shower and change. It won't take me more than fifteen minutes" he assures her.

"That's good; it'll give me time to try Snake again. Besides, I've got an hour before I need to be at work" she reminds him. "So please, take your time" she says magnanimously with a grin "take all the time you need."

"Snake, where have you been" Kat cries as Devon walks out of the bathroom and overhears her. "I called you yesterday. Why didn't you call me back?" she asks. "What, no. It's been on the whole time. If you did, why didn't you leave a message?" she demands. "At least I wouldn't have been so worried about you. Yeah, I did, why" she asks. "That's none of your business" she declares. "No, I'm not up to it, remember? Someone tried to kill me, day before yesterday. Fine, I'll be here. Just call if you can't make it," she says abruptly "bye."

"I don't need anyone to take care of me" she decides as she turns to face Devon. "I have to go, I'll drive myself but I'll see you later."

"What have you got Detective" Kat asks as she walks through the bullpen at Metro One. Detective Des is sitting in her small gray cubical.

"Not a lot, Lieutenant. I've been hounding the lab for the print results from those businessmen in Maui. It was good thinking on your part, grabbing those glasses off the table when you left."

"Thanks Des, glad you noticed the trouble I went to. What about the pictures off my cell phone? Any luck on those?"

"Not yet Sir, but they started the run on Interpol, so hopefully there's something there."

"Excellent" she says. "Calls?" she asks.

"I left the messages on your desk" she says as she follows Kat into her office.

"You look a little better today, if I may say so."

"Thanks" Kat says. "A little sleep makes all the difference."

"Is there anything you need, Lieutenant?"

"Right at the moment, no, but thanks. Let me know if

there's anything new, as soon as you receive it."

"Yes Sir" Des says as she heads back to her cubical.

"Lieutenant, I just got a call from the lab. They got a match on a picture you took."

"Excellent" Kat cries. "Which one?" she asks.

"The one of the bartender" Des replies; "they matched him through the department of homeland security site. He's been on the watch list for years, but they haven't been able to get a lead on him. They'll be after him now, though" she says.

"What's he on the list for?" Kat inquires.

"Terrorist ties, is all it says" Des answers.

"That could mean anything" Kat remarks with disgust. "Everyone and his brother are on that damn list. Alright, I'm heading over to capitol police headquarters. Call my cell when something else comes up" she orders.

"What's new here" she asks when she sees Devon.

"The department of homeland security has the bartender from Maui on their watch list."

"I should have clarified that more, what's new that I don't already know" she responds.

"I don't know what you know, so you'll have to bear with me. Are you still crabby Kat?" Devon asks.

"Maybe a little, but don't take it personal" she replies.

"They're going to pick up the bartender sometime today" he answers the unasked question.

"I hadn't heard that" she admits with a small smile. "I'm sorry Devon. That was uncalled for. I tend to be crabby when I don't feel well, and it's hard to feel good when everything hurts" she admits quietly.

"I can relate" he says sympathetically. "You do look slightly better today though" he admits.

"Thanks. A little makeup goes a long way. I don't' usually wear it, but it's good for camouflage. I hate people staring at me. So what's on the agenda?" she inquires.

"I thought we'd go back to Addy's" he says. "There are some things we need to look for and we didn't get the chance yesterday. But we'll go only if you can handle it" he warns.

"Let's go, I'm fine with it" she says decisively. "It looks

like we made it through the seventh day without another murder; I hope this is the new trend."

"Yeah, it would be nice" he admits as they head out for their trip to the garages.

"There are still people unaccounted for from the House. Some of them are known to take mini trips home, so that could be the reason we couldn't reach them" she says. "We're still calling all of the ones we couldn't reach yesterday. Traffic isn't bad today and at least it's not snowing again" she says as she tries to keep the conversation moving. I watched the news and the weather earlier. It looks like we're going to get hammered again with snow. They're saying by this weekend."

"That figures" he says.

"There's always something to fight with" she agrees.

"Here we are, are you ready to go in?"

"Yep, I'm good" she says.

"Let's do it then" he responds as he climbs out of the car. "We'll start with the garage and work our way upstairs."

"Sounds like a plan."

"After you" he says. "I'll take the high, you take the low"

"Fine" she says as she grabs her weapon.

"On three, go" and they enter with weapons drawn.

"Clear" they both report.

"Alright" he says in relief "let's dig. Let's re-examine Mike's truck."

'I'll take the driver's side this time" Kat says.

"Fine with me: there's a paper here, wedged in the seatbelt hook in the driver's seat. It says a name and a number" she murmurs "I wonder who it belongs to."

"What's the area code? Devon asks.

"It's a three one nine, that's out of state I think, it's an area code I don't know."

"How about we call it?"

"Sure, just let me finish with this first" she replies. "Hmm, here's something else. It's a matchbook from that hotel in Maui. Now this is going a bit far, don't you think?"

"I'd say so" Devon admits.

"How in the world did he get that" she wonders out loud.

"Maybe he didn't, but maybe someone he knows did" Devon replies. "That's no coincidence."

"Nope, no way it's a coincidence. Well, well, the plot thickens. So who do you think he gave a ride to that was at that hotel? It could be anyone" she says thinking, "but it sure will be interesting to find out. Okay, I think I'm through here" she says "how about you?"

"Make the call and then we'll move upstairs" replies Devon, "I'm done here too."

"Hello" a deep male voice says.

"To whom am I speaking?" Kat inquires formally.

"Who are you" asks the man on the other end of the phone.

"You first" she says with a little tease in her voice.

"I'm sorry, you must have the wrong number" he says and hangs up.

"Damn it" Kat says "he hung up on me!"

"Did you recognize his voice?" asks Devon.

"No, sorry" she says, frustrated.

"It's okay, we'll take it back to headquarters and let them find out who owns it" he says. "Let's go upstairs, you go low" Devon says as they reach the landing.

"Yeah, fine" she replies.

"On three, ready, go."

"It's still as messy as the other day" Kat says.

"Of course it is. No one's been here since we left. It was a sealed crime scene, but you never know. That didn't stop Addy or Mike from being here. They could have come back for something."

"I wonder if there's a secret entrance, and that's why we didn't see or hear either one of them yesterday" Devon says thoughtfully.

"That's true" Kat agrees in excitement. "It's an old building. It could have been built with a secret passageway."

"A lot of the old homes in the D.C. area were" Devon says.

"I should have thought of that sooner" Kat admits. "It could have saved me a lot pain and aggravation."

"No, I should have thought of it" he says. "I've been off all week now" he admits with disgust. "I need to start thinking

224

clearer."

"I've checked everything in this damn apartment" she cries in frustration.

"Okay, then start checking the walls and floor. There could be something behind or underneath one. I'm sorry, I know it's a long, tedious job, but if we find something, it'll be well worth it" he promises her.

"I found a book in the lamp on the wall in the bedroom" Devon yells.

"What? What lamp?" Kat asks.

"It's that old one near the bed. I don't think it's been used in fifty years, since there's no bulb in it. No one probably thought anything about it, it's so old. They just probably thought that age had made it stop working."

"The book looks pretty old. It looks like a bible or some-thing."

"Yeah" Devon says."We need to find someone who can translate this."

"I don't know anyone, but with your connections, you should" she says.

"Yeah, I'll call the office and give them a heads up. I'll be right back" he tells Kat.

Shit, she thinks. That's the same thing that he did day before yesterday. "I hope it has a different outcome" she mutters to herself.

"All right" he says as he walks back in quickly, making Kat jump.

"You startled me" she complains.

"So I see" he says. "I'm sorry, I shouldn't have left you, you're not yourself yet."

"I'll be fine, I just wasn't expecting that, that's all" she replies defensively. "I haven't found anything else" she answers his questioning look.

"Alright then, I guess we're done here. Let's head back and see what they can tell us at HQ. I'm anxious to see if this book gives us anything" he admits.

"We need something to get this investigation moving again" she says.

"Yeah, we don't have much" Devon admits "but what we do have can be added to anything more we get. It's all part of the big picture. Let's hope the picture is close to being finished."

"Did you find a translator?" Devon asks as soon as he gets off the elevator.

"Yes, we did" Mallory replies "he's on his way."

"Did I miss anything?" he asks.

"Not yet" she says as Kat walks over after having spoken with Eli. "The task force is still making calls, but we haven't gotten anything yet. Hi Kat, how are you doing?" Mallory asks as she hugs her gently.

"I'm doing well" she replies.

"You're still limping I see."

"Yeah, the legs still pretty sore, but it's definitely better than it was" she admits.

"Have you heard from Jacob yet?" Mallory asks.

"Not since I spoke with him first thing this morning," Kat admits, and just as she finishes saying that, her cell phone chirps."Hold that thought" she says as she turns away to answer the call. "Hello."

"Hey Kitten, it's me Snake. What do you need?" inquires Snake. "Wait, how are you feeling?" he asks.

"I'm doing alright; still a little sore but overall a lot better."

"Great" he replies. "So, what can I do for you?"

"What have you been up to for the past couple of days?" she asks.

"Been doing a little of my own investigating" he admits.

"What kind of investigating?" she asks suspiciously.

"You know; the one where you go and ask a lot of questions and sometimes get answers" he teases.

"Alright" she says in resignation. There's no getting around Snake when he's in this mood."So what have you found then?"

"I've been looking into my friend's interests, and I ended up with some questions that I thought he should answer. So I talked with him."

"Okay. What kind of questions, and what were his answers."

"How about if I talk to you and everyone else about this, in person" he suggests. "It's a little too involved for over the phone."

"Fine, when and where?" she asks.

"What about that same Italian place we went to the other day?"

"Hold on, everyone happens to be here right now, so let me ask" she replies. "Snake wants a meet tonight at Angelo's Restaurant where we met the other night. How about seven?" she asks everyone.

"I can make it" Eli offers first.

"Me too" says Mallory and Devon gives the okay with a shake of his head.

"It looks like it's a go with everyone, so meet us there at seven" she informs him.

"Great, I'll see you later" he promises just before he hangs up.

"He must have been in a hurry" she says "he couldn't wait to get off the phone. Okay, next? What's next on the list?"

"Well, we've found out a little about that book we found" Devon offers."It's the Quran, but not just the Quran; it also contained some writing on certain pages of the book. We're not sure what the writings relate to yet. We have the translators on that, but they sound like promises or threats if the wrong hands get them, which they did. The wrong hands being government hands" he clarifies.

"How long do you think before we get the report back?" Kat asks.

"Not long, I wouldn't think" replies Devon."The translators we have are good, so it could be anytime."

"I hope we get them back today" Kat says "It's almost five already. I feel like I've run in circles today, like a hamster on a wheel, run, run, run, but getting nowhere" she admits with a sigh. "Any information on the number we found in the truck?" she asks.

"Yeah, it belonged to a Steven Marlow. He's one of the businessmen that was with Tom Walters in Maui" Devon replies.

"Really" she admits "that's interesting. I wonder if that's what has Snake all excited. Alright, that covers that then, the cell phone number and the matchbook" she admits.

"No, not the matchbook" Devon corrects. "We're doing a fingerprint check on the matchbook also" he states, "but I doubt if that's connected to the same guy. That would be quite a coincidence."

"There's the call now. Let's hope it's the lab. You're sure" he asks? "There's no room for a mistake with this information" he says. "You've double and triple checked? Yeah, okay. I need that report on my desk ASAP."

"You're not going to believe this" he says. "This needs to be discussed behind closed doors, it's become a top security is-sue" he admits. "Let's go to my office, its close. Sit down. This doesn't leave this room, understand" he warns.

"Alright" Devon says with a huge sigh. "That was the lab, with the report that we've been waiting for on the matchbook fingerprints. It's definitely not what I was expecting" Devon admits. "The fingerprints that they found on those matches be-long to Jane, Jane Martin."

"What! Kat cries "how can that be, they must have made a mistake!"

"Nope, no mistakes" he insists "they rechecked their test three times."

"There has to be an explanation for this" Mallory says.

"She doesn't look like the type to keep that kind of compa-ny" Eli remarks.

"I have to agree with you there" Devon admits. "She seems awfully demure to have a friend like Mike Andrews. He's a loose cannon, as far as I can tell. With what he did to Kat, he's definitely not Jane's type."

"Wow, I'm speechless, I don't know what to say. Actually my brain doesn't want to accept this" Kat says. "I need to re-group, I think" she admits. "Has anyone ever done a back-ground check on her?"

"Probably, since she's the new Speaker of the House" De-von replies in disgust.

"True" Kat says. "I want to see her background check" she

decides. "We need to figure this out. If it's what it sounds like it is, it's bigger than any of us thought. Way bigger, White House big."

"Yeah, we can't talk about this with anyone" agrees Mallory.

"It's going to be hard to gather all the information we need without tipping anyone off" Eli says.

"What do you think of the department of homeland security?" Kat asks.

"Well, I'm not sure what to think now. This totally came out of left field for me. I'll have to reassess and then decide" Devon says.

What are the connections, Kat wonders.

"We asked this question before but never answered it. All four victims were high in the House of Representatives; they all had positions that enabled them to work closely with the President" Devon remarks.

"It makes me feel a little sick" Mallory admits.

"A little?" responds Kat."It makes me look at our government suspiciously."

"Sir" they all jump at the knock on the office door and then glance around sheepishly.

"Yes, what is it" Devon says as he answers the door. "Come in Dave. What's up" he asks of his best computer geek.

"I started that background check that you asked me to do, and it came up my security clearance isn't high enough."

"By whose authority" Devon asks.

"The Department of Homeland Security" he says.

"That actually makes sense" Devon admits."They usually monitor everyone, but especially those nearest and dearest to the president. No problem" he tells the tech "I'll take care of it."

"Thank you Sir."

"Get the phone Eli, please" Devon asks as he shuts the door.

"This is Agent Eli Callander."

"Yes he is, just a moment" Eli replies.   "Devon, its George Malik" he says as he hands the phone to Devon with a grimace.

"Wow" mouths Devon that was fast. "Yes Director, what

can I do for you?" Devon asks politely.

"We found her finger prints on a piece of evidence. We needed a background check, sir. That's the only reason" Devon assures him. "Yes Sir. No, we have plans to go and talk to her, probably tomorrow, since it's close to seven already. Yes, Sir" Devon replies while giving a disgusted look. "Alright, thank you Sir" and he whistles loud and long as he hangs the phone up and turns to face the group.

"They are extremely pissed that we tried to run a check on Jane Martin" he replies to their unasked questions.

"She seems to be well protected" remarks Kat

"I think we're going to have to leave" Devon says ruefully "it's time to meet Jacob.

TWENTY ONE

"I'll meet you there" Kat insists "I need to make a call."

"Do you want me to wait, we can ride together?" asks Devon.

"No, I need my car anyway. I'll meet you there, but thanks."

"That was pretty abrupt" Eli remarks thoughtfully. "Is something wrong between the two of you?"

"Not that I'm aware of, but she's been through an awful lot lately. Maybe she just needs space" Devon replies, troubled.

"Yeah, that could be. Let's head out, I'm starving" Eli proclaims.

"Thanks for getting the back room table, Jacob" Devon says after arriving at the restaurant.

"No problem. Where's Kat?" he asks suspiciously.

"She's coming, she had a call to make, so she's going to meet us here" he responds.

"So how's she doing?" asks Jacob.

"Good, she won't let anything stop her. She's a stubborn woman."

"She's been stubborn since I met her. I doubt that will ever change. Sometimes I think she's too smart for her own good" Jacob admits. "You don't mess around with her friends and you don't mess with her. She's got spunk and she's extremely loyal" he remarks with a grin and clear affection. "There she is now" he says.

"Snake, hey, how are you" she asks with a grin.

"I'm great, Kitten, and you?" he asks seriously. "You still look a little rough."

"Naw, I'm doing a lot better now" she insists.

"Is everyone here now?" the waitress inquires.

"Oh, yeah, sorry" Devon says.

"That's alright, what can I get you to drink?"

"I think we're all going with the house red" he says while glancing around and receiving nods from everyone.

"Yes sir. Is everyone ready to order?" she asks.

"I think so. You told me the special today was lasagna" and at her nod of agreement he states "we all want the special."

"Thank you" she replies and as she leaves, promises "those will be right up."

"Let's all catch up to what's been happening lately. We seem to have stepped on some toes" Devon says worriedly.

"How so?" Jacob asks.

"Well, we requested some background checks, run on the new majority leader, the new minority leader, and the new majority whip. Just routine checks, but when we tried to get the new Speaker of the House run, we hit a brick wall; a wall so high that the Director of Homeland Security called and put a stop to it. Our security clearances aren't high enough, I was told."

"Wow" Jacob says "that's weird"

"I thought so, too" Devon agrees.

"So what are you going to do about it?" Jacob asks.

"We aren't sure yet. We're working on it" he admits. "I do have some favors that I may need to call in."

"What about the backgrounds you were able to get?" Jacob asks. "Was there anything there?"

"Nothing that throws a flag at any of them, I think a deeper background is in order. Especially since the Speaker of the House is out of bounds" Devon answers.

"I agree" Mallory says.

"We should have been able to check them all. After all, it's what we do. But then the Director of Homeland Security stepped in and stopped it" Mallory complains.

"It's certainly enough to throw suspicion on everything" Eli remarks.

"This whole House of Representative issue has become a

nightmare, as far as I'm concerned" Devon says.

"It seems as if we've been blocked and misguided the whole time, with these murders" Kat adds. "I just don't like it" she says to Snake as he quietly takes in the questions, comments and emotions affecting everyone.

"You all sound a little put out by the directive. I doubt that it's personal" Jacob says.

"It can't be personal" replies Devon, "so what is it really?"

"Something's brewing on Capitol Hill" Kat says. "We'll figure it out; it will just take a little more time. What about you Snake" Kat asks "you said you had something to tell us?"

"Yes I do" he replies. "It's about Wes, the guy from Texas. The one that buy's the bikes for his friends? He let me in on some of the background for the new House Majority Leader, the one that was introduced as an American Indian. It's common for him to claim Indian Heritage, but he isn't blood Indian. He did live with some of them in Texas though and that's why he claims he's one. He feels like one" he says. "I informed him that he can't claim to be something he never was and that he needs to publically recognize his true background and to begin that process, he needs to talk with the President and inform him of his true heritage" says Jacob. "That's it in a nutshell" he finishes "that's my big news."

"Well, at least it's something" Kat says "like I said, we'll figure this out."

"Here's our dinner, let's eat. We can talk about something else for awhile. Everyone could use the break" Devon says.

"So, Snake, where have you been?" Kat asks. "I haven't seen much of you" she complains.

"I'm sorry Kitten. I had some urgent matters to take care of. But I worried about you the whole time" he promises.

"See, you tell me not to worry and what do you do" she teases.

"Yeah, yeah" he replies with a grin. "You know that old adage? Do as I say …well, that applies to you and me" he says with a laugh.

"So I see" she responds in kind.

"Well, I'm sorry guys, but I have an appointment. I promise

to keep in touch this time" reassures Jacob. "Call me if something happens, please. I'm no further away than a phone call" he stresses as he leaves.

"I'm going to hit the road too" Kat decides. "It's been a long day and I need my beauty sleep" she adds with a grin. "Good night everyone, see you tomorrow" she says as she hurries out of the room, hoping to catch up with Snake before he completely disappears again.

Unfortunately, there's no sign of him when she finally gets out of the restaurant. "Damn" she says with gritted teeth "you're too fast, Snake." What the hell is he running from, she wonders. It's too late to go and see Mike. I'm sure he's home by now. I guess I'll just head home, I really am tired. I could use some sleep myself.

"Good morning everyone! Mallory, Eli, Devon, what's new?" Kat asks. "Does anyone have any new information yet?" she asks hopefully.

"Nothing at the moment, but we're working on building the Congressmen's backgrounds, I want to know everything about them. Like who they know, for how long, everything" Devon replies.

"That sounds good" she says "maybe we'll get somewhere, finally. It sounds like everyone's working hard; it's noisy in here."

"There are other things going on here besides the Congressmen issue's" Devon replies, and as he's speaking, his phone starts ringing. "Deputy Chief Callander" he answers. His expression goes blank as he wonders what this call's all about. "Yes, Sir, nine a.m., yes sir. Thank you Sir" Devon replies as he hangs up. "Well" he exhales "that was strange" he remarks.

"What?" Everyone's now looking at him curiously.

"Let's go into my office, I think we need some privacy" he says.

"That was the Secretary of Defense, Nicholas Rantrall; he wants to see us in his office at nine this morning, all of us" Devon quotes.

"Now what?" Kat asks.

"Did we step on more toes?" Eli asks, confused.

"This has been a strange investigation" Mallory admits.

Everyone notices the quietness in Devon's replies. "I don't know what's going on here, but something is. Remember when we all said this was big. Well, I think we're going to find out just how big it is" Devon says thoughtfully.

"Kat, can you reach Jacob? He needs to be there also, by request" Devon says.

"Sure" Kat says "I'll call him right now."

"I wasn't able to reach him, but I left him a voice mail and told him where to be at nine a.m.

"Good enough" he says. "Gather up any paperwork that you might have lying around. Let's make this a top level security matter from now on. We're going to black it out, code word, Delta Congo. No speaking outside of sealed rooms, no paper trails" Devon reminds everyone. "Let's go to the Secretary of Defense's. It's about time we find out what's going on here."

"Please ladies and gentlemen, have a seat; Mr. Rantrall will be right with you." They all take a seat in a beautifully appointed outer office, on a comfortable couch and loveseat, with separate chairs. It all carries the blue theme around the room easily. Nice and bright, not dingy and drab like Metro, and the size of this office, its way bigger than my apartment. It must be nice. I definitely don't make enough, she decides to herself.

"If you'll follow me please, right this way" the secretary says.

"Jacob Callander is coming; he's just not here yet. Will you show him in when he gets here?" Devon requests.

"Absolutely Sir, it will be my pleasure" she assures him.

"Thank you" he replies.

"Mr. Rantrall, here are your requested appointments."

"Welcome, please have a seat" replies Nicholas Rantrall, a middle aged gentleman with a large muscular looking frame, and a military bearing as he rises in respect from behind an imposing dark cherry desk. A huge window behind him shows off a phenomenal view of the Capitol.

Looks like Snake beat us here, Kat thinks as she notices him sitting at the table with another gentleman of military means. This is some place she thinks. Snake looks slightly different in here, more official, more formal. It's definitely all been chosen to make an impression and very successfully done, she thinks as she takes a seat on one of the chairs set around a large rectangular table that seats ten and matches the desk. This is a huge office, she realizes.

"Thank you all for coming here on such short notice" Nicholas Rantrall says. "As you may be able to tell, this is a serious matter. We don't usually go through this, but it's a special request from one of my top operatives, and I have to agree with him. It's imperative that you know what you've stumbled upon. I need to remind you that this is top secret clearance only, none of your clearances are technically high enough to be a party to this information, but I have no choice.

"Since all of you are in law enforcement at one level or another, you understand the need for secrecy. By sharing this information with anyone outside of this office, you will only hurt my top operative. Since he trusts you with this information, I hope he will have no future regrets. His life may well depend upon your ability keep this information in complete confidence.

"After saying all that, I would like to introduce to you first, Mr. Eric Flannigan, the Director of U.S. Special Operations Command, (USSOCOM), and to Lieutenant Commander Jacob Callander of the Counterterrorism Operations Unit, U.S. Special Operations, Special Reconnaissance Division. As you can tell by the name of the unit, they are our front line defense against homegrown and world terrorists. Now please, ask your questions, but don't expect all of them to be answered. The less you know, the safer not only you are but they are."

"Jacob" Devon says in a quiet but shocked voice "I never had a clue. You just dropped out of our lives fifteen years ago. This is what you were doing? This is why we never heard from you again? I'm speechless" he says.

"Wow Jacob. I would have never guessed" Mallory cries softly.

"Awesome" Eli adds with a proud grin. "I knew you were going to amount to something good when we were kids, but this, this is over the top" he admits. Kat just sits and stares at

Snake, unbelieving and in shock of what her ears had just heard and her eyes had just seen.

"You will not say anything to Mom and Dad" Jacob orders. "The less people that know the smaller chance there is of anyone else finding out. I have put my whole adult life into this unit. I've managed to prevent my family from knowing anything. I will not put my parents in danger from a slip of the tongue. My goal will not be changed by my family. I never would have let any of you know, except these are extenuating circumstances. You've managed to stumble across something that should have never been noticed. We've been monitoring this situation for awhile now and now that things are starting to change rapidly, we've had to become more involved in the area."

"Just how involved are you in this whole operation?" questions Devon.

"Very, but to what extent, you will never know. There are many things that I cannot and will not divulge. These things could put my unit in danger. I've been working with some of them for most of my adult life. They're a lot like family to me, as I am to them. I will not compromise my Unit. I'm sorry" he says. "There really are no questions that I can answer for you. Just know that you four are not alone in this process. We are working for the same outcome, the safety of the United States of America and its citizens. You can still reach me by the same cell phone. I have not given this number out to anyone but the four of you. If ever the need arises and you find yourselves in trouble, don't hesitate to call me. It's part of my job, extracting U.S. Citizens from danger. We'll still be meeting together occasionally; I don't want any suspicions raised by acting out of character. I'm sure we've been watched frequently in the past."

"Any other questions?" asks Nicholas Rantrall. "Alright, take off Lieutenant Callander. We'll maintain our position for a few more moments to give you time to disappear."

"Thank you Sir" Jacob replies.

"Be safe, Marine"

"Always Sir" replies Jacob quietly as he disappears out the door. The room is so quiet you could hear a pin drop on the carpeting. Everyone seated at the table seems to be in some form of shock.

"You'll recover from this sudden notice quickly. Just remember that at no time, is it safe to even acknowledge that you were informed of anything untoward. If it's possible at all to forget this, I would recommend that. There are many people, the world over, that would love to know about Lieutenant Callander and his Unit. There is a rather large price on his head. Let's help keep him alive the way he does us. Thank you, ladies and gentlemen, for coming in today. We'll be in touch. I too, am available by phone should the need arise."

"Okay" Kat says as they reach the parking garage. "I guess I'll head back to Metro One. Talk to you all later" she says as she gets in her car and leaves.

Devon just stands there staring after her and thinking of his brother Jacob. The brother he thought was a lazy no good, the one that hurt his parents for no reason, the one he thought would never amount to anything.

"Earth to Devon" Mallory says gently as she waves one of her well manicured hands in front of his face.

"Oh, sorry" he says as he blinks and shakes his head as if to clear all thoughts and memories out of his mind. "I can't help but think"

"Yeah" interrupts Mallory "I know."

"Neither can I, but we don't want to draw attention to ourselves. So I suggest we head back to headquarters and get to work. The day must go on."

"Alright, let's go" Eli agrees. He looks the same as Devon, shell shocked. That's probably how I look too" she decides.

"Morning Detective" Kat says as she strides through the bull pen hurriedly, trying to gain the safety of her office for a few moments of privacy, a little time to think. But to no avail since Detective Rowald follows as quickly as Kat's walking. Shit, she thinks, there must be something new. "What can I do for you Detective?" she inquires as she stops in the doorway of her small office and spins around to confront Detective Des.

"I've got a few new reports, Sir, on the suspect that attacked you, Mike Andrews."

"Oh, thanks" she says as Des stops and hands her the reports. "I'll get to this in a moment" she promises. "I'm right in the middle of something else right now, so just give me a few minutes" she requests as she turns and closes the door before Des can enter. I need to think about everything that happened this morning. Snake, the Snake from the biker group, my Snake, a black ops guy? I can't believe it. Now, how am I supposed to act around him? I always thought of him as my friend, my protector, just Snake, but now I can't think of him that way, can I? He's not a just anything. I hate this. It makes me nervous.

Now I don't know how to act anymore. Stop, I can't think about this anymore, I need to work. "Detective" Kat says as she enters the bullpen. "I need the report on the horse rancher in Virginia. I want to go over that information, maybe go out and ask a few more questions. There's a connection between him and Mike Andrews. Let's see just what it is."

"Yes sir" Des answers.

"Alright, I'm heading out" Kat decides after she's gone over the report twice more. There are definitely some holes here that I need to fill. I'm sure Mark Jackman can help me out with those. "I'll be back in a few hours" she promises. "You can reach me on my cell if you need me" she informs Des.

"Yes Sir."

"Is Kat here" Devon asks as he walks into Metro One's bull pen.

"No Sir, she hasn't returned yet, you haven't spoken with her?" Des asks in a near panic.

"Nope, not today" he admits. "Where was she going?" he asks.

"She said something about that horse rancher and wanting to look around a little bit more, but that was yesterday afternoon. I just assumed she reported to Capitol Police headquarters instead of here, so I wasn't concerned" Des admits. "But now, I'm worried."

"Don't worry Detective, I'll make some calls. I'm sure it's nothing. Maybe she met up with Mike today or Snake. I'll give them a call" he assures her.

"Thank you, sir" Des responds in relief.

"Jacob, it's Devon, have you heard from Kat since yesterday?"

"No, she left yesterday around noon to head out to see that horse rancher in Virginia and hasn't contacted anyone since. Yeah, his name's Mark Jackman. He lives pretty close to the plane crash site. We went there after the crash and he showed us all the plane pieces and parts his ranch hands had located on his property, and then we had NTSB show up and pick them up for the investigation. He's the one that said he thought he saw it get hit, maybe with a surface to air missile.

"He seemed like a nice enough guy" he says nervously. "Yeah, great, thanks. Let me know as soon as you find her. Yeah man, thanks"

"Snake is heading over there. He said he's only about a half an hour from there right now, so we should know pretty soon what's going on. I'm sure she's fine" he reassures her.

"Thanks Deputy Chief Callander. She never misses work and she always calls when she's running late. I guess that's what has me so worried."

"I'm sure Jacob will call soon. I'll call you when I hear anything. I have to get back to headquarters; I'm in the middle of something. If she calls you before I do, just have her give me a call."

"I will, sir" Des promises.

I should be there within a half hour, Kat thinks. At least it's not too bad outside; cold and cloudy but not snowing at the moment. I'm grateful for that, she thinks. Snake, is he ever going to be my friend again she wonders as she almost passes the driveway to the horse farm. I forgot how beautiful this place was she thinks as she drives slowly down the long driveway.

At least he keeps his place plowed, and she pulls into a parking area back by the new horse barn. Maybe I'll start there, she decides, then changes her mind when Mark comes walking towards her from behind the horse barn.

"Lieutenant, what can I do for you?" he inquires.

I forgot how good looking he was, she thinks with a smile. I wouldn't mind getting to know him a little more, she decides as she puts a flirtatious smile on her face. This could be fun and besides, Devon and I don't have any ties, just casual sex, she reminds herself.

"I just remembered a few more things I wanted to ask you, Mark" she says.

"You drove all this way just to ask me a few more things" he says in disbelief. "Why didn't you just call?"

"I wanted to look at the areas on your property where you found the plane parts, and I wanted to see for myself if you had found anymore."

"You took quite a chance finding me home" he says. "I'm so seldom here for any length of time, that it's pretty much a hit or miss."

"Guess I got lucky" she says, and blushes after she realizes how she sounded.

Great, she thinks as she gives herself a mental kick in the pants. Now he'll think I'm a pushover, oh, shut up, she thinks. Let's take this back to business, she decides. "So, can you go with me around your property to show me where most of the parts from the plane were found?" she asks.

"Sure, how about on horseback?" he offers.

"Well, I've never really been on a horse, so I don't know" she says hesitatingly.

"I'll be with you and riding is no big deal, you'll do fine. You can investigate and learn at the same time" he adds coaxingly.

"Well, if you're sure" thinking this is going to be awesome and trying not to show too much excitement. "I've always wanted to try horseback riding" she admits.

"Great, than let's go and see which horse would be best for you" he decides. "How come you're here all alone today? Last time, there were three of you, so I just assumed you were partners?"

"No, we were just working together, not partners" she admits.

"But what about the female, wasn't she your partner" he wonders out loud.

"Yeah, that's Detective Des. We've been working so closely with the Capitol Police and the FBI that Des and I haven't had a lot of time to work together. She's been holding down the fort for me" she admits in a dwindling voice as she realizes just how much she hasn't talked with Des. I need to fix that, she thinks, I've treated her unfairly.

"Let's head to the big barn in the back. I keep extra saddles and stuff out there. We're still remodeling the new barn so we haven't moved everything up here yet" he admits. "You may want to drive back there, it's quite a distance from this barn" he suggests.

"Sure, jump in and we can take the car back."

"Thanks Kat" he adds with a smile. "Just park over towards the right" he says, once they reach the clearing for the old barn.

"I think you moving the barn closer to the house was a good idea" she decides after going down the long driveway. "It sure is a lot closer to the house that way. It must save you a lot of time when you go from barn to house."

"Yeah, it's a lot handier" he admits, "but this old barn, it's got a lot of things it's still responsible for" he says with a smile. "Let's go in the back."

"Who are all those guys over there" she asks after she spots six, maybe seven guys just hanging around the rear of the old barn.

"Oh, those are just the ranch hands" he says.

"They sure don't look like what I envisioned how ranch hands would look" she remarks. "But then again, what do I know about what a ranch hand looks like? I'm just a city slicker" she admits with a laugh.

"Here we are, the lights still work, since we're still using the barn" he says as he opens the rear door. "The saddles and gear are all over this way" and he leads her to the right rear corner of the barn.

"Hey, is that a motorcycle Mark?"

"Yeah" he admits "it was a gift from a friend."

"Nice" she adds "though I've never seen one like that" she

says while thoughts start racing through her mind. I'm in trouble here, I think. "The lights don't work very well over here" she says nervously.

"Sure they do" he insists "you just have to get into the actual tack room and switch on the overhead light for them to work."

"Oh" she says nervously. It's awfully dark in here she thinks when all of a sudden she's pushed into the blackest part of the room. She feels something grab her by the throat, and then everything goes black.

TWENTY TWO

Gray wintery light surrounds her as she wakes up choking on dust. Her hands are tied above her head and her feet just barely touch the floor. It must have been the pain in my arms that woke me up, she thinks. What the hell happened? I was just coming in here to get a saddle, we were going to go riding, she remembers. Mark? Why would he do something like this, she wonders, confused?

Everything's so dark, it's hard to see what's around me, she thinks foggily, still not a hundred percent awake.

"Kat, wake up now" Mark says. He pulls a string and a harsh light comes on and lights up the little tack room in the old barn. "I see you finally decided to join us" he adds with a laugh.

"What's happened, why are you doing this?" she asks in fear.

"Well, pretty lady, because you couldn't leave well enough alone, could you" he replies in disgust.

"This is all your fault you know. If you would have just stayed away, I wouldn't have had to resort to this."

"What are you going to do?" she asks in fear.

"Oh, nothing that you won't love" he assures her with a laugh. "We're going to enjoy each other for a while, then my "ranch hands" are going to have a turn, and I can tell you they're pretty excited by that thought. They all have special ways of entertaining women" he admits with a deep excited laugh. "That's why they have to wait till I'm done. There's not much left after they finish" he warns her with a small smile and an evil look in his eyes.

"I haven't done anything" she yells in a panic, "you need to let me go. There are people that will be looking for me" she warns him.

"Oh, honey, you were finished as soon as you showed up here alone. I can't let you go. There's too much danger for me in that. You know too much, saw too much. See, too much isn't a good thing" he laughs "at least not for you. For me, too much is great. Now hold still so I can undo your hands. There" he says after he picks her up and releases her hands from the hook that was holding them in the ceiling.

As her arms are let down, they start screaming in pain from the return of the blood flow. They're pretty much useless until all the feeling returns, she realizes in anger. But she still has her feet, and he doesn't know that she's a black belt. Unfortunately, the stab wound isn't healed completely yet, leaving her with a weak leg.

That will be a nice surprise for him she thinks until she realizes that he's been busy putting chains around her ankles, stopping her from being able to kick anyway. Damn it, she fumes, there's got to be a way out of this.

"Ready for some fun?" he whispers close to her ear. "What I'm going to do to you, you can't even imagine" he promises in a whisper. I thought he was so good looking, she realizes in fear. Evil comes in many forms, but I would have never thought he was like this, she thinks as she remembers her first meeting with him. Blonde, buff cowboy, she remembers with dismay.

I thought he was hot, damn it. He's nothing but a creep, an evil little scum bag.

"Let's play" he says as he pushes her onto an old piece of burlap that's lying on the floor. "I think we're ready for a little fun" he admits as he grabs the front of her shirt and rips it apart, buttons flying everywhere. Kat screams from the attack until he quiets her with the threat of a knife to the throat. "Make another sound and I'll use this" he promises as he just barely nicks her, and draws first blood. She shuts her mouth quickly and screams on the inside, knowing that there's no one

245

coming to her rescue this time. She's going to lose this battle. I can handle this, she says to herself as she feels her pants being cut off of her. My ankles are still chained together, but that won't stop this bastard, she thinks. He'll do what he wants, and then I'll just be leftover fun for his evil little friends.

"Well, aren't you a pretty thing, except for that cut on your thigh" he admires as he stands to study her naked body. "How does it feel when I do this" he asks as he sticks his finger in the cut and rips open the stitches. "It was nice, too bad it's all going to be destroyed" he remarks with pity after she stops moaning from the pain.

"No, you don't have to do this" she stammers in fear.

"Oh, but I do" he insists. "You just couldn't keep out of it. You had to come looking again. I think maybe I'll keep you for myself for a while" he taunts. "The 'ranch hands' can wait" he says with a laugh. "I'm going to enjoy this more than you know" he says on a big sigh. "Let's get started" and he kneels down to grab her by the nipples, tearing open the already bruised and cut tissue. "No screaming, remember. I don't want to kill you too soon" he threatens as he tears a rag into small enough pieces to stuff into her mouth. "There, no noise. Now I don't have to waste time shutting you up." He pulls her legs apart and moves in between them, freeing himself to begin. As he moves forward, he thrusts hard and fills her with a burning tearing pain. 'No' she screams on the inside as her head shakes back and forth. This can't be happening to me. Then the pain becomes so intense she feels a welcoming darkness approaching. Mark notices her losing consciousness and lets up. "Oh, no, no sleeping for you" he admonishes. "I don't want you to miss a moment" he insists as he sees her regain focus and he starts the brutal pounding again. Time has no meaning now, it's all about the pain, the all consuming pain. When he finally finishes, she's barely conscious and gray as the burlap she's lying on. "Wake up, Kat" he says as he slaps her lightly to bring her back.

In her mind she starts screaming again when she feels what he's done to her, the pain between her legs an agonizing burning pain, pain reaching up into her stomach and then her chest.

Tears leak out of her eyes and drip into the hair at the back of her head. I can't cry, she thinks, I'll choke on the rag.

"There you are" he says when he sees her eyes focus on him. He recognizes the fear that's in them now, recognizes the pain and he feels himself getting hard all over again, with excitement.

"Yeah, that's right, it's me darling. I did that to you, and I'm not through yet" he says as he smiles in anticipation. No, she screams on the inside, her head shaking back and forth rapidly, no, please, no more she's thinking as she feels him grab her arm and leg and flip her over.

Oh, god, no, not like this she thinks, screaming inside. She starts sobbing as she feels the searing, agonizing pain and loses consciousness quickly and completely this time. When she does wakes up, she's alone, but still lying on her stomach. The pain is so excruciating she can't take a deep breath, but she's alive, she thinks.

I can't believe I'm alive, just let me die now, she begs silently, please, let me die, please, I can't take any more. She just lies there, with her eyes closed and her spirit broke, as she swims in and out of consciousness. A noise wakes her up minutes, hours, or days later. I don't even know how long I've been here, she thinks in agony, as she tries to lie still, but the pain is so intense, she can feel consciousness dimming again and welcomes it.

I don't want anyone to know I'm awake, she thinks. I know I can't take anymore, either physically or mentally. The next time will kill me she knows. I hope Devon's not too upset. I know I'll probably never see him again, she realizes. I wanted him, I even thought I loved him, but he'll never want me again.

"Kat, are you awake" she hears. As soon as she hears that voice, she cringes in fear. Oh, please no, you bastard, not again, never again she begs silently, her body responding to the fear by releasing her bladder. It sounds different right now she thinks, less hollow, more like a regular room.

She slowly opens her eyes, just enough to see her surroundings. She's in a tack room, and all the horse stuff is lying around. But this is a different room than before, bigger and not as gray. There's a saddle and a mound of straw, and I'm not as cold as I was, she realizes. I've been covered with something, she thinks. Now why would he want to keep me warm?

Oh God, not again, she thinks in panic. Please, make this stop she begs silently, and then she goes into a total panic when she hears footprints. Her eyes well up with tears as she realizes whose footsteps those are.

"Kat, I'm glad to see you're finally awake" he acknowledges in excitement, when suddenly he hears an explosion off in the distance. He turns and runs to the door where a couple of his ranch hands meet him "go up to the gas fields and see if we had another mishap" he orders "you're of more use to me there than here right now" he says. He turns and refocuses on Kat. "Look at me" he commands and her heart jumps in panic.

As she slowly opens her eyes with fear, he notices and smiles that evil smile of his, his eyes cold and empty. So this is what pure evil in person looks like, she thinks. I can't believe I didn't recognize him for what he is. He's standing there staring at her when she hears a sound like a little kitten.

Meow... It sounds like its close. I wonder where it is, she thinks as she watches her attacker lose his concentration and slowly look for the kitten. "I don't have cats in my barns" he says slowly. "There had better not be one in here" he threatens as he takes a step to find the little invader.

The next thing she hears is a sound she recognizes from martial arts weapons training; a blade cutting through the air and striking its target. Mark staggers backwards grasping at his throat and almost lands on Kat, falling to his knees beside her. There's blood everywhere, she realizes in a daze.

What the hell is going on, who did this she thinks in a panic. Fear of the unknown is as strong or stronger than fear of the known for Kat, since her grasp on reality is off from the attack. As Mark gurgles and falls forward on his face, Kat notices a familiar figure enter the room out of the darkness. She closes her eyes and opens them again realizing that Snake has found her, and then she loses consciousness again.

"Wake up little kitten, you have seven lives and you're not going to lose one now." Kat opens her eyes and she's untied and wrapped up in something that smells like a horse blanket.

"Snake, how did you know I was here?" she asks weakly.

"Are you forgetting what family you're dealing with? Between the four of us, there's probably not much we don't know. Besides, Devon called and said you hadn't shown up for work today and I got a little suspicious, so I went on the hunt."

"Be careful, his hired thugs could be back at any time" she warns him weakly.

"Don't worry about them, a few friends of mine invited them to a party of their own. I don't think they'll be up to any more partying tonight. How do you feel?" he asks her in concern.

"I'm so sorry that you had to find me this way" she says as she starts sobbing.

"Shh" he gathers her closer, trying not to hurt her in the process, "it's all right now Kitten, you're safe."

"It's never going to be all right, Snake, never again" she responds quietly, between sobs. "I am never going to be all right. Just let me die now" she begs "please. I don't want to live this way" she insists. "I don't want anyone to know what he did to me" she admits.

"He was evil" he agrees quietly, a deadly look in his eyes "now he'll never be able to hurt you again" he says with a promise.

"It's too late Snake, what he did to me, it can never be taken back" she says in misery. "I'm surprised I'm still alive. I didn't know anyone could survive that" she says through the sobbing.

"I had one of my unit members clean you up and dress you, he's a medic" he says reassuringly. "I know what he did to you. You will be okay, with help, you'll be okay."

"He saw me" Kat says in shock, tears running down her face."Don't let him see me" she says in a panic "I'm disgusting" she groans "I can't let anyone see me ever again" she cries.

"Where's the party" they hear a familiar voice say as they turn and see Devon walk in. As he approaches, she breaks down in tears again. "God, it's so good to see you" Devon admits with a lump in his throat. "You had me so worried" he says as he holds her in his arms while gently stroking her hair "everything will be alright."

"I have to get out of here before anyone else shows up" Snake reminds them "but I need to talk to you first" he informs Devon "privately. Remember what I tell you, it's top security. Devon, you're the hero here. I don't exist. I was never here, and by the way, your unnamed skinned dead body, he never existed either" Snake says quickly and quietly. "Meet me outside to talk. You'll be okay for a couple of minutes, won't you kitten?"

"Yeah, just don't leave me for too long" she admits in an exhausted voice.

"We'll be just outside the door" he promises her.

"She's been hurt real bad" Jacob says quietly, so Kat can't hear him. "She needs a Doctor right away and probably a shrink in the near future. I have a friend about ten minutes from here that's a doctor; he just doesn't look like one. I'll call him and give him a heads up. She's not going to want to see one, but she has to" he informs him, anger in every word. "She's going to argue about this, but you need to insist and just take her, it's for her own good" he insists.

"Those so called ranch hands that were here with Mark Jackman are dead; my unit took care of them, the bastards. They were drawing straws on who got her next. Also, check out this barn, I think you'll find things that will help with the case" he suggests. "I'm going in to say bye to Kat, then I think I deserve a ride on one of my bikes, for a change."

"Kitten, I have to go" Snake tells her gently "but Devon promises to take care of you, so please let him, for me" he begs.

"Okay" she agrees quietly "if you say so" she murmurs, almost unconscious again.

"Good, I promise I'll see you later" he says and with a kiss on the forehead, he leaves the tack room, mounts the custom bike with the air brushed mural of a striking cobra on the side and roars off into the darkness.

"Well" Devon says "he blew out of here like a hurricane."

"Yeah" she whispers "he had to, remember?"

"That still seems unreal to me. Now, are you okay?" he asks.

"Yes and no, but I'll be okay" she says.

"You need to see a Doctor and let him decide if you're okay."

"No" she denies adamantly "No Doctor. I want no one to know what happened to me!" "**NO ONE**" she says louder, in a panicked voice.

"Shhh, it's alright" he promises a hysterical Kat. "I promise I won't leave you, but you have to see a Doctor, I promised Jacob and he's calling one as we speak."

"Please, Devon, don't make me do this" she begs, tears streaming down her face.

"I'm sorry honey, but Jacob told me you were hurt and that under NO circumstances were you to talk me out of the doctor's visit. What happened to you Kat? What would make Jacob so insistent?"

"Nothing" she replies and looks at the floor.

"Look at me Kat, you can tell me, talk to me." He begs her quietly.

No" she says "NO! I can't tell you, I can't tell anyone, ever!"

That son of a bitch, he raped her he realizes in anger, that son of a bitch. "The cavalry are here, I believe" he says when he hears the cars pulling up, the doors slamming.

"No" Kats says as she grabs Devon "don't let them see me like this, leave me some dignity, please" she cries, tears blurring her vision.

"Shhh, it's alright, I'll make everyone stay away, I promise."

"Thanks" she says wearily. "How long have I been here?"

"About twenty four hours, why" he asks.

"I've been locked up and tied up since I got here yesterday, I guess, since it's been twenty four hours." It seems like weeks, she thinks.

"Were you always in this room?" he asks.

"No, the first room was all gray and dusty and dark. I think it's towards the back corner of the old barn" she mumbles in confusion.

"Okay, let me go check in there for your clothes and coat. Who knows, I might get lucky. That seems to be the first order of business here, I'll be quick and be right back" he promises as he hurries out of the room. "I found it" he says as he runs back into the room that's kept Kat prisoner for a whole day.

"Want me to help you?" he asks.

"No! I can do it myself" she says fearfully. "Please, just stand outside the door so no one can come in" she begs, and so you can't see what happened to me, she thinks.

I wish I could take a long hot shower, I'd stay in it all day and I'd never get out. I could scrub him off me, she thinks tiredly. Soon, I need to go home. I might just go there and lock myself in forever, or maybe even disappear forever. No one would know then she thinks as she pulls on her pants, reawakening some serious pain. There's blood, she realizes, I wonder why I didn't think of that, and her shirt covering her bloody breasts, painful to the touch she realizes and there are no buttons left on my shirt, but at least I have a coat to cover that up. No one will be able to tell, dressed like this. I don't have a brush or a pony for my hair she realizes and starts crying again. Not having a pony is not a reason for tears she tells herself angrily.

"Okay" she says "you can come back in Devon, I'm ready."

"How do you feel?" he asks tentatively.

"Better now that I have my own clothes on, thanks."

"Are you ready to head out of here?"

"I've been ready since I got here yesterday" she admits.

"Let's go then, we have people to meet."

"Kat" Mallory cries when she catches a glimpse of her out of the corner of her eye, "are you alright?"

"I'm fine" she replies as she grabs Devon's arm and shrinks into his side.

Mallory stops dead in her tracks as her gaze flies to Devon's and understanding dawns. With tears in her own eyes for Kat, she backs away and continues with her small talk. "You look good Kat, I'll see you soon," she promises softly.

"Thanks" she says with a huge sigh of relief, as Devon

shakes his head in thanks.

"We have someone we need to see" Devon says. "We'll meet you back in D.C. We should be back by this evening, maybe tomorrow. I'm not sure but I probably won't get together with you until tomorrow. Make sure you search this farm from top to bottom. This bastard was into something and I want to know what" he orders with a vicious look in his eyes.

"Sure thing Devon" Mallory promises, totally understanding. "We have a whole group of agents on their way right now."

"Good" he says "then we're out of here. I'll talk to you tomorrow, or you can reach me on my cell, if it's an emergency."

"Will do" reassures Mallory as she watches them leave slowly through the barn, Kat's movements restricted and very painful looking.

This nightmare just won't end, Kat thinks as she's left in an exam type room, waiting for a Doctor to walk in. I don't need this, she thinks to herself as she hears footprints outside the door causing her to start shaking uncontrollably.

Oh, god, not again, she flashes to the barn. Please, God, not again, she repeats the mantra in her head until the door opens and someone says soothingly that "it's all right. This will help you relax a little." The next thing she remembers is waking up on a small cot in the corner of a bright and cheerful room. Wow, I must have been tired, she thinks before remembering everything that happened just before this. It wasn't a nightmare, she thinks in agony. It all happened.

"Welcome back Kat" Devon says when he notices her eyes are open. "You took a good nap" he says with a smile. "Feel better?"

"Yeah, I think I do, at least a little" she murmurs.

"Excellent. Do you think you're up to going home?" he asks teasingly.

"Yes, please, right now" she says hopefully.

"You bet. The Doctor said that you're going to be fine, you just need a lot of rest, more than this nap gave you" he says. "I promised him you'd get that at home. He said great, but he wants to see you first and then you can go. That's him, knocking" he says and calls come in.

"Kat, I'm Doctor Halle, how are you feeling?" he asks as he sticks a thermometer in her mouth.

"Better" she replies around the thermometer.

"Great" he says and starts to take her blood pressure. "Could you excuse us for a moment, Deputy Chief?" asks Dr. Halle.

"Sure, I'll be right outside this door" he promises Kat and with a small sharp nod, Kat agrees.

"Kat, I have a few things to tell you" the Doctor says. "You were brutalized, quit badly as a matter of fact. I've never seen so much bruising and tearing. You must be experiencing some major pain?" he asks gently. "But, you will get better, I promise. There are already signs of healing. Because of the things he did to you, you'll experience some pain for a few weeks at least." he says in pity. She absorbs everything he says, but it feels like it's coming from a great distance, actually it feels like a nightmare, not reality.

"It's alright Doctor, I understand."

"You need to contact your doctor and be watched" the Doctor insists "we don't want any more trouble. Because of what happened, there could be more" he warns her.

"I promise, I'll see my doctor. I want to thank you for taking care of me" she says quietly, without emotion, eyes empty of any feelings.

"Take care, Kat" the Doctor says as he leaves the room, sadness in his eyes and on his heart.

"Devon, time to go" she warns him when he enters the room as the doctor leaves. "Let's go now" she says as she struggles to sit up under all the blankets.

"Here" he laughs "let me help you."

"I think the blankets weigh more than you do" he teases. "Alright, next, shoes" he reminds her.

"Oh, yeah, I forgot I took them off" she says absently.

"It feels good to be home" she admits as she walks into her apartment after a long and uncomfortable ride. Even though it's messy, its mine, and it's safe.

"Let's call for takeout. What would you like to eat" Devon

asks.

"You don't have to stay" she says quietly. "I'm just going to take a long hot shower and then go to bed" she promises.

"I'm staying Kat, all night. I'm not leaving you alone. I want you to sleep and you won't if you're scared."

"Thank you Devon, I'll eat anything I guess. It's been a couple of days so I am kind of hungry" she responds as she gathers her pajamas and slippers and heads to the bathroom. "Just surprise me" she says as she closes the door.

"Kat, open the door, are you all right?" Devon yells.

She jerks awake, realizing she fell asleep in the tub, and the water that was so gloriously hot has gone chilly in the air. "Sorry" she calls "I fell asleep, I'll be right out."

"Devon, I'm so sorry" she says when she opens the door and moves into the living room. "I didn't mean to fall asleep" she admits in surprise. "I must have been tired. It has been a long couple of days" she adds as an excuse.

"No problem, Kat. As long as you're okay, I'm good. You do need to eat though. I ordered Chinese, for you Sesame Chicken."

Thanks for taking care of me. I really appreciate it. I appreciate all that you've done for me" she says as she moves in close and his arms close around her making her feel safe.

"Let's eat, then rest" he says with a smile. "I'm kind of tired myself tonight" he admits, trying to relax her and prepare her for bed.

"That was delicious" she declares with a yawn. "I can't eat anymore, but I'll save it for tomorrow."

"No" he says "I'll toss it, it's not good warmed up. Tomorrow we'll try something new. I'm ready for some sleep, how about you?" he asks.

With Kat sound asleep in his arms, Devon finds temporary peace, but no justice. He thanks Jacob for finding her. I wish it could have been sooner, but at least she's alive. She'll heal, the doctor said so, but she may be haunted by this for a long time, and with that thought Kat wakes up with a scream of pain.

"Shh, Kat, it's Devon, everything's all right, I promise. It's okay" he keeps saying until she quiets down and opens her eyes with recognition.

"I'm sorry, it was a nightmare" she mumbles. "I'm sorry" she keeps saying over and over through her tears.

"It's all right; you have nothing to be sorry for. You did nothing wrong. What he did to you, it's not your fault. It only matters to me because he hurt you. Not because of what you think" he says quietly. "You're still Kat, and I love you" he murmurs. Kat sighs with fatigue and falls quickly into sleep again, hopefully this time a more healing rest.

TWENTY THREE

"Good morning, darlin" Devon sings out in a happy voice. "How are you today?" he asks as he greets her in the hall with a fresh cup of coffee and a happy and normal attitude.

"I feel better!" she admits with surprise. The healing has begun.

"Great, let's have some breakfast. How would you like your eggs?" he asks.

"Scrambled please, with ketchup" she grins.

"Gross" he says with a wink. "Eggs are coming right up. There's today's paper and some juice, eggs will be just a couple more minutes."

"Thanks, Devon. I am so far in debt to you for all your help" she says.

"No way! You don't owe me anything" he says with a kiss. "What's on the agenda for today?" he asks.

"Since its Thursday" she says with a quick look to make sure she's right "then its work."

"You can take some time, before you go back into work."

"No, I'm ready. Work keeps my mind busy" she admits. "So it's work."

"All right then, let's get ready for work" he replies. She never gives herself a break. I hope this isn't a bad idea, he thinks. "We'll take my car; yours was being driven back by Eli, so we can pick it up later."

"Shit, it just dawned on me, my weapon and my shield. I had them with me. I have no idea where they are now" she says worriedly.

"Not to worry" he says with a smile, "I got them yesterday. You'll find them in the living room on the desk."

257

"Thank you again Devon, for always thinking ahead. I used to be that way" she says with a sigh.

"And you will again, just give yourself a little time Kat. The past couple of days were pretty bad, but they'll fade with time. They'll become less important in the future.

"I can't wait" she says with longing. "The sooner they go away the better. Okay, I'm all set" she decides, combing her hair and pulling it back, then changing her mind and leaving it lose. Pulled back makes me look bad, she realizes and I don't need that, it would raise too many questions.

"Good morning Devon, Kat" greets Mallory and Eli. "We were wondering if you'd be in today."

"Oh, yeah, we're both ready. What did you find" Devon asks while Kat maintains her quiet and looks tired and slightly haunted.

"You won't believe this" Eli says with enthusiasm.

"What?" Devon asks.

"A rocket launcher" Eli says with a grin.

"A what?" Devon and Kat ask together.

"You heard right, a rocket launcher. That ranch owner was the one that said he saw something like a ground to air missile hit that plane. He did, the bastard. He saw it because he launched it."

"Wow" Devon says with a whistle. "Things are starting to come together. Let's do a new board and start connecting them" he suggests.

"Devon, I need to check into Metro One, but I'll be back" Kat promises quietly.

"Are you sure" he asks as he pulls her off to the side.

"Yeah, I'm sure" she says reassuringly. "I need to do this."

"If you're sure, but if you can wait a few minutes, I can come along with you."

"No, I need to do this alone, Devon. It's my job.

"Alright, if you're sure, I'll see you later then" he agrees uncomfortably.

"Lieutenant, I am so glad you're back" Des cries. "What did you find out?" she asks with excitement.

"Find out about what?" Kat asks in confusion.

"The horse rancher, that's where you went the other day, isn't it?

"Yeah, that's where I was. Oh, Mallory and Eli found a rocket launcher in one of the old horse barns."

"Did you arrest him?"

"No, he's dead" she admits emotionlessly."There were a few problems. The FBI came in and to protect themselves they had to kill him."

"Oh" Des remarks, disappointed. "So no more information from him huh, that sucks."

"Yeah, it sucks" Kat agrees with a shiver.

"The Captain said to tell you when you got here that he's waiting for a report" Des informs her.

"I'll head up there now."

"Go right on in Lieutenant, he's been expecting you." Leslie informs Kat when she reaches his office.

"Thanks" Kat replies.

"What have you got for me Lieutenant?" Captain Hall asks.

"I visited that Horse Rancher in Virginia, Mark Jackman. He was the person who stated that he thought he had seen a land to air missile strike the Speaker of the House's plane. I wanted to look around the property one more time and see if he remembered anything, anything more about that explosion. Unfortunately, I found out the hard way that he was involved in the whole incident. I was attacked and held hostage right after I arrived there and unfortunately wasn't freed until the Callander's, with their special units arrived, and found me contained in the tack room of the old barn on Jackman's property. It was Jackman that put me in that room, and made sure that I couldn't escape.

"The Agents that went out to the property have discovered a rocket launcher located in that same barn and confiscated it as evidence. They're still searching the rest of the property, but expect to be done sometime today."

"Very good Lieutenant, your hostage experience did you no ill harm?" he asks with concern.

"No Sir, I'm fine, aggravated, but fine, thanks."

"Please keep me informed of any further news." Captain

Hall commands.

"Detective, my office" Kat snaps as she walks through the bull pen.

"Yes Sir" Des says.

"Take a seat Detective; I have a few things I want to say to you."

"Yes Sir" Des say's, a question in her tone.

"First, don't get used to this" Kat warns "but I want to apologize to you for not having you more involved with these cases. You've been doing a lot of the grunt work, the investigating, but it's been without me. Since I'm you're Lieutenant, I'm responsible for you and I should have been working more closely with you than I have been. However, I'm going to rectify that situation now."

"Thank you Sir."

"I hadn't realized that I had put you outside this investigation, but I had and from now on you go with me everywhere I go Detective."

"Yes Sir, thank you Sir."

"Now, we're working on some evidence which we found at Jackman's ranch in Virginia. I'm getting ready to head over there now. Get ready Detective; you're with me on this."

"Yes Sir" she responds.

"Devon, I need to talk to you about the Jackman farm" Eli requests firmly.

"What about it?" he asks cautiously.

"While we were searching the property, there was an area over by an old gas well that looked like the floor of a slaughter house. There was blood everywhere."

Devon stands very still for a moment and then says "Eli that never existed."

After thinking about it for a second Eli replies "right, I never saw anything."

"Good."

"Kat, welcome back" Devon says with a smile of relief. "We're updating the board and could
 use your memory on a few of these things."

"Sure" she replies expressionlessly.

"Alright everyone, let's go back to the beginning. The first murder Kat, please."

"The first murder was William Blaketon, the House Majority Leader, killed by a serial killer, or so we thought at the time because the person that murdered him had also killed someone in the same way, in Pennsylvania. We later discovered that the murderer was Elroy Wade, an ex-biker that rode with the Callander's brother, Jacob aka Snake.

Elroy Wade was found murdered by way of multiple stab wounds to the abdomen and then left in a house that was rigged to explode when someone stepped on a switch, located under the mat at the front door. The house was brought into question when a snitch of Deputy Chief Callander's told him he could find the murderer there. Deputy Chief Callander was injured in that explosion. Although we don't know at this time who it was pegged for, we believe it was Deputy Chief Callander, since it was his snitch that called his attention to that building."

"Murder number two" she continues "Karen Delrose, the House Minority Leader; her murder has been listed as poison. The Medical Examiner found it purely by hunch after he ran some very delicate toxicology testing. The poison was found to be from a species of jelly fish found only off the coast of Australia, but obtainable via the internet black market.

"The third murder, Jeff Stewart, died on the island of Maui, in the Hawaiian Islands. His death is also listed as poison, from a blow fish found only in Japan, however, obtainable also on the internet black market.

"The Medical Examiner on Maui did not make that differentiation; he had originally listed his death as an accidental drowning. The medical examiner for the department of homeland security retested the body and found the poison. The poison was absorbed through a slice of lime on his drink that got into a tooth surface that the victim had a hole in. It was relisted as murder.

"The last murder, the Speaker of the House, her plane exploded in air while she was flying it killing all on board, including her husband and two children. There were suspicions of a land to air missile, leading us to the horse rancher in Virginia who informed us that he had indeed found plane fragments and had put them in his barn. He also stated that he had seen the explosion and thought he saw a missile strike the plane just before the explosion. He also suggested that it was a land to air missile. After going back to the horse property it was found that he did indeed see a missile and that he or someone that was associated with him had used a rocket launcher, hitting the plane and causing it to explode.

I had gone to the farm to question him regarding the crash parts and possibly more witnesses. They found me locked in the tack room being held hostage by the owner of the ranch, Mark Jackman. He was killed in a fight that occurred when Agents showed up to release me" she completes by sitting down and placing her crossed hands on the table.

"Wow Kat, that was excellent. Nothing wrong with your memory" Mallory compliments with a grin. Kat thanks her with a slight smile and a head nod.

"Alright, thanks Kat. Let's look at the connection between all of these people. They were all members of the House of Representatives, all held elected positions. They were all killed on a Friday, exactly seven days apart. That has to mean something; we need to work on that. They were all killed differently except the two poisons and yet those were different also. There's another connection. All of their positions were filled less than a week after the last murder. That has to mean something, too."

"That's what we have so far, who can add to our information list?" Devon asks.

"I have some information to add" reports a unit member of Mallory's. "I've run some checks on purchasers of those two poisons on the black market, and I've come up with a list of companies. The next step is to check the companies themselves. Who owns them, where they're located, why they purchased those specific poisons? I should have some information about that later this afternoon" he guesses.

"The first reports that came in listed most of the companies as scientific development organizations on the cutting edge of creating antidotes for the poisons. They must have the actual samples to work with to create the antidotes. They look like up front companies and probably just find it easier to obtain black market samples rather than going through the thousands of pages of applications necessary to obtain legal samples. This business is so competitive that even a day poses the risk of putting them too far down on the list of discoverer's. There's no money in that, so they need to be at the top of the list in order to find an antidote to sell before anyone else. It does tend to create a huge window of competitiveness, large enough that it's a pretty dangerous game to be caught up in."

"Excellent work Agent, thank you" Devon says.

"Anyone else have anything?"

"I've been working on the businessmen angle" replies a unit member of Eli's. "I located a couple of connections to the Maui businessmen group. I ran the pictures you obtained from the hotel and have come up with only one match. He happens to be the new Majority Leader for the House of Representatives. He has some minor issues in his background, mostly from when he was an adolescent. As an adult he's walked the straight and narrow. I'm still waiting on names for the other three businessmen."

"Good" Devon remarks "see if you can push that a little faster. We need their names and connections as soon as possible. Eli, how do you feel about a trip to Maui? I think it's time to question the bartender. He's had long enough to relax; now it's time to put some pressure on him."

"Yeah, I'll set that up now. I would love to interview him" he adds with a grin.

"Mallory, we need someone to head to Texas and dig up information on the new Majority Leader. Why and how he's connected and who else belongs to that group. It's time to pull strings and see which ones break."

"I'll be out of here this morning" she promises with a smile.

"Kat, we have an appointment this morning with Director Malik, of homeland security. He's requested our presence at ten thirty, at his headquarters. If there's nothing else to add, let's go out and find more, Eli, Mallory, keep us updated" Devon orders."

"Kat, Detective, let's move to the homeland security head-quarters." Devon says. As the three of them prepare to leave, Kat's cell chirps.

"Hold on a sec" she says, "I have to take this."

"Kitten" Snake says from the other end of the line "are you busy?"

"A little, we're heading over to speak with Director Malik of homeland security. What's up" she asks as she turns away from both Devon and Des in order to concentrate.

"I want to set up a meet with everyone, as soon as possible."

"I'm sorry Snake, but that's going to be a little difficult. Eli and Mallory are getting ready to leave for Maui and Texas respectively."

"Oh, I didn't know that more information was found."

"It wasn't" she explains "that's why they're going there. They're on their way to interview the bartender and to look into the background of your friend from Texas."

"He's not my friend" he argues "an acquaintance, someone that has one of my bikes, but he's no friend. Fine, when are they due back" he asks after a momentary lapse.

"Probably not for three days or so" she says. "It takes about twelve hours to get to Maui, and I think they mentioned dropping Mallory off in Texas so she can get started, then going the rest of the way so Eli can spend some time with the bartender of the hotel that Jeff Stewart stayed in, prior to his murder."

"Alright" he admits "I give up. Would you call me please, when everyone is back so that I can set up a time for a meeting?"

"Sure" she agrees "as soon as they're back. Is something wrong?" she asks.

"No, not really, but I do need to talk with everyone."

"As soon as they're back, I'll call."

"Thanks Kitten, and hey, take care of yourself, please" he says.

"Yeah, I promise." After hanging up, she turns and remembers that she had an audience and that's why she turned away to begin with. Then she forgot, so it's with a jolt that she realizes they're still waiting for her and listening to everything she says.

"That was Snake" she says to Devon's questioning look. "He wanted to set up a meet with everyone, but I told him it would have to wait for probably three days or so now, until Mallory and Eli get back. He said it wasn't anything important, though."

"Okay then, let's get going, we're going to be late if we don't hustle" he replies.

"You know" Devon steams after they're scheduled meeting "that man thinks he's the most important individual this city has. Everyone had better drop anything they're doing when he summons. And then to not be here, that took a lot of guts. He could have had his secretary call and let us know that the meeting was canceled or that something else came up and he couldn't be there."

"Yeah, he's an ass" Kat says in agreement.

I wish I would have packed lighter clothes, Mallory thinks after deplaning in Texas. Damn its hot here she groans after wiping her face for the third time in ten minutes. After finally getting her rental car, she starts the three hour trip to Waco wishing the air conditioner would work faster. I'm going to be wilted by the time I get there if this stupid hunk of junk doesn't start cooling down pretty fast. According to the GPS, I should be arriving in the next ten minutes, ten long minutes she thinks, waiting anxiously to get out of her oven. I'm going to complain to the damn rental company about this POS (piece of shit) they rented me, she promises to anyone lucky enough to hear her bitch.

This is nothing but a small backwoods town, and I'm feeling pretty bitchy she thinks as she gets out of the car, tired and hot. Phew, at least there's a breeze, that'll help some. Now, some food would be good. She gazes down the narrow paved road, only a few cars to be seen. It seems pretty deserted around here.

This is a nice looking hotel though, a three story brick building with a beautiful trellis that climbs the wall next to the front entryway. A pink bougainvillea loaded with flowers, perfumes

the air as she walks towards the hotel entrance. There's a picture perfect wall waterfall on the other side of the entryway, the
sun glancing off the water causing it to glisten. There's a very
nice welcoming feel to the hotel and no expense was spared
here. Must be an up and coming town, considering where it's
located. Let's check this hotel out and see if they have a restaurant.

"Can I help you Miss?" asks the young male clerk behind
the desk.

"Yeah, I need a room for the night."

"One night, Miss" he asks with an appreciative eye.

"No, I'll probably need it for two" she answers absentmindedly, looking the foyer of the hotel over, emergency exit, no
one about besides the clerk. "It's pretty quiet here" she comments to the clerk as she glances back at him and smiles.

A full length mirror behind the desk covers the entire room,
showing tall pillars of flowers scattered about. Some antique
looking formal seating placed strategically for the guests comfort and a huge see through fireplace, quiet now but loaded
with firewood, waiting for its next opportunity to warm its
guests.

"This is some place" she comments to the clerk and with
her stunning looks and beautiful smile, he stammers and blushes from all the attention. She laughs to herself as she watches
his color go high, then low, then high, as he tries to concentrate
on the paperwork, and she scolds herself mentally. He's just a
kid for crying out loud, behave yourself.

"Here you are Miss; you're in room three-oh-four."

"So, is this place deserted?"

"Oh no Miss, we're almost full."

"What, why?" she questions.

"There's a conference in the town of Galopolia, about ten
miles from here. There are a lot of people attending it. You
were lucky that you got here when you did; you got the second
to last room available."

"Wow" she exclaims "I am lucky, thanks! Now, I hope you
have a restaurant here" she says in a questioning tone.

"Oh absolutely" he admits with a big Texan smile. "It's one

of the most popular restaurants for fifty miles. I recommend reservations if you're meeting someone here for dinner though. It's not easy to get a seat at dinner time."

"Oh, I'll just eat now and worry about later, later" she says with a wink, which starts his coloring flying high and then low. He's so cute; too bad he's so young. He can't be a day over eighteen, if that.

"Just point me to the restaurant and I'll move along" she promises.

"Oh, sure, it's out those doors on the left, then two doors down on the left. You can't miss it."

"Thanks so much" she says and picks up her purse and heads out the doors on the left.

Ahhh, I smell something wonderful she decides as she follows the clerk's directions and finds herself in a beautifully appointed restaurant, quiet and tastefully decorated. *You can feel the money in here* she thinks as the Hostess guides her to an intimate booth for two near the bar entrance.

"What can I get you to drink?" she asks.

"I would love a tall glass of iced tea, please. It's pretty hot out there" she says.

"You're from back east, aren't you?" the hostess asks with a smile.

"What gave me away" she replies with a grin.

"It's chilly out there for Texans Miss; it's only hot for easterners. You just came from a snow area, I'm guessing."

"Yes, I did, amazing" Mallory says "I thought it was blistering."

The hostess laughs with delight when she learns that Mallory came from temperatures in the mid teens and plenty of snow.

"Here you are, this will cool you down" she promises as she places a tall frosted amber glass of iced tea in front of Mallory, a straw next to it and announces that her waiter will be right with her.

"Thank you so much" Mallory says as she hurriedly opens the straw for that first wonderfully cold drink of tea.

"My name is Chris and I'll be your waiter today" a young

267

man says, with blonde curls and a diamond stud earring. "What can I get for you?" he asks with a smile.

"I saw that you have chicken salad as a special for today?" Mallory responds in inquiry.

"Yes Miss and it's delicious. It's one of our restaurants favorites."

"I'd like that" she replies "and a side of seasonal fresh fruit please."

"Absolutely, will there be anything else?"

"No, I think that will do it" she admits with a smile.

"It'll just take a few minutes, I'll be right back."

"Thanks" she murmurs as she takes her phone out of her purse to answer it.

"Hi Devon, yeah, I'm here. I was just seated for lunch, I'm starving" she admits. "It took me three hours to get here from the airport, so it's definitely out in the middle of nowhere, but the hotel is like a five star palace. It can't be too old; everything's too new looking for that. It was just shocking when I got into town. The town is a blink and gone town and yet this huge hotel sits on the main thoroughfare. Looks like maybe it's an up and coming town" she adds thoughtfully. "Wait; let me get my pen and notebook, okay, shoot. Yeah, I got it" she says "thanks. Yes, I'll stay in touch. Later" she says as she hangs up. Hmm, at least I have an address and phone number. That should make things a little easier, she hopes.

"Oh, thanks so much" she says to the waiter as he places her food in front of her. As she digs in, she wonders where in the area this address could possibly be. I'll have to look it up in my GPS. I don't want to start making anyone suspicious yet, she thinks with a groan of pleasure as the first bite is swallowed. Wow, that was really good, she decides as she's finishes her meal.

"How was everything?" the waiter asks when he comes back with the check.

"Delicious" she answers with a satisfied smile "please, just put this on my tab. I'm in room three-oh-four."

"Yes Miss, thank you and have a wonderful day."

"Oh, I will" she promises "wait, I have a question before

you go. Do you know this address?" she asks him.

"Not that one in particular but I know where the road is" he admits.

"Great, can you give me directions please?"

"Sure, it's easy. Just go out the parking lot exit and turn right. About a mile and a half on the right is this road. Turn right onto it and just keep going. It's a pretty new development, a lot of businessmen live there" he adds with a smirk. "You can't miss the big fancy houses."

"Alright, thank you" she says as she gets to her feet to leave.

Time to get back to work. I'll just head to my room, check it out while it's still light, then go searching, she decides. Nice room, one king sized bed, a large dresser and desk with a table and two chairs. Its expensive looking and smells new she notices with pleasure. No problem sleeping in this suite, she decides. The bathroom has a sunken Jacuzzi tub, a separate shower and marble countertops.

No expenses were spared in this Hotel. Maybe I should have checked the price first before I signed. Not bad she thinks for a hundred-twenty-five per night, after digging out the receipt. Checkout time is eleven a.m. Good, I'll stay tomorrow night also, and then leave, Eli's due back here day after tomorrow.

TWENTY FOUR

"Wow" she says when she gets halfway down the road. These are the biggest house's I've ever seen! People actually live in these, she wonders as she see's huge estates taking up every spare inch down the road.

Brick fences follow the lines of the property designating what property belongs to whom. Well, this will make things a little more difficult she decides when she notices that you have to pull into the driveway, then pick up a phone and listen for instructions. They must have some pretty intense home security systems on these big boys, I know I would. Now the address, she looks at her notes as she slows her driving so she can find the right number. Must be down further, no, almost, there it is, she notices in relief. Of course, it's the biggest freaking house on the road. It looks like a castle, with turrets and everything, it's pretty ostentatious. Why not just take out a neon sign with an arrow pointing towards the house blinking rich bastard lives here.

A car has pulled in behind her while she was daydreaming and it gives a little beep. When she turns to look in her rear-view mirror, she sees legs walking towards her, in some type of uniform. Oh oh, busted, she groans.

"Can I help you Miss?" asks the security officer.

"Yes, I mean no" she admits "I've come here to talk with Quinton Uqbahtor, the new Majority Leader."

"Well, you've got the right house, is he expecting you?"

"Probably not, I've just gotten in from D.C. and want to talk with him."

"He only sees people by appointment, Miss. I'm sorry. You'll have to call and schedule a time to see him before we can allow you on his property. Those are his rules, Miss, not ours."

"Thank you officer, I'll call for an appointment" she promises as she puts her car in reverse and waits for them to move.

While she's heading the way she came, she grabs her cell phone and makes the call for an appointment.

"Mr. Uqbahtor's office, can I help you?" asks a young sounding female.

"Yes, I would like to make an appointment to speak with Mr. Uqbahtor."

"Certainly Miss, let me look at his schedule. He has an opening on the twenty-fourth of April."

"What!" Mallory says in disbelief, "April! No, I want one for today."

"Oh no, we can't schedule one for today, he's got an early dinner engagement tonight and will be leaving within the hour. I'm sorry."

"Fine" Mallory says "thanks" and hangs up in a huff. These people think they're so important that they're making appointments two months in advance. That's ridiculous, she steams. Well, let's see, there's only one nice restaurant in the area, and they did say it was the most popular, so maybe he's going there. I'll go back to the hotel and see if I can get a glimpse of the reservation list. If I have any luck at all, he'll be on it in red, she smirks.

"Back so soon Miss?" the clerk calls out as he see's Mallory making a beeline for the
restaurant.

"Yep, I forgot to make a reservation when I was here earlier, so I want to get one in now"
she says as she walks by quickly.

"Amazing" he says quietly, people just don't listen, he muses as he shakes his head no slowly. Too bad, she's so pretty too. I wish I could help her, but they really don't care for me so I would probably make it worse, he decides.

"Can you help me?" a voice sounds behind him, so he turns and yep, there she is.

"What can I do for you Miss?" he asks politely.

"I can't seem to get a reservation for tonight. Can you help me with that?" Mallory asks sweetly.

"I probably can't, but I'll try" he offers grudgingly.

"Thank you so much" she says with a flirty smile. He just blushes and turns to the phone sitting behind him on the counter.

"I have a woman here that just checked into her room an hour or so ago and she needs a reservation for dinner. She's willing to take any seat available" he adds coaxingly. "Yeah, hold on a sec. They have a spot for one person, Miss, near the back of the restaurant. One that most people don't care for, since it's so close to the kitchen and noisy. You can have that one if you want" he offers.

"Really" she says excitedly, "Yes, I'll take it. You are a genius!" she proclaims to the red faced clerk and watches as his face turns an even brighter shade of red. I better stop; he could blow if he gets any redder she decides as she suppresses a smile. "Thank you so much" she repeats as she slips a twenty to him on the sly. "I better go and get ready for dinner" she remarks as she heads to her room for a shower. It's time to make Cinderella ready for the ball. If you're going to play with the big boys, then you have to look the part.

You look the part; she tells herself as she smoothes the rich satiny fabric of her favorite little black dress and studies her shoes that match. She grabs her evening bag and her room key and heads out. She sees a sharp dressed woman, elegant yet smart, where others see a beautiful, young, super model pretty woman in a form fitting little black dress that shows just how much of a woman she is, with diamond sparkles at her throat, wrists and ears. She looks like she's loaded with the green stuff, and is maybe from Hollywood. As she walks into the restaurant, all the men in the room follow her with their eyes. They wonder who she is and hope she's alone, including her mark for the evening, Mr. Quinton Uqbahtor.

Things couldn't have worked out better for her, she knows. Her table is just past his, close enough for her to hear everything that's said yet far enough away to make her look important.

She waits for the Host to pull her chair out for her to sit and helps her situate her in it and then she crosses her legs to show them off, puts her purse down on the chair next to her and glances up when she's finished to find Quinton staring at her intently. Plan A is a success, and now on to plan B. Then she looks back at him and gives him a sultry smile.

After ordering a drink, she looks over the menu while listening as his partners arrive for the evening. They're a noisy group. His table's almost all here she notices with a small sip of her beverage. Her waiter shows up to take her order and bring her another drink on the house, compliments of the gentlemen from the table near hers. She glances up with a smile and a mock toast in thanks for the drink.

After she places her order, she takes the time to look at the whole restaurant, notices how full it's gotten in the past few minutes and realizes the hard work the clerk went through to get her a reservation at such short notice. Then she notices someone walking her way, it's Quinton.

"Hello" he says.

"Hi" she returns.

"I wanted to introduce myself to you. I'm Quinton Uqbahtor, from Waco."

"How do you do?" she replies politely. "My names Malory Snyder" she says. "It's nice to meet you."

"I've been watching you" he admits with a small, enigmatic smile. "You're a beautiful woman" he states "but you seem to be here alone, so why don't you join us, Mallory? I would greatly like that" he says coaxingly.

"I'm sorry Mr. Uqbahtor."

"Please, call me Quinton" he insists.

"Quinton, thank you, but I was just finishing up. I have an appointment in about twenty minutes and I'll need to leave shortly. But thank you so much for the invitation. Maybe next time, a rain check?" she asks.

"I'm not here too often, but definitely a rain check" he agrees with disappointment.

"Thank you for the drink and the invitation" she says quietly as she rises to leave. I'll contact everyone once I get in the car. I don't want anyone overhearing.

"Devon, its Mallory."

"What's up?" he asks.

"I just finished dinner a table away from Quinton Uqbahtor and heard some interesting talk. They were speaking in Farsi, so I could understand what they were saying. They brought up Jane's name and her parents, which I found interesting."

"Why were they talking about Jane's parents?" he asks.

"Well, they mentioned how much her parents had worked for and sacrificed for, then they mentioned their connection to Jackman, and how he did a good job. I believe they were talking about the plane explosion and as far as I know, the only "job" he did was blow up the Speaker of the Houses plane.

We now have a connection between the Majority Leader and the murder of the Speaker of the House and some kind of connection to Jane Martin. Something's wrong in the United States, Devon. I need to talk to Jacob and tell him what I heard" she says quickly. "Can you get me the address for Jane's parents?" she asks in excitement. "I think I'll drop by and talk to them while I'm in the neighborhood."

"I'm not sure that's a good idea" he says "calm down Mal, no rushing off, this is probably dangerous. You might want to hold off on that, keep it under wraps. Let's get a conference call going, get everyone's opinion before you do anything" he suggests.

"Sure, I'll wait" she says "but I really want to do this" she insists.

"Alright, just wait, don't go far Mallory. Let me connect the other three and see what they think."

"Fine, I'll hold."

"I wasn't able to reach Eli, but the time difference is pretty big from here to Hawaii, let's try for Jacob. I've got Jacob on the line, Devon and Kat here and Mallory. I can't reach Eli but

I'll try him later."

"What's going on?" Jacob asks.

"Mallory's got a report and some questions, and I thought we all needed to listen and decide."

"Jacob, I'm in Texas. I just left a restaurant where I listened to Quinton Uqbahtor talk to his business acquaintances in Farsi. It was blatant, but I think he just assumed that no one in the restaurant knew the language, and would assume it was American Indian if they heard. I was only a table away and could not only hear what he was saying but I know the language.

"He talked about Jackman and the good work that he did, and he also mentioned Jane's name. That made me suspicious, but then he mentioned Jane's parents, and how hard they worked and how much they've sacrificed" she finishes in a rush. "I wanted to stop and have a chat with her parents, but Devon wants me to wait and get everyone's opinion. So I'm getting opinions, what's yours?" she asks.

"I'm not sure if confronting them is a good idea. We've already experienced the power of this group. They can be dangerous, especially if they think someone is getting too close to their secret. This whole problem is getting bigger, and it seems to involve top people in government. It's going to be almost impossible to find out just how big it is, but you already have involvement at the Speaker of the House level. The only one's higher than that are the President and Vice President. We're going to need more help" he states definitively.

"I'm going to have to let my boss know what's going on. Before we make anymore moves, we're going to have to orchestrate our movement. We want them all and we also want to know everyone who's involved. If we only take out the few we know, that leaves the United States open to future attacks. Mallory, don't visit the Martins yet, let me get some more information and call you back."

"Devon, do you feel the same way?" she asks "Kat, how about you?"

"Yeah, I agree with Jacob" Kat responds

"and so do I" Devon adds.

"Alright, I guess I'll just go back to my room and wait. Eli's supposed to pick me up the day after tomorrow, so if you change your mind, I'll have some time tomorrow to drop in on them."

"I'll get back to you in the next few hours" Jacob replies. "You too Devon, Kat; I'll call you in a few hours."

"Right, later" they all hang up.

"Jacob, it's Mallory again."

"Yeah, what?" Jacob says in frustration.

"Well, I just drove past the Martin house and was wondering if you could get some information for me?" she's asks.

"What information?" he says slowly.

"Where do Jane's parents get their income from? They have a pretty nice house" she informs him "nice enough that it costs a lot. I've never heard mention of where they work, so I was hoping you could find that out for me" she says.

"Mallory, you're not supposed to be that close to their house" Jacob says firmly "don't you know how to follow orders?"

"Yeah, I didn't stop and talk to them, I just drove by, so I did follow orders" she insists when she hears the anger in his voice.

"You followed your orders, not mine" he insists. "Just go back to your hotel room" he orders "and I'll call you with all the info you requested, as soon as I know."

"Fine" she says in resignation, turns the car around and heads back to the hotel.

TWENTY FIVE

Eli's wondering where that damn bartender is. He ordered his drink a good ten minutes ago and then the damn bartender just disappears. Finally, the waitress comes over carrying his drink. "Here's your drink sir" she says as she places the napkin and the drink in front of him.

After removing the lime from the side of his drink, he thinks, wasn't Jeff Stewart killed because of a lime on his drink? This isn't good, he decides as he glances up and over to the bar to see the bartender standing there staring at him. He's probably waiting for me to drink the drink and suck on the lime. Not going to happen buddy. So how do I get him over here to break the ice? I need some answers, before I can arrest him.

After waving the waitress over and ordering the fish sandwich and fries, he waves over Casey, the bartender. "I'm sorry to bother you" Eli says "but you don't happen to know
where I could surf around here, do you?" he asks with enthusiasm.

"No, sorry, I don't surf" the bartender replies flatly.

"Oh" he feigns disappointment. "You can't point me to the surfing beaches; since you live here? I figured even if you didn't surf, you'd know where to send me."

"Oh, well sure, I know a little about where they surf. It's on Maui here but it's the other side of the Island. The beaches are a lot better over there. That's where I usually go to watch some of my friends surf; they have better waves over there."

"Great, thanks" Eli says. "Is there a special time they all surf over there?" he asks with enthusiasm.

"No, they drop in frequently and check for waves. We have good ones usually every day, but at different times, so they're always checking."

"Thank you" he replies. "What road do I take to reach the other side?"

"Oh, that's Mandarin Bay road" Casey replies. "It's easy to find, it's the only four lane highway on this island. You want to go west when you get on it" he says.

"Thanks again" Eli says as Casey walks away.

A buzzing feeling takes him by surprise until he remembers he put his cell on vibrate so he wouldn't be disturbed when he was talking with Casey. "Hello?" Eli answers after he gets his phone out, throws some bills on the table and wanders out the door to talk in privacy.

"Eli, its Mallory, where have you been?" she demands.

"Working Mal, why, what did you think I was doing, playing cards?" he asks sarcastically. You're not the only one working this case, you know."

"Yeah, I'm sorry Eli, I wasn't thinking."

"No problem" he says on a big sigh. "So what's up?"

"I connected Quinton Uqbahtor with Arabs and with Jackman. He's in on the whole process somehow; we're all working on that right now. He also connected Jane to this whole process along with her parents. We tried to include you in on a conference call earlier, but you didn't answer."

"Sorry, I'm undercover, remember. I can't be available all the time when I'm working."

"Okay, okay, sorry" she mutters "I understand."

"Thanks" he says dryly.

"Anyway, I wanted to stop and visit with the Martins but Jacob doesn't want me to. He wants to find out more information on them first, so I'm just hanging around now and wasting time until dinner is over. I don't want Uqbahtor to see me return too early. He asked me to sit with him and I had to give an excuse of having a meeting and being unable to. Now I'm just wasting time. So what do you think about my meeting with the

Martins?"

"I have to agree with Jacob" he says. "It's better to be more prepared than just stopping in" replies Eli. "You know better that that" he reminds her. "It sounds like your letting emotion get in the way of work" he warns.

"Your right, I am, but it's hard not to, when I think of Kat and what they did to her."

"I know, it's been hard for all of us, we just want to take them all out, but not without everything in order, it has to stick" he remarks.

"Yeah, you're right, thanks Eli for getting me back on track."

"No problem, so let me go, I have to get some work done here before we leave tomorrow."

"Eli, how did it go" she asks when she gets on the plane that's been waiting for her.

"It went good. Casey, the bartender, is in custody in Maui for the murder of Jeff Stewart. He swears he was only following orders, but he's refused to give up the name of the person giving the orders. We'll get the name, though" he says with confidence. "I left him with my toughest unit members; they'll get the name and call me as soon as possible. They'll break him," he assures her "I have no doubt."

"Excellent" she replies.

"How about you?" he asks.

"It went okay. Like I said on the phone yesterday, I was able to listen in on a conversation between Uqbahtor and his group of businessmen. He spoke Farsi and they all understood him just fine, but so did I, which he was unaware of" she adds with a smile. "That's when I heard him talk about the good job that Jackman did, and also how the Martin's did such good work and sacrificed so much for what's happening."

"Wow" he whistles. "That's excellent! Now we know for sure that there's a connection."

"Yeah" she replies. "I wanted to kill him, when I heard him mention good job and Jackman in

the same sentence. All I could see was Kat's face. It was hard, not being able to do something right then."

"I know" he soothes "but we have to have everything tied up, we can't afford to go off half cocked."

"I know" she replies miserably "but it didn't make it any easier for me, to find out and then walk away, with no justice for Kat. It's a crock" she complains.

"Soon" he says positively "we'll have them all" he guarantees.

"Welcome back Eli, Mallory, glad you made it. We've got a time set up to meet with Jacob at a place he designated. He says no one can get into this place and there's no way anyone could have bugged the place, so we can talk freely.   We'll leave here about five p.m. It's about a thirty minute drive, into the woods near the Washington-Virginia border. I guess it's his place, at least it sounded like it when he explained, so we'll see" Devon says.

"Great, we can talk about everything then. That gives me about an hour, enough time to run home and change, put my stuff away and be back here to leave" Mallory declares.

"Yeah, I'll go with you" Eli says "since I've been staying at your place anyway. We'll be back by four-thirty.

"That was fast" Kat remarks. "They must be in a big hurry, so I guess we'll talk at Jacob's."

"Right" he agrees. "Let's get these desks cleared off, gather up any papers we need with us, and get ready to head out."

After traveling on a long and narrow dirt road for the past fifteen minutes, Devon starts to get agitated. "This road is never ending" he complains when he finally see's the road Jacob told him to take, for the final leg of the journey.

"It sure is quiet out here" Kat says uncomfortably. I hope it's not the wrong way, she thinks.

"We should be there in the next few minutes" Devon says and after going another mile or so. He turns into what looks like the woods until he moves a little further forward and comes across a small hunting cabin.

"Nice" says Eli. "No one around for miles, nice hideout" he declares just as he spots Jacob standing towards the corner of the cabin.

"Come on in, everyone, I'm all set" Jacob invites. "Welcome to my hunting cabin" he says with a small smile.

"I didn't know you hunted" Kat says in confusion.

"Of course I do" he replies after studying her for a few minutes, trying to see into her mind."I hunt people."

"Yeah" laughs Mallory "I guess you do."

"Come on in" he says as he leads the way into an average size room, with a dining room, kitchenette and a bed all in the same room. Enough room to sit on the comfy looking old couch, lie on the bed or sit at the table, a bathroom off to one side, no TV, and no radio, how boring Kat thinks.

"It doesn't look like much" he admits "but it's more than it looks" he grins. "We're going to take this to a different level" he promises "after I get rid of the car. I don't want anyone to know you're even here" he says "so toss me the keys and I'll put it away, then we can get down to business." After returning no more than five minutes later, he steps in and says "alright, follow me" and he proceeds to walk over to the wall that's empty, taps gently on one spot of it, it looked like a random spot, but must have been pre-placed, and then the wall swings forward and an elevator appears.

"Wow, cool" Kat says.

"Talk about high tech" Eli murmurs "this must have cost a fortune."

"Yeah, it did" Jacob says after he overhears the comment "but it was worth it" he continues. "We've done a lot of good with this facility. It's a high security facility, so it goes without saying, no one knows anything about this and we want to keep it that way" he continues as the elevator comes to a stop, the doors open and a long well lit hallway appears. They all start to walk down the hallway to the first door.

Doors appear all the way down the hall, off to the right and left. The walls are a soft yellow, the floor concrete covered in a light colored tile. It's a nice place, no dampness, and bright enough without any windows to make you forget you're totally underground. "Very nice" Kat murmurs.

"Thanks" he says "I figured you'd like it" he admits with a

grin. "We'll go in here" he says as he opens the first door.

"Are there any more people down here?" Kat asks.

"Yeah, there are a lot" he responds "but you won't see them today. I won't endanger anyone for myself. You all know me, and now you know where this is. It is top secret, so you can't say anything to anyone else. However, under duress or torture, you may divulge this place. They won't figure out, and if they do, they won't actually find this part of the facility. But if tortured, you could give up names and I can't take that chance with the lives of the others that work here" he states firmly. "But we can talk here without worrying that someone may hear us, there's no way anyone can, each room is sound proofed and monitored. Have a seat" he says as he waves everyone forward.

The room is larger than it first appeared. There's a rectangular table with 10 chairs, room to walk around it and a small kitchenette with required coffee pot, a few cabinets for dishes, refrigerator and microwave. It has all the amenities for a comfortable office. "Alright, let's talk about what Mallory found out in Texas" commands Jacob.

"I was seated next to the table that Quinton Uqbahtor and his friends sat at. While seated there, I could hear what they were discussing. Even though he spoke in Farsi I still understood what he was saying, since I'm fluent in seven languages and Farsi happens to be one of them." Jacob looks surprised and pleased by that announcement.

"He used Mark Jackman's name and added to it that he did a good job. I'm sorry Kat, I'm not trying to dredge up anything, but I have to report on this."

"No problem" she agrees with a small smile, even though she lost some color in her face when his name was mentioned. Hmm, Snake decides, still have a problem there. I'll have to see what can be done and looks at Devon who shakes his head no, almost imperceptibly, so Kat doesn't see him. Snake moves his head slightly down in an affirmative.

Mallory continues with the information gained regarding Jane's parents and how Uqbahtor mentioned them by name and talked about what a good job they were doing in spite of all the sacrifices they made. "I'm really suspicious of Jane Martin" she comments "since her parents are involved with Uqbahtor. He's involved with the Arabs and connected to Westfield, Jacob's motorcycle buyer."

"We're making connections that all seem to have Arab ties, which makes this sound suspiciously like terrorism." Eli states. "I've watched some of these things occur and it never turns out beneficial for us. I know Mallory's been in on some of this information also. Now we can see where's this is probably heading. We just aren't sure why the House of Representatives and what good did killing four of its members do?"

"Let's think, people, what did the four dead House of Representatives have in common?" Devon inquires brusquely. "There has to be something there" he admits "granted, some of the militant groups kill just because they can and like to, but it also draws attention to them, something they all usually want. This is totally out of context when it comes to the Arabs, since we've heard nothing about anyone claiming these murders."

"They like taking credit for the things they do, but they normally don't use three different means to accomplish things with. They normally just strap on a bomb and take out their target and as many innocent bystanders as possible. That's always been their modus operandi, at least up until now, but these are different.

"There were either a lot of outsiders involved in this or they've converted a lot of Americans into Muslims. Either way it looks like the good ole U.S. of A. has been infiltrated. Now we just need to figure out why. We've pretty much figured out the who, but the why is still unknown" he admits.

"Hold up there brother, we aren't exactly sure of 'the who' yet. We have a general idea, but it's not exact and it has to be exact before we can begin the operations. That's all we need to do, go after a religious extremist group without positive identification and we would have every religious group out there crying discrimination or something else as farfetched. This is where we take the ignorant stand, until we obtain proof. We can get proof; we just need to know where to start. I'm focusing on the House of Representatives, since they're the ones that have been so affected by all of this. Does anyone else have anything?" Jacob asks brusquely.

"Eli, what happened in Maui?" Jacob asks.

"I had the bartender arrested and I left him in some extremely capable hands. A couple of my personal team stayed back to work him up and get him to talk. It looks like he was a hired hand. I was actually afraid to drink my drink after I noticed a lime in it, so I sent it all off to the lab for testing. If nothing else, we can get him for attempted murder of a Federal Agent, that'll put him away for a nice long time. I'd still rather have proof positive and the name of the person who hired him for the murder of Jeff Stewart. Hopefully we'll get a break there."

"Good work Eli, thanks" Jacob says. "Okay everyone; let's plan another meeting in a few days to go over what's happened. We can meet here again, plus I'd like to get together with you all for dinner some evening. We could go to that Italian restaurant again. That place is pretty good" Jacob admits with a grin. "It gives me the opportunity to use my undercover persona, ask more questions, plus I can be seen in public with you that way, but not as a Lieutenant."

"Fine" Devon agrees "what evening?" he asks everyone in general.

"How about tomorrow night" Kat suggests, "that will give us time to get a little further in the investigation before we meet, not that we can talk about it outside of this place, but it may give us an idea when we need to meet here again."

"Sounds good to me" agrees Mallory and Devon together while Eli shakes his head yes at a look from Jacob.

"Alright, tomorrow night at seven, sound good?"

"Yep" they all answer as they get up to leave.

"I'll take you all up" states Jacob as they near the elevator for their return trip to the real world. "I'll get your car for you, and be right back. Want to go along, Kat?" he asks.

"Um, sure" she says uncertainly as she looks at Devon for approval. He just squeezes her hand and says sure.

"We'll be right back" Jacob announces. "Five minutes, that's all" he reassures everyone. "So Kat, how are you doing" he asks as soon as they're alone.

"I'm okay" she says quietly.

"Really?" he asks.

"No, I guess I'm not, I can't sleep and I'm never hungry anymore" she admits discouraged.

"Yeah, you look like you've lost some weight and you don't smile anymore, do you?"

"Not very often, there's just not much to smile about."

"Sure there is, you're alive" he says with force.

"Yeah, I'm alive" she states flatly, "that's about all, though. It feels like I was robbed of everything I loved, all I found fun. I can't feel any of the happy things anymore" she says with tears in her eyes.

"You will" he reassures her. "I know someone good you can talk to, would that help?" he offers.

"No it wouldn't. I don't want to talk to anyone, tell anyone. I'll get better on my own" she insists."I can still do my job and when I can't do that anymore, then I'll look for help" she states firmly."I don't want to talk about this anymore" she says with fervor."I can block it during the day with work, but not at night. There's nothing there to stop my brain from reliving everything, especially all the mistakes I made that put me in that position" she says adamantly."I'm ready to go" she says decisively "where's the car?

"Right over here" he says, saddened by what she endured and how she's handling it. A quick no shake of his head to Devon informs him that he had no luck with her either. Someone has to help her, I just don't know who.

"I'm heading into headquarters" Devon says "where does everyone want to go?"

"I'll go back to headquarters, too" Mallory and Eli say.

"I'll see you later" Kat tells everyone as she gets in her own car.

"Lieutenant" says Detective Des, once she reaches Metro One. "I've got a message for you from Mr. Malik."

"Yeah, what's he want" she asks tiredly.

"He wants you to call him as soon as you get back to your office. He didn't say what it was about, but he sounded angry."

"Mr. Malik please" Kat requests when the operator answers the phone."Just a moment please" she's told and then put on hold. After waiting close to ten minutes for the arrogant bastard to answer his phone, he announces that he wants to see her in his office ASAP.

I really don't like that man, she decides again when she hangs up and gets ready to go. "Detective, with me" she says. "We have to make an appearance at DHS Headquarters. He didn't say what he needed to see me for, but I guess we'll find out" Kat admits.

"Yes Sir" she replies quietly. I hope she doesn't blow, that man is enough to make anyone lose their temper.

"Lieutenant Thomas to see Mr. Malik" Kat informs the receptionist.

"Yes Lieutenant, it'll be just a moment" she's told as the receptionist phones him to notify him. "Please go right in Lieutenant, he's waiting."

"Thank you" Kat replies as she moves forward to open the door.

"Come in and have a seat. Thank you" he replies after they've complied.

"You're probably wondering why I needed to see you Lieutenant. I promise that I won't keep you long. I have to inform you that you do not have clearance to look into the background of Jane Martin. She has Homeland Security clearance, has worked for me for a number of years and was cleared through this office. She now answers directly to the President and Vice President of the United States. I will not tolerate your office trying to gain information without clearance. This will stop or I will report you to your Captain, do you understand?" he demands with arrogance.

"Yes Sir, I understand, but I disagree" Kat says flatly. "We are investigating multiple murders and I need that information. You are getting in the way of this investigation sir, and even though you are the Director of the Department of Homeland Security, that does not give you license to inhibit an active investigation. If you must contact my Captain, then you must but I will not now nor in the future let you stop me from doing my job, are *we* clear, Sir?"

"I beg your pardon" says George Malik in a loud voice.

"You're out of line Lieutenant and I will not tolerate insubordination."

"So report me" she replies. "Need I remind you that you are in the way of this investigation, of which is unlawful? I can and will arrest you sir, if you do not cease and desist, are we clear, sir?" Kat demands.

"I'm going back to work, if you need to speak with me again, use the phone. I don't have time to jump at your every whim" she finishes as Des and her storm out of the office. The secretary's eyes are wide and unbelieving when she sees Kat, since she just heard everything that went on in that office. She gets busy with her work, before the Director see's her sitting around and takes this out on her.

"Wow, Lieutenant that was awesome" declares Detective Des.

"Thanks" Kat says dryly "but it will make life miserable for me, at least for a little while. I'm sure he's on the phone now, with Captain Hall."

"But you were right sir; he is getting in the way of the investigation."

"Yes he is, but there was no reason for my behavior except anger and if I can't control my anger then I can't do my job" Kat states tiredly.

"Sir, he pushed you beyond the bounds and I'll tell Captain Hall that, too" she says in support of her Lieutenants actions.

"Thanks, but I can handle my own problems, I don't want you putting your job on the line with mine. Let's see what kind of collateral damage there is from this" Kat says as she pulls up in front of Metro One.

TWENTY SIX

Walking through the bull pen is usually a noisy process, except for right now. Something big is going down. That was awfully fast, but I knew it was coming.

"Captain, I didn't know you were in here" Kat remarks when she enters her office.

"I just got off the phone with Director Malik and he is definitely ticked off" Captain Hall replies to Kat's unspoken question.

"Yes Sir, I expected as much" she admits with a sigh.

"Did you think you could get away with speaking to the Director of Homeland Security the way you did?" inquires the Captain dryly. "I understand you have a problem with him, but there are other ways to handle this than yelling at a superior and accusing said superior of getting in the way of an active investigation. Have you forgotten how to interrelate to others without resorting to yelling?" Captain Hall demands in anger. "Look, I don't want to remove you from this case, since you've been on it longer than anyone else, but that is exactly what he wants, and he has the President's ear, friends in high places. So if I don't do this, he can and will make life hell for this office."

"This doesn't just affect you now Lieutenant, it affects the entire force, so I am formally notifying you, you're suspended without pay until further notice. Do you understand me Lieutenant?"

"Yes Sir, I understand you."

"Hand in your weapon and badge" he demands. "Now, you are off all cases until further notice, Lieutenant."

"Yes Sir."

"Dismissed" he responds in disappointment. "I'll do whatever I can to get you reinstated Lieutenant, so stay available."

"Yes, Sir, thank you Captain" Kat responds and leaves her office.

"Detective" Kat says after Des enters her office, "I'm no longer on the case, but that doesn't mean the case is closed, you still need to work it and get any and all information over to Devon for processing. Keep up the good work, Detective. I'll be in touch."

"Yes Sir. I too will help the Captain in any way I can, to get you reinstated" she informs her with emotion.

"Thanks Des" Kat says with tears in her eyes. "I'm heading over to Capitol headquarters now" she says.

"I can't work the case from here, but I might be able to help over there. You can reach me by cell if you need to" she says as she turns and leaves.

After getting close to Capitol headquarters Kat decides to make a detour and stop in and talk with Mike. After parking a block away, she gets out of her vehicle and heads to the coffee shop.

"Mike" Kat says just loud enough to be heard over the din. "How are you?" she inquires as she stands at the counter.

"I'm great" he replies. "What brings you to my neighborhood?" he asks with a smile.

"Well, I have some time and I wanted to see you and say hay" she responds "so here I am" she grins.

"It's good to see you Kat."

"It's good to see you, too" she responds "I've been so busy that I haven't had much of a life, but for a little while today, I'm going to enjoy this freedom" she says.

"Did the cases get solved?" he asks in surprise.

"No, not yet, but we're getting close" she answers.

"Then why aren't you working" he asks

"Well, you know the temper that I have? It got me in trouble today. Just a little trouble, then I can go back to work" she admits with dignity.

"You got suspended?" he asks in surprise. "That's a first"

he says puzzled. "You've never had that happen before, have you?" he asks in confusion.

"No, but it was deserved" she responds quietly.

"Oh, boy, who did you yell at, the President?" he asks with a smirk.

"Not quite, but maybe just as bad. I gave the Director of Homeland Security a piece of my mind" she admits sheepishly.

"Well, you don't seem too torn up by it?" he notices with a questioning tone.

"I'm not, I shouldn't have done it, but someone needed to do it and I guess I was the only one willing to go that far" she admits with a sigh.

"Yeah, you need to learn patience Kat and diplomacy, something you still struggle with" he says with a smile.

"Stop Mike, I know all my short comings, you don't need to remind me" she says disgruntled.

"Okay then, how about your favorite cup of coffee" he offers with a small smile. "I say you deserve one, so let me get it for you."

"Well, well" says Mike as he goes around the counter. "Look who the cat drug in" he adds with a laugh as Kat spins around to see what he's talking about.

"Snake" Kat cries happily. "Now I have someone to sit with me for a little bit."

"Hi Kitten, how are you?" he asks quietly.

"I'm good now that you're here" she admits as she puts her arm through his in a gesture of camaraderie. The first natural emotion she's demonstrated since her attack. She's getting better, he decides as he agrees outwardly to sit with her. \

"So what are you doing here" he asks after they take the table in the corner, back to the wall.

"Are you on vacation?" he asks in surprise because she's here during the middle of an active investigation, pretty unusual. Maybe all isn't right with the world.

"Nope" she answers quietly "just suspended for awhile" she admits.

"Suspended!" he repeats with surprise.

"Yep, I'm suspended."

"Okay, what did you do" he asks warily.

"I told the Director of Homeland Security that he was getting in the way of an active investigation" she admits. "Technically he is" she replies quickly to his amused look.

"Ah" he says "you actually told him in no uncertain terms" he questions with a grin.

"Yep, you know me Snake. I just say it, no beating around the bush" she admits with a guilty shrug.

"Yeah, I do know you, you were going to work on your political correctness, weren't you" he reminds her.

"Yeah, but he just steamed me so much that I totally forgot about any PC stuff" she says in defense. "He needed to be told, so I told him" she states.

"Alright then" he replies. "So how long are you suspended?" he inquires.

"Until further notice, pending review of my case, probably" she admits.

"Well, are you allowed to work the case?" he asks.

"Not officially" she says guiltily "but I plan on going over to Capitol police headquarters and helping Devon on the qt."

"That sounds like a plan" he admits "but how about working with me instead?" he asks. "I have a couple of things going on and could use your help."

"Really?" she says in excitement. "I've never had the opportunity to work with you before, but I would love to. What do you need me to do?" she asks enthusiastically. "Oh, I don't have my weapon, do I need one?" she asks. "They took it and my badge when they suspended me."

"Don't worry, I'll get you one to use" he promises.

"Thanks" she says. "So, what's first?" she wants to know.

"First, we leave this place, because we can't talk here, remember" he reminds her quietly.

"Yeah, sorry" she says.

"We'll head west" he says "let's go."

"Okay, hold on a sec. Mike, I need to go, I'll call you later" Kat promises.

"Sure" he says with a wave while busy at the counter.

They ended up at Snakes camp, in less than twenty minutes

thanks to a short cut he knew. "We'll work out of here" he says when they head inside."I've got a sting going on you might be interested in" he offers as he motions for her to follow him. Once down stairs, they pass all the hall doors she noticed before and continue on to the very last room that sets at the end of the hall. "Not many people can get in here" he states as he leans forward for a retina scan.

"This is the top security clearance room" he says after opening the door for her to precede him. "You will only have access to this room while I'm with you. When I leave, you leave" he states firmly.

"Sure" she says agreeably as she glances around and sees flat screen monitors everywhere with technicians sitting at different consoles and running different programs.

"This is my unit" he says. Kat's amazed at the quietness of the room. It's a huge room with light blue colored walls, thick carpeting that matches the walls and muffles sound, and then there are monitors that are at least fifty-five inch minimum. Every monitor is hooked up to a different technician who appears to be doing multiple things at once. It's busy, but quiet. You can feel the tenseness in the atmosphere, yet it all looks calm on the surface.

"Some of these people are monitoring the President and Vice President, twenty four hours a day, seven days a week. Others are monitoring different things, like the Pentagon, the DHS and all the air transportation coming in and out of D.C. We also do searches for people, and we monitor the Arab states" he says quietly.

"Wow" she says. "You cover a lot of territory" she remarks.

"We have to, the lives of American citizens and the heads of the U.S are protected here, we have a large responsibility" he remarks.

"This is a department that no one knows about. Our safety and the safety of this country is on the line should anyone find out about this. The Department of Homeland Security does not know about this department, the President doesn't like to have all his eggs in one basket. This department was kept out of general knowledge so that we can be completely non-corrupt.

Everyone that works in this department takes a special oath, promising never to divulge anything about this, or their lives are worth nothing.

These are the most dedicated people of the country. I'm proud to be a part of this unit. You are only here because I swore that you were safe, don't make me regret that, Kat" he says.

"Never" she promises "I will never divulge anything nor will anyone ever hear about this department from me. I'll swear an oath to you if you want me to" she offers.

"Not necessary" he claims."Okay, let's get to work" he says as he leads her to an office off the back of the room. "Sit down" he orders as she enters a room that looks like the previous one, only smaller. After moving around to the back of a black lacquer desk, he takes a seat and quietly opens a compartment on the desk. "I should have done this earlier, but I never got the chance" he says by way of an apology. "This could have saved you a great deal of pain and anguish, so I want to apologize to you Kat. Can you ever forgive me?" he asks quietly.

"For what?" she asks in confusion."You haven't done anything to me" she reassures him.

"I neglected to put this on you" he says "and for that you have suffered."

"No, any suffering done was not done through you" she swears adamantly. "I made decisions and some of them put me in jeopardy. Nothing that you did has ever caused any harm to me" she repeats determinedly.

"Thank you for that Kat, now please, let me get this set up for you" he states. "It's a GPS device that goes in the hair, where it can't be detected and is attached until we remove it. It can't be washed out or brushed out" he promises. It takes on the property of hair and is microscopically small enough to bye-pass any type of detection device. We monitor this twenty four/seven so that you don't have to worry. You saw the technicians in the other room; they are monitoring these types of things all the time while doing other things.

So you see, I could have stopped your attacker, but I hadn't gotten one of these to you yet. I am deeply sorry, you'll never know how much" he adds with regret.

"Thank you Snake" she says tearfully. "That means so much to me" she admits all choked up, with tears streaming down her face. "It's been tough" she admits. "Devon doesn't understand and he doesn't know what to say or even how to act with me. It makes me constantly remember. The only place I could escape was work and they took that away from me today when they suspended me" she says tiredly.

"There happens to be someone here that wants to talk to you and probably can help you" offers Snake.

"I'm not sure" she replies suspiciously. "I haven't talked with anyone since the incident" she admits.

"I know; that's one of the reasons I wanted you to come here today. I think this person can really make a difference for you. He may be able to help you get some rest, before you crash. You're still losing weight and you look like you haven't slept in a month" he remarks. "Let's get this over with so that you can move on."

"I thought you had work for me" she responds in panic.

"I do and it will be ready for you after" he states firmly, taking control away from her and using it to help. "Let's go" he says as he stands and ushers her out the door and through both the office and the unit room.

"This place is huge" Kat says as he ushers her into yet another room.

"Come in" says a deep voice that causes Kat's heart to skip a beat.

"Greg, this is Kat. I've spoken with you about her and I've finally convinced her to see you" responds Snake to the un-voiced query he's see's on the face of the counselor. "Kat, this is Greg" he introduces as she takes a moment to get her heart back under control.

"It's nice to meet you" she says automatically to the gentleman behind the large oak desk, with the blonde hair, gray eyes, military hair cut and compassionate face.

"I've known her for close to fifteen years" Snake says, trying to ease her discomfort, giving her time to relax. "I met her at a friend's coffee shop when she was what, fifteen?" he asks.

"Yeah, I was young but in college. He saved me then, just like he's trying to now" she adds with a grimace.

"I'll leave you to it" Jacob says "since I have some pressing matters to attend to at the moment. Just give me a call when you're done and I'll come and get her" he promises as he takes his leave.

Step one in the recovery process; at least it's a step in the right direction. She'll be better for it, not cured maybe but able to cope, which is all anyone can hope for. Jacob requests the last four hours in Director Malik's office be brought up on screen three. Let's see exactly what happened to get her suspended.

"Hmm" Jacob whistles after viewing the footage from her meeting. She's got spunk, he decides with a grin. He deserved everything she said to him, besides all she did was tell the truth. She would have handled it better if she hadn't been on the verge of an emotional break, he defends her. Poor Kat, you're always trying to deal with everything on your own. You've always been so stubborn about your independence, too. Okay, we'll file that for later and move on. "Bring up the House please, last four hours."

"Did you hear what he said to her?" he asks his operatives. "There is definitely a connection between Malik and Martin. It almost sounds like she's running him, and that's absolutely not the impression of the man that I have" he murmurs.

"Get me an in depth background on George Malik, please" Jacob requests. "I want everything, his personal life, his bank accounts, what he spends and on whom, and where they're connected" he decides.

"Mallory, it's Jacob, I have a few questions about Quinton Uqbahtor, and I'm hoping you have some answers."

"A few" she says cautiously "but not all, what do you want to know?" she asks.

"Is there a connection to George Malik?" he asks outright.

"There is a small one" she admits "but I haven't been able to figure out what, just that there is."

"Okay, what is it?" he asks.

"They're connected by a church" she says slowly. "Actually it's the minister of a church" she corrects herself.

"A Church?" he echoes in disbelief. "That's not what I was expecting" he admits.

"I know, me neither" she admits ruefully.

"Alright, what's the name of the church, the name of the minister, how are they connected and for how long?" he questions rapid fire.

"They're connected through the small town she comes from, just outside of Waco. Hey, that's your state, Texas, so you should know who I'm talking about?" she replies with a question.

"My state is not Texas" he disagrees with grinding teeth. "Wait; don't tell me, it's Jerald Johnston, from In His Name Ministries, of Texas?"

"Yep, you guessed it" she laughs, "right the first time" she teases.

"Well, well" he murmurs while he's deep in thought. "I never saw that one coming?" he admits in disgust. "That minister has the largest congregation in the world, he broadcasts worldwide."

"Yeah, cool huh" agrees Mallory.

"No, not cool" he denies. "That's going to be a tough number to get into since I'm sure he's well protected by various specialists, from computer to bankers to fellow churches and ministers." This thing just keeps snowballing, he decides as he envisions all the branches. "Have we ever heard the Director or Jane Martin mention this connection?" he queries.

"Nope, I've never heard anything about this connection, which means they're being awfully cautious about this staying private and to me that screams hiding something."

"Yeah, that's the feeling I just got" he acknowledges. "Okay, I'll put some people on it and we'll see what we can find" he decides, says bye and hangs up. Damn, I just can't seem to Comprehend this connection, this came way out of left field, he grumbles.

"We have some information, Lieutenant Callander" one of his unit members announces.

"What is it?" he asks.

"It looks like Jane's parents, the Martins, are founding members of that church, they were in on the ground floor" he says. "The church started up around thirty four years ago, just before Jane was born. Background says they helped build the church and increase its congregation."

"That's interesting. What do we have as background on the Martins?" he asks.

"I'm working that up right now Sir. It says that they moved to Texas from their country of origin, Iran, in nineteen-seventy-four and became citizens of the United States in seventy-five. They helped to start the church "In His Name" in seventy-six. They had Jane in seventy-eight, an only child; she never had any sisters or brothers. They were totally dedicated to the church and the raising of their only child. There is no illegal information in their records; never had a ticket, never went to court, never did anything wrong" he says in disbelief.

"You sound amazed agent" he asks "why?"

"Well, sir, I've never seen a record so clean. I have a hard time believing that these people actually exist, let alone live in the U.S."

"I have to agree with you, this sounds like a record that was created" he remarks thoughtfully. "Anyone could have created this, but the first thing they usually learn is to make it sound real, a person who gets speeding tickets or parking tickets. Since no one is perfect, their records should reflect that. This was obviously created by an amateur or maybe someone that doesn't believe this will be looked at. Now we dig" he says "let me know when you get anything else"

"Yes Sir."

"I have something for you Lieutenant" notifies another agent looking into the backgrounds of the Martins. "I found the connection to their home country of Iran. They were originally part of an insurgent group that they broke away from. When they left, it was to preserve their lives, according to these records. They were spirited out of the country, made their way here via Canada as Canadian citizens, landed in Texas and laid low for awhile. Then they took their citizenship tests to become official. The father is the only one that has worked, and he has always been in sales. He worked at a shoe store in the local mall until he retired about four years ago, but they still have a decent income. It looks, on the surface, as if they invested well, or someone has been generous to them with gifts of money. It also could be because of the church. They did help form the church and have been with it every step of the way, as it's grown. It's now considered the largest non-denominational Christian church in the world, with an actual membership of over a million and a worldwide network. Wow, the only church bigger is the Catholic Church.

"Let's get started on the minister for this church" Jacob orders. "I want to know everything there is to know about him. Start with where and when he was born and to whom, etc. You know what we need" he says as he walks back into his office. Just as he starts to sit, the phone rings and he grabs it with a gruff "Callander"

"Lieutenant, Kat's finished here. You can come and get her anytime."

"Thanks Greg, I'll be right there" he says and heads out the door.

"How do you feel Kitten?"

"I don't know" she admits. "The same, but different, I guess. He said it will take awhile to get through this but that I've made a good start."

"That's good then" he responds as he grabs her hand and holds it all the way back to his office. "I'm here for you, kitten. I always will be so anytime you need to talk, you know how to reach me."

"Yeah" she admits with a sniffle. "Thanks, Snake, I love you!"

"I love you too, Kitten. Okay, enough with the mushy stuff, we've got work" he says.

"I think I'd better give Devon a call, if that's alright?" she asks.

"Sure, you can use my office, I have things to do in here" he offers as they walk into the ops room.

"Devon, its Kat?"

"Where are you Kat, I've been going crazy looking for you. There's been no sign of you for hours."

"I'm sorry Devon. I went with Snake today to help with the investigation. I got suspended at work this morning, for insubordination to the Director of DHS."

"Yeah, I heard" he says. "How come you called Snake and not me?" he demands to know.

"I didn't" she says in denial, "I ran into him at Mike's and he talked me into helping him with the investigation until I'm cleared to go back to work. I thought it was a good idea, so here I am."

"Where is here?" he asks suspiciously.

"You know I can't tell you that, Devon, you can't trust any phone system" she replies heatedly.

"Sorry" he admits. "I've had a bitch of a day" he states in frustration "First you get suspended, then you disappear, then you won't tell me where you are and you're with my brother!"

"Yes, to all of those, and I am sorry" she says formally. "But it's not always just about you" she reminds him "this goes both ways, you know?"

"Yeah, I know" Devon replies with a deep sigh. "Are you coming back today, or am I not allowed to know that either?" he asks sarcastically.

"I believe so, but we're in the middle of something, so I'm not sure what time. I'll let you know as soon as I know" she promises.

"Alright, thanks Kat and I'm sorry" he says sincerely.

"It's alright" she responds, "its fine" she says hoping it will be, at least for now.

"Kitten, we were just getting ready to go over some information on Jerald Johnston, the Minister from the 'In His Name' church in Texas."

"Okay" she says in confusion. "Why are you looking at this minister?" she asks.

"Long story, short version is the connection that's between George Malik, Jane Martin and Jerald Johnston."

"Oh" she says in understanding.

A minister, they're supposed to be above these things she

thinks, remembering her minister from her home town. A nice old guy that always smelled of moth balls but was always ready with a smile and a kind word. He was a dear old man. They're all dead now though. First it was Mom and Dad and then a month later Pastor Reilly, all dead within months of each other. What a shame. She remembers each one and realizes how much she still misses the people that helped form the person she is, today.

"Earth to Kitten" she finally hears after he says it three times.

"Oh" she gasps in dismay "sorry, I was thinking."

"So I see" he admits with a smile. "But we need to work on this right now, so if you could join us?" he says.

"Jerald Johnston, age fifty six, born Ocaw, Texas to Bridget and Jeffry Johnston, now deceased. Graduated from Ocaw High School in seventy-three, completed his Christian education from Forever Hope School of Ministry, out of Trent, Montana. He started the "In His Name Church" in Waco, Texas with the help of some local investors and has built the largest non-denominational church in the world. He's never been married, and is quoted as saying he's married to his church. He speaks all over the world looking for new memberships. The church has membership drives every month and he has increased his television time to four evenings a week, U.S time and twice a week on weekends for other countries. He also ministers in their languages, thereby surpassing the language barrier. The people who follow him love him. There's never been a hint of anything illegal coming from his church or himself. That's all I've been able to get, Lieutenant, but I'm sure there's more. I'll stay with this until further notice, Sir."

"Thanks" he replies.

TWENTY SEVEN

"This case is going to drive me batty" he says to Kat as they take their leave. "I'll contact them later to see if there's anything new, but I have to get you back to town or Devon will hunt me down" he says with a grin.

"Yeah, right" giggles Kat. "He probably would" she says as she sighs with exhaustion.

"I'm sorry; I'm just a little tired tonight. It's been a long week."

"It sure has" he says quietly, hoping she'll close her eyes and rest finally.

"I see some things don't change very fast" Kat says as it starts snowing like a banshee as soon as they reach D.C. proper. "I'm so ready for spring" she complains. "I really hate this weather, at least this year. It's caused nothing but trouble for the last month."

"Yeah" he replies in agreement "but sometimes you can use it for your benefit. It's excellent for tracking" he says with a grin.

"There's a spot "she cries" hurry before someone else decides they're going to park there."

"Got it" he says gleefully after pulling in quickly, knowing how precious and few parking in D.C. is.

"It's ours now; let's go see what's been happening at headquarters."

"Hi Mallory, how's it going here?" Kat asks after getting through the lobby and into the inner sanctum of the headquarters.

"Good" she replies "everything seems to be moving in the right direction now. We've had a call from Jane Martin, earlier, and she set up a time for all of us to meet with her regarding this investigation. It's scheduled for six-thirty. Devon was really hoping you'd be back before then, so he's going to be relieved when he see's you."

"Speak of the devil, there he is now" she says as she points to the back of the room where his office is.

"Kat, Jacob" he cries in relief. "I'm glad you made it back here. I wanted you both to be included in the meeting with the Speaker of the House" he admits with relief. "We have to be there in about an hour."

"What can I say" Jacob replies with a shrug "timing's everything" he adds with a wink.

"So, what's does Jane want to talk to us about?" Kat asks in curiosity.

"We aren't sure, but I'm hoping she's going to have a lead or two for us that we can actually work."

"This should be interesting, but because of my cover, I can't come along" Jacob replies thoughtfully.

"Of course you can't, what was I thinking? We better get ready" Devon says. "Eli, Mallory, are you ready to head out for this meeting" he yells.

"Yep, let's go" they all reply in unison. Devon decides to drive since "my vehicle" is in the garage so I won't need to clean it, it's snowing pretty good out there now" he remarks with disgust.

"I'm a little tired of the snow; we've gotten more snow this year than we have for a long time. I wouldn't mind if it stopped anytime soon" he says.

"Yeah, we're all pretty sick of it" they reply.

"Now wait just a minute, I'm not used to any and here I've been stuck with it for the last few weeks, ever since I've been here" remarks Eli. After the ten minute drive took twenty five, they all piled out of the car just to get some air.

"Whew" Kat says "it was awfully tight in there with all of us in our winter clothes. There was barely room to move, let alone breath" she complains. "If you don't mind, I think I'll walk back. Besides, it will be faster" she says "than it was getting here."

"Go right on in" Jane Martins secretary says when they arrive in her office. "She's been waiting for you" she admits with a smile.

"Thanks" Devon responds as he continues to move in the direction of the main office. This is some office, antique furniture everywhere, crystal chandeliers, heavy duty shine and sparkle from every surface, a heavy plush carpet that your shoes really sink into.

This is our tax payer dollars at work. What's wrong with this country, he wonders. There are children starving and people think nothing of surrounding themselves with the most expensive, or sending the American dollar that's not worth much nowadays, overseas to help those poor countries. What about our people. I sure am glad no one can read my mind, I have very radical thinking, he admits to himself.

"Deputy Chief Callander, Agents, Lieutenant, please come in and have a seat, I've been waiting. Welcome everyone, and thank you for agreeing to meet with me on such short notice" Jane says as everyone takes a seat. "I felt it truly important to talk with you about the investigation that's been taking up so much of your time" she says with a smile.

"First off, I would like to answer any questions that you may have regarding me or my new office" she offers with sincerity.

"I do have a few questions" Devon admits. "Question number one" he ticks off on the fingers of the one hand he's held up, "Why is your background blocked from everyone except the Department of Homeland Security? That's not only thrown suspicion on you, but also on the Director of DHS. Question number two; are you trying to impede this investigation, because of your friendship with George Malik? Question number three; what is your friend George Malik's background when it comes to Iran?

"Hold on" Jane says. "Let's work on these three questions first, then we'll add to them."

"Number One, my background has always been restricted, that was done by a Presidential directive. The President's Secret Service investigated me a few years ago, found nothing, closed the investigation and sealed my records. Since they found nothing suspicious about me, they believed me when I told them that I am just a plain Jane, nothing interesting or hidden. Any further questions about that?" she asks politely.

"Yeah" Devon admits, "I've been with the Capitol police for close to fifteen years and I have never seen someone with a sealed background that has nothing to hide."

"Well, now you have" she reiterates with a smile. Funny, she's smiling, but it sure isn't reaching her eyes. Good actress Kat wonders or the truth. As she listens to more of the story, she decides to watch this one closely, there's something not quite right.

"Question Number two" she continues. "I would never try to impede an investigation. Those people that were killed, they were my friends. I want their murderers caught as badly as you want to catch them" she reassures them mildly. "Anything else regarding this question?" she asks.

"Yes actually" Devon admits with a smile. Jane just smiles slightly and rolls her eyes while waiting for the next comment. "I tried to do a background on you. Shortly after I had initiated the process, I got a call from Director Malik, warning me to cease the investigation. I was denied any and all access to your information, which raised a red flag, obviously" he states. "Any idea why?" he asks politely.

"Not really" she admits "I can only think that George is trying to protect me, which he doesn't need to do since I'm guilty of nothing. But he comes from the same state as I do and we actually travel in the same circles. Needless to say, he tries to act like my father when I'm in D.C. What can I say? he's just being nice to me. I don't want to damage our relationship over something as minor as my background, of which I have none, if you remember. I will talk with him" she promises "I doubt he realizes how that has made me look and since I'm so new to this position, I can't afford any negative publicity" she assures them.

Smooth answer, but is it the truth? She's pretty practiced on these questions, she may have been prepped. "If there's nothing else, I'll move onto the next question?" she asks. Devon gives a nod of approval to get her started.

"Question Number three; my parents came from Iran a few years prior to my birth. They wanted a better life for their family. I understand they got mixed up with a Muslim extremist group. I also know, after having been detained by a similar group a few years ago, that the only way to truly break free from them is to leave the country and start over. New unknown names, new life style, practically hiding out for fear of your life. They've managed to do all of those things while raising a daughter and helping to build a church. I give my parents great credit for all they've overcome. Their backgrounds were not sealed, so you were able to look at them and know that what I tell you is the truth" she remarks firmly.

"I will not have my parents treated poorly, just because you are doing an investigation. My parents have nothing to do with my position, as you can see from their backgrounds. They've never even been out of Texas, not in the thirty-five years that they've been there. They are simple people that just want to live their lives' freely and in peace."

"Alright" Devon says "I have a couple of more questions, if you don't mind?"

"Go ahead" she replies impatiently.

"You stated that you and George Malik are friends, are more than mutual acquaintances. Did you also know Abdul Adl Thayer?" he asks.

"I have heard of that name" she admits. "I believe it was through George Malik though, why? she asks. "What does he have to do with this investigation?"

"I'm sorry, Madame Speaker, but I can't comment on that, this is an active investigation" he responds to her question.

"Wait" she says, "you won't find a clearance higher than mine" she reminds him impatiently.

"Regardless" Devon responds "this is an active investigation, I can't comment on your question."

"Fine" she says impatiently "If you can't be forthcoming,

305

than I believe our discussion is over. Now, I have a pile of work to do, so if you'll excuse me?"

"Way to go Devon" Jacob says with a smirk after he's briefed on everything that happened during the meeting. "You sure know how to create enemies!"

"Yeah, yeah, whatever" he says impatiently. "I got some information, but she got pretty defensive with that last question. I saw guilt there, didn't you? I think we'll push her buttons some more with Addy. This could get interesting" he says as he rubs his hands together. "Let's put out a bolo on Addy. I want to see him" Devon says. "If we put a little pressure on him, he may crack and then poor George, what will he do if he says something he doesn't want known? I get the feeling there's a lot more to Malik than they want anyone to know."

"Deputy Chief Callander, I've got some information on Addy" a unit member of Mallory's says. "He was last seen in a small town outside of Tehran, Iran."

"Wait" Devon says. "He's in Iran? How the hell did he get out of the U.S? He's part of this murder investigation and he gets out of the U.S. and into Iran? That's bullshit" he replies in anger. Well, doesn't that make things easier? It's just one more problem in the never ending list of problems with this damn investigation. Someone always seems to be a step ahead of us. He glances around at the ops room at headquarters. If we have a leak, it could be someone in this room. Who's giving out information, he wonders.

"Alright people, check and see how he obtained his flight to Iran. I want to know just who's backing him. If it is Director Malik, we're going to have to take him down

"Devon, I'm heading over to Metro One. I want to catch Detective Des before she leaves" Kat says.

"Fine, I'll come over later" he replies with a quick squeeze to her hand. "We can order takeout" he suggests with a grin.

"Sounds good to me" she replies.

"Where are you going Kat" Snake asks as she walks by lost in thought.

"Oh, sorry, I was thinking about something else" she admits. "I'm heading over to Metro One for a few minutes" she answers carefully. "Then I'm going home. Devon's going to meet me there and then we're doing takeout" she adds with a smile.

"Great" Snake says "I have a couple of things I need to do tonight, so I'll leave you knowing you're doing okay" he says.

"I am" she replies. "I'm going to be fine now, thanks to you" she admits, hoping it's true but knowing it's not.

"Not thanks to me" he denies "it's all you Kat, this is all you."

Yeah, she nods in agreement; it is she thinks, too bad.

"Hold on" she yells over the music that's playing, probably too loudly, in her apartment, but it's okay, it's just what I need. "Time to drown out life" she says as she checks her peep hole to make sure it's Devon before she unlocks the door and ushers him in.

"Hey" she says "I'm glad you're here."

"Me too" he says as he grabs her and holds her close. "I've wanted to do this since you got back" he admits. "You look different, quieter, more relaxed." he says.

"I feel better than I have in a while" she realizes. "Whatever that counselor did, he helped me, I guess."

"Yes he did, about time too" Devon agrees fervently. "I need to thank Jacob big time for getting you back for me" he admits.

TWENTY EIGHT

"Lieutenant, I've got some information on George Malik, Director of DHS."

"What is it" Jacob asks after he returns to his op's center.

"We've gone over the time period before and after your visit to the Speaker of the House and what we found is interesting. There was a phone call made to Jane Martin minutes after you let her office" he remarks. "Obviously, the Director of DHS knew when you arrived and when you left" he says. "What we don't know, is where he got the equipment that enables him to listen or even view what's going on at the Capitol Building, in the Speaker of the House's office, no less."

"Well, don't sound so shocked" Jacob remarks dryly. "After all, we do the same thing, just on a wider scale, you know?"

"True" he agrees "but I didn't know anyone else had our high tech capabilities. I thought this was sole proprietary and that we were the only ones that had this" he admits in confusion.

"Well, all I know is if we can have this capability, then others can also. We got ours but it didn't stop it from going elsewhere. Money is a strong arm, and it buys its way everywhere, so there's no such thing as sole proprietary. For the right price, everything is available. Yes, this will make our job a little more difficult" he admits "so we're going to need to go back to the drawing board to figure a way to stop the blocking. Let me see the Malik video for the time before and after the visit to the speaker's office."

"Here it is, notice how you can see and hear everything just fine and then all of a sudden there's nothing. You can't even see him in his office, yet we know that he's there. He's found a way to jam this. We need to find out what he's using, where he got it, and how to stop it" the agent admits.

"Wait" Jacob says "go back slightly and watch his right hand" he adds with intensity. "See, there" he says as they stop the video feed.

"Yeah" says the agent "I see it."

"It looks like a pebble, just a normal pebble, maybe from that water fall he has on the corner of his desk. That is an awesome way to hide something like that. Intermix it with others that look like it but aren't and you can leave it in your office with no one knowing."

"We'll have to get in there when he's not around" Jacob says. "What do we have that can be used to jam his signals? I don't want him to know that we were visiting, but we do want that jammer and any others he may have. Let's set this plan in motion, we only have a few hours left before everyone arrives for work again" he reminds them. After an intense evening that moved into the early morning hours, trying to gather all the equipment they could get to do this job, they're ready.

"Let's hope our jammer is strong enough to jam his equipment" Jacob says as he takes the lead to Malik's office. "I don't want my picture broadcast anywhere," even though he's made up to look like black ops, clothes, hat and face all blending into black. No way could anyone identify him. Twenty five minutes later they're on their way back to their ops center with no one the wiser. Now it's going to be fun watching his video and seeing recognition on his face when he finds he's got nothing. I just wish I could have been there in person, he grins wickedly.

"Alright, here we go, let's see what we've got. Report on the jammer."

"Yes Sir. We have one identical to this Lieutenant. We were supposed to be the only one with its capabilities, unfortunately, it looks like someone either broke under pressure or went for the cash. I do know that it was ours first. We've made some changes to it over the past few months, but it's still recognizable as ours" he states. "When we find whoever did this Sir, I'd consider that person a traitor."

"Agreed" remarks Jacob, "unfortunately these things usually go to the highest bidder. I just didn't know that DHS had that kind of budget." I'll have to look into that, he decides, I know they don't have our budget, no one does.

"Mallory its Devon, is Eli there with you?"

"Yeah, why" she asks.

"I have a job for him, or you if you're interested?" he replies.

"Depends, what is it?" she asks.

"Remember Addie?" he asks.

"Of course, what about him" Mal asks?

"I need some more background on him and his twin brother. I'm looking for any connections to Malik" he says.

"Oh, that's interesting. Do you really think they knew each other before now?" she asks.

"Yeah, I think there's a connection, big time. I know Jacob's looking in the same direction; I just thought we could help. I want this murder ring, if that's what it is" he says. "We're going to clean house a little" he admits.

"Alright, I'll let Eli know and we can put both our units on it" she offers."I'll get back to you later today."

"Thanks" Devon says "appreciate it."

"What was that about" Kat asks when she gets out of the shower, after jumping in it to get ready to go back to work, her suspension cancelled due to suspicions of a Malik conspiracy. "Malik and Addy, I'm hoping for a visible connection, so we can start that house of cards falling" he admits with a grin. "I have a gut feeling that they're involved and have been for a long time.

"Malik's not the person he wants people to see him as" Kat says thoughtfully. "I get a bad vibe every time I have to be near him" she admits.

"Me too" he says thoughtfully.

"I just thought it was me" she admits."I've had a few rough weeks, so I thought it was my feelings that were messing things up, but I don't think it is. It seems to get worse every time I'm near him."

"I know what you mean" he replies. "Let's head out to head-quarters, we'll start searching too. The more eyes, the better chance there is of finding something faster, I figure" he says. "Who knows, we just might uncover something big."

"Lieutenant" Detective Des says. "I've been running the search you asked me to do on George Malik. Most of the areas are not accessible" she admits in resignation. "My clearance isn't high enough" she says, disgruntled.

"Yeah, I know about that problem" replies Kat. "We'll just have to try something else," she says. "How about doing a run on his parents?" she suggests. "Maybe we can get in the back door, and get some information that way"

"Alright, I'm on it Sir" replies Des.

"I'll be in my office" she informs Des as she walks past the bull pen.

"Patterson, I want to see you" she says on her way past.

"Yes Sir" he replies with a touch of sarcasm.

"Have a seat, Officer" she orders when he wanders in.

"You're probably wondering why I wanted to talk with you" Kat says at her most formal. "I don't like the attitude that I've been getting from you lately" she says while he just looks at her with no expression and says nothing.

"Have nothing to say?" she inquires.

"No, Sir, I don't."

"Really, you have nothing you want to say to me, Officer?"

"No, Lieutenant, nothing" he denies.

"Oh I think you do" she insists "since you don't seem to have a problem saying things behind my back, do you Offic-er?"

"I don't say things behind your back, Sir" he denies.

"Yes, you do" she states in a flat voice, anger simmering just beneath the surface. "You've been saying negative things about me for over a month now" she declares "and I won't to-lerate it anymore! This is a unit officer, we work as a team. If you can't join us without saying anything derogatory about your commanding officer, I will suspend you without pay. Is that understood, Officer? Having any trouble understanding me now?" she asks.

"You'll just have to suspend me then Sir, because I say what I think and I don't think you should be my commanding officer."

"Fine, then get out, Officer, you are officially on suspension until further notice, without pay, did I include that" she asks with a snarl.

"Yes, Sir, fine, I'm out of here."

"Hold officer, I need your gun and your badge before you leave this office. Thank you" she says after he jerks the badge out of his pocket and the gun out of its holder and tosses them on her desk.

Well, that was unpleasant she decides, but justified, now on to more important matters. "Detective, how's that background coming?" asks Kat as she walks back into the bull pen.

"Good, better than it was. At least I'm getting somewhere now, since you don't need clearance for the parents" she adds with a smile. "They're being treated as normal citizens, and that's nice for a change" she sighs. "I have found a connection, as it were, between George and Quinton Uqbahtor. Granted, they're from the same town, and the circle of acquaintances is small which makes it more feasible for them to have a connection, but this connection seems to go back to Iran."

"What?" cries Kat. *"Iran?"* I'm hearing that country's name way to often here she realizes. The big connection has to be Iran. But what the hell is it, she wonders?

"Alright, print that information out Des and I'll take it to Capitol headquarters, since I'm heading that way anyway.

"Keep working on the Malik's. I want to know about his parents, their connections, everything. The last time they went to the doctor and what it was for" she adds.

"Hi Eli, how are you?" Kat asks after she arrives at Capitol headquarters, after having a difficult time finding parking. "I had to park on the roof of the parking garage. I don't know where all the damn cars come from, there don't seem to be that many people here, but the parking is always so bad!"

"Yeah, it's always like that" Eli agrees with a grin."You

can't let it get to you since there's nothing you can do about it; you just have to go with the flow."

"That sounds like a California way of life" she remarks teasingly. "You're showing your colors."

"Yeah, I know and I'm really starting to miss L.A. The weather there is so much nicer" he adds with yearning.

"Yeah, I know, this year has been a tough one for the D.C. area. Of course, it's all because you're here" she adds with a straight face.

"Right, now the weather's my fault too" he says with a grin.

"So, what's new over here?" she asks.

"Well, let's see, we found Addy, he's in Iran at the moment."

"How the hell did he get there" she demands.

"Your guess is a good as ours" he admits in frustration.

"Great, we can't get to him there. That would be a different department. So now, what are we going to do?" she asks as Mallory and Devon wander over to where she's been talking with Eli.

"Hey, Kat" Mallory says while Devon just smiles at her. "We're waiting for the Malik information to come through. They think they'll have something pretty soon."

"Good, it seems we're at an impasse at the moment" she murmurs.

"I have a report" Eli yells after he hangs up his cell. "The lab has just confirmed that the poison in the lime of my drink was the exact same one as the one that killed Jeff Stewart. The bartender is being brought back to D.C. to stand trial, he's being charged with murder one and attempted murder of a federal officer. That should get him the needle for this. That's one down and a few more to go. At least we know who killed Stewart, but not who killed Delrose. We know who killed the Speaker and that was Jackman. The only one still out there hanging is Delrose's murderer, but we'll get him or her, or whomever. We also know that William Blaketon was killed by Elroy Wade, the serial killer. He used his signature style, so he was easy to figure out, it's just too bad he's dead, Eli says wistfully. "We could have put him in the cell next to the bartender."

"We have a little bit more information on Malik, unfortunately, he's checking out clean" Devon remarks in frustration."I know his records have been altered to even the most minor of details and that whoever did the altering was a pro."

"I think that with the information we do have, if we head over there, it might shake him up a little. Maybe enough for him to make a mistake."

"Alright, I'm in" Kat says "but I'm not driving. I had to park on the roof of the parking garage. I'm not moving my car until I go home tonight" she insists with determination.

Devon laughs and says "you might not be able to see your car by that time, it will be a snowman. It's snowing that hard right now."

"Great" she grumbles in disgust. "Anyone heard from Snake today" she asks as they all get on the elevator to head to the parking garage?"

"Not yet, why?" Mallory asks.

"No reason, I was just curious."

"We're here to see George Malik" Devon informs the receptionist.

"I'm sorry Sir, but he isn't here yet."

"Not here? Is that usual for him?" Devon asks.

"No Sir, he's never been late that I know of, and he's never missed a day of work either. I'm not sure what happened today. Maybe he got called somewhere else this morning and forgot to let me know" she replies doubtfully. "I'm not even sure when you can expect him, since I don't know where he is."

"Have you checked the parking garage, to see if his car is here?" he asks.

"No, I didn't even think of that" she replies in astonishment. "I'll call security and ask them to check his parking spot right away. Oh, dear" she mutters after she hangs up the phone and looks at the people staring at her, trying to read her expression on whether or not his car is there."They said it was parked in its usual spot. Sir, now I really don't know where he could be" she admits in confusion and fear.

"Have you checked his office?"

"No Sir, the door was closed when I got in, just like it always is, so I just assumed that he wasn't in yet. I haven't heard any noises coming from his office this morning, either."

"Mind if we check his office" Devon asks out of courtesy, he's going to look anyway if she minds or not, she just doesn't need to know that.

"Sir, I can't let you do that, he doesn't like anyone in his office if he's not with them."

"I'm not going in his office alone" he promises "you can come with me so that we'll have witnesses."

"Oh" she replies nervously "I don't know" she says in confusion. "Maybe it would be alright, since we are worried about him. Alright, here are the keys, we'll go in, but don't touch anything" she adds in fear "that way, he won't even know we checked his office."

"Fine" he replies as he moves in to open the door with the key.

"Kat, Mallory, Eli, there's a problem in here" he says after he cracks the door open.

"You better stay back Miss, this is going to be bad, I think" he admits after he smells the ripe scent of death permeating out the crack in the door.

"No, I can't let you go in there without me, Sir, we made a deal."

"Yeah, well, you can go in, but don't blame me if you get sick."

After a shocked gasp, the receptionist teeters on rubber legs and notices the room dim around her as she collapses in a dead faint. George Malik is sitting at his desk without his skin.

"We have another murder" Devon announces.

"It looks like the first only reversed" Eli remarks.

"Yeah, it does look like the Blaketon murder, except the skin is missing this time" Kat says.

"I'm going to call this in, someone get the receptionist out of here before she comes to, she'll just pass out again if she sees this" Devon orders.

"We'll get her" Eli says as he and Kat help move her while

Devon pulls out his cell phone to notify the coroner.

What the heck is going on? We just start getting close and boom, something else happens. It's not going to be easy keeping the media out of this one, he decides after he hangs up from dispatch. "Mallory, let's work the crime scene a little until the medical examiner gets here."

"This can't be where this whole thing occurred" she says. "There's not enough blood pooled around and in order to do something like this, it would leave a lot of blood and tissue. It's just not possible for this to be the kill zone."

"I'll start checking the hallways after I notify security to lock down the building. No one leaves and no one enters" he states.

"Devon, maybe you should call Jacob. He's got live feed from this sight. He may know something already" Kat suggests.

"Yeah, I thought of that, I'll call him" he agrees.

"What?" Jacob demands. "No, we haven't heard or seen anything from that sight. Let me check, I'll get back to you in a minute" he promises and hangs up.

"Shit" yells Jacob to the agent at the desk. "Didn't you wonder why he didn't come in to the office this morning, has he ever missed a day of work?" he demands. "You should have been suspicious! Damn it, we knew he had a jammer, I thought you'd taken care of it" he yells at the agent.

"I had, Sir. There must have been another jammer. Something different than the one we found, one that was just as strong if not stronger" he admits in confusion. "That's the only way anyone could have pulled this off!"

"Great, just great" Jacob yells angrily. "Now we have the Director of DHS dead in his office, skinned like the first murder, only this time the skin was taken and the body was left. And, need I remind you, we don't have a video of what happened. I'll be in my office" he grounds out as he stomps to the back of the room.

"Devon, its Jacob, we have no fucking video of what happened. Someone had a jammer that messed with our surveillance. Yeah, I know. I don't know, since we didn't see anything happen. Yeah, I've got guys on that right now. We can at least see who came and went during the night. I'll let you know" he promises.

"Well" Devon says "Jacob sounds like he's spitting tacks. They didn't get any video feed from this office, because whoever did this jammed it with some kind of electronic device. He's looking now at all the video feed he does have, including the parking garage. He's hoping that he'll be able to pick up on someone moving around suspiciously. He said he'd call with any news."

"We have someone; we're running a facial recognition program on him right now to see if it's someone we have in the data base. Unfortunately, it looks like a professional hit. If that's the case, we don't have many hit men in our base. But we'll keep looking" Jacob promises Devon.

"What have you got?" Jacob asks.

"We're still working the scene, but we do know that Malik, if that's who the body is, wasn't killed here."

"The primary crime scene is still being searched for. We have a news bulletin going out at the two o'clock time frame notifying the public of the murder, and asking them to be on the lookout for the remains, or a bloody crime scene. We're also setting up hotline numbers as we speak. We hope someone finds the actual crime scene before it snows anymore and destroys any more evidence. The coroner just removed the body, along with any evidence he saw. The crime scene techs are working the office now. Hopefully we'll get a hit on something, soon. In the mean time, the medical examiner is sending a DNA sample out to have it tested, to determine who the body belongs to. We should have some answers by this evening."

"Oops, hold on a second Jacob, I've got another call coming in. Shit" he says as he gets back on line. "It's Jane Martin. She wants to see us as soon as possible. We'll have to go and see her, as soon as we get the chance" Devon decides with disgust. "People just have no clue what we do and how busy we get after a murder."

"I hear you" Jacob says sympathetically. "I'll get back to you if I get any more information."

"Yeah, ditto here" Devon promises and hangs up.

"Ms. Martin, I'm sorry I had to put you on hold, we're a little busy at the moment. What can I do for you?" Devon asks.

"I need to see you and Lieutenant Thomas and Agents Mallory and Eli Callander, as soon as you're available."

"It may be a while; we have a case to work while it's hot. We need to gather evidence before it gets destroyed, so I doubt we'll be able to make it anytime today" he says firmly.

"No, you don't understand, I need to see you about the case, immediately. I may know who did this" she says quietly.

"Really?"questions Devon."Alright, I'll try to gather everyone up as soon as possible. It's a zoo outside, with all the media vans and people. We have to get through that before we can head out. I'll try to be there in the next half hour. That's the best I can do" he admits apologetically.

"Fine, a half an hour is fine" she says quietly."I won't be talking to anyone else until I've spoken with you" she assures him.

"Listen up guys" Devon says to his siblings and Kat. "Jane Martin wants to see us as soon as possible. I told her we could be there within the next half hour, so we need to tie things up and hustle. Make sure this place is locked down when you leave" he orders the crime scene techs, "we'll be back later to go over more of it" he reassures them.

"We almost made the half hour mark" he says with a sigh. "Now, let's see what the Speaker of the House knows, I'm really hoping it's some good information."

"Capitol Police to see Jane Martin" Devon says to the receptionist.

"Go right in" she advises "she's been waiting for you.

"Ms. Martin, Deputy Chief Devon Callander, along with Agents Mallory and Eli Callander and Lieutenant Thomas of D.C. Metro One are here. May we come in?" he asks as he knocks lightly on her door.

"Please, come in Deputy Chief, Agents, Lieutenant and have a seat."

"You told me on the phone that you might have some information on the killer of George Malik, Ms. Martin?"

"Yes, I do" she says. "It's someone by the name of Abdul Adl Thayer. I believe he's involved with this." After a quick glance at Kat, Devon responds with "are you saying a person by the name of Abdul Adl Thayer, also known as Addy, might be involved with this murder?" he asks incredulously.

"Yes, that's right. He's known to hire professional hit men, and one of his favorites is someone that kills in the same manner as George was killed."

"Jane, were you aware that William Blaketon was killed in this same manner?" he asks in a too calm voice.

"Yes Sir, I was."

"Why didn't you come forward at that time?" he demands.

"Because I knew it wasn't Abdul that did it that time. I questioned him personally, and he denied it. I had no cause to disbelieve him, Agent."

"Since you're not a law enforcement professional, you had no business questioning him and withholding evidence Ms. Martin. You did something we call obstructing justice, which means that I can and will have to arrest you."

"Wait, you can't arrest me" she says shakily "I haven't done anything wrong."

"By not informing us of this earlier, you have obstructed justice. We could have arrested Abdul Thayer and then George Malik would be alive today. So yes, you did do something wrong."

"I think I need legal counsel" she says. "I need to call the President too, he's not going to be happy about this, not happy at all."

"He wants to talk to you, Deputy Chief" she informs him and hands him her phone after reaching the President.

"Yes Sir, I understand Sir, Mr. President, we'll wait. I promise not to arrest her until you've seen her. He's on his way" Devon reports to the other Agents."He said to give him ten minutes and he'll be right here."

TWENTY NINE

"Jane, what have you done?" asks the President of the United States as he enters Jane's office preceded by a couple of Secret Service Agent's with their weapons drawn and followed by a host of them.

"Sit down everyone, while I talk to Jane, please" he orders everyone in the room. They all sit as they watch the President talk quietly and quickly to Jane while the Secret Service surround the room, checking all entry's and exits, windows and doors."Clear" they report to each other quietly. Now that they're done searching the room, they stand back against the wall and wait quietly while the President continues to talk with Jane. "Good" he says as he finishes what he was saying and turns to look at the agents in the office.

"Ladies, Gentlemen, we need to talk" he states as he takes the seat behind the desk, Jane standing at his side. "Jane informs me that she requested you to come here and talk with her. That she *thought* that she knew the person that could be responsible for the murder of our Director of Homeland Security? She informed me that when she told you, you threatened to arrest her, as if she could have anything to do with this. I don't understand why this happened" he remarks. "She was trying to help and you want to arrest her for that?" he asks in confusion. "No wonder the public refuses to help the police in such matters. They're afraid that you'll arrest them, innocent citizens, just because they want to help. It looks to me like we need to overhaul our justice system. People should feel comfortable coming to our safety forces to help them when they can, not feel threatened by them."

"As it is, you were lucky it was Jane that contacted you and was able to talk with me, since we can't have innocent people being accused of *'obstruction of justice.'* I believe that was your term. We must begin allowing people to come forward to help when they can without the threat of jail. This is unacceptable, Agents. I want you to go back to your offices and figure out who was responsible for this murder. If you can't allow the public to help then I would have to say you are on your own. This ends here and now" he states.

"She has retracted any and all information that she willingly wanted to give you. You are back to square one, do you understand me?" he demands.

"Yes Sir, we understand" they reply.

"Thank you, you are dismissed."

"Well" Devon says after they get back in the car and head away from the Capitol. "How do you go up against the Commander and Chief of the United States? He's the highest power in this country, and he knows it."

"We can't go up against him" Mallory replies quietly. "Jane knows something, so now I guess we'll have to start with Addy. Even though he's in Iran, it doesn't mean that he didn't hire someone to do this murder. We heard her, maybe he was responsible for the murder of Blaketon too, who knows."

"That will be a hard one to prove" Eli mutters "but we can work on it."

"Let's talk to Jacob and see what he can offer us by way of connections and equipment. He's done this a lot more than we have" Mallory admits. "I mean, it's his life, so let's talk to him, tap into his experience."

"We'll get him on the phone again, when we get back to Headquarters" Devon agrees.

"We need to regroup and get this investigation pointed in the right direction. We can schedule a meet time, sometime after the media blitz."

"Shit" Eli says as he hangs up his cell phone. Oh, oh, Devon wonders, now what?

"That was one of the agents I left in Maui. He said that Casey Bellwood, the bartender that we had in custody, tried to escape as they were getting ready to transport him to the airport to bring him back here.

"He decided to run, started to cross the street and got hit as soon as he stepped off the curb by a bus that was going about forty-five miles an hour. He was practically vaporized. So now we have no one to bring to justice for the murder of Jeff Stewart, and the attempted murder of me. These murders are all related, yet we can't seem take anyone responsible to court because something always seems to happen to them."

"Crap" Devon says aggravated, "I'm getting pretty sick of all the coincidences that seem to be surrounding these murders. We've been foiled at every stop, snags everywhere."

As soon as his cell starts to ring, he grabs it and hears "It's Jacob, Devon, can all of you come out to the cabin? I think we need to talk and go over some of the things that have happened lately."

"I agree" Devon says "and so does everyone on this end. We can head out there right now, since the Speaker of the House is taking over the media blitz that I had planned to do. We don't need to stick around for it now, so it will give us a good opportunity to escape while everyone's busy. Do you have directions or a different route for me? I want to take every precaution to make sure no one is able to follow us. I'm even going to change vehicles to one I know they won't think to tap."

"Yeah, I'll get them to you after you change vehicles. That way there's no chance of anyone intercepting that information. We've run into more corruption than I thought possible, in a really short amount of time. Let's hope we can do something about this." Jacob says.

"Welcome everyone" he says as he meets their car at the cabin. "I'll move the car after you go on in, and be with you in just a minute. I don't want to leave any chance of discovery out here" he explains as he drives their vehicle further away. After everyone is gathered, they head downstairs to the war room.

Kat's been in it, but none of the others have, so they gaze around the room in amazement. Who would have thought that anything like this exists, in the underground of a cabin that looks like any of the other hunting cabins that are dotted throughout the area? This is awesome, Devon thinks as he realizes just what he's looking at. People are monitoring every important office in D.C., plus the outside of some and the parking garages of others, it's shocking, the capabilities that we have. After viewing everything that's going on and realizing the capabilities, they all head for Jacobs office at the back of the room.

"Now we can talk freely" he says as he sits behind his desk.

"Jacob, I had no idea that such a place existed" Devon admits. Eli agrees silently and Mallory just stares in awe at her brother.

"I never had a clue" Mallory admits in shock. "You're a pretty important person, aren't you? This all reminds me of some of the fictional books I've read in the past, where everything is hush-hush, and things like this exist. I was suspicious, but didn't really know that this was a reality!"

"Well, they say if you can think it up for a book or movie, then it's probably real somewhere. And now you see that it is" he smiles ruefully. "Everything is real here, but also top secret. No one, not even the President, really knows about this place except for those of us that work here, and now you four. The President knows something like this exists but he has no idea where or what is real and isn't. That gives us some room to work in safety, which we need since we face the worst of the world in these walls, and survive them."

"Alright, let's make some plans" Jacob says. "I heard what happened to your murder suspect in Maui, Eli, and I'm sorry about that" he admits in sympathy. "That sucked, but with everything that's been happening, I can't believe it wasn't set up. When something like that happens, it could be a coincidence, but that would be amazing to me, since I really don't believe in coincidence. It goes against my training to think that way. So if I act suspicious, you'll know why."

"We're going to need to stick together closely with this" he adds "but you'll have to be constantly on guard, now that the Speaker of the House doesn't trust you. This will just make things more difficult. I have already watched the video of what went on in her office this morning. You were definitely in the right when you threatened her with arrest. I'm really not surprised that the President came to her rescue and twisted it all to make you look incompetent. That was his goal and he did a good job with it. So I would have to say, fight the battles that can be fought, and walk away from the ones that can't, it's good for your health. It will help to keep you alive. I would hate to see anything happen to any one of you, we're all family, you know."

"So, let's look at what we can actually do for these murder victims. They're depending on us, since we're the only ones that want to find justice for them. There are going to be a lot of things said in the near future, so prepare yourselves. You didn't pick amateurs to attack, you found the pros and they don't and won't back down easily, because they're good at what they do" he warns. "I've been watching some of them for a long time and they seldom make mistakes, everything they do is for a purpose, a greater purpose than you can imagine."

"Alright, so now we need Addy, somehow brought back, and in the near future. We have a general idea of where he's at in Iran, but they don't extradite, hell, they don't cooperate at all with us. If I'd have to pick a country that hates us most, it would be them. We also know that there will be a funeral for Malik, probably a pretty big one because of his position in the U.S., I'm sure it will be huge and probably televised on every station in the country, which means security's going to be very heavy.

I have no doubt that anyone with any position in our politics will try to make an appearance. Next year is a voting year, so you can imagine that they'll all try to use this as a free commercial for their polls. I don't see anyone bypassing this opportunity 'he says resignedly "which means that this unit is going to be pretty busy. We have to monitor everything, to protect the president, plus the secret service will be in constant contact with us until this whole ordeal is finished."

"Now, we need proof that it was Malik in that desk chair. Kat, will you call the medical examiner, please?"

"I'm on it Snake" Kat promises.

"Devon, we need to hear what the forensic team has to say about the crime scene, so can you call them?"

"Mallory, Eli, I need you to help watch some of the video feed from last night. We're going to try and see who did this murder, if we can get a visual on anyone. Since that falls in both yours and Eli's area of expertise, I'd appreciate your help. Alright, that covers things for now. Let's get to work and we'll report back here when we know anything or on the hour if not. Thanks" he says as he gets up and leaves.

"What have you got Kat?" he asks at their meet on the hour.

"I talked with Dr. Zorgath and he confirmed that it was indeed George Malik that was murdered. He had a bit of a problem even doing the autopsy, because the coroner for the Department of Homeland Security showed up at his office and demanded release of the body before the autopsy was completed. He said he had to do some underhanded fancy stepping to get around that, but he managed to hold on to the body long enough to finish. The Department of Homeland Security is a pretty aggressive department, but he withstood them and got the results he was after. They definitely weren't happy with him for that, but what can you do?" she shrugs with a grin.

"Excellent" he says "how about you Devon? Anything at the forensic end?" he asks.

"They're running some prints that were found on the desk and on the corner of the door, but with so many people coming and going prior to collection, they aren't very comfortable with finding anything. I did hear through the grapevine that a funeral is going to be held for George Malik on Sunday, at the Chapel on the Hill, and that it will be televised, but only members of the congress, senate and DHS will be allowed to attend the funeral. There simply won't be enough room for the world to be there" he says with a smirk "so that part of the process is now scheduled."

"Good" Jacob replies. "We'll start getting our stuff set up so we can monitor everything that goes on. If we get lucky and the murderer shows up, we'll get him.

"I also heard that Jane Martin will not be attending the funeral. She's headed for Texas to be with his family and friends from back home. She stated that she wanted to attend her church to honor Malik's memory with the other people in the world that cared for him. 'He was a friend, after all' she's said to quote. So we won't be able to watch her, but I'm sure she'll be in touch" Devon finishes.

"Good" Jacob says.

"Mallory, Eli, anything on video?"

"We watched the footage over and over, of the building, sans Malik's office, of course, and we did see something that was dark. A shadowy shape, but no matter how many times we watched it and how much we tried to enhance it or clarify it, or how many different angels we tried, we got nothing. Your guys are excellent, Jacob, so I figure if they can't get it clear, then no one can."

"Yep, that's pretty much true" he agrees in disappointment.

"Alright then, what's next?" he asks of the room in general.

"I think we need to get ready for the funeral, since it's the day after tomorrow" Devon responds. "I want to be ready in case someone shows that shouldn't. Also, I think someone needs to follow Jane to Texas. I'd still like to keep my eye on her, even though she won't be at the funeral. Something could change or happen and we need to be prepared."

"I agree with you on that Devon and I've already set up a team that will go and infiltrate the church that she will be attending for his other funeral. I've also activated them so that they'll leave in the morning and get there ahead of schedule. I want to use some of our electronics, monitor everything, and listen to everything. We can watch to make sure that everything stays normal there."

"Alright people, listen up. The funeral starts in about two hours and we want eyes and ears everywhere. We can't afford to have anything happen today. This is going to be televised in so many different countries that we need to have everything covered. The President and Vice President will be attending this funeral, and the President may even appoint someone to this position after the funeral service. We aren't sure of anything at this time. We'll just have to take the watch and see attitude."

"Everything seems to be in order" Jacob comments as he watches the live video feed from the church. "I'll bet the scent of flowers is overwhelming. There are so many flowers you can barely see the casket. I thought they were supposed to donate to charity instead of sending flowers. None of those people are any good at following orders. The casket is sitting up on the stage area, so everyone can see it, but the flowers almost overwhelm it. The chairs for the President are near the head of the casket. That casket probably costs more that I make in a year" he remarks. "Of course, Malik would have insisted on an expensive box. I believe Jane picked out the majority of things for the funeral and then decided to go to her home town and be at the church that both she and Malik attended in Texas, for the funeral" Mallory adds.

"We're coming down to less than a half hour before the service begins. We have twenty five different angles going, so if anything suspicious occurs, we'll see it" he comments. "People are starting to fill the benches in the church, but I don't expect the President until the exact time, if not a few minutes later. So keep your eyes tuned in, let's not miss anything today."

"The Vice President just arrived and is taking his seat on the stage. The President should be arriving momentarily. I bet he walks in with the Minister of the Church. They'll all be sharing in the service, to honor Malik. There he is and there's the Minister, following. This is about to begin" he warns his unit. "Let's not blink people, we need to see everything. The Minister is rising to call the service to order, after that, the President will begin speaking."

"I want to thank everyone for being here today" the Minister says to the packed room. "Mr. George Malik was an outstanding individual and a good man; he contributed greatly to our lives and to our country. He took his placement and his office very seriously and would help any and everyone who ever called upon him for it. He will be greatly missed. Great men like George Malik are few and far........B O O M !

"Oh my god" screaming ensues live at the church, on the video. All you can hear from every monitor in the war room except the ones destroyed by the explosion are screaming, yelling and panic. "There's been an explosion, from the casket at the front of the church. The smoke is so dense that it's impossible to see anything. The President and the Vice President were sitting within feet of the casket. We can't see that part of the church, so don't know what happened to them. We won't know that until we're able to see what's going on.

The Church has been swarmed with every FBI Agent, CIA Agent, DHS Officer and Capitol Police Officer in the nearby vicinity. Its mass chaos, as you can see. This is Sydney Norwood, live from the Chapel on the Hill."

"What happened to the President" yells Jacob. "He's not moving around, not that I can see. Bring up the other feeds; we need eyes and ears everywhere. This is un-freakin believable" Jacob yells. "Quiet people" he yells till he's almost hoarse "this has been a shock, but we have a job to do here and we need to remember it."

"Report, the President, any sign of him?" yells Jacob.

"No Sir, not at this time."

"What about the Vice President?"

"No Sir, nothing."

"Damn it" he growls. "Who cleared the building after it was checked?"

"We had the team go in yesterday and check absolutely everything. They found nothing; they also guarded the building through the night up until the service began today, Sir. No one could have gone in there and planted anything without our knowledge."

"The place was clean, Sir. The casket, though, wasn't brought to the church until this morning. It had to have been the casket. That's the only thing that we had no control over. It came from the funeral home, so we didn't check it. It looked like the casket was actually the point of explosion, it must have been planted in the casket before they put Malik in it" he says.

"That's just conjecture, at this time. Trust me, we'll get the facts. Contact whoever was in charge at the Chapel. I need to know if the President and Vice President are alive, and I want that information now, before the media gets it" Jacob demands.

"Sir, I have Morgan on the line, he was responsible for the unit you sent there yesterday."

"Go" Jacob says into his headphone "what have you got?"

"It's mass chaos here, Sir. We've not been able to locate either the President or the Vice President. The Minister's missing also, and the casket, there's not much left of it. I would prepare for the worse. From what I can see, there is a very low probability of either the President or the Vice President surviving this."

"This is unbelievable" Sydney says as the cameras pan back to her, standing near the media van, not near the church. "As you can see, the smoke is heavy, thick and black. The President and the Vice President are still unaccounted for. They may have escaped out the back before this happened, although from what I hear, it's not probable. As soon as we find out what happened to the President and the Vice President, we'll let you know. Remember, we are the first with the news for Metro D.C, this is Sidney Norwood, live."

"I need the team that went with the Speaker of the House to contact me immediately" Jacob orders.

"Yes, Sir, I have them on Comcast two Sir, Mike Harold."

"Agent, I want you to listen closely. You must monitor everything that happens at the church where the Speaker of the House is right now. The Secret Service have rushed her out of the church, and are preparing her for Air Force One, to take the oath of office for the President of the United States, since neither the President nor the Vice President have been located post explosion.

"The United States cannot be without a head, and the Speaker of the House is the next in line. The Secret Service has requested that you be put on standby and join the motorcade that's transporting her to the airport. Consider yourself part of the security force that's protecting the President. Report to me anything unusual, and I'll pass that information on to the necessary parties."

"This is Sidney Norwood, live at the Chapel on the Hill with breaking news. There has been a huge explosion at the Chapel on the Hill during the funeral for the Director of the Department of Homeland Security. It is mass chaos, as you can see in the distance" she reports with a pasty white face, suffering from shock at what she just witnessed. "This is as close as we can get due to the nature of what just happened. The President and the Vice President were both attending this service and have not been located as of yet. I repeat, the President and the Vice President were both attending this service and have not been located as of yet.

"They were sitting in the blast zone, from what an informant has told us. As you can see, its total chaos at the Chapel on the Hill. You can hear the screaming and hysterics from this distance that are still occurring, and see people trying to leave. Security is at the highest it's ever been and the police, FBI, CIA, and DHS are questioning anyone who attended this service. We're hoping to be able to interview someone who was in the chapel at the time of the explosion. We can pass more information on to you as soon as we receive it. The death toll looks to be high, but we won't know that for sure until they can get the area cleared and start taking a census."

"This was a terrorist attack on our country, against our President and Vice President. Until they've been located, we have to assume the worst. The Speaker of the House was not attending this service. She had gone to Texas to be at the service there, since that's where both George Malik and she are from. Since they were friends, she felt it appropriate to spend this time with the ones that were closest to him. I heard only moments ago that Air Force One has picked her up from Texas and are en-route to D.C. She is prepared to be sworn into the office of the President as we speak, on Air Force One by a Supreme Justice. We'll let you know more as soon as we find out. This is Sidney Norwood, live at the Chapel on the Hill."

"Bring up sector two" Jacob commands. "Let's see what's left of the casket and the stage where the President and Vice

President were last seen. The smoke seems to be clearing out. We should have a better visual now. Shit, there's nothing left of the casket, except for small pieces. Pan over to where the President and Vice President were sitting. Nothing, absolutely nothing except some smoldering pieces of the casket, wilted roses and blood red rose petals lying all over the stage. There's a small part of the podium that the Minister was standing at, with no sign of the minister or of any chairs either. This isn't good" he remarks. "The blast area was strong and contained to the area near the head of the casket where the President and Vice President were sitting."

"It looks like it was definitely set to take out the President. The blast also took out parts of the first few rows in the front of the church. It's a good thing people always fill the church from the back forward, there probably weren't as many people in the first few rows. But after looking at the scene, I can't believe anyone could have survived that kind of explosion."

"Whoever did this was definitely serious. Somehow whoever it was, slipped through our defenses. It's official, we just had a terrorist attack against the United States, taking out the biggest target in the free world. Since we didn't find anything prior to the blast, it had to have been lining the casket. It was probably some form of plastic explosive, which is not easily detectable to equipment. You can bet there'll be some kind of retaliation for this attack. Let's contact our foreign agents and see what the news is, where this attack came from, and what faction is trying to take responsibility."

"Alright people, let's get out there and start our own investigation. We know that every other law enforcement agency is already out there or will be real soon, but that doesn't mean we can sit back and wait for their results. We need our own answers, and we need to look at the things they aren't looking at, so let's do it" he commands. "Information passing is on a need to know basis only. We share when we hear what they know, not before and we never share everything" he reminds them all as they leave.

THIRTY

"This is Sidney Norwood; with breaking news live from WKTL Channel 7 News, Metro D.C Area, your only full news channel. We are live and have been since the horrible explosion that occurred at the Chapel on the Hill church of D.C. This is the site where the President and the Vice President of our United States were killed while attending the funeral service for George Malik, the Director of Homeland Security, who was murdered earlier this week. Our law enforcement agencies have been combing the explosion site for hours now with no sign of either the President or Vice President. The worst has now been decided; that both Bruce Wellington, the President of the United States, and Joseph Masey, the Vice President of the United States, were killed this morning while attending a funeral service for George Malik. They were killed by a bomb that was concealed in the casket holding the body of the Director of Homeland Security."

"That explosion also killed the Minister of the Chapel on the Hill Church, during his eulogy and killed and injured numerous others that were seated in the front of the Chapel.

The medical examiner's office is still investigating the scene, along with borrowed forensic technicians from multiple surrounding neighborhoods. They're hoping to have the crime scene completed within the next twenty-four to forty-eight hours, barring any complications at the scene. Stay tuned for further updates as we receive them."

"This is Sidney Norwood, WKTL Channel 7 News, Metro D.C., with more Breaking News. We have just been informed that Jane Martin has been sworn in as the new President of the

United States on Air Force One, and has already arrived in D.C. She will be holding a press conference approximately one hour from now, to reassure the Unites States public that, and I quote "the running of the Government and the safety of its people are and always will be at the very top of her priority list."

"This is Sidney Norwood, WKTL Channel 7 News, Metro D.C with more breaking news. The President of Iran, Murabbi Abdul-Majeed has just announced that his country is greatly saddened by what has occurred on United States soil and to our President and Vice President of the United States. He wants to offer any and all investigational help in finding the person or persons responsible for this reprehensible act. He is also offering help to the new President of the United States in finding the responsible parties, as a gesture of goodwill. The Queen of England has also offered any help and all of their condolences to our country on behest of the President and the Vice President's deaths. Leaders from all over the world have come forward and offered their help and condolences at this tragic time. This is Sidney Norwood, WKTL Channel 7 News, Metro D.C." she finishes white faced and with tears in her eyes, "stay tuned for more breaking news as we receive it."

"Devon, it's me, Dad. What are we going to do son? This is a terrible thing. Your mother and I are really upset by the senseless murder of our own President and Vice President. What should we do? Should we leave town. Is it safe here, and if we leave, where would we go that's safe?"

"Dad, Dad, calm down. You don't need to leave town, you're safe where you are. This was an attack on the President and Vice President, not on the citizens of the United States. Relax, you don't need to worry. You're safe. The armed forces of the United States are on alert, and in position to strike should anyone try anything. The United States is not allowing anyone in or out of the country right now, we are officially in lock down. Things will be a little tight for awhile, until we can get a handle on this, but it shouldn't affect you or Mom. You're both safe here, I promise."

"Are you sure Devon, can I tell your Mom all this. I'm not sure I feel safe staying in Washington at this time. What happens if they blow up the White House or the Capitol Building or even the Pentagon?"

"Dad, it's alright, I promise. Don't worry. There's no way anyone's going to be able to bomb anything. They would be shot out of the sky if they appeared in our airspace. All flights from everywhere in the U.S. have been stopped. This is being treated as an attack on United States soil. Air space is restricted until further notice, so don't worry, you'll be fine. Just stay home, stay away from any large groups of people. People become irrational when they're afraid and I'm sure there's a lot of panic going on right now. Just stay home, stay inside and keep your doors and windows locked for a few days. Just until the police can get a handle on any groups causing trouble, and break them up or arrest them, if need be."

"Alright, Devon, if your sure. I don't like this, but I'll follow your instructions. Will you call us with any new information, please? I think that would help your mother and me a lot if we knew we were being told everything. We trust you Devon, to tell us what's going on."

"Sure, Dad, I'll phone you as soon as I learn more."

"Thank you Devon. I feel better now. You stay safe out there, and if you see Mallory, Eli and Jacob, oh and Kat, tell them I said to stay safe. We're living in dangerous times Devon, I just know it" Joseph Callander says in his doomsday voice, before he hangs up.

"Oh, boy" Devon says to Mallory.

"Dad, huh?" she replies to the look on his face.

"Yeah, he and Mom are pretty shook up."

"What's up?" Eli asks as he walks up to Devon and Mallory.

"Dad just called. I should have called them after this happened to reassure them, but I didn't think about it, everything's just so crazy. Now they're in a panic and ready to run to a different state to be safe. They have that whole doomsday mind set going on, so they're afraid. I told them to stay put, that they aren't in danger where they are, but not to go out into the public. People act crazy when things like this happen, there'll be looting and vandalism, just because they'll think the police are too busy to deal with that kind of stuff. I think I calmed them down, and I promised to call if I found out anything else that will affect them."

"You're a good son" Eli remarks sincerely to Devon, "thank you for taking such good care of them all these years."

"This is Sidney Norwood, WKTL Channel 7 News, Metro D.C reporting live from the Chapel on the Hill church. Earlier today the President of the United States, Bruce Wellington, and the Vice President of the United States, Joseph Masey was killed in an explosion during a funeral service for George Malik, the Director of Homeland Security. That explosion destroyed one third of the church, the casket that held the remains of George Malik, the Director of Homeland Security, and the Minister as he was giving his eulogy. So far the totals for this bombing are seven deaths and seventeen injuries, one critical. The new President of the United States will be coming forward in the next couple of minutes to talk with the public. Jane Martin, the previous Speaker of the House, was sworn in to the Presidency a few hours after the explosion that killed the President, on Air Force One during her flight back to D.C. According to the Presidential Succession act of 1947, the Speaker of the House is next in line to become President should anything happen to the President and the Vice President. The House Majority Leader follows the Speaker of the House. I believe that means that Quinton Uqbahtor will be the new Vice President of the United States. That announcement is expected to be made by the new President during her speech and acceptance of her role as the new President."

"This is Sidney Norwood, WKTL Channel 7 News, Metro D.C with more breaking news. A few remains have just been found that confirm that the President and the Vice President were indeed killed in that explosion. The remains were discovered by cadaver dogs that were brought in to help with the search for the dead, and are being transported to the medical examiner's office for positive identification" she reports excitedly. "This is Sidney Norwood, with Channel 7 News, Metro D.C., your most trusted source, always first and always fast with your up to date information."

"This is Sidney Norwood, WKTL Channel 7 News, Metro D.C. The new President of the United States is going to appear in just a moment. She's in the oval office and will be making a speech to the citizens of the United States. Here she is."

I am Chief Justice Chenowith, and I would like to introduce to you Jane Martin, the President of the United States, and Quinton Uqbahtor, the Vice President of the United States. She would like to address the public during these trying times. It's all yours President Martin."

"Thank you Chief Justice Chenowith. I want to thank you for being here during this terrible time and to say it is with great sadness that I inform you that my good friend Bruce Wellington, the President of the United States and another good friend, Joseph Masey, the Vice President of the United States, were involved in the explosion at the Chapel on the Hill church earlier today while attending the funeral service for the Director of Homeland Security, George Malik. They have been confirmed dead."

"I was in Texas at the time of this terrible incident, attending a different service for George Malik who was murdered earlier this week. Since he was from the same small town in Texas which I am, I thought it honorable to be there to say good bye with others from our church. The Secret Service informed me as they were picking me up, of everything that has happened. They had with them Chief Justice Chenowith, in case that I needed to take over the President's office. Since this happened, he swore me into office earlier today, while onboard Air Force One. This country was never without a President.

I promise you, the American people, that I take this office seriously and will run it according to the wants and needs of the American public and the laws of this country. I will never give up the search for the ones that are responsible for this terrible deed, the assassination of our beloved President and Vice

President. I will do my duty seriously and with great pride, for the United States is a great country. Since the Vice President was also murdered, Quinton Uqbahtor will be moving into that position.

According to law, he is in line for that position and I welcome him, he will be of great assistance to me while I learn all that I need to, to maintain the position of President of the United States, and run this great country.

I will speak to you in more depth later tonight, when you've had time to digest all the things that have occurred, and I have had time to discover as much as possible about what exactly occurred this morning at the Chapel on the Hill Church. Do not be afraid for you are well guarded during this time. All air space has been restricted in and over the United States until further notice. We have fighter jets manned on the ground ready to intercept anyone that breaks our no fly zones. They will be shown no mercy should they attempt to penetrate our air space. We have also activated every branch of service, in protection of the United States during these uncertain times.

We take seriously the protection of our country and its citizens. You are safe. Please do not be afraid for your lives. We have taken control of this situation and will allow no harm to come to our citizens. I pray that you will feel comfortable in your own homes, and on your own streets. Thank you for taking time today to listen to me and I will be talking to you more thoroughly this evening."

"This is Sidney Norwood, WKTL Channel 7 News, Metro D.C. We just finished listening to the new President of the United States, Jane Martin, who was sworn into office earlier today after the explosion at the Chapel on the Hill church. President Bruce Wellington and Vice President Joseph Masey were in attendance and killed in an explosion that occurred during the funeral service for the Director of Homeland Security, George Malik. He had been found murdered earlier this week in his office on Capitol Hill. He was the fifth person connected to Capitol Hill, murdered in the past six weeks.

And now the President and Vice President, both gone in a horrific explosion that occurred during his funeral. We have not heard from any extremist groups claiming to be the ones that have done this, but I have been assured that no stone will be left unturned while looking for those responsible. We will have more live coverage on the President this evening, she has promised to talk with the American people. Remember "This is Sidney Norwood, with Channel 7 News, Metro D.C., your most trusted source, always first and always fast with your up to date information."

"Anything guys?" asks Jacob, after finishing their preliminary search via planted cameras at the Chapel on the Hill, for explosives.

"Not yet, but the casket is in tiny bits, which demonstrates the primary area of the explosion. The explosion was extremely strong, I'm thinking overkill. There's a group out there that uses similar means when setting up explosive devices. I've got people checking on that and listening for chatter."

"Someone is going to claim this, I have no doubt" Jacob predicts. "The problem is when? The sooner the better it is with these factions. Now, let me make a call. We need to hear from the group that was dispatched to the funeral home. They need to bring in whoever had the opportunity to line that casket with explosives. I want to talk to him ASAP."

"The President of Iran is having a news conference this evening. He's quoted earlier as saying "How saddened he is by the tragic loss of the President and Vice President of the United States." I find it difficult to believe, it's definitely not characteristic of him, since he's always been totally negative of the West, especially the United States. How we are the great corruptor of the world. Now he seems to be backtracking, and that sends up flags." Why now, all of a sudden. What's the connection?

"Good evening, this is Sidney Norwood, with Channel 7 News, Metro D.C., your most trusted source, always first and always fast with your up to date information. Jane Martin, the new President of the United States is scheduled to appear any minute now, with a message for the People of the United States. Directly after that, we will broadcast the President of

Iran's message to the United States, so stay tuned to Channel 7 News, Metro D.C. for all upcoming news events."

"Here she is, the President of the United States" announces Sidney as the cameras pan in and focus on Jane Martin as she walks to the podium "a woman of average height and thin stature with plain brown hair, who always seems to be wearing the same suit, pale face, flat shoes. She doesn't put on pretenses, she just is" Sidney murmurs quietly.

"I want to thank you for your attention to this serious matter. It has been determined that an explosive device was hidden in the casket of George Malik, the Director of Homeland Security and that during his funeral, his casket was used as a weapon to destroy the two most powerful men in the United States. His murderer has not been discovered yet, but is being looked for by every branch of our military. The United States will not sit still while there are assassins out there that have attacked our country, our very own President and Vice President, with no regard to life.

"This will not be tolerated. I have given direct orders this afternoon to search every country, every border, every suspicious individual, and to watch for any behavior that could lead us to the people or possibly the country responsible for the murder of the top government officials of this country.

"In the past five weeks, we have not only lost four individuals from our House of Representatives, but our Director of the Department of Homeland Security, and finally, our President and Vice President of these United States. This must stop now. I believe I speak for the citizens of this great country when I say that there will be no stone left unturned during our investigation.

"We will find those responsible for this unwarranted attack and we will not rest until we have found, apprehended and disposed of this and any threat to the United States. The citizens of the United States need not worry about their future. Your future is secure with me in this office. I will not rest until everything in this country is as it should be. We will make every change that needs to be made to protect our own. I will not be taking questions today after I'm through with this discussion, but questions will be answered later during the week, when we have more information. As of this moment, we have little information. However, I know that in a few days we will have a lot more to offer. Until then, I want to thank you for listening, and now please allow me to do my job. Thank You."

"This is Sidney Norwood, with Channel 7 News, Metro D.C., your most trusted source, always first and always fast with your up to date information. Well, that was brief, to the point and abrupt. What should we think of that? Is she having difficulty taking over the power associated with the Presidency? Who will she appoint to the Director of Homeland Security position? We all have so many questions without any answers. I must say she needed to be more specific as to 'the who's and why's' and less abrupt.

"She told us, but never bothered to even try to answer any of our numerous questions. Questions I believe the public has the right to know the answers for. Granted, she assumed this position under extreme circumstances and hasn't held the Office of the President longer than, what, four hours and this was her second appearance for the media. So I suppose we need to give her a break. I'm sure she'll be more forthcoming in the near future.

"I'm turning it over to you Gerry; we'll be back as soon as there's more breaking news."

"Thanks, Sidney, well be waiting" replies Gerry Partell of World Vision Now, reporting live from New York City. "We have some curious things to report but right now we have live coverage from the President of Iran and his condolences. He is close to beginning his speech, live at his presidential headquarters in Tehran."

"Thank you for joining us during the unstable times that have occurred in the country of the United States of America. What has happened there is a terrible thing. I want to offer my support to the new President of the United States, Jane Martin, to help her with the discovery of the party responsible for the murder of the President and Vice President of the United States. I am offering our help, the help of the Iranian country and its people, to locate any and all persons involved in the assassination of those two people. They will be found and dealt with as quickly as possible. This behavior cannot and will not be tolerated. To Jane Martin, the new President of the United States know this, we are glad to help you during these trying times."

"Well" Gerry Partell of World Vision Now says. "That was quite a speech" he remarks, looking confused. "The President of Iran has never shown any kindness to the United States and has, as a matter of fact, proclaimed for years his dislike of the United States. I'm not sure what this was all about, but it was definitely not expected."

"Lieutenant Callander, we have the suspect from the funeral home. His name is Charles Brighton. He's responsible for cleaning and preparing the casket for the placement of the body. He didn't want to come in, he actually ran, grabbing a gun. I think he was hoping to escape so he didn't have to face anyone. But one of the unit's sharp shooters took out the hand holding the gun. He's slightly injured, although nothing that should get in the way of your interrogation. We should be at the base within the hour."

"Excellent" Jacob replies. "I'll meet you there."

"Devon, I need to talk with you" Eli says into his cell phone. "I'm at the rear of the church looking for remains. We've found a few, so far. I'll come to you" he says as he starts to the front of the church, where the explosion originated.

"What's up?" Devon asks as he straightens up from his crouched position, groaning in relief. "I'm sure not getting any younger" he admits with a groan.

Eli just shakes his head and responds. "You're not that old, you just need to hit the gym more often."

"What's up, Eli?" Devon asks with a mock glare.

"I'm heading out; I need to get back to headquarters. I want to be near the monitors since they're bringing in that person of interest from the funeral home, Charles Brighton, for interrogation at Jacob's base."

"Okay, I'll round everyone up. We can get there probably in the next thirty minutes."

"No, you don't need to round everyone up unless you want to watch the monitors too."

"Yeah, I think we should" Devon decides. "I just thought since we couldn't be a part of the interrogation that we could keep in direct touch of the procedure through our feed to Jacob's base. He informed me when I requested permission to attend this interrogation "to trust him, you don't want to know what's going on. One of his specialties is interrogation, and he never lets anyone watch. And he quoted "just take my word for it; you don't want to be a part of this."

"At least he promised to share what he learns, and he went on to say just because you can't be in on the interrogation doesn't mean I won't tell you everything. We're working together on this, and we all need to keep open channels. His remarks for all of us" Eli says.

"He did promise to contact us later, as soon as he knows what went on and who this can be traced back to. He wants the name of the Muslim group of extremists that are responsible. There are so many of them that we need that information as soon as possible."

"Detective, what have you found?" Kat asks. "Anything useful, that we might get a lead from?"

"Not yet, Lieutenant" responds Detective Des tiredly. "I've searched everywhere and there's nothing."

"What about interviews with the survivors from the front of the church? Then of course everyone, not just the ones sitting in the front. I want the bird's eye view. Feelings, thoughts on how things felt, smelled, anything that could pin point what happened."

"That I can do, Lieutenant, as soon as they allow me to get near the survivors. The other departments have been questioning them since they got here; and most of them don't want to be re-interviewed."

"Yeah, I know" she responds with fatigue. "We'll do it anyway, with whomever we can talk into it."

"What did you get Jacob?" Devon asks from Capitol headquarters, talking to the video monitor.

"Not a lot, actually, but I got a name which will interest you" he admits with a grin of success.

"A name, anyone we know?" Devon asks.

"Actually, yeah" Jacob replies.

"Mind sharing it?" Devon asks, impatiently.

"Sure, I thought you'd never ask" Jacob responds annoying Devon even more. I must be tired, I'm sure not up to this verbal banter, he decides.

"Spill it Jacob, I'm tired of the games."

"Fine, the name of the person that contacted the gentleman at the funeral home is Addy!"

"You've got to be kidding me!"

"Nope, it was Addy. He was contacted via cell phone from a private number, giving him detailed instructions, and telling him where to find the c-four for the explosion. He was even given instructions on how to set it up, where to hide it and how to make a timer to use for a specific timed explosion."

"Awesome" declares Devon. "Where is he right now?"

"Last we heard he was in Iran. I don't think he's moved since our last information update. I've sent unit members in to Tehran to start looking for him. I bet he belongs to a Muslim extremist group. I just haven't got a name for it yet, I promise you I will, though."

"I have to take this information to the President. She's going to want this to let the citizens of the United States know that she keeps her promise."

"As soon as we can get a visual on him, I'll call the President and let her know."

"No, wait. I'll call you and you can go to the White House and let her know in person. Phone lines are bad right now. I'm sure most of them are being monitored, so you wouldn't stand a chance of telling her if you wait. I think you need to be the one to let her know" Jacob decides.

"I need to see the President" Devon informs the Secret Service agent at the front door. "I have information pertaining to a suspect from the explosion at the Chapel on the Hill church, early yesterday. She's going to want this information as soon as possible" he informs the guard.

"I need ID" the guard states, and after looking at it he pulls out his radio and asks for a check on Devon Callander of the Capitol Police. After listening to the response for about five minutes, five long minutes, he then hangs up, requests Devon's weapons be handed over and then allows him to enter, informing him "you can pick up your weapons at the rear door of the building, but you'll need to show you're picture I.D." he's informed. "Just turn left at the end of this room and let them know who you are" the guard says.

"Thanks" he replies to the brief directions. Security is tight, but after yesterday's disaster, it has to be, no more chances. This was difficult enough; the public would go nuts if it happened again.

"Madame President, I have some information and was told to bring it to you in person."

"What is it Deputy Chief Callander?"

"We have a name for the person that hired the gentleman at the Funeral Home. He told us he was contacted by a gentleman he believes was of Middle Eastern heritage after hearing him speak with an accent. He was then given the name of Addy and told to contact that person should anything happen or should he need anything else" Devon says as he watches for any kind of expression to cross the Presidents face. No expression. I bet she's really good at poker. She can certainly wipe all expression from her face, even her eyes are blank, nothing there. It's really strange, but interesting.

"Hmm" replies the President as she thinks. "Thank you for that information, Deputy Chief, do you have his full name?" she asks.

"Yes, it's Abdul Adl Thayer. He a owns a building on the south end of D.C. that houses a livestock hauler. The truck driver was the one responsible for disposal of the first body, the one that was skinned, the Majority Leader of the house. He also had a twin (identical) brother that was killed at his place, by mistake. At that time it was Lieutenant Thomas of D.C Metro One police department and I that discovered the truth. That Addy was still alive and his twin was the one the hit was taken out on, accidently. It's the same Addy that you brought to our attention and then took back because of the President."

"We didn't have enough to keep him in jail longer than the required twelve hours, so had to release him. If we could have kept him" he admits "we may have been able to stop the assassination of our President and Vice President."

"I'm sorry" replies the President, "but you can't go back and I'm sure that you did everything you could. Sometimes the law actually ties our hands before we can do our job" she murmurs in understanding. "You can be assured that something will be done with this information. This person will be found and brought to justice, and any prior acknowledgment of this person was off. I never knew this person at all. I'm not sure where you received that false information from."

"Thank you Madame President, I'm sorry for the mistake" Devon replies as he turns to leave.

"Deputy Chief, let's keep this information out of the mouths of the media until we have the chance to find and obtain this individual. I don't see what good it would do for anyone in our country to hear what you just told me. I think that information should be kept inside this room only, and never spoken of again. Your cooperation in this matter would be appreciated."

"You have my word Madame President, thank you. This information will not leave this room" he reassures her.

"Thank you Deputy Chief Callander, your word is good with me. I will be speaking of this matter at the appropriate time. Let's hope it's in the very near future."

THIRTY ONE

Alright, Devon thinks as he gathers his weapons and leaves the White House for Capitol Police headquarters.

"Jacob, its Devon" he says as he makes his way through the congealed streets of D.C, en-route to headquarters after dialing Jacob on his cell.

"What's up, Devon?"

"I just wanted to let you know that the information you gave me was handed to the President, personally. She was grateful for the information and requests it be kept confidential until she has the opportunity to do something with it.

"She said she was hoping it would be quick, but didn't guarantee it. I assume she'll let me know when she decides something and will be notifying the public. Nothing will endear her more to the public than bringing the parties responsible for the assassination of the President and Vice President to United States justice, so you know she'll have a big push going with this. I would expect to hear something soon."

"Thanks Devon, for the word. I'll be on the lookout" Jacob responds before hanging up.

Excellent, Jacob thinks when he's notified that the President is on the line waiting for him. "I'll take that in my office" he orders as he hurries to the back of the room, where his office is located.

"Madame President, what can I do for you?"

"I have a name for you, Lieutenant and since I know that you work directly for the President, I'm assuming that it holds true for me and my office now?"

"That's correct, what can I do for you?" he repeats.

"I have the name of the person responsible for hiring the funeral directors helper, and I want you to find and apprehend him, bring him back to the United States. I believe he can be found in Tehran, not far from the President of Iran. I'll contact the President of Iran personally and inform him that he is harboring the assassin of the President and Vice President of the United States. I'm sure he'll help to return this person to our country for justice. I'll call him as soon as I get off the line with you and once I find out what he says, I'll let you know."

"Thank you, Madame President. I'll be awaiting word, and I'll also let my covert operation in Tehran know what's happening and to be prepared."

"Thank you Lieutenant. I appreciate all of your help and your loyalty to this office. I'll be in touch shortly."

"This is Sidney Norwood, with Channel 7 News, Metro D.C., your most trusted source, always first and always fast with your up to date information. In approximately two minutes, the President of the United States will be coming on stage to notify the citizens of the United States about a person of interest that they have found, regarding the assassination of the President and Vice President. She has obtained some information regarding this suspect and wants to let the citizens of the U.S. know what plans she has developed. Here she is" Sidney says quietly as the new President of the United States walks on stage.

"Thank you everyone, for being here with me on such short notice. We have discovered a person of interest regarding the assassination of the President and Vice President and have located him in Tehran, Iran. He is the leader of one of the largest terrorist cells in the world. I'm preparing to get in touch with President Majeed to discuss the necessity of bringing this man back to the United States for justice. I believe it would enable you, our citizens, to overcome this tragedy easier by becoming a part of the decisions regarding this person. How to punish him and who shall do it. It's important for me that the citizens are satisfied. I never want to cause the people of the United States any problems. My job is to help, not hinder, the forward progress of our great land and its people.

I will do my utmost to ensure that this stays the land that we love and the home of the brave. I'm sure I will be requesting another news conference within the next forty-eight hours, after we have had time to apprehend the person of interest, and transport him back here to the United States. I guarantee that you will be involved in all the decisions regarding his punishment. Thank you and good night."

"President Majeed, this is Jane Martin, the President of the United States. I just received some information pertaining to a person of interest who may have been responsible for the assassination of our President and Vice President. He's been spotted in Tehran. As a matter of fact, when you had the press conference offering help to the United States during these difficult times, he was seen in the background, standing in the crowd behind you. If you would be kind enough, we could use your cooperation in capturing him and allowing us to bring him to the United States, for questioning."

"Madame President, I would be happy to help you in this matter. I will dispatch some of our best to find and apprehend him. I will also meet out swift justice, so that you will never have to worry about him again."

"Oh, thank you, President Majeed, but that won't be necessary. We want to bring him to our country for justice. I believe it is in the best interest for the recovery of the United States citizens to decide the justice for this man. He did assassinate our President and Vice President, and the American people need to decide on what the payment for these transgressions should be. I believe it will help them accept the matter and move forward from it, after they decide what should be done with him."

"If you're sure Madame President, then of course, I will do as you wish. Your country may send in its finest to apprehend him and if we see him first, we will capture him and await your escort to take him to the United States. I promise you no harm will come to him through my government."

"Thank you President Majeed, your cooperation and help during these trying times is greatly appreciated. I'll be in touch, sir, to let you know what our citizens decide the punishment will be for this individual. He goes by Abdul Adl Thayer, and is responsible for the largest known terrorist cell in the world. A name no one in the world will soon forget. Again, thank you President Majeed, I'll be in touch."

"Lieutenant, I've just finished speaking with President Majeed and he has assured me that he will help in any way he can to apprehend this man and hold him for pick up by our military for transport to the United States. So you now have the go ahead to pick him up and begin the process of deportation to the States. I've been assured by President Majeed of his cooperation and that he is waiting to be contacted by our military. So please, you may put this in motion as soon as possible."

"Thank you President Martin. I'll notify my unit that the plan is a go. You should probably expect him within the next twenty-four hours" he assures her.

"Thank you Lieutenant. I look forward to talking with you again soon" she replies and hangs the phone up slowly, what a day. This job is all consuming right now. I guess that's probably normal, considering the circumstances. Oh, well, I'll rest later, right now, duty calls she decides with a grimace as she gets up and moves on to the next problem.

Jacob hangs up the phone, deep in thought. Why is the President of Iran helping us, he wonders? This is a totally backwards thing. He's always been first in line when it comes to condemning the United States for everything, including the U.S. corrupting the rest of the world. Maybe the President of Iran knows Jane personally, and he likes her or maybe not, he decides. I don't see how they could possibly have any connection to each other, but then, who knows.

After giving the order for his unit in Iran to pick up Addy, he phones Devon to let him know. "Yeah, we'll be picking him up within the hour" he predicts to Devon.

"Excellent, this is finally starting to move somewhere" he says thoughtfully. "You said that Majeed, the President of Iran offered to help us detain him, awaiting pick up by your special forces group? Isn't that an extremely unusual thing? I mean, that guy has caused more trouble for the United States than any other country in the world."

"Yeah, I know" he agrees "but I haven't got any hits on the why of that yet. I will though, I'm definitely going to look into it." Why does he suddenly have a change of heart regarding the United States? Whatever, it's just creepy he decides as he hangs up.

"Devon, what's going on?" Kat asks as she walks into Capitol Police headquarters. "I haven't talked to you in a day or so, so figured I'd stop in and find out what's going on. Anything I don't know about?"

"Well, I just hung up with Jacob. We'll have Addie in custody within the hour and are deporting him back here to stand trial in the U.S. This is all per the Presidents orders. She wants him to receive justice in the United States since this is where he committed the crimes. I believe she's going to try to allow the United States citizens to help make the decision somehow of what and how he will be treated.

"She's smart, knowing that this is an unprecedented move and will definitely win over the citizens of the country. It will make them feel responsible for the justice they decide on for our deceased President and Vice President. He's due back here sometime within the next forty-eight hours. He'll be presented to the President and then put in holding somewhere secret so that he can't be harmed until he's judged and sentenced. I don't have a clue how's she's going to pull this off, but I'm sure it will be via the media. She seems to know how and when to use them. I don't think anyone has given her enough credit. I think she has been one underestimated woman"

"I agree, at least something is finally going to happen." Kat says quietly.

"I understand, Madame President. I'll be sure to spread the word" Devon promises.

"Listen up folks" he announces to the office in general. "The President of the United States has requested a news conference at zero-eighteen hundred hours today regarding an assassin by the name of Abdul Adl Thayer, aka Addy, the probable assassin of the President and the Vice President of the United States.

She'll be talking about justice and will also be interviewing Abdul Adl Thayer, live, in front of the citizens of the United States. She'll then allow him to speak briefly, so that the people of this country can actually make a decision on what will happen to him. This has never been done before, not in the history of the United States. I'm sure there will be world coverage. Be prepared for unrest" he warns. "We may have to be out on the streets in full force with every other law enforcement agency, just to keep things under control after this televised speech. Let's hope it doesn't rile the world, like I think it will."

"All right, we'll keep this station tuned in. Sydney Norwood is the favorite newscaster in the D.C. area, and this is her channel. Let's go and get an early dinner" he suggests to Kat. "We may not get the opportunity after the news conference, so we better grab the chance while we can."

"Okay, I guess I am a little hungry, so how about Italian?" she suggests.

"Fine with me, I'll drive, let's go" he says.

"I'll have iced tea please" she orders and the "spaghetti and meatballs. Devon, what do you want?"

"I'll have the same" he informs their waitress.

"I'll be right back with your order" she says.

"So, how are you doing Kat?" he asks sincerely. "I haven't even had the chance to talk to you lately."

"I'm okay" she says. "I've been sleeping a little better, so I think I'm moving on, although there are still occasions where I'll experience a flash back. But those are getting farther apart, so I believe I'm on the mend."

"Excellent" he smiles after hearing that. "I'm so glad that you're moving forward, and putting this nasty experience behind you" he says.

"Yeah" Kat agrees, but thinks it was more than nasty. People just don't understand how really bad this was. I'm not sure I'll ever be normal again, but at least I've learned how to suppress it to show a different face to the world. It makes people stop remembering and that's my goal. If they don't remember, then they won't ask and I'm good with that, she decides with a smile on her face.

"Here you are" the waitress says as she places their plates in front of them.

"Mmm" Kat says as she picks up her fork and digs in. "I was hungry, thanks Devon."

"You're welcome" he says distractedly.

"What are you thinking?" she asks when she notices his mind seems to be somewhere else.

"I was just thinking about the news conference scheduled for tonight. There are so many strange things going on lately. It's hard to believe everything that's happened in the last six weeks. The course of the whole world has been thrown into an upheaval. More has happened in the past six weeks than has happened in the past two hundred years!"

"I know what you're saying, it's true" she remarks, thinking of all that's happened in the past six weeks. "Unbelievable" she states emphatically and puts down her fork. I've lost my appetite again, she realizes. Too much stress lately.

"I guess it's time we head back to the office. I want to see the Captain before he leaves for the day, let him know about the news conference at tonight eight, and what to expect."

"I'm ready, let's go." Devon says.

"Thanks for the ride, Devon."

"I'll see you later" he says as he walks back into headquarters after dropping Kat at her car.

"Yeah" she says quietly. That relationship will never be the same. Even though it happened to me, he knows and can't accept it, so the *us* is pretty much gone. Too bad, I really like him.

"This is Lieutenant Thomas, what can I do for you?" she says when she answers her office phone.

"Kat, it's Snake, how you doing kitten"?

"Good, why, what's up?" she asks suspiciously.

"I was just wondering if you're set to watch the news conference tonight."

"Oh, yeah, but it's not for a couple of hours yet, so I'm not sure where I'm going to watch it."

"That's why I called. Why don't you join me? I have a

huge TV and it's ready to go. We can watch it together and then discuss the problems that are being created after we see what's she's going to say."

"Alright, let me finish up this report and I'll leave. I should be there in a half hour."

"Great" he says "see you then."

"If it keeps snowing out there, I may not get back tonight" she admits after she arrives at Snakes base.

"I'm sorry, I didn't realize how much snow we had gotten" he admits, chagrined. "If I'd known, I never would have had you drive all this way."

"Well, you didn't force me to do anything. I chose, so stop with the guilt" she answers tartly.

"Alright" he laughs. "I never could get away with anything around you, Kitten."

"That's right" she replies and smirks in satisfaction.

"It took you longer than I thought, so we only have a couple of minutes to get ready for the news conference. Let's get in there. I don't want to miss any of it."

"Yeah, me either" she admits.

"Here she goes" he says quietly as the President starts speaking.

"Thank you for joining me, again with such short notice. I promise in the future to give you more warning before I do another news Conference. But you should plan on a lot of them. I want you, the citizens of this great country to be informed constantly, about everything, not just what others think you should know. So I know we're going to become great friends and you're going to be more informed than you've ever been" she promises. "Tonight, we are here so that you can see and hear what the person who killed your President and Vice President this past week, has to say for himself. I believe that the American citizens have the right and the responsibility to listen to what happened and why. Since you're going to be the judge and jury for this assassin, it's important that you are informed. If you will bring out Abdul Adl Thayer, also known as Addy, to the stage, I will ask him some questions. Thank you" she replies after he's brought out, and guards are stationed nearby.

"Now, Mr. Thayer, do you understand American English?"

"Yes, I do" he states without inflection. "I know your language perfectly" he brags.

"Good, then would you mind answering some questions?" she asks.

"Not at all" he replies in perfect English.

"The first question is, did you kill the President and the Vice President of the United States?"

"No I did not" he denies.

"Wait" the President says "let me rephrase that question. Did you kill the President and the Vice President by assigning someone to place a bomb at the Chapel on the Hill Church?" she asks.

"Yes, I did" he replies in arrogance.

"Did you preplan this bombing so that the President and the Vice President were sure to be killed?"

"Of course" he replies. "I would not have planned something that would not be sure to kill them. That would be ridiculous" he admits. "I take pride in what I do and I have disposed of the two worst people in the world. The American infidel's deserved to die. The country of the United States of America is the harlot of this world. She shames our world with her very existence. I have tried to reform her, by disposing of the two most powerful men in this country. The only thing that saddens me is that I could not kill the whole country of all of its citizens. Only then would the world be free from the infidels that are disgracing us, our very existence" he admits with a smile.

The crowd at the oval office, consisting mostly of news reporters, suddenly gasps with indignation and jump from their seats, as all pandemonium breaks loose. The President steps forward to take charge of the microphone, and yells into it to be heard above the screaming and yelling masses "please, take your seat. Remember, we are live on television and we must maintain our dignity. Do not allow this man to bring you to his level of idiocy. Please, take your seats, so that we may continue with our news conference." As everyone suddenly realizes what happened to them, they start to sit as the President directed.

"Thank you, and I must say, what he said was shocking. But it's not as if we've never heard that before. We need to think about everything that he said, and then calmly and rationally make a decision on how we want to treat this prisoner. As I said before, the American public will decide on how this prisoner will be treated. He is not a citizen of this country; therefore he does not deserve our lengthy judicial system decision. We will not waste our hard earned money on this foreign perpetrator. We will treat him as they have treated us in their country when they have decided to kill American citizens for whatever thing they had been accused of. He has actually admitted to the world what he has done. Now he will pay by the choice of each and every one of you. This was his trial and now you will be the judge. This will be done next week, a vote will be taken.

"The people of the United States will vote on-line on the decision of how to treat this assassin. The question is simple but the answer will be just. You tell us what you want done with him. You will only be allowed to vote one time and only if you are an actual citizen of this great country. You will need your social security number to validate your citizenship. The polls will open in approximately seven days. You will then have twenty-four hours to decide and on that day you will place your vote. Never again will the people of this great nation not have a say in how we treat the people of the world when they have used terrorism against us. This deed must be dealt with swiftly and without our judicial trials that take years to do. This must be taken care of now, so that the world will see that we are no longer going to sit back and make empty threats. That those, who continue on in this manner, will not be tolerated."

"The United States of America will stand tall and strong and swiftly deal with these situations. The people that commit these acts have no rights and will not be treated like our citizens. They will be treated like the criminals that they are. I want to thank you for voluntarily donating your time tonight to hear what this man had to say. I will be talking again with you since I believe that you, as American Citizens, have the right to know what is happening in your country, and in the world that affect each and every one of you every day. Thank you and good night" she finishes, turns and leaves the stage.

"Holy shit" remarks Jacob after he and Kat finish watching the broadcast. "Do you realize what she just did?" he asks in dismay.

"Yeah" she replies in horror. "This is going to create fights and murder among the people in the United States. I know how people react, the one that says let him go will be lynched by a mob that says kill him. This is really bad" she warns. "I better contact my boss and see what he wants me to do" she mutters as she pulls out her cell phone.

"Yeah, I'm going to check all our video feed starting at the time the announcement was made and see if things are firing up out there. We're going to have major problems with this. She has created a monster out of the American public by letting them do this. Mob mentality is a terrible, destructive thing. I wonder how many innocent people will die because of this decision," he mutters in disgust.

"Yes sir, I'm on my way" she replies to her Captain on her cell. "It's started" she says to Snake when she hangs up. "People are gathering in the streets. You know what they'll be talking about and then the fights will start. If we can't keep control of the situation, then we'll have to institute marshal law and then the people really won't be happy. I think she's going to need to go on the TV again and hold another news conference. She needs to tell the people that if they can't control their emotions and opinions, this will be the only time this will ever happen. That from this point forward, she will bring the decision making back to the judicial levels. Maybe they'll calm down and move on."

"I'm not sure, that sounds more like wishful thinking than reality. I'm sorry Kitten, but it is what it is. We just have to work with what we have and hope for the best. You take care of yourself out there, it won't be easy, but you can do it. Just don't get in the way of any cross fire. I like you the way you are, alive and well. It's a lot better than the alternative" he adds firmly.

Kat's cell phone rings as she pulls onto the highway to take her back to D.C. "Hello, I'm on my way."

"Kat, its Devon, where are you?" he asks worriedly.

"I'm just leaving Jacobs base. I should get into town in about a half hour or so, what's up?"

"All hells breaking loose in D.C. The police are going out in force with their riot gear on. We may need to call out the National Guard to get control of the situation. Things are wild right now."

"Yeah, I figured" she admits sadly. "That's what happens when you get a novice in office, and they do something stupid like our President just did. She isn't experienced enough to be aware of what she created when she did what she did."

"This should show everyone her lack of experience in matters of justice," he says.

"But because of what she did, the American people are going to love her. They're not going to condemn her for this chaos. They're only going to remember that she put them in charge of this decision. No one will ever go against her because of it. It's the damned if you do and damned if you don't theory" she quotes. "I'm on my way, but if it's as bad as you say, it may take me a lot longer to get there. I'll call when I'm back" she promises and hangs up.

Forty eight hours after the televised news conference, the President is holding another one. "Thank you for joining me today" she says formally. "We experienced some disappointing behavior after the last news conference. If you, the American public, can't think responsibly and act accordingly, then we may not be able to continue in the same direction as we started two days ago. I want this to work because I firmly believe that you deserve to have a say, a vote as the case may be, for matters concerning our great United States of America.

"We need to show the world that we are not the harlot, but intelligent individuals that can and will make important decisions affecting our lives and our country. We have not shown the world what we are truly capable of, which is the important decision making principles that we all should have done. We have only shown them that as Americans we can't keep our emotions under control long enough to get the job done. It also shows them that we aren't capable of ruling the world, in a thoughtful and decisive manner."

"I can't stress the disappointment that I have experienced since the last news conference. We must change our thought process and move into the future. A future that allows you to be such a large part of the world, by making decisions that will affect how we are perceived by other countries. Now, you either want these rights, or you don't. If the chaos continues, then I will have to assume that you do not want these responsibilities. I will step in and take those decisions from you and make them myself. Do not let me down, people of America! Stay in control of yourselves. Make the decisions that need to be made to bring you strength of character. To bring you back into the rightful position of power that you should hold in the face of the world. You're behavior will be the deciding factor on whether or not there will be a vote five days from now. If the chaos and destruction continue, there will be no vote, the decision will be taken out of your hands and put into mine."

"That was a pretty powerful and demanding speech" Kat says to Devon, after watching it in silence at Capitol headquarters. "Think it will help?" she asks tiredly. "I'm about done in here" she says through a yawn. "It's been a long two days. Two days of constant work, with little or no sleep. None of us can keep up at this pace" she warns "so this had better have made a difference."

"Yeah, I agree with you there" responds Devon, Eli and Mallory, all looking exhausted, and in need of sleep, too.

"We can't keep up like this" Mallory insists "it had better work. We'll just have to wait and see" she responds as she sits heavily in a chair.

"Don't close your eyes Mal" Eli warns her "you'll sleep until next month."

"Don't I know it" she admits as she stands back up, finishing her power sit, ready to hit the streets again.

"Two days before the election and all is finally quiet in the streets all over the country. I wonder if they'll be able to handle the decision" Devon says to all the unit leaders at headquarters. "If not, then we'll start over again after the vote tally and who knows how long that will last. We may never get it to stop" he says with thoughts of the street chaos that occurred after the announcement of the vote. "Alright, let's get some rest, everyone, we don't know what's going to happen in the next two days, but for now, we have a reprieve, so let's take advantage of it and rest. I'll meet you all back here tomorrow at zero-seven hundred. We can start here and see what needs to be done. Hope for a quiet day" he says as everyone starts to disperse. "Kat, wait" he demands. "Where are you going?" he asks.

"I thought I'd take a ride and talk with Jacob. The last I saw of him was when the streets exploded after the Presidents first news conference. I was just curious about his take on things."

"Oh, no rest, huh" he asks with a yawn. "Not right now, but you go ahead and I'll see you later" she promises as she leaves.

"Right, later" he says quietly as he gathers his things to leave.

"Kitten, what are you doing here?" Snake asks when Kat pulls up to his base.

"I just wanted to talk to you and see how the past couple of days have been for you" she admits tiredly.

"How come you're not home in bed?" he asks quietly.

"I can't sleep, so I thought I'd get updated and plan for two days from now."

"Yeah, we've all been making plans. Let's hope peace prevails after the vote. After Jane Martin got angry and pretty much put the United States in their place, it hasn't been too bad. I'm really not sure what's going to happen after the vote. I believe she'll have a better handle on it this time. Last time she had no experience, this time a little more, so who knows. But I think the general public will want to keep her happy. She seems to have that affect on everyone. She may just make a good President, all in all. Only time will tell" Snake says thoughtfully. "Anyway, I have a spare bed here Kat, so why don't you try to get some rest. At least for a little while, later we can have dinner together and talk, if that sounds okay to you?" he asks.

"Yeah, that sounds good, but I don't know if I'll be able to sleep. I'll try though, if it makes you feel better" she promises with a sigh.

"It makes me feel better, so follow me and I'll get you all set up."

"Here it is, it even has its own bathroom and a coffee pot and a small fridge with water and pop, help yourself. Those are room darkening shades, so pull them and it will be just like night. Sleep good and I'll wake you at around seventeen hundred, then we can have a bite to eat."

"Thanks Snake" she says tiredly.

"Kat, wake up, it's okay, it's just a bad dream" Snake says soothingly as he pulls her into his arms and tries to get her to come out of it. "So, is this why you don't want to sleep?" he asks after she shows some clarity.

"Yeah, I haven't been sleeping very well, so what's the point in trying" she admits as she pulls away and tries to sit on her own. "I'd rather not have the nightmares, so I don't sleep. It's just easier, you know?" she responds nervously.

"No, I don't" he replies heatedly.

"Don't be mad at me" she begs "you're my only friend. I couldn't stand it if you were mad at me" she pleads tearfully.

"I'm not mad" he reassures her "but there's no reason for the nightmares. Why didn't you say something, why isn't Devon helping you with these?" he asks.

"Um" she starts "he's not, we're not, you know, we've grown apart" she admits. "With everything that's been going on and the city in such a mess, we haven't had time for anything but work. Besides, he's acted differently since, you know, anyway, we aren't as close as we were" she finally finishes.

Hmm, he thinks, anger building inside him. How dare he treat her like this, none of this was her fault, he needs to man up that bastard. Am I going to have a talk with him, he decides to himself.

"Oh, well, whatever" he says "how about something for dinner. I'm pretty hungry" he says to change the subject.

"That would be good, but can I take a shower first, I'd probably feel a lot better after one" she admits.

"Sure, kitten, take your time. I'll meet you here in a half hour, okay?"

"Perfect" she says, "that would be great. Oh, and Snake, thanks. You have no idea how much I appreciate you."

I never paid attention to how pretty she is, he realizes as he watches her over dinner. She sparkles like a diamond; her eyes are beautiful, with full thick black lashes and green as an emerald. I better back off or we're going to end up as more than friends, he decides as he finds himself thinking of her in a more than friendship manner. "So, besides work kitten, what have you been doing?"

"You're kidding right? There's no such thing as more than work, at least for the past few weeks there hasn't been. Plus I just begin to think that I'm finally over what happened to me and then slam, it's back with a vengeance. I know that's normal, but it's still frustrating. I'll get better, but it's going to be a long process, I think" she admits.

"What happened to you was a very terrible thing" he says in compassion. "But you're strong and you have to remember that you didn't do it, someone else did that to you. It wasn't your fault, even though I know you blame yourself. You tell yourself you weren't vigilant enough, strong enough. That was a fight you couldn't win. No matter how good you are in self defense, you're still a small person. He wasn't, so he already had an advantage. He also knew what he planned, and you didn't, so you were at a big disadvantage. Always remember, it was just your body, not you as the whole. Don't let him take that from you, because then he wins and you lose. You're no loser Kitten; you're a winner all the way."

"Thanks Snake, I do tend to get out of perspective and I can always depend on you to drag me back to reality. I need that; I need your friendship. Please don't ever take that from me" she says with emotion.

"Never, kitten" he vows. "I'll always be there for you."

THIRTY TWO

"Well, the last news conference regarding the Assassin is today at twenty hundred. Every channel will be covering it, so there's not going to be a problem watching it. It's only four-teen-thirty so let's work on the other cases. We need to official-ly close the William Blaketon case, the original suspect. He was killed by Elroy Wade. Since then we've had George Malik killed in the same way, even though the crime scene was oppo-site of the Blaketon crime scene.

We found the skin of Blaketon but not the body and we found the body of Malik but not the skin. It's almost like whoever did this is playing games with us, leaving us opposite clues. We do know that whoever did this has experience with a knife. Skinning something with as much precision as they did, took a lot of talent. It's actually creepy, knowing that there's someone out there that can do this so easily. It can't have been Wade; he was already dead weeks before Malik was killed. Who else is capable and talented enough to pull this off?" De-von asks Mallory, Kat and Eli.

"I've been thinking about this a lot" Kat replies, thoughtful-ly, "I just can't come up with someone that would do this, or even could. Maybe the FBI's BAU could give us a profile, and turn us in the right direct. At least we'll know approximately what this person could look like or be."

"Yeah, your right" he agrees."I'll contact them and bring them in on the case. Give me a half hour or so, and we'll meet here again" he says as he leaves to hit the elevator.

"This is Sidney Norwood, with Channel 7 News, Metro

D.C., your most trusted source, always first and always fast with your up to date information. The President is scheduled to appear in just a few moments. She's preparing for the vote, tomorrow, on the prisoner Abdul Adl Thayer, who committed the assassination of the President and the Vice President. Tomorrow, the people will vote on how to handle this crime against the United States. She's supposed to announce the on-line voting address that the public will use. This is a first, for the United States, and hopefully not the last. From what we've heard while going out and talking to the public, this is what everyone wants, the choice and the chance to make a difference for our country. Sidney says quietly "here she comes, Jane Martin, the President of the United States."

"I want to thank you for allowing me to be heard today, the day before the big day for our country. I believe this will change the course of the United State's future. We will be seen as the powerful country that we have always been, only this time we are finally on the right track. Everyone will see the difference that tomorrow will make, for the future of our world. It's time we took back everything that was ours, and will be ours again."

"I would like to introduce you to my good friend, counselor and our new World Peace Goodwill Ambassador, Mr. Jerald Johnston from "The Peoples Church" in Marlin, Texas. He will be helping us with our transition into our new way of life. I trust him to guide me in the ways that are right and good and help me to give this country back all that had been taken away, because of ignorance and greed. This is the future; we need not plan any longer for it because we are going to be too busy living in it, instead of wasting our time waiting for it. I hope you're as excited as I am, to embrace the new United States and release the old. Reverend Johnston, do you have anything you would like to say to our people of the United States?"

"Yes, Madame President, I do."

"I want to thank you from the bottom of my heart, for your eagerness to accept President Martin into this office and your willingness to listen and even agree with her visions for our country. It's time that we make some changes, changes for the better, to re-earn the dignity and honor that belong to us, to show the world the new tomorrow and all that we're capable of. This is a monumental step that you have chosen to take and it is with honor that I am allowed to be a part of this whole process. I will gladly accept the duty of greeting the world in your name, and allow them to see and understand what the new United States stands for. We are proud to be Americans, we have said that for years, but it is only now that we truly mean what we say.

We ARE proud and the world will recognize that, after tomorrow, when we show them that we, as a group, know what is best for our nation and we will begin doing those things immediately that will give us back our dignity. We will no longer be looked down on. Terrorism will be looked at in a different light. All will think twice before terrorizing our citizens ever again. I am looking forward to the changes that we are making for the betterment of our country and of the world. I want to thank you President Martin, for starting the change that our country has needed and for allowing me to be a part of the whole process. I will help you in any way that is needed as we continue with this change."

"Thank you Reverend Johnston and I want to tell you that I'm glad you accepted the position of World Peace, Goodwill Ambassador. I look forward to working with you for many years."

"Ladies and Gentlemen of the United States, tomorrow is the day you have all been waiting anxiously for. Tomorrow you will decide how we will treat the Assassin of our beloved President and Vice President of the United States. How you decide will change laws that have been on our books for a long time, good laws that belong to the past and were useful in their time. It's time to rewrite a part of our history while gazing strongly into our new future. I look forward to announcing to you on the day after the vote, what your decision has been. I will then make the determination of how to best carry out your wishes. Tomorrow is the vote for justice. Thank you for your time tonight and I will be speaking with you again the day after tomorrow. Goodnight" she says, turns and leaves the stage with Reverend Johnston on one side and Vice President Quinton Uqbahtor, the other.

"She's so small she's dwarfed between them, but she actually looked pretty tonight. I don't think that word has ever been used with her name before, but she really did look pretty, she even had a new suit on. Glowing, I would say, she must have been happy, having her good friend beside her. Her position is not as hard when she can surround herself with friends. She was definitely thrust into a den of vipers in the beginning, but she stood strong, she truly has backbone" voices Sidney in awe.

"Listen up, everyone" commands the Director of the FBI. "Tonight is the completion of the vote for justice. We should have a little information about what way this is leaning soon, but I don't have high expectations about knowing for sure. There are a lot of people voting, the internet is probably jammed and it will most likely take the rest of the night to finish. Then the vote will be tabulated by the computer program that's monitoring it. We probably won't know what the final decision is until we hear it with the rest of the world, tomorrow night at twenty hundred hours.

I do know that the neighborhoods are quiet, it's almost as if the world itself is holding its breath, waiting anxiously for the outcome. This is definitely a history making day, so take note, and always remember what occurred during your lifetime, on your watch" says the Director of the Federal Bureau of Investigation."Thank you and continue on, keeping our country safe."

"The voting process was quiet, literally quiet, not like some of our past votes. Doing this on-line was a smart idea. It kept most of the citizens at home, where they could vote in peace and completely anonymously. Tomorrow is the day of reckoning, if you will" Devon says. "We had a good day today, really nothing of interest, an actually boring day" he admits with a quiet chuckle. "If it keeps on like this, we may be out of jobs" he says with a grin. "Let's go and eat" he suggests, just as Jacob walks in, in his undercover clothes.

"What's going on everyone?" he asks when he sees his brothers and sister grabbing their coats.

"We were just going to go out to get some food, want to join us?" Mallory asks.

"That sounds great, but where's Kat?" Jacob asks.

"She's at Metro One, I presume" Devon responds. "Why?"

"Don't you think you should invite her along?" Jacob challenges.

"Fine, call her, she can meet us there" he responds with an *'I don't care attitude.'*

"We're going to that little Italian place, the one we've visited frequently in the past" Mallory says with a confused look at Devon.

"Fine" Jacob says "I'll give her a call."

"We'll wait for you in the car" Devon says as he walks out the door.

"Devon, wait" Mallory yells as she hurries to catch up with him. "What's wrong between you and Kat?"

"Nothing, absolutely nothing" he replies."She was just a date a couple of times" he admits "and now, nothing, so it's time to move on, I guess. She probably has already, anyway."

"I thought there was more between you two, I'm sorry, I must have been mistaken."

"No problem" he replies calmly."Everyone changes and moves on. You know how it is in the dating world."

"Yeah, I do, unfortunately" she admits."Alright, let's not talk about this. Is it going to bother you if she joins us for dinner?" she asks.

"No, I'll be fine."

"Good" Mallory replies distractedly. I know I saw more than just a date in their relationship, something must have happened. I wonder what it was.

"There they are" she exclaims as Jacob and Kat enter the restaurant.

"Back here" she waves to get their attention. "Here, sit here Kat" Mallory offers.

"Thanks Mal; did you all order yet?"

"No, we were waiting for you two. We told the waitress to

come back here when she saw that we were all here. Here she comes" she says. "I think we're all going to hold with our old ordering style, the house choice and a couple of bottles of your house red wine, to go with it."

"Very good" the waitress replies. "I'll be right back with you drinks, after I put in your order."

"It's not very busy tonight." remarks Kat.

"No, everyone is probably at home voting and doesn't want to chance missing anything, just in case the President goes on the TV early" Mallory offers.

"This whole world seems topsy-turvy to me lately" she admits. "The norm is now the abnorm and the abnorm is now the norm. It's all crazy, almost like what we called opposite day when we were kids. Who would have thought, that two months ago, all these things could happen to change our country, our laws and our lives?"

"Yeah, our lives have definitely changed" Kat admits. "It will never be the same again." If only we could turn back time, then maybe the world would be normal again. But that's impossible, there's no going back. You can only go forward.

"Dinner was great guys, thanks for thinking of me" Kat says as she stands to put on her coat and leave. "It's time to go home and get some rest" she admits with a smile. "Tomorrow's going to be a big day, I'm thinking. I want to be ready for it, so I'll see you all later, and thanks again."

"Devon, can I talk to you before you leave, in private" Jacob asks.

"Sure, I'm about ready to leave anyway, so we can talk now, on the way to the car" he offers. "Thanks Mal, Eli, I'll see you both tomorrow" Devon promises.

"I just have a couple of questions" Jacob says. "What the hell are you doing to Kat" he asks with a snarl. "You're making her nuts and hurting her. I promised myself that she would never be hurt again after what that bastard did to her. The bastard I killed, remember? It's just too bad you can't kill the same person over and over. I really don't like it when Kat is hurting!"

"I'm not doing anything to her" he denies. "We dated a

couple of times, that's all. I think we both decided to move forward. She's not interested in me and I feel the same about her. We're adults, passions change, people change and move on. You know that" he accuses Jacob.

"Yeah, but are you sure she's moved on" Jacob asks menacingly.

"Yes, I am!"

"Alright, you've moved on, so you wouldn't have a problem if Kat and I started dating, would you?" he asks nonchalantly.

"No, do what you want" he says, aggravated. "We're done. Go ahead, knock your socks off, you have my blessings, yada, yada."

"Thanks for your blessings Devon, but you can keep them, I never did want them from you anyway" he adds in disgust as he turns and leaves. Walk away, he tells himself, just walk away, anger never did you any good with your siblings. Just walk away.

"Kat, it's me Snake, let me in."

"Coming" she yells as she grabs a robe.

"What's the matter? I was just getting ready for bed" she responds to his impatience.

"I was worried about you so I decided to come over to make sure everything was okay" he answers her questioning look.

"Oh, well, I'm fine, but come in. I promise not to fall asleep on you again" she teases.

"You can sleep on me anytime" he winks and laughs.

"Want something to drink?" she asks as she leads him into her postage stamp size living room. "Here let me put this away, have a seat" she says as she rushes to tidy up a little bit.

"Relax, I don't care if your place is a mess. I came to see you not your place."

"Right" she says in agreement, "something to drink?"

"Sure" he says to shut her up "I'll have whatever you have" he says to calm her down.

"Okay, let me get it" she says with a smirk. "I'm having this green tea, it's so refreshing, don't you think" she grins as she hands him a large glass, with some watery green stuff in it over ice.

"Thanks" he responds automatically

"Ahhh" she says after taking a long drink, "wonderful and cold, just perfect" she says as she waits for him to follow suit.

"Yeah, that was good" he manages to get out, while trying not to gag in her face.

"Give me your glass" she laughs "I was just kidding, I was going to let you drink all of it but I just can't" she admits as she laughs again.

"That was very funny kitten! I might have to get even with you for that one" he threatens with a grin.

"So, what's the real reason you're here?" she asks.

"I wanted to make sure you were okay, and that's the truth."

"I believe that, but what else?" she demands.

"Well, I wanted to find out what happened to you and Devon" he says as he watches her face closely for any distress.

"Yeah, we aren't seeing each other anymore" she admits.

"When did this start?"

"Well, it started, actually it was probably my fault" she admits guiltily, "but it started after I was raped. I'm just not interested in him anymore or in anyone right now. It may take me a real long time before I decide to get intimate with anyone. I'm just not ready for that yet" she adds in humiliation. "I don't know when or if I ever will be" she admits uncomfortably.

"Why didn't you tell me?" he asks in disappointment.

"I can't even say it out loud to myself, let alone my best friend" she says tiredly.

"Kat, I know people that can help you, remember?"

"Yeah, I remember, but that was one of the hardest things that I've ever done" she admits, "and I didn't want to have to do it again."

"Was his talk that bad?" he asks in surprise.

"Yes" she cries adamantly. "It was terrible, some strange man asking all these intimate questions, and waiting for me to tell it all. It was really bad, and I won't do it again. That's why I avoid your place as much as possible. I know it was his job, but to make me tell him everything, emotional feelings and physical feelings, describing the pain and what I was thinking at the time, I just can't do it again. I won't do it again" she insists.

"Kat, I had no idea" he admits. What the hell. He was supposed to help her, not make her relive the agony to get him off. I will be speaking to him, as soon as possible, he decides.

"I'm so sorry kitten. I had no idea that's what he did. Why didn't you tell me after you talked to him?"

"I was in shock again" she admits. "I couldn't think; all I could do was remember, everything, absolutely everything that happened to me. It was almost worse the second time than the first, because I had already experienced it. Then I had to re-experience it. I'm done, Snake, I can't take any more personal stuff. All I can do is work and think about work. It's the only way I can function. Now, if you don't mind, I need to go to bed. I'm pretty tired and I have to get sleep when I can" she says with regret. "Thanks for coming though. I really do appreciate it, even if I don't act it."

"Sure kitten, I'll leave, but I want to hear from you tomorrow? I need to make sure you're alright" he insists.

"I'll call you in between the murder and mayhem in the city" she adds with a laugh.

Finally morning, Kat thinks as she watches the sun come up from her living room window. Another night with little or no sleep, hopefully one day soon, I'll be able to sleep most of the night instead of toss and turn all night. This lack of sleep is going to do me in. He should have just gone ahead and killed me. It would have been a lot easier. I wouldn't have had to remember anymore or re-experience anything anymore. That bastard took my life from me, and I want it back. Maybe I should hit the gym and beat the crap out of someone. It might make me feel better. I know, I'll call Snake; he can be my sparring partner. If anyone can keep up with me, it's him.

"Snake, its Kat. Are you in town?" she asks.

"Yeah, why, Kitten?"

"I need a sparring partner and I thought you might be interested. I need to get rid of some energy and I thought you were probably one of the only ones able to keep up with me. So, what do you say?" she asks eagerly.

"Sure, where do you want to go?"

"I usually go to Gurley's Gym. It's small but clean. I've been going there forever" she admits."It's on Wellington Road, southeast."

"I know where that is, I'll meet you there in half an hour."

"Awesome," she cries, thanks. "I'll see you soon."

"It took you long enough" he says after Kat enters the gym.

"Sorry, my Captain called just as I was walking out the door."

"Problem?" he asks casually.

"No, they want to bring in extra man power for tonight after the vote, just in case the people get riled up again when they hear what the vote was and what the next step is. I'm hoping for a more peaceful evening, but you never know."

"Okay, let's go" she says after she ties on her gloves and climbs into the ring. "Now be careful, I don't want to hurt you" she teases as she starts dancing.

"Watch out Kitten, I don't want to hurt you."

"Alright" she says with a grin and her first right cross. Well, she has quite a right cross, and not bad power behind it, he decides with a grin. This will be fun. After twenty minutes of non stop fighting, they both stagger over to the edge of the ring and sit down, trying to breath.

"You're not bad" he says as he wipes his face so he can see her.

"Neither are you" replies Kat with a grin, hair hanging in wet tendrils down her face, sweat dripping in her eyes."That was great" she responds, gasping for breath."I guess I'm a little out of shape" she admits with a groan as she tries to stand up.

"No, you did fine, you just didn't expect me to give as good as I got. You figured I was an easy win, didn't you Kitten? You forgot I'm special forces, didn't you" he asks with a smirk.

"Yeah I did, to me you're Snake, not Lieutenant Callander."

"That's what I figured" he admits with a laugh. "I'm both, actually. Now, I need to shower and head in to work. It's going to be a crazy day, getting ready for the vote results tonight. We better be ready, I feel a big problem coming after the announcement of how the vote went. People that want it to pass will be happy, but those that don't, not so much. I don't see either side sitting down for the results. They'll take it to the streets" he predicts.

"Me too" she says as she heads to the showers. "Thanks again Snake, I'll talk to you later today, I promise."

"Welcome Kitten, stay safe, I'll see ya later."

The office turned out to be mass chaos, all the regulars mingling with the extras pulled in for today and probably tomorrow. Everyone talking about assignments, as Kat walks past the bullpen that is way fuller than normal and a lot noisier too.

"Detective Des, my office" she says loudly to be overheard above all the background noise.

"Yes Sir" she replies as she jumps up to follow.

"We hear anything?" asks Kat when she gets to her desk.

"Not yet Sir, the Captain just wants everyone to be on standby in case it all goes downhill after the voting results. He's being slightly paranoid" she says quietly.

"No, I don't think he is" Kat denies. "He's being careful, he remembers the evening after the vote choice was discussed by the President and how everyone started fighting in the streets over guilty or not-guilty. He has every reason to err on the side of caution and be ready, rather than being caught with our pants down again" she remarks.

"Yes Sir" replies Des.

"Detective, we will be spending the evening at Capitol Police headquarters, watching the breaking news with the Agents there. The Captain can reach us there or we can start out from those headquarters. It's just as close as this place is, and it will allow us to see what the Capitol Police and the FBI is doing after the vote. We'll probably start outside and sweep the streets, looking for any trouble makers. Hopefully they'll stay home and be satisfied with the results."

"This is Sidney Norwood, with Channel 7 News, Metro D.C., your most trusted source, always first and always fast with your up to date information. The President is scheduled to appear on stage within the next five minutes, to inform the American Citizens what their voting results were from two days ago. On what the decision is of what to do with the prisoner that is being held for killing the President and Vice President of the United States. Never before has the American public been responsible for making a decision of this magnitude, deciding the future of the prisoner being held responsible for the deaths of the President and Vice President. Whether the prisoner will live or die. This is a big decision, holding a lot of power and emotions. How will the public hold up as judge and jury? Here she is now" says Sidney as the cameras pan to the President as she enters the stage in the oval office, along with Reverend Johnston and Vice President Quinton Uqbahtor.

"I want to thank you, ladies and gentlemen of the United States of America. Today is the big day" she announces calmly with a smile. "Today we will inform you of how your vote went the day before yesterday. Everything seems to have worked flawlessly" she admits with another smile "and I am so very proud of all of the American citizens. The voting not only went extremely well, but there were also no angry words and no fighting, in spite of some of the lines that occurred at coffee shops and libraries, schools, anywhere that you had to go to vote, if you didn't have a computer available to you at home."

"Since we're going to vote much more frequently than ever, I do suggest that everyone have the capability to vote at home, since that would streamline things even more and allow us to carry out your duties as an American citizen. I promise to look into the prospect of ensuring that all citizens have a computer at home, and to that end I will enlist the aid of one of my cabinet members to begin the process of looking for computer suppliers for the general public."

"Now to the vote" she says. "We voted on the day before yesterday, the decision of what will happen to the prisoner that we have in custody, responsible for the murder of the President and Vice President and countless others that dreadful day. Also, for all the severely injured from that same bomb. You have decided, you cast your vote and the guilty vote did win with more than three to one votes. Officially, you have found the prisoner guilty of his admitted crimes. I promised you that you would vote and be responsible for what happens to him."

"We have decided that by all fairness, he be put to death

373

immediately for the deaths of both the President and Vice President. He will be put to death on television so that all of you may watch the proceedings knowing that you are responsible for the justice that has finally been chosen and carried out. He will die by decapitation, as they like to do in the Middle East, to our American citizens when they hold them hostage. This will show the world that not only is America a strong country but it is a fair one, also. We will show the world that this is how we shall treat our prisoners when they are found guilty of terrorism against the United States. The laws will be re-written to include the clauses needed to carry out this justice from now on and into the future. This is an exciting day" she proclaims "for the United States of America."

"We are taking back our country, one person at a time and will no longer allow other countries to carry out their evil purposes on the great United States. Nor will we spend our hard earned money on lawyers and judges that like to drag these problems out for years, to make as much money as possible. Remember that these people are guilty of their transgressions and have been judged by you, the rightful judges, the citizens of our United States. Their sentences will be handled swiftly and with justice for what they have done. I am proud of you, each and every one of you" she proclaims with emotion, as she dabs at her eyes. "You have made the right decision and by allowing you this opportunity, you have started to make the right move for the future safety of our great country."

"We will televise this capital punishment tomorrow at twenty hundred hours, or eight p.m. nationwide. Please be advised that this will be graphic and hard for some to watch, so beware and keep your children safe. You decide who needs to watch this procedure. You are the parents or guardians. Thank you and we will meet again tomorrow evening for the final act of justice. Goodnight" she says and turns and walks off stage to where the Vice President and Good Will Ambassador awaits.

"Well" Kat says. "I'm surprised yet not surprised. He was guilty and is being treated as they treat us when they capture American Citizens, which I guess is fair. It kind of makes me feel bad, even though I'm sure the prisoner never felt bad about what he did. I just hope it does make the statement that she proclaims it will, although I'm not so sure it will. It may turn our public into bloodthirsty individuals. It does remove some of our humanity, and that will always be a dangerous thing to do.

"Yes Captain" Kat says after answering her cell phone. "I had no idea, this has been a strange day, from start to finish" she says. "I guess that's good, yes Sir, I will."

"The Captain was letting me know that there have been no problems as of yet, in the streets. It's as if the people are afraid to leave their houses, for fear of what they could face" she informs the group at the FBI Headquarters.

"Yeah, that's what I just heard from the Director, it's too quiet" Devon replies puzzled."The general public has never taken anything so quiet."

"I think we should all hit the streets and see for ourselves what's happening. I find it hard to believe that it's so quiet out there."

"Yeah I agree" says Mallory and Eli backs that up too.

"I'm out of here" Kat decides as she heads for the door to the elevator. "I'll call you all later."

Wow, she thinks as she wanders around the area of D.C. Metro One. It's never this quiet out here, not even on Christmas when everything is closed. This is just weird; she thinks when she heads over to Mike's Coffee Shop. "Hey Mike" she says as she walks in. The usually noisy place is quiet as a church, one lone customer sitting in one of the booths that he had installed recently, replacing all the regular tables in order to give his customers more privacy.

"Hi Kat, how are you?" he asks quietly.

"I'm fine" she answers and looks around the deserted shop, then back at Mike in question.

"I don't know, Kat. It's usually a lot busier than this on a Wednesday night. But after watching the President and hearing what she had to say, I can understand why everyone just wants to be home today. I definitely have mixed feelings about what happened. I voted for the justice vote also, but I didn't expect to feel this bad after finding out the decision and what happens next. I feel responsible for putting that criminal to death. Isn't that weird?" he asks.

"No, I think that's probably what everyone's feeling and that's why they're all home, hiding from the fact that they chose to kill that man. That's a tough decision, even if it was for the assassination of the President and Vice President. The public has never experienced anything like this and they're probably confused and maybe a little numb, or even scared. All normal feelings, I'm sure" she says comfortingly. "They're probably just waiting for tomorrow, to actually see if this is all true or just a bad dream" she observes of the empty coffee shop.

"I hope so" Mike exclaims,"I can't afford to have my business down to nothing for any longer than one night. I hope business comes back tomorrow."

"I'm sorry Mike; I hope it comes back soon, too! I better get out of here. I'm going to make sure the streets are still quiet."

"I'll talk to you tomorrow" he says with a small salute.

I'm going to head home, Kat decides after wandering the deserted streets of Washington D.C for the past four hours. "If there were going to be problems, they'd have started by now, I believe" she says to Mallory and Detective Des.

"Yeah, I agree. No point in wasting time out here, the streets are too quiet. Tomorrow we'll be back to normal, probably" Des says.

"In the mean time, I need to get home and get some sleep. It's been a long day," she replies as they all head for their cars.

THIRTY THREE

"Good morning Kat" Snake says after she answers her cell phone while walking out her apartment door for work the next morning.

"Hey Snake, how are you?" she asks.

"I'm fine, but you didn't call me last night" he reminds her.

"I know, I'm sorry. I wandered the streets until around eleven pm, looking for possible trouble, but there was simply no one out last night, and then I came home and tried to get some sleep. It's been pretty illusive for me lately" she admits "and last night was no different."

"I'm sorry" he says. "Maybe if I start sleeping at your place, you'll be able to sleep" he offers suggestively.

"Maybe so" she admits before realizing what it sounded like. "I mean" she stammers

"stop" he says jokingly, "I was kidding."

"Oh, yeah, thanks, I knew that" she says, trying to regain her dignity.

"So what's going on today, until they televise the decapitation?" he asks.

"We're going to get out on the streets and see what the public is talking about. We're trying to figure out what to prepare for" she admits. "This whole thing is just freakin weird."

"Yeah, it's weird. I've never seen the streets as deserted as they were last night, not even on Christmas when everything is closed."

"That's what I said last night to Mallory and Des. It was

strange" she admits. "Usually the streets are crowded, even in the middle of the night. I've never seen them as empty as they were last night, it was freaky."

"Hey, you have time for breakfast?" he asks.

"Yeah, probably, where do you want to go?"

"How about that friend of yours, Mike, his coffee shop?"

"Sure, we can go there, but he doesn't serve cooked food, just cold food like muffins, donuts, pastries, things like that."

"Yeah, that's fine with me, how about you?"

"That's fine, I'm not that hungry anyway" she admits.

"I figured as much, but you can eat a little, right?" he demands.

"Yes, Snake, I'll eat a little" she says to keep him of her back. "See you in about ten minutes."

"You bet" he replies.

"Thanks for meeting me here" he says to Kat when she walks in the door."

"Sure, of course I'll meet you, not a problem. Did you order anything?" she asks as she looks over her little menu.

"Yeah, I've got a couple of donuts coming and a pastry, you can choose whatever" he offers.

"Thanks, let me go and get a coffee before we start talking" she says as goes to the counter.

"Hi Mike, how's business today?"

"It's a lot better than last night" he admits "but still not back to normal, hopefully by tomorrow though" he replies.

"I hope so" she says absentmindedly after she gets her latte and turns to head back to Snakes table.

"I'll talk to you before I go" she promises Mike.

"So, how did you sleep?" Snake asks after studying her quietly for a moment.

"Not good, maybe an hour's worth, which is better than none, and has become the norm for me."

"We need to do something about that" he reminds her. "If you aren't sleeping, then you'll get sick. You've already lost more weight than you should have, and not eating or sleeping isn't doing you any good, so what do you believe will help you sleep?" he asks.

"Well, let's see? How about going backwards a couple of months, before any of this weird stuff started happening; I would probably be able to sleep if nothing had ever happened to me" she replies angrily.

"Kat, Kat" he murmurs to her heated outburst. "I'm not judging you, I'm just worried" he says in self defense. "Let me help you, please?" he begs.

"I don't think anyone can help me" she declares tiredly. "I don't have the energy to fight you, so please, just leave it alone. Look, I need to get to work. It's going to be a long day, but I'll call you later Snake, I promise" she says as she heads out the door.

"All right, listen up everyone; this is going to be a rough evening for most people. You'll have those sick ones out there that will totally enjoy what happens tonight, but for the most, it will be a very disturbing viewing on the TV. I hope that it won't carry out into the streets or even into the homes of people. Under the circumstances, I don't have high hopes."

"We are all, as of this moment, working nonstop until we can get our cities under control. It may take the whole day; it may take more than twenty-four hours, but we will prevail. Be prepared to work and then work some more. There is no time off until we gain control of all of the problems that may occur because of the beheading that they're planning on showing on every news channel tonight. If people want to escape from it, there's nowhere on television that they can go, so let's hope this stays quiet and safe."

"Be vigilant, watch for any small nuance that may prelude big trouble. Stay in touch with this office via radio and cell phone. If there are any problems, call immediately for back up. Thank you everyone, now, head out there and stay safe. Return here to watch the scheduled news report."

"This is Sidney Norwood, with Channel 7 News, Metro D.C., your most trusted source, always first and always fast with your up to date information. The President is scheduled to appear on stage within the next few minutes. Actually, there they are now."

The President, Vice President and the Good Will Ambassador have all walked onto the stage, followed by Addy, in hand and leg cuffs. He's smirking at the audience, with a "know it all" look, and mumbling under his breath. As he takes the seat moved to the stage for him, he starts yelling out loud about Allah, and how he will die for his cause.

"The cause of the evil one, the American's, they have contaminated the world with their hypocrisy. The people of this country will see what the Muslims have been warning them of. They will pay with their souls for the terrible thing that they are about to do. I am not afraid" he yells at the stunned audience, the Senators and Congressmen that have chosen to attend this punishment in person.

Jerald Johnston moves close to Addie and offers him salvation for his soul and Addy yells even louder about how they are insulting him, at this important time in his life. "I would rather die a martyr than live with these people that are destroying the world, just remember, I am but one in a legion of warriors."

After all the yelling is finished, the executioner moves forward, grabs Addy by his hair, pulls his head up and back and with a swift motion, slices through his neck, while blood gushes outwards everywhere, then he removes his head. As the camera's scan the President she's just standing there as if nothing untoward has happened, until she realizes what she actually witnessed, then she suddenly tears up and starts weeping.

"Oh my God" mutters Kat after watching the beheading. "I can't believe that we've reached bottom so quickly. I can't understand how we got to this place in our history."

"Alright, it's time" the Captain yells in the madness that's occurring at the station. "If this is happening here, what's it like out there in the streets? Get out there and stop the craziness as quickly as possible. Maintain calmness, control the situation. I know that the streets are going to be worse than this station was and that was bad enough. Be safe people, and stop the craziness. Keep in contact with the precinct" he yells at the retreating backs of his police officers.

"Stop" Kat yells at a robber when he doesn't hesitate to clock an old woman and grab for her purse. The Captain was right, she decides as she wrestles him to the ground and slaps cuffs on him while he squirms and screams in madness. The town has gone nuts. "I'm going to need a wagon" she squawks into her radio "at Twenty Sixth and Main. I have a suspect in custody awaiting transport." The streets aren't quiet tonight, she notices while waiting for the ride. They are absolutely crazy, just like the Captain feared they would be.

At least we seem to have enough police visible or maybe not, she decides as she watches a robbery take place right in front of her. The suspect just looks at her and grins, almost as if he's saying, so, what are you going to do about it? They all seem to have gained confidence from what they witnessed on TV tonight. This is not a good thing.

"Captain, I think we have bigger problems than we first thought. Have you heard anything about bringing in the National Guard?" Kat asks. "There's no way we can control this madness, there aren't enough of us. We need the National Guard out here, or a police state to be declared."

"I'm working on that Lieutenant. It's much worse than I anticipated. We have to get control, before any more murders take place."

"I agree Captain. I'll await word from you."

Forty-eight hours later, things seem to have quieted down. At least we can hear ourselves think now. It was bad, they all agree, after Kat arrives at Capitol headquarters and finds Devon, Mallory and Eli all taking a short break.

"You guys look terrible" she says after seeing them for the first time in two days.

"Have you looked in the mirror lately?" Mallory asks. "You don't look so great either" she says dryly.

"No, I haven't had time, what day is it anyway" she asks tongue in cheek.

"It's Sunday" Eli says.

"What" Kat screeches "Sunday?"

"No, just kidding Kat" he admits with a short laugh. "It's Friday, you only lost a day and a half, not four days" he admits with a tired smile.

"Thank god" she replies with a groan, "I must be tired or you would have never gotten me with that."

"We're going to set up a video conference with Jacob when he has a chance" Devon says "if you want to join us, it will probably be in the next half hour, at least I'm hoping it will."

"That sounds good. So, did you arrest anyone interesting?" she asks.

"No one unusual" he replies, "just your normal everyday trouble makers. They seemed to have a lot more guts though. I hope that's not a prequel to the future."

"We had enough trouble on the streets before the execution, and now, it's ridiculous."

"That was Jacob" Devon says after he hangs up from his cell. "He says he's ready for the video conference, let's go to my office" he suggests tiredly.

"Have a seat everyone and I'll dial him in."

"Hey Jacob, how are you holding up?" Devon asks.

"We're doing pretty well on this end, how about you guys?"

"Well, we all just got in, we've been on the streets for the past two days, and even though it feels like a month, I think it's pretty much over here."

"Yeah, I agree, it was a bitch of two days though."

"Absolutely" everyone agrees with tired nods or shakes of their heads.

"You guys look pretty rough. No sleep for any of you in the past two days?

"Someone had to do it and we were needed, so we worked it."

"So what's next?" Jacob asks.

"I'm not sure" Devon replies, but Mallory announces

"I'm headed home for some R & R, well deserved and long overdue."

"Yeah, me too" Kat agrees quietly "I thought I'd study my eyelids for about twelve hours, who knows, maybe even more. Night everyone" she says as she leaves Devon's office and heads for home.

"This is Sidney Norwood, with Channel 7 News, Metro D.C., your most trusted source, always first and always fast with your up to date information. The President will be holding a special news conference this evening at nineteen hundred hours. It will be telecast on Channel 7 News in its entirety, commercial free. Please join us in the discussion of the execution and the ramification it's had to the general public. I believe she has some opinions she wants to share on what happened this past week after the execution. Since this was the first time anything like this has happened in the United States, she has information on how it went.

"I believe she received reports from all the major cities in the United States and what happened in them after the execution. She will be adding her opinion to the cause. Please join us at nineteen-hundred tonight on Channel 7 News, your most trusted source, always first and always fast with your up to date information. I'm Sidney Norwood and I look forward to you joining us this evening."

"Shit" Kat complains to her living room in general. Will this never end? I'm getting pretty sick of these news conferences, and the President. She's been on TV more than any President in the history of the U.S. I'm not watching it, she decides. I'm going out, maybe get a little drunk. Who knows, maybe then I can sleep, she decides as she grabs her coat and heads out the door. No cell phone either and she turn's it off. Freedom, just freedom from everything for a little while and she smiles as she walks into her favorite little bar, within a block of her apartment and so small that not too many people know about it. It makes it more personable.

"I'll have a whiskey, neat," she orders, and when the bartender hands her the drink, she thanks him and heads to a table in a corner. I'm good, she decides, as long as the people just leave me alone. I shall drink and drink until I'm bleary eyed and then I'll go home and sleep, for a good long time, she decides to herself with a small smile. Ah, that's good she decides as she orders her fifth drink.

The bartender asks her if she drove and she just looks at him like he's crazy. "Of course not" she declares in a bit too loud of a voice.

"I'm going to have to cut you off" he says "you won't even be able to walk home soon if you're not careful. Is there anyone I can call for you?" he asks.

"Oh, sure, I think so" she says drunkenly, "I have a phone somewhere, maybe someone in it can get me" she says stupidly with a grin.

"Let me see it" he says as she searches all her pockets twice.

"Here it is" she admits with a loud "yippee. Just call one of them and they'll come and get me" she says to the air in general.

"Alright, I'll call. Is this Snake? This is the bartender at the Happy Green Tavern. I have a woman here, I think she goes by Kat? Anyway, she's not able to drive, actually she's really not able to walk home either. She's had a few too many, is unsteady and came in here alone.

"She told me just to call someone on her phone, anyone, and they'd come and get her, so I called you, because your name came up first. She must have called you last, so it put you at the top of her list. Yeah, I understand, she'll be here, she's sitting in the corner alone anyway. Alright, I will thanks."

"He's on his way" the bartender says to Kat who just looks at him like he's an alien.

"You stay here" he says "and I'll get you another drink, how's that sound?"

"Good, good" she says with two longheaded nods. Fifteen minutes later, Kat's laid her head on the table and is almost out for the night when Jacob walks in, heads straight for her table, studies her for a minute and then shakes his head and tries to talk her up. She get's halfway up and then goes back down and after her third try he just takes matters into his own hands and hauls her out of the chair, holds her up and walks her out the door after telling the bartender thanks for calling him.

"Kitten what am I going to do with you?" he asks. "I guess you aren't listening to me, are you" he says as he gets her into his car and heads to his bunker. She'll sleep better there, he decides. Besides, he's on duty early and doesn't want to leave her alone all night like this.

"Good morning Kat" Jacob says loudly the next morning.

"Oh, stop, don't you think you're talking a little too loud" she complains as she takes her pillow and places it over her face and head. "I know I drank too much, so there's no need for you to yell, now is there?" she complains. "I'm an adult, so don't treat me like an adolescent, please. I deserve better treatment than that" she complains.

"I'm sorry Kitten, you're right. It's not like you do this every day, is it? I don't think I've ever seen you drunk before, come to think of it" he replies.

"I may have done this one time before, but even then I don't think I felt this bad, so I must have drunk more than ever last night. I'm sorry that you had to go out and get me; that was very inconsiderate of me" she admits as she removes the pillow from her head and squints into the light of the room. "I promise it will never happen again."

"Kat, you're allowed to over imbibe occasionally, but not for the reason that you did."

"Oh, and what would that reason be, Mr. Know It All?" she demands in anger.

"Your attack, and your inability to overcome that, forget it and start moving forward" he quickly replies.

"STOP" she yells, starting to simmer in anger. "I'm sick of you telling me to move forward, forget what happened, don't let it get to me" she says nastily. "It did get to me, it's been what, eight weeks and I'm supposed to forget and move on" she states in disbelief. "Well, sorry Lieutenant, but that ain't going to happen."

"I obviously can't move forward yet, and it did affect me, so bite me" she says in anger. "It affected something deep inside me and I can't change that, no matter what I do. I've tried a lot of different things and the pain and the memory keeps coming back, so leave me alone. I'll face it the only way that I can and I will get better, but only when my body decides to forget. For now, it is what it is and if it bothers you that I can't seem to get over it, then leave me the hell alone" she yells. "Right now, I do not care" she says as she stands up from the bed and tries to straighten her clothes and then her hair. "I am fine with myself. I have to be" she admits to Snake a little quieter as she calms down slightly. "If you're not, then I'll leave and you can just forget about me. I can and have taken care of myself since I was fifteen. So, to change the subject" she starts "how did the President's News Conference go last night?"

"You didn't watch it?" he asks.

"Nope, I was busy, remember?"

"It was a big deal actually," he says. "I have it on tape," he offers, "if you want to watch it."

"Yeah, maybe in a little while, let me try to wake up a little more, and shower, if that's alright with you?"

"Sure Kitten, help yourself. I'll get some coffee started and then maybe some breakfast?"

"Sure" she says, really not interested in food but too tired to fight anymore.

"Alright, I'll be back in a half hour, how's that sound?"

"Sounds good" she responds as she starts walking towards the restroom and the shower.

"There's a spare tooth brush in there so help yourself" he says as he leaves the bedroom. Wow, she's got a temper; he decides with a grin. I forgot about that.

"Alright, I'm as a normal as possible" she admits when she sees him again. "So, let's see what the president had to say."

"I'll turn it on for you, but then I need to get back to work. I'm on duty today."

"Great, thanks." At least he won't be hovering, she thinks, looking at the huge breakfast that he expects her to eat.

"This is Sidney Norwood, with Channel 7 News, Metro D.C., your most trusted source, always first and always fast with your up to date information. The President is scheduled to appear within the next few moments to address the people. Here she is, live from the oval office:

"I want to thank everyone for joining me tonight for this spur of the moment News Conference" Jane Martin, President of the United States says. "There have been so many good things that have happened in the past few weeks. There have been really bad things too, not that I want to make light of those. I just want everyone to focus now on the positive and the direction that this great country is heading in. We will always remember those we lost but we also honor them by following the things that are in the best interest of you, our great American public and this great country. In so doing, we will keep their places close to our hearts knowing that this would be what they would want. Just before the end for our last President, he had a few things that he was working on that would benefit you, the American people. I want to continue on with his efforts, in memory of him."

"His dream was to take care of each and every one of you by finding a way to make sure that every citizen in this great country could have health care. To that end, he worked closely with some of our top scientists and discovered a way that would truly benefit this country and her people. It is an extremely small electronic chip that each person in this country would have, implanted into their hand, near the thumb. This would enable each one of you to have your complete health history available with a swipe at any Doctors office or in any hospital in this country.

For those with Medical problems, every medication they take, every reaction that they've had, any problem that they have would be available to any medical professional. This will save thousands of lives while helping to do away with medical errors. That in turn would do away with medical malpractice problems, allowing this country to come out of the free fall of the expensive health care costs that we are experiencing right now. It would allow you, the people, to feel more secure knowing that if, say, you were in an accident and unconscious, your treatment would still be the same. All because the doctors and hospitals would be able to scan your hand and know exactly how best to treat you.

"This does away with waiting to hear from someone that knows you and has your health history. This will saves lives, because treatments can begin immediately, without the wait. This will also enable the United States to have the health care reform that it so desperately needs, by saving all the money spent on litigation and putting that into actual health care. Insurance companies will no longer be ruling this country. The ruling will be left to those that you elect and not to those that only benefit from how deep your pockets are."

"After going over all the information available, I have found that this is the best thing for this country, and in order to protect you from not only costs, but wrong care, a House Bill is being drawn up as we speak, to help you with this process. We will be taking a vote on this, similar to the one for the execution. It will be an on-line vote for the American Citizens only, using the same method, your social security numbers, to allow you to vote. This will also help us with the problems that we seem to have with illegal aliens. Only actual citizens will be allowed to have this chip."

"Without the chip, you will not be allowed to use our health care. You will not be allowed to do anything, even to the point of the buying of food, in the future. This chip, in the future, will allow us to control what we so desperately need to, the illegal's in this country. If they become legal citizens, then they will be allowed to have the chip implanted, and not until then. There are so many good things that can be done with this chip that I cannot see how anyone could vote against it. I, Jane Martin, President of the United States will guarantee that you will all benefit from this device greatly."

"Please remember that when you log on to vote. This is a special item, just for our citizens of this great country. No other country has advanced as far as we have and are as close to streamlining health care and life safety as we are."

"Expect the voting to be available and ready within the next few weeks" she promises with a smile."We have our top scientists working furiously on this chip and your elected official's drawing up the bill with the utmost speed. I have a deadline of two weeks and then the voting will occur. Be prepared for one last news conference, the week before the vote, so that I can go over the bill with you personally. The law that was put into effect prior to the execution can be found on-line at the Presidents website. Please feel free to read this at your leisure. A well informed citizen is the best citizen. I would want to know it all before I voted, and so should you."

"Thank you and I will be talking to you again next week, once the bill is ready to be read and voted on. Goodnight" she says as she leaves the stage.

Well, well. An implantable chip, supposedly to help streamline our safety and health. Just what the people of this nation worry about constantly, she muses. I think I'll read that execution law she decides as she gathers her stuff and prepares to leave the bunker.

"Snake, oops, I mean Jacob, sorry, can I see you for a moment?" she asks. "Just a minute" he says as he finishes whatever he was doing on the computer.

"What's up?"

"How can I get back to D.C.?" she asks.

"My shift ends in about a half an hour, after that, I'm all yours" he finishes with a grin.

"Excellent. That will give me time to start reading the execution law that's available on the Presidents website. I'm just curious" she answers his questioning look. "I just want to see exactly how this law was worded."

"Well, let me know, I hate reading and that's got to be one long boring law."

"I'll let you know" she promises as she turns and goes back to her borrowed room.

"I think we should have a meeting at our Italian restaurant, Angelo's" Kat suggests on the way back into D.C. "You want to call the troops and let them know to meet us there tonight?"

"Sure. All set" he says to Kat's bowed head. "What are you doing?" he asks.

"Finishing reading the execution law" she says absently while she finishes the last page.

"That took a while" he says as he speeds around a slow moving vehicle.

"Yeah, it's a long law and there were a lot of things added to it that I'm sure the public is unaware of," she replies. "The people of this country are in big trouble" she exclaims when she finally turns her full attention on Snake.

"Why?"

"That law doesn't hurt or execute just known terrorists, but it includes any and all people that would be against anything in this country. It looks like it's a safety measure to guard the country for the President, against all persons that could cause this country trouble. They get to define trouble, and just like the execution, there is no place in the bill for a trial and jury of your peers. They have pretty much done away with all lawyers and judges. The people that judge you are your neighbors, and if they're in a bad mood, look out, you could end up dead.

Guilty or innocent, all one has to do is point their finger at you and poof, you're being judged and if found guilty, death. No more prisons, no more long term jails. This all happens within seven days of being judged and found guilty. Then the vote and the decision are carried out within two days. It's bad, Snake, we are in huge trouble in this country. First this law, then the chip. Is this making the country safer or is it turning it into a jail, with the smiling jail keeper, Jane Martin, Darling Jane, the newest President of the United States?"

"Let's hope for a vote against this chip. I can't honestly see where this chip would make anything better. It just opens up everything about you to whoever has the ability to read the chip. It's not a good choice" she mutters. "I'm not having it implanted, which could cause me to be looked at in a bad light, can call me forward as a troublemaker for the U.S. and send me in front of my neighbors who get to vote if I live or die."

"This is a terrible thing," she mutters "terrible. Sure there are other things that have occurred and been good, but when you top those things off with this one law and another that will take away from the people any sort of privacy they think they have, most of it makes terrible sense. This country has become a dangerous place to live. I think I may even look into moving out of it and becoming a citizen of a different country. Maybe Australia" she says seriously.

"That bad, huh" he replies absently. "How can I protect this country when the President is throwing things like this at the people who are wandering around in the nonchalant way that they normally do. My job can't be done if I have a chip in my hand, showing everyone where I am," he says angrily.

"We need to talk about this, but I'm not sure that the restaurant is a safe place to talk" he says. "Anyone eavesdropping could say that we are all traitors to this country, those who don't want to follow the laws. We'll eat and then go to one of our houses to talk, somewhere that's hasn't been bugged. I don't want this discussion to go anywhere else," he says decisively.

"Hi Mallory, how are you now, after your rest?" Kat asks.

"I'm much better" she admits with a smile. "I think I slept for twenty eight hours straight" she admits as she takes the seat next to Kat.

"Excellent! I just wish I could do that" Kat remarks in envy.

"You will, soon. Sleeping problems normally resolve themselves in a few weeks" Mallory answers knowledgably.

"Thanks Mal, appreciate your answer" she says as she turns to greet Eli and Devon who walk in together.

Wow, they sure do look alike, she realizes, seeing them side by side. I tend to forget they're quadruplets. You sure can tell as they both laugh at something that Snake says. All three of them could be identical. It definitely isn't a hardship looking at any of them, they're beautiful people, she thinks with a smile.

"What, oh, thanks, yeah" she says to the question of ordering the house special. "I'm good with that" she decides with a laugh. "I've never had a bad meal in this place and I've been coming here since I was fifteen."

"Yeah, their food is extremely good" Mal agrees. "I love this little place. It's kind of like home, only with a lot better food then you'd find at my place" Mal admits with a laugh.

"I don't think there's any food at your place, is there?" Eli asks, confused.

"Of course there is" she says with a wink. "I always keep a can of tuna in the house, just in case."

"Tuna, yum"….Kat adds with a grimace.

"Let's head to my place" Devon offers."I have a living room that's big enough to hold all of us comfortably and I sweep it daily for bugs, just to be sure. In my line of work, or really in any of our work there's always the possibility of someone bugging us, just to gain inside information on who knows what" he admits.

"Yeah, that's true" Kat agrees, while Mal shakes her head in acknowledgement. "We are all in that precarious of a position, but as long as you're diligent, you won't have a problem. And as long as you update the type of bugs to sweep for, you'll be fine."

"So when was the last time you updated your bug list?" Jacob asks.

"It's been about a month, so I guess I better do that today, before we sweep, so I get them all" he says ironically. "Thanks for the reminder, Jacob."

"Welcome" he replies with a grin.

"Alright, the place is all clear" Devon informs them all as they walk in to his living room. Quiet, calm colors of dark cherry, waxed to a shine on all the wood surfaces and the blues and grays of the furniture with the crisp clean lines that men seem to prefer; colors that calm the soul. It's overall a modern man's home, but a comforting one. He has the eye of an artist, Kat decides as she studies all his artwork sitting on wood surfaces and hanging on muted walls. Nicely done, then she realizes what her place looks like and grimaces. I need to do something with mine, she decides. I don't have a picture on the walls. Shame on me.

"Kat, h.e.l.l.o., Kat?"

"Oh. Sorry" she says to Devon as she blushes. "What?"

"You were going to let us know about the law regarding the execution, remember?"

"Yeah, sorry, my mind wandered, but I'm here now, so, about the new law. This is the worst law that I've ever seen put on paper and voted for. No one should have voted until this was read by at least most of the citizens of this country. We are now in big trouble" she says hotly. "Just thinking about what's in that law makes my blood boil" she admits with red cheeks.

"That bad, huh" Eli exclaims. "You don't rile easily Kat, so it must be bad."

"It's real bad, Eli, real bad."

"Alright, let's hear it" says Devon, "just spit it out."

"The supposed law that protects us from terrorists and allows us to get rid of them when they are found not only includes terrorists, be they citizens or not, but it also includes any and every United States citizen, and any illegal. If you are accused of doing something wrong, whether it's against the government or even just a neighbor, then you face the same voting process as did the terrorist who was executed. That voting is done by your neighbors; there are no longer lawyers or judges. The people have assumed and been given that responsibility. If found guilty, which is usually the case, you are then executed within two days, which is their max time for holding a criminal after the voting has taken place. This is the law that the people passed just prior to the execution of the terrorist that killed the President and Vice President."

"Are you sure that you read it right?" Devon asks.

"Yes I am. I happen to have a law degree, so I know how to read those things" she admits.

"You have a law degree, yet you're a cop?" Mallory exclaims in confusion.

"Yes" Kat replies. "I can be called a lawyer, since I passed the bar, but I never wanted to be a lawyer, just a cop. I got bored in school so just kept taking more and more classes until I could get on the police force. I had to be twenty one to be able to join the force, so I had five years to kill. I took law in school out of boredom and got my law degree. It's no big deal" she admits with a blush. After everyone in the room stops laughing, a chuckle heard now and then, she continues "this law has corrupted this country of ours. We now live in the most dangerous country of the world. The next thing that the President wants to pass is the chip with all your information on it. Can you imagine? There will be no where you can hide from Uncle Sam. He will know absolutely everything about you, maybe even more than you know. You can't access the chip, but others can, therefore, others could say whatever they wanted to say about you. Call you a terrorist, condemn you and kill you all within days of each other." After she finishes, everyone sits with white faces and shock in their eyes.

"I never expected this" claims Mallory quietly. "What are

we going to do?" she asks tearfully. "What about all the innocent little children? How will we be able to protect them from
their own country? What have we done? God help us all" she
moans as Eli gathers her close to comfort her.

"Wait, this can't be right" Devon insists. "You must have
read the law wrong" he says in denial.

"Nope" she replies. "It's the truth. Why do you think they
want this thing passed so fast?"

"The faster they do this, the less time you have to oppose it.
It's never been the passing of things that had the problem; it's
always been the opposition that irritated the White House.
They gain too much momentum when they have time to spread
a negative word. Opposition is and always will be the safety
net for the U.S. Unfortunately, our safety net now has a huge
hole in it. Everyone will vote for this because the President
backs it and she can do no wrong! Look at her; she's meek as a
mouse and just as nice.That's what she leads with and has most
of the country convinced of."

"Yep, we're screwed" she states in fear."The only thing that
I can think of" she says thoughtfully "is to start an underground.
We need to be prepared; this is all going to go through. If we
don't want to be a part of this, then we need to do something to
stop it. It can't be stopped now, at this stage, but we can make
it more difficult. Snake, is there anything like this chip that
black-ops uses? I know you put a GPS hair in my hair, so that
you could always track me, just in case."

"What?" Devon exclaims "you planted a GPS on her?"

"Yes, I did. After her incident, I felt it was in her best interest to have a GPS planted on her so that I could always locate
her. I never wanted her to go through anything like that again.
She's had it on for the past few weeks and she probably doesn't
even know which hair it is, it blends so flawlessly and isn't
picked up by your de-bugger program."

"Well" he exclaims in disgust "I had no idea" he grumbles.

"Why would you? It has nothing to do with you, does it?
We might have something like the chip they're trying to get
implanted in every citizen of the U.S. I'll have to talk with my

tech people and see what they have to say."

"If we need to go underground, then it's going to require some work, and if we go underground, it will be too dangerous to ever come back to this way of life. It will be permanent" he warns quietly. "It will be a very difficult thing to do. The only thing to compare it to would be as if you all had to go under-cover, so deep undercover that even your own mother wouldn't know you, you would become legend. I've done that to a cer-tain point and it takes an emotional toll. I hope you can under-stand what I mean and what it would mean to you" he says.

"Yeah, I hear you" Eli responds quietly. "But it may be the only way that we can save this country, save our people and protect them from their own President. Make this a country once again that has joyful people and children running around happily, instead of with fear."

"Alright, let's all take this information and investigate quiet-ly" Devon suggests. "Let's find out what we can and meet again in a couple of days, to compare notes."

"Fine" says Mal as she gets up to leave, Eli protectively holding her hand as she gathers her things.

"I'll look into what I can, as quietly as possible. It wouldn't do to tip anyone off about what we know and what we suspect" Kat admits. "Where will we meet again?

"Here" says Devon, "how about the day after tomorrow at nineteen hundred?"

"Good for me" agrees Mallory and Eli. Kat and Snake just agree silently with a nod.

"Be safe out there" Kat says "and watch out for big brother. They'll be looking for anyone acting differently" she assures them "so protect yourselves and beware on the computer. They can already track you there, and will probably have something set up to tell them who visits the site about the laws and about the chip. I would use the computers at the libraries or other public places and use them randomly with a fake I.D. You can't be too careful now" she assures them sadly.

"I can't believe this is happening, Snake" Kat says. "We have a big problem, so big it almost unimaginable! Remember, we only have five more days before the President's next news conference. She'll cover the chip and the laws governing it, to some extent, but you know she'll leave out any future issues with it, or anything negative. There have been previous problems, according to the scientific journals, of the chip breaking down and causing a serious sore area because the body starts fighting it as a foreign implanted body.

That's seen to be happening in approximately five out of one hundred cases, according to a study that's been done in the past year. This has been in development for about ten years now, and they believe they can produce enough of them to begin the implants within the next month. People will be voluntarily receiving them free, at their local Health Departments. The implant is simple, done with a needle, and not more painful that receiving an injection. They propose to place these in the area of your hand between the thumb and forefinger. A simple procedure, with no side effects, unless your body is one of the five out of a hundred that wants to reject it. They're also looking into placement near the forehead, at the hair line. We don't have a lot of time before they have enough for everyone to receive the implant. It's coming fast" she warns. "We don't have a lot of time before this begins. I think we need to obtain some cell phones that can't be traced. Who can we get them from?" she asks.

"Let me handle those problems" Jacob offers. "I have access to more electronics then you do, so I'll deal with everything that we're going to need."

"Thanks Jacob" replies Kat and Mallory. "What else do we need to do?"

"My suggestion" responds Jacob "is to decide what you're plans are going to be for your future. Will you stay here and act normal, or will you join the underground?"

"We have to think about more than just us" Devon says. "We still have loved ones here that will need us, remember" he says dryly to Jacob, "Mom and Dad."

"Of course" Jacob replies "I haven't forgotten about them, I never have, much as you want to believe otherwise. Just because I couldn't see them didn't mean I ever forgot them" he assures everyone. "We can bring them underground with us, it wouldn't be a problem."

"Maybe not for you" Devon exclaims "but what about them? They're not that young anymore, and a big change like the underground may be something they couldn't do. Besides, they have a life and friends and they might want to stay around them, like normal. They deserve to be able to make that choice."

"We'll just have to wait and see after the next news conference with the President, how things go. If I know them, they're going to be upset. I know they won't be getting the implant, which will start them thinking about staying or going. Things are about to change radically in the very near future" Devon says worriedly. "This world is changing faster than anyone expected, in just a few months, look where we are already."

"I need to get going" Kat says. "I have things to do tonight, before work tomorrow, so I'll see you all later."

"Give me a ride, Snake?"

"Sure, Kitten, let's go."

"Night Kat" says Mallory and Eli "see you soon."

"Remember we're just a phone call away if you need anything" Eli offers.

"Yeah, thanks. Just drop me at my apartment; you don't need to come in."

"Of course I'm coming in" he replies indignantly."You are never facing anything alone again, you got that?" he demands.

"Yeah, thanks Snake" she replies meekly "you have no idea how much I appreciate you, but it's probably going to be a long time before I feel normal again" she admits sadly. "Looks like everything's the same" she says after she enters her apartment. "It seems like I've been gone a long time and not just twenty four hours, but as you can see, all's quiet."

"Alright, you're home, safe and sound Kitten and I'm heading back to base. You call me if you need anything, I'll probably see you sometime tomorrow. I'm off duty after tomorrow, for the next few days, so I'll be working on what we discussed earlier" he says. "Night Kitten" he says quietly and kisses her on the cheek.

"Night Snake" she says as he leaves, touching her face after the heat of his kiss. I never thought of you that way, but I should have. You were always just like a brother, but not anymore, she thinks with a smile. Not anymore.

THIRTY FOUR

"Has anyone talked to Snake?" Kat asks three days after he dropped her at her apartment.

"No, why?" asks Eli.

"Well, he said he'd see me the day after he dropped me at my apartment, but that was three days ago, and he didn't. I've called and left messages, but he's never called me back" she says in confusion.

"I'm sure he's fine, but he is black-ops you know and he never knows very far in advance what he's going to be doing and where."

"True" she says, slightly relieved. "I tend to forget that Snake is Jacob and he has a dangerous job."

"Yeah, we all do."

"It was a shock finding out what he really did. I just thought he was a biker" she admits. "It's hard for me to keep that in my brain, I'll work harder on it" she promises.

"Don't" Eli says. "If you forget, than that's information that no one else can get from you. The less you know, the safer you'll be."

"True" she admits. "I've been a little out of it lately, though, so hopefully I'll get my act in gear and stop being stupid" she adds with disgust.

"Kat, there is absolutely nothing stupid about you" laughs Eli. "You are probably the smartest person I've ever known."

"Thank you Eli; that was the nicest thing anyone has ever said about me. I appreciate it" she admits with a smile.

"The news conference is coming up and we thought we'd watch it together at Devon's. It starts at nineteen hundred so we're going to meet there and have dinner."

"Really" Kat says in surprise. "Who's cooking?" she asks suspiciously.

"I think Devon is ordering out."

"Oh" she adds with a smirk. I should have thought about that one. "Alright, let him know that I'll be there. I'm working tomorrow, but after I'll head over" she promises.

"Detective, report, my office."

"Yes Sir" Des says in surprise. "I didn't know you'd be here tonight Lieutenant."

"I decided I needed to work, to catch up" she explains. "We have those arrests that I've been working on, the Captain is still planning for the next news conference, which is tomorrow. I believe the Captain is expecting problems again and has advised all of us to not be surprised if we have to work for the two days following the conference."

"We've been actually pretty quiet considering where we are," Des admits. "It's very unusual for this city, and the crime rates have definitely dropped in the past month."

"Yeah" Kat says on a sigh.

"That new law has everyone afraid to leave their homes anymore. Even the restaurants and the bars have been pretty slow, lately" Des remarks.

"This country is not the same as it was four months ago" Kat says quietly. "It will never be the same again."

"Alright, I'm going to head over to the Capitol headquarters and check with them on any news."

"Yes Sir, I'll see you later" Des says.

"Anything new, guys?" Kat asks as she walks into Capitol Headquarters.

"Not right at the moment. We're gearing up for after tomorrow's conference. I think things will probably pick up after that and it won't be for the better" Devon admits. "I know there are going to be a lot of angry people out there after that conference."

"True" Kat replies."I guess I'll see you tomorrow, at your place, right?" she reminds him.

"Yeah, we'll all be there" he assures her."I'm having food delivered by Angelo's."

"Awesome" Kat says at the mention of her favorite restaurant, "I'll be there" she promises as she leaves. I'm not busy right now, maybe I'll ride out to Snakes base and see why he hasn't called me back, she decides after she gets in her car.

"Snake, is anyone here?" Kat calls after she enters the cabin, no guards anywhere. I've never been here when someone hasn't greeted me. This is weird. No one's answering either. "Hello" she calls as she pulls out her weapon and heads for the stairs. It sounds deserted; it's kind of hollow sounding, nothing in here, no furniture, nothing. Very strange she decides as she heads downstairs. "Anyone here?" she yells to the empty halls. Something's wrong, she knows as she opens the door that held all the high tech equipment and monitors. It's empty and she gasps in surprise. There's no sign of anyone or anything. Where have they all gone, she wonders in a panic. I know this is the right place. I've been here enough times to know where I am. Oh god, what if something happened to all of them.

He left me, she screams silently in her head. He promised he'd never leave me alone. Her heart starts to pound louder and louder. They have to be here, she thinks as she runs from room to room, finding nothing. No sign of anything, or of anything ever having been here. There aren't even any holes in the walls for wires. What the heck is going on here? She runs back upstairs just to make sure it's the right place. Am I really losing my mind? She runs down the drive that led to the garage where Snake always hid their cars while they were here. There is no garage, just an empty spot where one could go. Oh my god, they destroyed them, all of them. I need to get out of here she thinks as she races back to where she left her car. This can't be real she decides as she gets in and starts it.

I better call Eli and Mallory and Devon, they must know something. They have to know something!

"Devon?"

"What is it Kat?"

"I'm out here where Jacob had his base."

"Yes, what about it?" he asks impatiently.

"There's nothing here" she admits."Nothing. The cabin is here but there is absolutely nothing in it" she stammers. "Nothing, the garage is gone, not a sign of it on the property" she repeats. "No sign of anyone having ever been in that cabin" she says tearfully."There isn't even a hole in the basement walls were there could have been electronics. Nothing" she keeps repeating over and over. "Nothing"

"Kat, listen to me."They probably had to leave, remember? We talked about it, underground, remember?"

"Yeah" she says as she rubs her forehead."I remember, but why like this, why didn't he say anything, where did they all go" she asks in a panic.

"I don't know" he replies quietly."He must not have had time to let us know, or he was afraid to use his communications. He's probably getting all the new stuff that he said he'd take care of, remember" he says soothingly.

"Yeah" Kat says with a sniff. "But"

"Kat, listen, turn your car around and head back to D.C. Meet me at my apartment and we'll try to figure this all out. I'll let Eli and Mallory know and they'll be there waiting for you, okay? he asks calmly.

"Okay" she says sniffling."I'll be there in about an hour" she replies after wiping her face from all the tears and gathering her thoughts so that she can actually drive.

"Good" he says. "We'll see you in an hour at my place" he reminds her.

"Okay, bye Devon" she says as she starts the long journey back to D.C. She was really afraid, for the first time in her adult life, for someone else. Devon answered the door at her first knock, grabbed her by the hand and pulled her quickly into his apartment.

"You made it" Mallory says in relief as she walks toward her.

"Yeah" Kat says, still dazed."I'm here. It was a long drive and there was more traffic than I was expecting" she admits.

"That's alright" Mallory adds soothingly."Here, have a glass of wine. You'll feel better" she promises as she drapes her arm around her waist and leads her to the couch.

"Thanks, I needed this" she admits after taking a long drink.

"We know you did" Mallory agrees wryly."Here sit down and we'll talk."

"Now" Devon says after Kat's had time to relax a little. "Tell me what happened, when you feel up to it."

"I'm fine" she says in a quiet voice."There was nothing there" she repeats. "I told you all of it on the phone."

"I know you did, but tell all of us again, please" he insists.

"Alright, I drove out to talk to Snake and arrived at the base they'd been using. It was strange, even when I first pulled in, because no one met me at the car. Someone always met us outside, remember? As soon as we pulled in, someone was standing there, usually Snake. But not today," she repeats, "no one. Then I went into the cabin, just like normal, same porch, same door. The door wasn't locked, but I didn't even think of that until just now. I walked right in. There was nothing in there. No furniture, no wall hangings, nothing" she repeats. "It was completely empty. There wasn't even a shadow where there could have been a picture that was taken down from the wall. Everything was just blank, as if the place had never been used before. Clean but nothing else" she says as she shakes her head to clear her thoughts again.

"Then I went to the basement door and opened it. I went downstairs and all the rooms that were down there were gone. There's no sign of any walls to separate the rooms like there were, no electronics, no holes in the walls or even in the woodwork to show that there had ever been anything down there. It looked like a huge basement that was ready for someone to move into, but one that had never been used. It was almost as if I had imagined everything" she admits, confused. "You were there, right?" she asks."We were all there, weren't we?" I am not having a nervous breakdown, she says to herself. "I know that was the right place" she insists as Mallory starts to rub her shoulder in sympathy.

"We were all there" Mallory reassures her."You're not having a nervous breakdown" she says firmly.

"Thank you" Kat breaths out in relief. "Thank you, you have no idea what that means to me" she says brokenly.

"I think we do" she says quietly. "I would have had the same reaction" she assures her "if I had faced the same thing. Am I going nuts? That would have been my first reaction."

"It sounds like they've gone underground" Eli says. "Everything that you've described is what happens when someone goes underground. They can't leave any type of proof that they ever existed, it would be too dangerous for them. He'll contact us as soon as he can" Eli assures her.

"Hey Detective, anything new?" Kat asks after walking into Metro One.

"I've been trying to tie up old cases, Lieutenant."

"Excellent" Kat responds with a smile. "I want to close up any files that can be closed before we get hit with the next wave. We need to finish all these things before the news conference. I have a feeling all hell's going to break loose after the conference, and if I'm right, we're going to be working nonstop for days afterwards."

"There's a special news bulletin scrolling across the screen, Lieutenant. Check it out" she says anxiously. After turning up the volume so that they could hear the message, Kat listens closely.

"This is Sidney Norcross, News Channel 7, Washington D.C. with a special news bulletin. We have just learned that President Jane Martin has appointed a new Director to the Department of Homeland Security. A Mr. Eric Flannigan, he's a Five Star General with the U.S. Marines, and the previous Director of USSOCOM, which is an elite group from the U.S. Special Operations Command. He has been appointed to the position of Director of Homeland Security, starting immediately."

"This is exciting news" Sidney remarks. "It's been a few weeks since the former Director of Homeland Security was murdered so viciously, and then the previous President and Vice President assassinated, using the poor man's casket. Let's hope that all of the previous problems are finished, since we have a new President, and she has moved the United States in such strong ways. This is Sidney Norwood, reporting live outside the White House. Tune in to our evening news for information on the President's next news conference."

"Well" Kat says."That name sounds familiar to me. I think I may have met him before." When was it she wonders? Devon and I met him, when he introduced us to Lieutenant Jacob Callander. Yeah, now it's clear. He was a very professional man, she remembers. He was a very important man, even then. Now even more so, being Director of Homeland Security.

Well, this was a productive day she decides as she finishes cleaning her desk. It's time to hit the road; maybe stop for some dinner and a drink, then home and bed. One of these days I'll get to sleep without dreams. I'm sick of the nightmares. A drink or two might relax me enough to sleep through the night, as long as I remember to stop and not get stupid drunk like that one time. But then again, if I do, maybe Jacob will show up again to help me. No way, she decides. I haven't talked to him in days. He's gone again and god knows where this time. I wonder if he'll ever get in touch with me again.

"Lieutenant Thomas?"

"Yes" Kat responds to the sudden knock on her apartment door. "Can I help you" she asks of the delivery boy standing in the hall with a delivery receipt.

"I have a delivery for you" he says, but when Kat just looks at him like where, he admits "I can't bring it upstairs. I left it safely downstairs near the street. Will you follow me please?" he asks nervously.

"Sure, let me get my jacket" she says. "After throwing on her jacket and sliding her weapon into its harness, she descends the stairs right behind the delivery boy.

"There it is Lieutenant. Will you sign for it please?" he requests.

"There must be some mistake" she exclaims. "That's not my bike."

"It says your name right here" he insists as he points to the

405

delivery receipt. "You are Lieutenant Kathleen Thomas, aren't you?"

"Yeah, that's me" she admits.

"Then this is yours, too" he replies as he pushes the signature pad at her again.

"Alright, let me see that" she says in resignation."Yeah, it says me, but it doesn't say who it's from."

"It doesn't have to" he says "as long as you are this person here, then that's all I need" he insists.

"There's an envelope that comes with it attached to that box. Maybe it will say in there who it's from. But I wouldn't turn that down" he admits with longing, "even though it looks like a girls, I'd still like to have that, it must be worth thousands" he says, "It looks like its custom made."

"Yeah, it does" she admits as she walks around the Chrome and pink "mean looking" motorcycle with the painting of the black panther crouched in attack on the gas tank and underneath it the word Kitten, written in script.

"It's beautiful" she says in awe as she reaches out to glide her fingers over the cat. "Thank you" she says to the delivery guy.

Where am I going to put this, she wonders as she grabs the box that was sitting on the seat and heads for her apartment again. I need a special storage place for that; it certainly can't sit out there in the street. Maybe Mike will let me store it at his house. He has a garage, he might let me park it inside there. I'll call him as soon as I see what's in the box. After tearing open the box she discovers a helmet that matches the bike down to the Black Panther painting with her nick name, exactly the same as the bike only proportioned smaller to fit the helmet.

It has to be from Snake, she realizes, her hands starting to shake in excitement as she opens the envelope.

"Kitten, this is yours. I wanted you to have a constant reminder of what I told you. I will never leave you, you are never alone. You'll understand more when you put the helmet on. Just remember, YOU ARE NEVER ALONE. Snake. Wow, Snake, where are you? she murmurs as her eyes well with tears.

After adjusting the helmet straps so that she can get it over

406

her head, she sits on the sofa and waits. After about twenty seconds of having it on his voice comes out of it loud and clear, "YOU ARE NEVER ALONE KITTEN, when you need me, just put on this helmet and tap the button over your right ear. I'll get the message and call. I'm sorry I had to leave like I did, but in a few days you'll understand why. I will be back, when you least expect it, but until then I wanted you to have something made just for you, from me.

"I love you Kitten and I promise to show you as soon as possible, but until things have changed and I'm able to leave the underground, I can't be there in person. I'm always there in thought though. This is the only time you will hear this entire message, the next time you put on your helmet, you will be reassured of never being alone. That is a constant reminder for you, and also that I'll be back very soon, I promise. Sleep well Kitten, as if I am sitting right by your bed. Goodnight."

No, don't stop talking to me, she panics. After hurriedly taking off the helmet and putting it back on, his voice comes through about twenty seconds later, YOU ARE NEVER ALONE he says in his beautifully deep rich voice. Then there's nothing. Just the one message, as if the other message never existed.

Snake, she thinks with tears streaming down her cheeks. When will you come back, when, she screams in her head, I miss you, she sobs. After about an hour of putting it on and taking it off just so she could hear his voice over and over, she decides to stop the insanity and call Mike. I need to store that beautiful bike somewhere safe and Mike's is probably the safest. After talking to Mike and telling him what she needs he offers to come over and follow her to his house.

"Thanks, Mike, since I've never even ridden a bike, I'm not sure what to do" she admits.

"That's okay Kat. I'll help you. You want me to get a trailer for you?"

"Yes please" she says. "I won't ride this bike until Snake himself teaches me how. I'll save that for the future."

"Good" he says in agreement. "I'll be there in about an hour."

"Thanks Mike."

Finally, Kat decides as she climbs into bed after midnight. This was a long day she sighs in fatigue. I just need to hear him one more time she thinks as she puts the helmet back on. "YOU ARE NEVER ALONE KITTEN" she hears and a few minutes later she falls into a deep sleep. A healing sleep, she'll discover tomorrow when she wakes after sleeping all night. The first all night sleep she's had since her rape, and all because of a helmet from Snake.

"This is the big day Lieutenant" Detective Des says when Kat walks into the station at zero seven hundred, the morning of the scheduled news conference. "You look good Lieutenant."

"I feel great" she admits with a smile. "I slept great" she adds in a happy voice.

"Whatever you did, it worked for you."

"Thanks Des. We should go out sometime, like we used to" Kat says with nostalgia.

"Yeah, let's plan something for the weekend" replies Des enthusiastically.

"Sure, that sounds good to me, unless we end up working the whole weekend because of the news conference."

"Let's hope we don't. I wouldn't mind some mindless fun."

"Yeah" Kat says, laughing, "me either. I'm leaving here around eighteen hundred. I'm supposed to be at Devon's. We're all meeting there to watch the news conference together. Well, most of us. Eli went back to L.A. He said he was tired of our cold weather and had a desk full of paperwork that he needed to get done, and Mallory's back with her whole team. I think they're out in Missouri somewhere, on a case. So it will be just Devon and I, unless he invites his parents over to watch it with us," she says quietly.

"Good" Des says. "I'm going to watch it from home. At least I'll have a little time at home in case all hell breaks loose again after the conference. Then we'll all be back here and out there" she admits with dread.

THIRTY FIVE

"Come on in Kat. My mom and dad are coming, too" Devon says in apology.

"Good" she replies with a smile.

"You're not mad that they're coming" he asks in surprise.

"No, why would I be? I like your parents, Devon" she admits.

"Thanks Kat, I appreciate you saying that. I have some beverages and snacks set out; help yourself" he offers as the door bell rings again and he turns to answer it.

"Hi Mrs. Callander" replies Kat to her greeting.
"Please, call me Sandra" she insists.

"Sandra" says Kat as she receives a hug from her.

"Mr. Callander"

"Joe" he insists with a smile. "It's good to see you Kat, how have you been?"

"Good, really good Joe, thanks for asking."

"Let's all go into the living room" Devon suggests "and we can have some snacks and some cold drinks."

"Thanks Devon" replies Sandra. "The news conference will be coming on shortly. Let's get the right channel on so we don't miss anything."

"This is Devon" he says as he answers his phone.

"Devon Callander"?

"Yes, what can I do for you" he asks as he walks into the kitchen so he can hear, away from the TV.

"This is Eric Flannigan, the Director of Homeland Security."

"Yes Sir" responds Devon. "What can I do for you, Director?" he asks.

"I'm looking for your brother, Lieutenant Jacob Callander. Is he at your place?" he asks.

"No Sir, he's not."

"Can you tell me where I can find him or how to reach him?" he asks.

"Actually, I can't Sir. I haven't seen him for over a week now. I've tried all the usual ways to contact him with no luck. So I really have no idea where he is.

"Hmm" replies the Director. "I assumed that if anyone would know you would, but you're saying you have no idea?"

"That's correct Sir. It's not unusual for me to not know where he is or to hear from him. I went fifteen years without knowing if he was alive or dead. So, no Sir, it's not unusual at all," Devon replies bitterly "only this time, my parents are going to want to know where he is and I can't tell them either, since I have no idea, again."

"I'm sorry to upset you Devon. I'm sure he's fine, just missing again. Would you contact me if you hear from him?" he asks Devon.

"Yes Sir, I promise, as soon as I know where he is, I'll let you know."

"Thanks Devon" replies the Director of Homeland Security.

"Here it is" Devon says when he walks back into the living room, the news conference just beginning.

"Thank you for joining me tonight" says the President of the United States, Jane Martin, flanked on one side by Quinton Uqbahtor, the Vice President and the other side Jerald Johnston, the Minister of the Peoples Church from Texas and the new Goodwill Ambassador of Peace for the United States. This is the evening we have all been looking forward to, she says with a happy smile. Tonight, we, the American people are going to move into the future, a place that we have been trying to get to for many years. After years of preparing, we finally have an answer to our health care dilemma."

"We know, as compassionate and caring people, that all of

our citizens of this great country should be taken care of equally and honestly. We have found a way to do this and not raise your taxes. We have found the perfect answer to this decades old problem. Our great scientists of this age have developed a very special microchip. Technology is so far advanced that they have been able to create something so small that it is hard to believe all the information that is contained on it. With our capabilities, we have moved into the twenty second century, farther than anyone else in the world.

"This technology will permit us to not only protect our citizens but to help them when the time comes that they need help. These microchips are no larger than a grain of rice. Yes, a grain of rice that holds the history of you, every tiny bit of information, your health, you medications, your allergies, and your medical history. No one, besides your own physician or hospital in an emergency will be able to have access to this chip. This chip may save your life. I am so very excited about this capability that I wanted to show you my acceptance and willingness to experience this new product by having this microchip implanted into my own hand, tonight.

"You will witness the very first microchip to be implanted, into your own Presidents hand. I am not afraid and I wanted you to witness that, so that you too can think of these things in the most positive way only. Along with my microchip being implanted, is the Vice Presidents. He, too, has agreed to have his microchip implanted and Reverend Johnston also has agreed.

"We all wanted to show you, through our act, the easy and painless process that is being used. The microchip, once implanted, will be connected through the wireless society, to a large data base that has all of my information in it, just like yours is. After it's implanted, it is then filled with all of that information. You can't feel it," she assures the country. "The only thing you will actually feel is the implanting and that is a very small and very fast procedure. Even a small child will not mind having this done."

"The microchips are all numbered with a unique number that only one microchip will have, every individual will have their very own number. The implantation occurs, first by a technician; your information is already waiting to be transmitted into your chip and as soon as they finish the implantation, your information is sent. All this occurs within approximately one minute. How easy that is" she exclaims. "One minute of my time may save my life in the future, a big plus. Another big plus is that for you, the citizens of this great country, there is no charge for this. Only American citizens can get this chip, absolutely free. All of our hard work and the many years of testing and producing and there is no charge. I find that exciting," she exclaims. "Finally, we have something to offer you, with no hidden charges and a wealth of good that it will do for you."

"This is a big night" she admits with a laugh. "Let's start this implantation process" she urges. "I want to show everyone how easy this is." The technician walks out while a computer is wheeled out and another technician sits at it in preparation of sending the information to the Presidents chip. "Please, show everyone watching; exactly what the chip looks like" the President requests.

The technician places a small object onto a white piece of paper and requests the cameras to zoom in. "Next to the chip is a small grain of rice" explains the technician. "The rice is the cream colored item. The grey item is the actual microchip. You can see that it is almost exactly the same size as the piece of rice. We use a very small chip implanter to place this microchip into your right hand between your thumb and forefinger. The reason that area was chosen is because it is a softer area with less chance of being injured. Once the chip is in, there is no lump, no sign of it. You will probably forget exactly where it is once it has healed and becomes a part of your hand" reassures the technician.

"Thank you" the President says with a smile, "let's do this" she orders the technician.

"If you'll come over here President Martin, and please have a seat" he requests when she gets to the chair. "Now, your right hand please."

"Make sure the cameras can see this" she orders the technician.

"Yes President Martin" agrees the technician. "Can you see what I'm doing?" he asks of the camera man.

"Yep, all clear" he replies.

"Good. The next step is to cleanse the area with a moist alcohol swab, ensuring that no bacteria can enter the area while I am implanting the chip. It is a common procedure" reassures the technician. "Now, as soon as that area dries naturally, I will be using this small instrument to implant the chip."

"It's quick, so watch closely. If you take your eyes off the screen, you'll miss it" he promises with a smile. After waiting twenty seconds, he places the tip of the implanter on the spot that he wants the chip to go and pushes the cap, a quick click noise as the implanter pushes the microchip into the hand, he moves the implanter and complete. The chip is implanted and there is no sign of any damage, and the President never flinched. She smiled the whole time and watched as the chip was placed into her hand.

"That's it?" she asks. "I didn't feel anything" she admits. "I expected at least a tiny feeling of something," she says in confusion, "but there wasn't anything. The worst thing was the cold alcohol swab" she admits with a laugh.

"You're done President Martin, and the computer technician has just nodded her head, telling me that all of your information is completed and now resides on your chip."

"Wow" the President exclaims "that was quick, and absolutely painless, it's less than a minute after I sat down and it's done. Unbelievable" she repeats with a shake of her head and a grin.

"All right Quinton, it's your turn" she says with a laugh. "He's a guy, it will probably hurt him" she admits with a smile at her audience. Quinton sits down in the spot just vacated by the President. The technician takes out a fresh alcohol swab and cleans the right hand of the Vice President, places the implanter on the spot where the chip will go and clicks the button. He almost immediately removes the implanter and again, no sign of anything. No sign of the chip, no bleeding, nothing.

The Vice President just looks stunned that he felt nothing as he's given the okay by the technician and rises to his feet.

"You're all done Mr. Vice President" the technician assures him.

"Wow" exclaims the Vice President "you were right President Martin. I felt nothing" he admits with a smile. "I don't mind having things like that done when they don't hurt" he says to the country. "That was the easiest thing I have ever done" he admits in surprise.

"Reverend Johnston, you're up" says the President. As he walks over to the seat, he glances quickly at the camera to see where it is and notices it following his every move and probably every expression on his face. How can I get out of this, he wonders, without creating a problem? I don't want that chip in my body anywhere, he thinks in dismay.

She really put me in a bad position. But then, I wasn't given notice of this in advance and definitely had no opportunity to say no. It was pretty much a direct order from her. Fine, I'll get it, but then I'll remove it myself at the next opportunity I have. I will not keep the damned chip in my hand. He sits in the chair motioned to by the technician and offers his right hand. The tech cleans it with an alcohol swab and waits for it to dry. He then places the implanter tightly against the area were the chip is to go, pushes the button on the implanter and moves it, all in the same smooth motion. He glances at the computer technician; she nods and informs Reverend Johnston that he's done.

"Wow, that was fast and painless" he replies. "We three are now safer than anyone in this country. If anything happens, the doctors and hospitals now have all of our information available, at the touch of a button, amazing. They don't even need to know who you are, the chip will tell them. This is so awesome."

"I want to thank you for tuning in tonight to find out how best to keep yourselves safe. We have demonstrated to all of you just how simple and easy this was, no pain involved and free. How can you not like all of those things? On the day after tomorrow, a vote will be taken on whether or not we want to use these chips. I cannot see why anyone would not want to use this, so make sure you get on the computer and vote. That process is much harder than this one was" she adds with a smile. "I know I can depend on our citizens to make the right decision" she assures everyone. "Thank you and goodnight" she finishes and walks off stage with the Reverend and the Vice President.

Total silence fills Devon's living room. Everyone is shocked by what they just watched. "Um" Joe says "I don't think so. I don't want to have a chip implanted in my hand" he says. "I don't believe that it would be just for health reasons and health care. If that bill passes, the government will be able to find anyone and do anything.

They won't stop with just health care, I'm sure of it. They're too corrupt to stop at something like that. They'll use it in the most corrupt way. They'll be able to track you and hunt you down. No" he says adamantly, "No Way."

"I agree" Sandy says. "This is one of our worst nightmares" she admits. "We saw this coming, but were hoping it wouldn't ever get to us. The time has come, I guess. What are were going to do Joe, how can we stop this?"

"Spread the news" he says. "Tell everyone not to vote for this. To make it fail. It's the only thing we can do" he adds with dismay. "That's not much, but at least it's something. We have to get the word out; this is not what everyone thinks it is. This is something much worse."

"Yeah, I agree" Devon adds with a serious face, staring at the now blank TV. "This is a lot bigger than people think. This is not just for health care reasons. You're right Dad; this is total government corruption, at its most insidious. We need to be prepared. The vote will pass, you know it will," he says. "Once that's done, no one will be safe. They'll enforce it, because you know that will be in the fine print of the bill that passes. It will become a law; there will be no choice for anyone. Everyone must do it or you will be judged by your neighbors and found guilty, thanks to the first bill that was passed, then put to death. This country is so totally screwed up."

"This is the most dangerous President we've ever had" he admits. "She's turned everything upside down and because of her meek attitude and appearance, she gets away with it. The streets are going to be a mess after the vote, Kat. We'll be scraping people up off the streets like so much trash. The vote will pass and then the United States will be in the biggest trouble it's ever been in."

"We need to come up with a plan, to help all those poor people that don't want to get this chip. You know they'll start hunting them down. They must have some kind of instruments that can tell if you have the chip or not. They'll start visiting people's homes, looking for those without it and either forcing them to get it or arresting them, and then their nice neighbors will accuse them and they'll be found guilty and be put to death. We saw how that worked after the first bill passed."

"Yeah" Kat admits in fear. "I'm not getting that chip" she says loudly. "No freakin way. Not going to happen."

"Don't worry Mom, Dad, we'll think of something. We have to" he assures them. "You don't need to worry today; the voting isn't until tomorrow, so we at least have a day. We'll think long and hard and see what we can do for you and all the other people that won't receive the chip."

"How about if we tell them it's against our religion" asks Sandra with hope. "We have religious freedom in this country, don't we? We should be able to say no to anything because of that, right?"

"No, Mom, I'm sorry, but that doesn't work anymore. It was written into the first bill that passed, that religion is not allowed to be used to try to get out of a law."

"The President made sure that was on the bill. The bill is totally against humanity and gives anyone rights against anyone. That new bill really is guilty until proven innocent, and there is no more innocence left" Kat replies.

"We're doomed" sobs Sandra as Joe tries to calm her down. Devon just watches quietly and sadly.

Those bastards. They're hurting the very people that helped to build this country strong. They have taken away everything from them, he thinks. Bastards, he yells inside as his anger and determination starts to build. We have to do something. Jacob, where the hell are you, I need you today. Of course, you're never around when you're really needed, so what's new.

The day of reckoning (what she's been calling voting day)

arrives with sunshine and warmth. It's a beautiful late spring day, all those cherry blossoms that covered all the trees a bright pretty memory. They did their job and moved on, looking at the grass covered in petals. If you didn't know what today was you'd never believe it. I used to love my job, five months ago anyway. So much has changed and so many have left since this all started. If only we could go back, she dwells. At least four months, maybe even five, she decides before all the craziness started, before that first murder, before Bill Blaketon, before his mom let the cat out. Things were so much easier then, if only they could be again.

"Last night sucked" Kat admits to Des when she gets to work. "There was a lot of crying going on" she admits.

"Crying?" Des asks in surprise."Why? The news conference was good, didn't you think?" she asks in confusion.

"That depends" Kat says. "If you agree to the chip then yes it was, but if not, then no it was bad."

"Why would anyone not agree to the chip?" Des asks in confusion. "It's free and it could save your life" she says "and it doesn't hurt to have it implanted."

"That's true" Kat agrees "but what about the other uses they have for it?" she asks.

"What other uses? They didn't say anything else about it, just that the doctors and hospitals would have your information immediately, so they can save more people. There's only good about this thing" she adds indignantly. "I can't wait to get it. It will take a load off, and I'll never need to show my insurance card again, it's all good!"

Wow, Kat realizes as she continues on to her office. Sample one of a yes person. I didn't expect that, but if the only way you look at it is the way they want you too, then her opinion is going to be the most common. We're in big trouble, she decides. As she closes her office door, she remembers how good she slept last night. Only with my helmet on, she admits with a grin, but hey, if that's what it takes, no problem. Thanks Snake, wherever you are, stay safe for me please, she pleads quietly. I wish he'd call, but he probably can't. If only I could talk to him, I'd be happy. Someday soon, she hopes.

"Lieutenant, the Captain wants to see you in his office" she's told as she heads to her office.

"Okay" she says and turns around to head to the elevators to take her to the second floor, where her boss is located. Probably a little nervous about tomorrow, she thinks as she's given the nod to go on in by his secretary.

"Captain, you wanted to see me?" she asks.

"Yes Lieutenant, please sit."

"Yes Sir."

"You're probably wondering what I want to say. Well, today is a momentous day for the United States. We are being moved into a new direction that is going to require some getting used to. I'm sure everything will work out, the only thing that's changing is I will no longer be your boss."

"What?" she asks in disbelief, "Why not?"

"I'm here this morning only to clean out my desk. I've decided to retire from the department. My wife and I, along with my family are moving. I can't take anymore of the day after votes. We want to be gone from D.C. within the hour. Our goal is to live quietly and happily somewhere with less people, somewhere out west maybe. We haven't decided that yet, but it won't be here. I'm too close to the White House here and there are things going on that I disagree with. Lieutenant, that's for your knowledge only, please do not share that with anyone else. I'm not leaving a return address. No one will know where I am or even who I am. I believe this is for the best, and I wish for you health and happiness Lieutenant. You've been a very good officer. I'll miss this station and many of the people in it, you especially. It's been a pleasure Lieutenant, thank you."

"Goodbye Sir. It's been my pleasure also. If I can ever do anything for you, please call me. I don't know where I'll be, here maybe, but you'll find me. I wish you good health and safety Sir." The Captain just quit, she realizes. I wonder who's going to take his place. I wonder if he knows something that I don't?

After a long thirteen hours, it's finally time to call it a day. The voting will be complete soon, and the results announced within hours. I have some time, she decides. I think I'll go see

Mike. I haven't kept in very good touch with him. Hope he's not mad at me. Maybe I can go to his house and see my motorcycle. Before the vote announcement it'll stay quiet, so I won't have to worry.

"Mike, are you back there?" she calls when she enters the coffee shop.

"Yeah, Kat, I'm in the back, I'll be right up" he promises as she hears more slamming and then he comes through the swing door. "Hey Kat, how are you?"

"I'm good, how about you and the family?"

"Great" he admits "great. Want a coffee?"

"Sure, my usual please" and she waits for the cappuccino machine to stop making so much noise.

"Well" he remarks "that's weird."

"What is?"

"It never fails, just about every time you come in here, he shows up. It must be ESP or something" he adds with a grin as Kat swings around quickly and squeals with happiness, takes off running and is picked up by a biker dude with jet black hair, caught back in a pony, electric blue eyes and a smug grin.

ABOUT THE AUTHORS

Dennis (D) and Cheral (C) live in Northeast Ohio, namely the snow belt area, with their two dogs, a King-Sheppard, (Sasha) and a Golden Lab mix (Buddy). They live near their four wonderful children and their eight amazing grandchildren.

They have been blessed with life and love for more than thirty six wedded years. You can catch them at their wesite
www.dcwhite.org
or find them on facebook, twitter, linkedin, tumblr.

Use Capitol Angst in search.